I0650642

Broken Orbit

Book Two in the *Gravity* Series

by **Karma** *Rose*

Broken Orbit,
First Edition

by Karma Rose

ISBN: 978-1-7344914-0-1

First paperback edition, published 2020

© 2018 by Karma Rose. All rights reserved, including the right
to reproduce this book or portions thereof in any form
whatsoever. No part of this book may be reproduced or
transmitted without written consent of the copyright holder.

Book cover image © by Karma Rose. Cover design © by
Andrew H. Arroyo. Neither are to be reproduced or transmitted
without written consent of the copyright holder.

This book is a work of fiction. Names, characters, places, and
incidents are products of the author's imagination or are used in a
fictitious manner.

This book is dedicated to several people. First, my mom, who wanted us from the very first meeting and still hasn't stopped. I hope I was able to write the good and ugly well enough to portray adoption honestly.

Next, my great-grandfather, for showing me early in life that anyone can be a writer. All you have to do is write.

Lastly, I never thought I'd get a dad to thank, but it's nice to be proven wrong sometimes. Thank you for giving me a place to work on my future and showing me that good fathers don't have to be works of fiction.

A special thanks to some of my longest-supporting friends and family for encouraging me no matter how poorly written some of my work has been, and for nagging me when I was having writer's block! It's a good reminder that even if I'm not confident in my work, other people like it enough to get mad at me for taking my sweet time finishing it. I love you all!

To every Cory, Katelyn or little pixie out there, please keep shining. You make the world brighter for all of us.

The Fairytale

Spring is the start,
With an open heart,
And nothing can compare

As Summer's heat,
Turns the knees weak,
With naught to do but stop and stare.

Yet Autumn will follow,
To turn the heart hollow,
And prepare us for the fall.

For the finale's uninviting,
Its icy chill biting,
Winter comes to end it all

<u>Prologue</u>

Robert Smith was average, ordinary. A married man with two children, a nice home, and a steady job. Too plain to pick out of a crowd with his brown hair and eyes—he dressed very simply. Even sitting in the less than average old farm home, across from his keen-eyed companion, he was unremarkable. The man they discussed, however, was anything but.

"Still no word from Cory, then?" asked Lisa worriedly.

Robert shook his head, regretting how he did not bear better news. "No. Nothing. And the demon sightings have dropped off the radar, too."

"At least the man hunt's stopped," she laughed scornfully. Her eyes drifted to a particularly damaged space on the table, fingers tracing old wounds in the wood. "He's out there, I just...I wish he'd come home. Him, my brother, and for good. That last visit wasn't enough. Not even close."

"You two were that close?" he asked. They had been meeting regularly since Cory's disappearance. While Lisa had divulged plenty of childhood stories and secrets, Robert was always eager to glean more—as much as possible. Should his friend come back, he wanted to be ready for anything if he was needed.

Lisa smiled wistfully. "Yeah. Cory was the best big brother I could've asked for, and I had three to choose from. He'd play with me, help me braid my hair before his claws really came in. He was always extremely protective of me, from when I was tiny to my first boyfriend, all the way up until college. Then he encouraged me through the hard work that took, too."

Robert smiled. "It sounds like he was a good brother."

She nodded and laughed, "Yeah, he was. We were almost inseparable for a few years before I really got into school. We used to drive Mom crazy, I'm sure. I was the mastermind, and he could reach the high shelves. Then it was a matter of who would rat out first since Mom always knew if something was out of place."

"It's good to know he had some happy times," chuckled Robert, trying to imagine a younger version of the giant demon behaving immature and mischievous. "At least when he was younger."

"Oh, they weren't all happy," sighed Lisa, still tracing the scarred wood. She frowned, lost in a memory. "I always tried to help him when he hit a bad season. Especially when Grandpa Charles was visiting. Cory would get the occasional spell of depression, but what Grandpa did was something else."

"I'm sorry, who?" Charles? Was this where he got his middle name, then? Robert scowled, unsure if Cory had forgotten to mention the character accidentally or intentionally. "Cory's never told me about him."

Lisa blanched, looking like she had confessed the worst of secrets unnecessarily. "Oh. Grandpa Charles was...something else. Set in his ways, Dad always said. He didn't like that Dad had settled with a poor farmer's daughter to start, and then there was Cory, and Mom insisted on Cory Charles for some reason and I know that just poked the lion...

"I don't know what all he did to my brother, since some of it was in private, but what I saw was inhumane and cruel, plain and simple. He always treated Cory like he wasn't any better than an animal and it showed. Anytime Grandpa was going to visit, Cory would get in this mood and just—"

The phone rang loudly, startling the both of them from their conversation. Robert saw the relief on Lisa's face when their discussion was ended there, and he wondered just how terrible Charles must have been.

Set in his ways? Robert considered the words while his companion left to answer the landline in the other room. He mulled over the era and the physical differences which he had stopped noticing so profoundly with Cory. His stomach dropped nauseatingly, thinking over what kind of man would not approve of a poor woman or Cory, the secret son.

An excited shout interrupted his pondering; he sighed gratefully at the distraction. Lisa returned, nearly skipping in her excitement, a grin on her face clashing with the more somber look in her eye.

"Cory's back! Pastor Ericson just called, he's at the church," she gushed. Her sadness came to the forefront as she continued more quietly, "He said Cory's not ok—"

Robert was out of his seat and grabbing his jacket as he dashed for the door, unwilling to hear an explanation when he was sure Cory needed a friend right now. After all, with so long away, he certainly had plenty to talk about? Robert was sprinting for his car, more concerned for his friend than the steady rain coming down. He remembered the stories, had driven around here enough by now. If he made it to the diner, he had gone too far, he knew. How hard could it be to find a church?

He was buckled with the ignition turned faster than he could think to move, shifting the car into gear.

"Hang on, bud. I'll be right there."

Broken Orbit

My dearest Katelyn,

I love you. I never said it enough. I always thought I would have a lifetime to say it. I'm sorry. I love you.

This letter is useless to write. By now, I imagine you think I have passed away in this hell. For your sake, I hope it gives you comfort to know you can finally move on. Forget me.

I love you.

Tell my parents...Mom, Dad, I only hope I made you proud, somehow. You deserved a better son than whatever cowardly thing I am. I'm sorry.

I love you.

With any luck, Paul will follow along with my wishes and play the part I need him to. You will never read this, I'm sure, but I still cling to the possibility I might deliver it someday. If I ever escape I will find you, my dear, and I will find a way to repay the neglect of these lost years.

I love you.

If I cannot have you—or my home, my family— please forgive me for what I do. I cannot bear remembering the things I've lost.

Please, Kate, forgive me where I cannot.

I love you.

> *Always yours,*
> *Cory*

Karma Rose

Chapter One:
Faces

Eight Weeks Previously

Nearly seventy years with a demon among them and the humans never could have imagined this. They never could have conceived of other demons living in a world beyond the forests, through a gateway of trees. No one could have foreseen the splendor waiting there, untouched by greedy hands or hearts.

With the land covered by emerald trees and lit by topaz in the sapphire sky, the demon people waiting for us on the other side of the gate seemed right and natural. They were all a variance of red, some nearly as orange as Braxen while others tended to the other end of the spectrum with light lavenders and vivid violets.

In this first, overwhelming moment of wonder, I forgot the world behind me with its cities and the monsters which roamed them. Like a faded dream, it left my mind to make room for all of the beauty before me.

"Pure-Horn," one of the demons greeted Braxen, giving me and my family a guarded look. He continued to speak in a fluid, exotic language that was both unbearably sharp and unerringly soothing.

Braxen responded in the same tongue, nodding in our direction and rolling his eyes. My, but it did look peculiar! I smirked at the thought as he turned his attention to us. Dawn finished breaking to light the world beneath the canopy, and I finally took in our demon guide, Braxen.

By comparison, he was pale, nearly marigold beside my crimson, with amethysts for eyes as he scrutinized my family. His face was thin, undefined but experienced—so spoke the nose which had quite obviously been broken several times over his life. A single tattoo crossed over the edge of his left eye; piercings were the only other decorations he bore.

Pale white horns tipped with black curved back protectively over the burn scars on his naked scalp. A solitary patch of hair was woven into a braid which fell down his back, just past his tail. He stood not an inch taller than me—both of us towering a full head over the next tallest of our company—and wore nothing more than a loincloth to display completely his lean, wiry build.

Despite the entirely alien appearance of this man, every part of me recognized him as well as I would recognize myself.

"I apologize for speaking in words you don't understand," he said, his exotic accent much more pronounced when I had his untamed eyes to look into. His tail flicked the air lazily. "My companions haven't had as much opportunity as myself to learn the languages of humans."

Kate remained tensed, either unimpressed by the

surroundings or refusing to become distracted by them. All the same, she was intimidating. "So you're the ambassador, then?"

"Ambassador?" Braxen took a moment to mull over the word, nodding slowly. "Yes, yes in this instance I am the *il'tha*, peacemaker, representing our village. I will take you there."

"Where, exactly?" she demanded, and he froze at her tone, stunned. She stared him down fearlessly. "My children are hungry. They haven't eaten in hours and I haven't had a straight answer since your *angels* first showed up. Forgive me if I refuse to follow anyone anywhere without a bit of information first."

Braxen looked to another demon for help, but she shrugged, as lost for words as her "*il'tha*" appeared to be. He turned back, bewildered. Though I could see he was unaccustomed to allowing such an attitude from anyone, he seemed to be having trouble accepting such a small adversary.

"Our village is larger than most, although we've lost quite a few wings recently. It isn't far: just through the forest to the tunnels, and from there we'll reach our home."

I nodded, as pleased by the answer as Kate seemed to be. "Thank you."

Braxen simply nodded, taking this as his cue to begin the trek to the tunnels he spoke of. At first, the path appeared to be rough, barely distinguishable among the underbrush. The other demons seemed to know the way, however, taking such carefully measured steps or precise routes. We followed close behind, and as I watched I saw a pattern emerge in their movements. The larger scarlet demoness was far lither than Braxen, who was still more graceful than the deeper purple demons who crashed through the forest, by comparison. Those closest to these colors were similar in skill. It was an oddity I could not help admiring silently.

Not too much farther ahead, I saw the path become clear. I was surprised to see the trails trampled and dug into the earth. After trekking the barely used path behind us, it may as well have been a concrete sidewalk. While I was absorbed by the anomaly, the demons in the lead halted abruptly, sharp eyes alert as they listened.

I stopped to listen as well, and I heard it—a quiet hiss slithered in the air some distance away as it turned to a sharp screech like nothing I had ever known before. A shiver ran down my spine and through my tail, the smell of their fear rank in the air. The only one to remain calm was the scarlet woman, her tail moving slowly back and forth as we waited.

Kyle shifted uneasily, asking rather loudly after the stillness, "What are we stopping for, Grampa?"

The woman answered before I could, "It's just a sound, one of the *kruuta* is hunting. We'll be safe in a group."

It was clear he did not understand a word of what she said, the same as myself, but he still answered confidently, "Oh. Good."

Braxen gave a quiet sigh and motioned us forward again. "Keep moving. I'm not going to be lunch to save anyone who falls behind."

In one fluid movement, we were making our way

10

forward once more. The animal kept at its noises, never getting too close, this *kruuta*. What kind of creature even made such a sound? It was piercing even in the muffled walls of the forestry, and so very chilling as every call shivered up and down my spine again and again. As abruptly as I had arrived, this new world had turned as terrifying as it was beautiful.

Just ahead, the trees were beginning to thin enough I could see where the activity was in this place. The demons did well to hide their presence, but I saw those details which I knew scarred every place I had ever been to. There were claw marks in the bark, scratches in the earth, and even the growth of the branches showed where I imagined they stretched their wings.

Towards the center of all of this, there was a knot of roots which, when I looked, were created by a trio of the tallest trees I had ever seen. Astonishingly, this seemed the norm, every tree as massive or tall as those three. Their roots, however, formed an archway and from what I saw, the infrastructure which held the tunnel beyond in place.

Without a word, the demons all aimed for the tunnel, their excitement apparent in their faces and how light their footsteps suddenly became. I, on the other hand, fought back a moment of dread as I approached the impressively large tunnel. Inside, the darkness was all-consuming, devouring any trace of the sky or the freedom I possessed where I stood. All the same, before anyone could see me hesitate, I took the step.

I would not allow the past to steal this moment from me.

Karma Rose

The tunnels swallowed us all whole, with plenty of room for us to spread out and be lost to the group. My wings pressed tightly to my body, a shiver running down my spine and through my tail. Being without the sky was mortifying, even now when I could see daylight ahead of me. While the other demons had similar reactions, they were calmer about the transition, able to control themselves in spite of the solid stone and earth above us.

"Not much farther now," reassured Braxen with an inquisitive glance towards my family. I quickened my pace to come between them and the demons, instincts flaring to protect them. As he had said, the tunnel was coming to an end, the light ahead reaching out to banish the darkness of the road behind.

When we entered the main cavern, it was all I could do to not collapse in amazement at the awe-striking scene. Above us, a massive crack in the earth provided our sky, the sun at midday now as it moved through the deepest of blue skies I had seen since years before my captivity. At the edges of this fissure grew small shrubs of vibrant greens, blooming flowers spotting the wall with a full rainbow of colors. In the higher branches I saw eagles nesting, while the further down my eyes fell, the thicker the foliage became and the smaller the avian dwelling there.

Cutting through what I guessed was the center of the cavern—as it was difficult to make out the other side—was a river. Demons were clustered around some of the banks, and it took me a moment to understand that they were fishing. Tens—no, nearly hundreds of vibrant skins surrounded me—running, walking, crafting, working, flying. Demons of every height, width, and color I could have imagined were all there, pausing to watch me with as much interest as I observed them.

In the distance to what I guessed as the east of the cavern was a small village of sorts, huts, and fires set upon a hill away from the wall. Braxen led us to the center of this encampment, to a rather large pit of blackened wood and ash. Benches were set around it for when the fire would have been blazing and warm. Now, however, only the faintest of coals remained from a bonfire I assumed we had missed in our evening of travel.

The demons began to gather around us, trailing in from their work in the cavern. All of them had wide eyes, as though they had never seen strangers before. It took me a moment to realize why they stared, murmuring so excitedly to one another. It was not my face they found so alien, it was my families' faces—*human* faces—which disturbed them so! At that moment the strangeness of the thought had me laugh quietly, simply amazed.

Braxen stretched out his wings, a signal which silenced the growing din of voices around us. I caught a glimpse of the undersides of his membranes, stopping short for a moment when I saw the tribal designs tattooed into the skin depicting a sun and moon. My wings ached for him, wondering how it was he could have borne the process. The way the others respected him had me assume he was their leader. Perhaps the tattoos were a symbol of such?

He made his announcement in a strong, self-assured voice which echoed across the chamber boldly. The words made little sense to my ears, the language one I was completely unfamiliar with. Their demon tongue, I supposed. I could hear where his accent came from, listening to the sharp, guttural words rolling into soothing purrs. The demons around us were all nodding. When Braxen had finished speaking they gave him a barking growl, sounding like an assent.

As Braxen returned to our small group, the rest of the crowd dispersed. "We will show you to your hut now."

"Wait, what was *that*?" demanded Kate. I could only imagine how she was able to continue her defiance through the wonderment of this place.

Vladimir was the one to reply, startling me. In all of the excitement, I had forgotten his presence. "It was part of his ambassadorial duties. Now come on, or you can sleep outside."

Kate huffed but followed along with us, if only indignantly. "Are you going to elaborate on those duties, or do you just really enjoy being an overly cryptic pain?"

"Aw, not even a day and it's like you've known me for years." He feigned his being emotionally moved, obviously pleased by his sarcasm. Without answering Kate's initial question, he pointed ahead of us at a relatively large hut appearing to have been grown from the trees around it. "That's where you'll be staying. It's a palace by local standards, so keep that in mind while you're judging it.

"The river water is potable, meals are communal and signaled by the drums. If you need to relieve yourselves, there's a bucket inside. Put it out at night and the cultivators will collect it in the morning. Goodnight," he finished abruptly, sounding bored of us before vanishing unceremoniously with Braxen barely a step behind.

I saw Katelyn fighting the urge to demand answers of the nearest demon, so I smiled broadly with a grand gesture towards the hut. "I always did love a humble home. Children, how about you run ahead and see what all is inside, hm?"

We released them to their excitement, listening to their giggles as I turned to Kate, "I know these conditions are far from preferable, and I understand if you would rather take the children home."

"No," she snapped firmly, fire in her depthless gaze. "The kids can learn to adapt, it'll help them build a bit of character. But I *am not* and I *will not* break my family apart for any reason. Do you understand, mister?"

I nodded, the exuberant cries of Sarah cutting off my reply, "Grandma! Cory! There's animal furs in here, it's so cool!"

"I can't wait to see what all you found!" Kate called back, pulling me down to give me a quick kiss on the cheek before hurrying in after the children. "All right, where are these animal furs?"

I took one last glance at the majesty of the vast cavern, every demon in sight staring at me in return. How strange, to be seeing so many of these faces like mine.

That I am not the queerest member here, I thought. *And if I am, it is the strangeness of my clothes or my manner, not the severe inhumanity of my visage.*

I spent just a moment longer to enjoy the difference before making my way into the hut. I was greeted at once by childish laughter and a comforting wave of heat—likely from both the number of bodies in such a small space and the dying pile of embers in the center of the entryway. While the hut itself was far from spacious, it was open and expanded a foot or so above my horns.

Where I first entered was an open space I thought would be the equivalent of a living room, given the fireplace and seating marked by well-worn logs. Across from the entrance, the hut branched into two equally open spaces, both laden with furs in a mess for sleeping. Kate and the children were toppled over in one of these piles, laughing as the fur tickled their faces. I took a deep breath and smiled, setting aside everything I was carrying to join them.

"I see you somehow found us in the vast maze of this shack," greeted Kate, but her venom sounded half-hearted.

"Perhaps the children are not the only ones in need of building a bit of character," I teased in reply. Picking up Kyle to make space for me to sit, I set him on my lap. "Oh, these are soft, and I am exhausted."

"Me, too, Grampa." Kyle yawned widely, his tiny body swaying as he fought to stay awake. He looked past me tiredly. "Who's that?"

I looked over at the entrance, startled to see Braxen looming there silently. He made a gesture with his hands, crossing his wrists with closed fists, before speaking in a quiet purr, "I'm sorry. I didn't mean to scare you. I followed to see that you had everything you need."

Kate glanced at me before fixing the demon with a

16

firm glare as sharp as her words, "Food. We need food, the children are hungry."

Braxen was unfazed. If anything, I thought I saw him resisting a smile. "I understand. Our early meal should be ready soon. Just follow the drums when you hear them. You can rest while you wait, or I can show you the village."

She seemed to relax a bit at his compliant reply, finally receiving some answers and an offer of aid. "I think we'll rest for now, but after we eat I'll take you up on seeing where everything is, thanks."

He replied in his exotic language, switching again to reply, "Of course, while you are new here. If you need anything in the meantime, ask for me; the others will help find me." He turned to leave, adding as an afterthought, "You are all welcome and safe here."

Not a moment after he was gone, Kate was laying herself down with Sarah on one side. I lay myself down on her other side, keeping myself closest to the exit, Kyle already nearly asleep in my arms. Kate began to hum quietly, halting any protestations from Sarah before they could begin. I smiled, fatigue taking a swift and firm hold over me. I looked over at Kate, meaning to speak but falling short as I slipped away beneath the sweet veil of sleep.

~~ * ~ * ~ * ~~

Twisted images haunted me, distorted voices calling my name. Demon faces met me at every turn, frightening me more than they should have. I was no longer alone. Not a day before, I never could have imagined seeing a face like mine. Now, there were hundreds of demon eyes staring through my dreams at me, their clawed hands reaching out to rend me.

They all wore thin, malicious smiles hissing at me, cursing the humanity I so desperately sought in all my years of social damnation. They mocked the claws which I had filed for my family's safety, my gentle tones which I had practiced endlessly to keep others from feeling threatened.

"Weak!"

"Human."

"Traitor!"

"I did not know, please!" I cried desperately, seeing nothing but their angry eyes and vicious fangs bared at me in disdain. "There was no other way! I only wanted to belong."

Braxen stood out suddenly, the angels on either side of him. Daggers were protruding from his chest and bandages where his horns should have been. He hissed, eyes half-feral as he yelled at me in his language, a gorgeously aggressive sound. One word stood out, and I realized that I understood it as one of my own as he yelled it again and again, angrier every time.

"Skyborn!"

~~ * ~ * ~ * ~~

I started with a gasp as I woke from the nightmare, looking around in a panic. My heart raced painfully in my chest as I took in the small hut's structure. Soft, warm furs

18

both covered me and cushioned me from the earth floor.

It only took me a moment longer to recall where I was, and I leaned back with a tired sigh of relief. The demons, of course. Braxen and the angels had taken us here, to Paradise.

"How will we get there?"

"The Hrexis tree. Just walk through."

My mind supplied the recollection of the gnarled old trees entwined together into an archway, lit by a moonless background of stars. I groaned and looked over at Kyle nestled into one side of me, Kate in the other. In her arms, Sarah was also sleeping soundly. I smiled in relief, tired enough to hope Braxen's word was true regarding our safety here.

~ * ~ * ~ * ~

I woke again mid-afternoon, this time alone. Outside, I heard the children laughing while Kate was speaking to a much deeper, almost sultry voice I did not recognize. With a groan, I left the bedding and—stepping around the small fire pit in the center of the hut—went to the flap for a door. Hesitance took me for a moment before I pulled it back, blinking into the soft sunlight of a new world.

Around me, many other huts were built and demons were wandering through them, with no pattern which I could discern. Some women were weaving, others appearing to tattoo one another. Several demons stopped to stare at me when I stepped out, a hush befalling them.

I nodded once, smiling awkwardly in greeting. Looking for Kate, I found her behind the back of the hut we had slept in. Kyle and Sarah were not twenty feet away, tumbling in the grass with another young child, perhaps Sarah's age if not slightly older. I was startled when I realized it was a tiny demon girl, light red with vivid yellow eyes.

I worried about their safety for a moment before recalling how, when I was the young girl's size, my claws had yet to fully develop. So I went to join Katelyn, curious about the demoness she was speaking with.

"Oh, Cory, this is Krasha," she said when I approached. I looked at the woman she motioned to, still amazed despite recognizing her from the journey the day before. She came up to my chin in height, with scarlet skin just a shade lighter than my crimson tone. I kept my eyes focused on hers to avoid staring at her barely-clothed body or the bone ridges covering her.

"A pleasure," I said quietly, giving her a nod in greeting. Krasha answered with a disquieting, sharp-toothed grin which startled me.

"Braxen was right. You are very...different," she chose the word with care, although I had the feeling she had a cruder one in mind.

"Ah, yes," I agreed awkwardly, glancing over at the children out of habit and seeing the act too late to stop it. The girl had Kyle's arm and, amid of their wrestling, bit into him. His next scream only confirmed the damage I knew would come from such cruelty.

"Unhand my son!" I yelled impulsively, towering over them both in an instant. The girl wrenched away from him, scrambling over to where her mother was now gaping at the scene in shock. Everyone was staring, all with the same stunned expression. Yet their eyes never followed the girl. No, they were trained on me and my reaction as I scooped up my sobbing boy to help him.

"Hush now, you're all right, Kyle, it's all right. Let me see your arm," I told him, and he showed me the bloody mess. Where she had bitten the wounds were deep, and the tears in the skin were obvious from when she had pulled away. Thankfully, she was still too tiny to do anything more unconscionable. "Oh, it's all right. We can fix that, I promise. Hush, Kyle, hush."

I looked around, ignoring their faces while listening for water. As lost as I could be, I relented and returned to the hut. Kate was right behind me with Sarah at her side. She went to the small collection of things we had brought with us, pulling out a first aid kit. I staunched the bleeding with my shirt, heart aching when he screamed at the pressure on the wound.

"It's all right, you'll be perfectly fine, Kyle," I told him gently, looking him in the eye. He stared at me for a moment before he steeled himself, pursing his lips to keep quiet even as rivers of tears cut across his cheeks.

Kate brought me the kit. All of the lessons from observing my mother and Paul—though rusty—were still at my disposal. I drew more from how Paul helped me treat my scars than anything. Wiping as much of the blood away as I could, I then pulled out an alcohol wipe to dab around the wound at first.

"Are you ready?" I asked Kyle. The tiny child I knew stared at me again, and a resolve far too mature for his face took residence there. "Very well."

I disinfected the wounds, expecting him to pull away or scream but he only stared intensely, alternating between his arm and my face. When I was finished, I assessed the damage before finally allowing myself a smile of relief.

"No need for any stitching," I told him, and he smiled back. He was quiet and patient while I applied ointment and bandaged his arm, crawling into my lap to collapse as soon as I was finished.

Kate sat beside me, rubbing Kyle's back. "You were so brave."

He looked at us both, then at his arm. "As brave as Cory?"

"Braver," I said, for the first time realizing why he had stared at me. He was seeing the scars, trying to be as brave as I had been helpless when receiving my own. "Kyle, you were much braver."

"Do you find it odd?" I asked Katelyn in a hushed tone when we made it to the fires for supper. I was painfully aware of the stares the other demons fixed our family with, divided between us and where the children were exploring the food available. It was with a poignant twisting in my gut I reminded myself I was not what they stared at. Not my face, at least.

She looked up at me, eyes mercifully brown as they danced with the firelight of the meal we sat at. Her lips turned up into a wry smirk. "What's odd, mister?"

"Demons, this place, how humans have never discovered it. *Magic*." The word was sharp as it slid off my tongue. It felt wrong, making the memory of my blood turned to acid nearly unbearable. In this new place, I could not deny the things happening to me and write them off as lunatic hallucinations. Not when walking through portals made of trees was offered up as everyday humdrum.

Kate shrugged easily, picking thoughtfully at the meal we had joined for. "I guess it's like fireworks."

"Fireworks?" I could not help but chuckle in my incredulity, staring at her face and how easily she accepted it all.

Her nod was confident. "Yeah. I'm sure people thought they used to be magic, too. But there's always some kind of explanation, no matter how outlandish things look at first—like fireworks."

"Fireworks," I repeated the word, hesitant despite her certainty regarding her assessment.

"It's how I've always thought of you," she told me, her smirk turning to a grin. She nudged me playfully, at ease now she had found some bearings in this village of demons. Her footing here was far better than mine, to say the least. "You're like fireworks."

"Hm." I mused over her easy outlook, the world much more bearable with it. I did not have long to practice with it, however, with the children returning from their scavenging at the food. They sat between us, each gabbing on about their day between starved bites.

Fireworks or not, I was grateful for the time to bond with them better.

23

Karma Rose

~~ * ~ * ~ * ~~

Beneath the blanket of the starlit sky, the world was quiet; I could hear the wind rustling through the trees in every direction. In spite of the excitement of the last several days, I could not sleep. Any time I closed my eyes, all I could see was this gorgeous world and the endless host of possibilities it held for my family and me. Instead, I wandered across the vast cavern to where I knew the river emptied into a lake, the air still warm enough to bear what would no doubt be icy water.

As I made my way to the river, a second sky appeared in the earth, shifting and quivering with the rippling liquid. The slight babble of the river put a smile on my face, walking along the length of the water with the stars above and beside me. Sooner than I expected, the lake materialized before me, stealing my breath as I nearly drowned in its majesty.

Lain out before me was a velvet carpet, softer to the eyes than I imagined it would feel falling between my fingers. Strewn across its surface, the stars were alive and dancing with light as they winked at me, as if they teased me with the possibility of catching one of them in my eager palm. Yet I knew they were empty promises— breathtakingly gorgeous though too far out of reach.

It took me a moment to remember to breathe, and another moment still before I could recall what I had intended to do here. Regretful of disturbing the nighttime splendor, I scanned for any demons which may be lingering in the area. Once I saw I was alone, I allowed my guard some relaxation, undoing my shirt's buttons.

I tossed the article aside, checking again that the lake was abandoned. As well it should be at such a late hour. Stripping off my pants, I stepped into the cool water with a sigh, wading out until it lapped at my chest. Behind me, I heard the rustling of footfalls on the path.

I whirled, well aware that they were too heavy to be Kate, calling out, "Who is there?"

From the depths of the shadows, Braxen slunk forward, ever-fluid in his movements. "No one you need to fear. I came as a companion, curious as to your," he deliberated for a moment, "*adjustments* into this village, given it is rather different from the norm."

As soon as I saw him, I hurried deeper into the shadows of an overhanging willow nearby. My skin burned, painfully aware of how bare it was with my scars showing freely before this stranger.

"I am perfectly comfortable in solitude, but thank you for your concern, Braxen." I lowered myself into the water, still feeling too vulnerable before this savage.

He shook his head with a laugh. "As evidenced by your aversion to even leaving your hut. What, do our women frighten you?"

I assumed his tone meant a playful jibe, yet I could not understand if there was a hidden meaning. This culture was so far from anything I had experienced, I felt as though I was treading on the thinnest ice.

"Ah..." I looked for an escape, some way to flee the watchful eyes of this demon.

"Come now, the lake is always better with an extra pair of wings." With that he leaped in, creating a rather sizable splash.

While he was under, I attempted to slip away, shouting in surprise when he materialized from the water before me. I shook my head, somewhat breathless from fear, "Fine! I will bathe another time. However, I would appreciate it if you gave me the privacy I seek while I dress."

He belted out his laughter. "Oh, you sound so human! What could you possibly need privacy for when you are no First?"

"I am unaware of what that is, but I am well aware of my discomfort with being naked before strangers. Particularly someone as unpredictable and uncivilized as you!" I was mildly shocked by my sharp tongue, although I did not show it. He simply shrugged before diving back beneath the water, unconcerned.

I sighed and hurried from the water, snatching up my clothes and towel before scurrying back to the tree's shadows. There, beneath the tree, Braxen resurfaced for air.

"Oh, hello."

"I thought you agreed to give me my privacy!" I snapped, glaring at him in annoyance. This demon and his utter lack of respect for my requests!

"Well, yes, I was. It's not my fault that you're still here in a very open area, is it?" Orbs of water rose from the lake, circling him slowly. I would have been surprised, had these strange things not been happening around him since I arrived.

Fireworks, I reminded myself firmly.

I faltered for just a moment, "No, I suppose not,

although you could respect my request more sincerely in the future."

"I thought I had? Why are you demanding things of me that I should tend to you?" he asked honestly. The inquiry grated against my patience.

I bit my tongue and sighed, assuming this to be another cultural difference between us. I flinched reflexively at the thought of being seen bare-skinned but continued dressing, every scar burning as my shame solidified in my stomach. As I finished, Braxen was stepping from the lake, what little coverings he wore soaked through. A strange look of understanding reached his eyes. It was still an alien face to me—the emotions he shared even more so—like a raw interpretation of an untamed force.

"Never mind," I dismissed it all, grabbing my towel and turning toward the village. Braxen stopped me before I could make my escape.

"Wait! You've been a hermit for days. Would you like to see the village?" he offered, and when I glanced back he seemed genuinely hopeful I would agree. If I was learning to read these demon expressions correctly, at least.

I kept myself from sighing, wanting so desperately to flee back to my hut and hide there, away from these people and this culture. It felt as though it all mocked me. My efforts to be accepted by humanity, the struggles I had faced along the way. Every last moment my life had been built upon was being challenged; the man I had become as a result felt as though he lacked the resolve to face it. Either I had to endure the fight all over, or embrace the opinion that I had simply gone insane. A deliciously tempting option, in light of this new world.

Braxen must have seen my inner turmoil, adding gently, "The village is asleep; it would just be us, and the look-outs above."

The reassurance comforted me more than I felt was healthy, both from the avoidance of others and the innate trust I could not help feeling with this particular demon. At least the disconcerting sense of being split had ceased since the first day we met, replaced instead by a calm, intuitive insight into his next actions.

Regardless, I did need to explore this place. It would also be refreshing to speak to someone, especially a demon. I could learn about our people and, hopefully, begin adjusting to such different faces.

"Very well," I agreed, reminding myself how this is what I had so desperately desired time and time again, to not be alone, to belong. Why, then, was there such reluctance to learn about these people—*my* people? "Lead the way, then, sir."

I saw the relief in his eyes before he motioned to the village, setting a welcomingly leisurely pace. It was a long moment before he finally turned to me and asked, "Where would you like to start?"

For how many years in my youth had I imagined this encounter when I could finally ask every question which haunted me and my nightmares? Now, standing with this fantasized scenario before me, I could think of nothing but running back to the safety of my human family. Why did I want to deny this world, damn my ties to it? Why, in the face of youthful dreams, did this final reality terrify me so?

Glancing around the massive cavern, I began with the obvious, "Have you always lived here?"

Braxen's eyes shimmered as he smiled openly. "No, not always. This area is sacred. It was a place where those who sought peace could come to find relief. The walls and tunnels were made by the Earth Elementals before our gods rose to the skies.

"Now, it is a refuge, one of the last safe havens which have not been ravaged in recent years," he continued. His smile faded as ghosts danced through his expression and brought tears to his eyes. "We are very nearly all that's left of our people. There are only two other villages now."

I stopped, a strange sense of dread slithering down my spine. "What happened?"

"Angels." The look he fixed me with was torn between hatred and an endless hurt of the most unexpected betrayal. How I knew the feeling well. "They've slaughtered us by burning the forests we live in, collapsing the mountain caves. My home was in the desert, where they poisoned the water."

The absolute horror of it all made me feel sick, although there was something even more perturbing about his words. "I apologize, Braxen, but I thought you said *angels* did this? Why? Surely, they were justified somehow?"

A murderous rage flashed across his face, but he breathed in deeply as he warned in a controlled tone, "I will be patient with you, Cory, but don't *ever* say those words again, especially to the others. We did nothing to deserve watching countless families suffer, to sit helplessly and listen to children burn alive or loved ones have their insides destroyed by acid water. Don't *ever* suggest that again. There is never a crime which justifies the forced suffering of another creature."

Chagrined, I nodded, mumbling, "My apologies, Braxen."

The anger drained from him, replaced by a strangely humble manner. "Thank you. I'm sorry for my harshness. I've seen many of these things happen myself, I can be...overwhelmed, by the memories."

I nodded. Yet another thing I could relate to in this, if not through the same experiences. "I think I may be too tired to continue. Please, excuse me."

"Wait." His hand caught my wrist in a firm grip, eyes wide and worried like a child's. "I never meant to frighten you. Please don't judge us too soon, Cory. These are good people. If you meet me at the morning meal and follow me, you might see that and more. We are your people," he added eagerly, a hint of desperation in his voice.

I nodded in agreement, relieved when he released me. Without a word, I hurried back to the hut, finding my family deep in the embrace of sleep. Trepidation was all I found in my thoughts, a deeper feeling welling in my chest as I considered what Braxen had told me.

He was right, in how no crime would ever justify the images now running rampant through my mind. Why would angels hunt out and murder demons if they were innocent? Unless he was lying, but to what end? There was no use in lying to me or my family, certainly. After the life I had lived it would be bigoted hypocrisy if I judged these people too soon, particularly for crimes against them.

As my mind began to calm and sleep beckoned once more, a singular thought stood out to me, vivid as it burrowed deep into my core. Whomever these people were, I needed to learn more about them. If they truly were the good innocents Braxen claimed, I needed to help them. Somehow, I needed to ensure the needless deaths in my nightmares would not be in vain.

Remembering all Kate had once endured, I knew that I could not stand idly by again.

~~ * ~ * ~ * ~~

A little over a week in the village now, and I was beginning to lose track of the days. With so little urgency stressing every moment, nor any schedules nor deadlines to speak of, it was easy to put such concerns aside while I explored this new world and its culture. So I spent time every day learning what I could, usually with Braxen all but dragging me along. As I gradually made my way to my family's hut I smiled, grateful he had been too caught up in his responsibilities to terrorize me today. The Shaman was exhausting, however well-meaning I knew him to be.

Lost in thought as I was, it was a wonder I noticed the world around me when my body stopped mid-stride, halted in place by the scene before me. An adorably tiny demoness was carrying a basket on her hip as she walked, coral skin shimmering faintly in the filtered sunlight. She wore more cloth to cover herself than the others, and I recognized the shy, shameful hunch to her shoulders with a sickly familiarity. I still warred with the feeling regarding my scars. Yet she still held her head up, a faint smile dancing on her sky blue lips.

None of this cemented me in place. It was in the instant which followed my spying her as a gaggle of other, more sizable women approaching did the trick. Their jeering tone was obvious no matter the language, my heart mournful for the poor demoness. The group had nearly passed when one knocked the basket from the coral woman's hip with a swat of their tail that I knew could not have been purely accidental.

I rushed over quickly as the contents spilled out, kneeling to help collect the items. "Here now, allow me."

"Oh." Her surprise was hesitant, watching my hands with a practiced caution which worried me. She seemed such a sweet little creature to be so paranoid! "Who?"

I smiled gently, handing her one of the rolls of parchment. "My name is Cory."

Her copper eyes lit up with excited recognition. "Oh!"

"Who are you?" I asked, gesturing to her with all of the ingrained care I used with humans. Anything less seemed egregious. She looked like a delicate, gentle fairy, with her glistening skin and bright eyes, an infectious smile dancing on her comparatively soft face.

She pointed to herself in question, and I nodded. "Leilani."

"It's a pleasure to meet you, Leilani," I chuckled,

surprised by myself and the ease of speaking to her. Of course, after so much time with Braxen, I imagined dental work on a crocodile would be quite a simple task. Certainly more preferable, at least. I caught sight of something on one of her parchments, a charcoal sketch of a home woven from trees. "Is this your work?"

Leilani stared at me, politely confused as she laughed nervously, "No words."

"Oh. Of course." I smiled awkwardly in the face of this barrier, collecting the remaining scraps quickly. She straightened them in her basket with a practiced hand. Her eyes were wary as I reached for the receptacle, standing with it and gesturing for her to lead the way. I had little else to do beyond avoiding Braxen and whatever fresh torment he had conceived of next, the obnoxiously energetic monster he was.

With another hesitant glance at me and her basket, she pursed her lips but led me through the village. Despite her size, her feet moved her along quickly, a graceful flash of sunrise made flesh as she flitted around the other demons and across the uneven terrain. My mass put me at a disadvantage, and I felt all the more uncoordinated as I struggled to follow while maintaining some shred of my dignity.

I began to recognize the area as she stopped at a minuscule hut. "This is near my family."

No sooner had I said the words than I heard the excited outcry of Kyle, spotting him a moment later as he charged at me. I passed the basket off with a quiet laugh, noticing her caution vanishing to the brightest smile when she spied the young boy. I caught his running approach with a grunt, hefting him up with a grin.

"And what is so urgent, my boy?" I asked sternly, wiping at a smudge of dirt on his cheek. He turned his head in protest, revealing an even larger stain on the other side of his face. Oh, dear.

"Playing tag," he gasped, grinning broadly. He saw the little demoness beside me. "Hi, Leilani!"

"Hi, baby," she cooed, enthralled by the little human I held.

"Oh, you know her?" I should not have been surprised. He was such an outgoing young man, he must have met every demon in the village by now.

Kyle nodded. "Yeah, she teaches how to make stuff."

I nodded slowly, recalling his sudden obsession with braiding and weaving. "Well, now, let's hope she teaches you how to stay clean soon. Perhaps then something about the idea might stick beside the dirt."

He squirmed impatiently, my jest lost on him. "Grampa, I need to keep running, before the others find me!"

"Very well," I sighed, setting him down and watching him sprint off. Only a second later, Sarah bolted by, hot on his trail. "Oh, the joys of children."

Leilani smiled politely, nodding to her hut and excusing herself wordlessly. I returned the smile, meandering off toward my abode. Perhaps Katelyn would be there already. With a glance at the sky, I saw that the sun had long since peaked, now halfway through its steady descent.

My family's hut barely in view, a familiar hand

wrapped itself in mine. "Hello, mister."

I smiled broadly, overjoyed at the touch. "Hello, my dear."

"I see you met our neighbor," she commented, nodding toward the comparatively diminutive hut I had come from.

"Ah, yes," I sighed, content with our lulling pace. "Unfortunately, I did not catch the names of the women tormenting the poor thing."

"She seems to be less than a favorite," agreed Kate with a worried frown. She shrugged, a smile breaking free reluctantly. "But she's good with the kids. Cute for a demon, too. Like a *really* tiny doll."

"You two could almost be sisters," I chuckled, holding the "door" open for Katelyn before following her inside.

Kate raised one brow skeptically, no doubt questioning why she would ever be compared to anyone so timid. "Right. Enough with the weird hypotheticals."

"How else am I to be entertained? Braxen seems to have abandoned me today." I smirked mischievously, glad for my freedom.

Her hand left mine, resting on my arm as the other flitted to trace across my inner membrane. She grinned at my maddened expression. "Kids should be busy for a while."

In an instant, the world fell away, and all that mattered were those depthless black eyes which captivated me so completely.

Chapter Two:
Fireworks

"Braxen!"

I looked up, the name as right as it was wrong in this dream of a memory. I recognized the faces in front of me, although a part of me wondered how that was possible. They were the Avatars, old and wise, the ones who represented our gods as people.

Why was I here?

"It doesn't pay attention well, does it?" asked the Avatar of Jeckat scathingly.

"He's young," my father sighed defeatedly. He hadn't been feeling well lately, always sad for some reason.

"And you're certain, about what he is?" asked the Avatar of Yurick, my grandmother's eyes severe.

"I'm a Shaman," I chimed in eagerly, holding out my palm to demonstrate. A spark of fire came to life and disappeared in the same second, pitiful at best.

Dad nodded shakily. "Yes, I'm certain. First his mother, now he's doing things...like that, and more. I'm a crafter, I can't train him."

"Of course not," agreed Grandmother. "We'll take it from here."

"Train me for what?" I wondered, nervous as my father stood to walk away. My grandmother stopped me from following, her claws digging into my shoulder. "Dad?"

"Braxen, you don't have a family anymore," said the Avatar of Jeckat, cold and detached. "You never had one."

"But—"

"You're a Half-Child, Braxen, nothing more," explained Grandmother sharply, gripping me harder. "The only thing you need to worry about now is training to serve your Master."

I felt a spike of terror, remembering the stories I'd heard about Half-Children in our legends. They all ended up dead or disfigured. I didn't want that. I just wanted to go home with my father.

~~ * ~ * ~ * ~~

As the memory faded, it left me feeling empty. I came to my senses, alone in the hut as I sat up and tried to shake away this sudden feeling of despair. Hot tears streamed down my cheeks, the knot in my throat catching as I gasped for air. I missed the man like I missed my father, and all I could recall was him walking away from me. Why?

With a sniffle, I wiped the tears from my face and shook the desolate grief from me, reaching for a clean shirt and pants. I could not waste my time thinking these things, not when I had this world to explore still. Three weeks, and I still felt as lost as I had when I first stepped foot into the village. I sighed and stretched, making my way outside as I buttoned my shirt beneath my wings. I caught sight of my arm with a habitual wince. At least no one stared at the scars here.

"Human!"

The sudden cry startled me, although Braxen's grin was no surprise at this point. *"Please,* stop calling me that."

He chuckled and threw an arm around my shoulders for a quick—if awkward—hug. Demons certainly had little concept of personal space. "And what else would I call you?"

"My *name?*" I suggested a bit sharply. I sighed, rubbing the remaining sleep from my eyes. "My apologies, I had little rest and my temper is short."

Braxen groaned in frustration, the sound turning into a strangely choked growl. "Why do you apologize for everything? You'd apologize for the rain if I blamed you for it!"

"Why are you tormenting me so early in the day?" I moaned, already exhausted by his antics. "I thought you had tasks to attend to, diplomacy or whatnot."

"And leave you to navigate our village alone?" he chuckled. His mirth was so genuine I was startled to realize how many years it had been since I had heard such heartfelt humor. "You would wander off someplace you shouldn't and be dead by sundown. No, I'll help you keep your bearings. You're much more fun than my usual, how do humans say, duties," he said the word with obvious confusion. The sound of it hitting my ear was wrong as it found its way from his fanged lips and forked tongue.

38

Broken Orbit

I shook the oddity from my mind, still so unaccustomed to seeing such features outside of a mirror. "Please, find another pastime. Vladimir asked me to see him today, and I imagine I will need all of my energy for whatever this meeting has in store."

After all, last time I met with him at his request he was the bearer of more than startling news. Breaking away from Braxen, I caught myself walking without thinking through this new little village. As though I had lived here for years, I was dodging the running children and working mothers expertly. I knew their patterns better than I knew how to breathe. Yet another curiosity which I had little time to consider, between how lost I had felt only a moment prior and how restlessly I had slept.

Before I knew it, my feet had stopped at the entrance to Vladimir's office. Well, more or less an office, as he called it. Any respectful businessman would barely acknowledge the space for the hovel it was. Disregarding my rather judgmental thoughts, I knocked twice against the frame before hearing his call to enter. I ducked into the space.

The interior was much more refined than its shell, showing an obvious talent for decorating within primitive means. At the center of the room—as it was surely spacious enough to be called such—was a massive stone, the outermost layer chiseled and polished until it lay flat. Into said surface was carved a map, detailing an astonishingly large expanse of land.

There were smaller paper maps spread about in a disorganized pattern that only the maker could understand. Small figurines were smattered here and there across the mess like a haphazard game of chess. Several chairs were placed around the table, seeming sturdy despite being woven out of what appeared to be tree branches.

"Good, it's you. I was starting to worry you wouldn't show." Mesmerized as I was by the startlingly sophisticated space, I had neglected to observe Vladimir lurking in a darkened corner. His red eyes were as piercing as always. He cracked a smile at my obvious fright. "Sorry. Didn't think a big demon like you would scare so easy."

I composed myself quickly, making a point of ignoring his comment. "My apologies for my tardiness, I slept rather poorly. What did you wish to discuss?"

His smile was gone as suddenly as it had appeared, following my cue. "You. What are you doing to help the community?"

"Ah, well, I—"

"Yeah, whatever it is, it's not going to continue," he interrupted quickly, motioning at a chair to offer me a seat. I tensed at his cool approach, biting back the urge to hiss at the unnerving similarity to Beth's mannerisms. As he realized I intended to stand, he shrugged and took a seat for himself, lounging back into it. "I want you to start combat training."

The words were so surprising I laughed. "My apologies, but...Combat training? I am an elderly cripple. If you want me, you must be desperate."

"We are," he retorted flatly, eyes narrowed as they boasted ancient wisdom which made my tail shiver. "I'm not sure Braxen's told you, but we're at war here. And every able-bodied man has a responsibility to protect this place."

"Are you *drafting* me?" I asked incredulously.

"If that means mandatory military experience, yeah," he replied with an oddly cheery demeanor. "Which also means that you start training today."

"I get no choice in this? But my family—"

"But nothing," he interrupted sharply, agitated by my protests. "I don't tolerate cowards, Mr. Lawrence, I punish them. Are you a coward?"

"No." My immediate reply came from a place of habit, one Vladimir was reawakening with disturbing ease. I cursed how I was not more in control of myself.

"That's a lie," he accused me with a bored sigh. He smiled a wizened, twisted smile. "You're lucky, though. Braxen specifically requested the opportunity to be your instructor. He's a good fighter and he's a hell of a lot nicer than I am," he added with a sadistic glint in his eye.

"Very well, then. When do I begin?" I asked submissively. I wanted this meeting to be over with, to be away from this demented man who reminded me so much of an even more demented woman.

Vladimir motioned to the exit. "Don't catch your tail on the way out."

I fought a reflexive glower at the flare of indignation I felt. Instead, I gave a curt nod, turning sharply to leave. My tail cut the air like a whip. All I heard behind me as I left was an amused cackle. The sound faded quickly with the distance I put between myself and the nightmare from a memory.

I had not realized it previously, but my heart was

41

racing, hands trembling. Whether from terror or rage I could not care, letting loose a rabid snarl and sinking my dulled claws into the nearest tree as best I could. I gasped for air, the sensation of having my claws buried helping burn through my anxious energy.

A few minutes later I was finally able to breathe deeply and evenly, releasing my grip on the bark slowly. I sighed as my hands dropped back down to my sides, struggling to sort out what I should do next when I realized I was not alone.

"You followed me," I accused flatly, turning an irked glare on Braxen's calm demeanor as he lounged against a neighboring tree.

He shrugged. "I wanted to save time tracking you down later. Vladimir was less than gentle with his news, then?"

"As pleasant as a kidney stone," I grumbled, sighing when Braxen tilted his head in curiosity. "Pleasant as a snagged claw?"

He winced in obvious discomfort. "I'm sorry on his behalf, Human."

"That is *not* my name," I snapped irritably, shaking my head slowly. I turned to rest my back against the tree I had mauled, sliding to the ground tiredly. A sigh escaped me numbly. "What do you want from me first?"

Braxen followed my lead and took a seat on the loamy earth. "A moment to understand what you're fighting for, then we can start practicing basics."

I leaned my head back to rest against the cool bark, staring up at the light filtering through the leaves above. "How do I tell Kate? We only just found each other again, and now this...I wonder if it would have been better had we never left home."

He made no effort to hide the difficulty of the question I presented. His scowl contorted his demonic visage, although where I would have anticipated an aggressively horrific expression I was gladly disappointed. My expectations gave way instead to see his impassioned concern. "I have no easy answer, and it shouldn't be easy. This is not an easy world. You should know how you're going to tell yourself these changes, Human. You can't explain this to her if you can't explain it to yourself."

I scoffed, laughing bitterly, "Ah, yes, and you are just so helpful, Braxen. How did I ever hobble through life without you?"

He took a moment to puzzle over my tone, and I had to wonder what he thought of such sickly sweet sarcasm. His reply was caught at his lips as his expression faltered before I heard what gave him pause. I silenced my breath, listening intently. I could see other demons frozen mid-action, just as focused on this singular task.

Drumbeats shattered the abrupt quiet, deep and commanding. My body trembled in time with their bellow as it echoed across the cavern walls. Every face looked up and around with me, but where I was curious they were horrified.

I looked to Braxen, seeking answers. "What does the pattern mean?"

His face was torn with grief, eyes tired. "Refugees. That beat means refugees. Bliss attacked again."

Before I could ask for an explanation, I watched him hide his upset behind the strong face of a leader.

Standing fluidly, he held himself with such graceful composure he seemed unreal. Braxen motioned for me to follow him as I was already clambering to my feet to shadow him towards the main tunnel. The drums began to fade away, leaving the cavern to suffocate beneath the imposing weight of this new silence. It felt as though no one was breathing, all of us waiting for the next moment to break the tension.

The wait was anything but easy, the anticipated arrival coming slowly. It was several long minutes before the first refugee stumbled out of the tunnel. I saw their face, a woman, bloodied and bruised. One of her eyes was missing, leaving a gaping hole to stare at us in its stead.

Braxen moved in an instant to her side, bounding across the distance with a powerful urgency. He greeted her quietly, a flash of blue emanating from his hand. She smiled gratefully and collapsed against him. He called loudly to the other demons, passing the woman off to one I recognized, Krasha, as more refugees arrived. Every face was injured in the same way, one of their eyes simply missing.

The initial shock began to fade, leaving nothing but horror to flood my chest. I made my way as fast as I could to where Braxen was, still emitting those blue flashes before passing off exhausted, wounded people. I lifted the first body he shifted in my direction, turning and sprinting off after Krasha towards the medical huts. My shoulder burned in protest, legs aching, yet the moment I had given my passenger to the Healer I was already on my way back. Next I knew, another tired body was in my arms, shivering and clinging to me.

I found myself murmuring comforts reflexively, my cradling arms becoming an embrace. "It's all right now. I have you, you're safe here."

Then the Healer took them, leaving my arms empty as I whirled around again. The endeavor blitzed by in a blur of burning lungs and muscles while desperate claws clung to me as I struggled to comfort them. I did my best to remain calm and confident for them, only ceasing when I returned to find a weak Braxen with no more refugees before him.

I gasped for air, finally caving to the relentless fire in my lungs, wheezing, "What else can I do?"

Braxen looked to me, in an instant relieved as he replied with a weary sigh, "We need to arrange hunting parties and any extra wings with Healing knowledge."

"I can join a hunt, and Kate has basic experience with medicines. Whom should I inform to gather others?" Despite my body's protests, I found that I could not cease in my efforts. Not whilst I knew those poor wounded faces needed for anything.

"Start with Krasha," he instructed faintly. I noticed then just how pallid his face was, his hands shaking. "If you see him, Yagin is a good hunter."

"What about you? Braxen, you can barely stand," I noted, all but lunging forward as he lost his balance. He caught himself and waved me away. "You need to rest."

"I will rest once this is over," he replied firmly, fixing me with some hidden bitterness. "Those people need me."

"Braxen, you are no use to us if you cannot even stand," I protested earnestly. He stumbled again, and this

45

time I ignored his indignation as I went to his side to help him brace himself. "Please, Braxen, I am useful for very little. Let me find you someplace to rest before I assist the others."

Despite the arguments I knew he wanted to spit back at me, his fatigue won out and he caved to my bargaining. I helped him to my hut, just as good a place as any for him to recuperate. Kate was giving the children firm instructions when we entered, already focused on the next task at hand. I could only assume she had seen the faces.

"What can I do?" she asked as I approached. She was pushing up her sleeves, hair pulled back and eyes fierce. "I've already talked to the kids, they'll stay here for now."

I nodded. "Good. Braxen needs rest. Go find Krasha, help her gather others to assist in the medical huts. I'll be leaving on a hunting party shortly."

Her hand brushed my free arm, the words she did not speak giving me a small respite. "Be safe, Cory. I'll see you soon."

"Soon," I agreed, watching her purposeful gait exiting the hut. I sighed tiredly, seeing Braxen to the bedding and helping lower him to the furs. "Sleep or don't, but you need to rest for the moment."

I then turned to the children, kneeling so that I could meet their worried eyes. I motioned them in for a quick hug, holding them tight. "Both your grandmother and I need to go help now, but we will be home soon, all right? Stay inside and listen to Braxen, even if he leaves as well. Do you understand?" They both nodded reluctantly. "Good. Everything will be all right. I love you both," I finished, giving them one last squeeze before I had to stand and leave.

"Bye, Grampa," sniffled Kyle, waving as I left the hut. It broke my heart to leave, though I knew they would be safe and my efforts were needed elsewhere.

Letting out a shaky breath, I forced back my nervousness and tears. I scanned the village for anything which might resemble a hunting group, but it was still chaos. Without Braxen's firm instruction, it seemed these people lost all sense of direction in a crisis. I saw so much fear and uncertainty, my heart broke anew.

What could I do? What had Braxen done? He had simply jumped into action, yet there was no apparent course available here. Regardless, everyone was so distraught I doubted they would notice anything less than a rude shock.

I inhaled deeply, letting out a deep, monstrous bellow which halted the panic. The resulting quiet turned to stare at me expectantly. I shuffled my wings awkwardly. Now what? What did they need?

"I am assisting Braxen while he recovers. I need all experienced wings to the Healer's huts to speak to Krasha." The voice which escaped me sounded like mine, but the confidence it commanded felt as though it came from someone else. My heart pounded in my ears, tongue numb, but I continued, "Those who are able, I will be coordinating the hunting parties to feed the extra mouths. We need to have the fires going to cook what we catch, as well.

"If you do not have those skills, focus on your

own. We will need blankets, clothing, fresh beds, and homes. If you can assist with children, come speak to me. If you need assistance with children while you are otherwise occupied, meet the volunteers as they come up.

"There is no task too small if the immediate concerns are otherwise met. We will get through this together. Everything will be all right," I finished, more for my benefit than theirs, watching as there was renewed hope in their faces and they began to disperse. A handful went to the Healer's huts, a gaggle of others more took up their crafts with a new purpose. Still more approached me, waiting for my instructions.

I faltered for a moment, fighting back my panic before I addressed their concerns. "If you are here for hunting, please step to the side there," I gestured to a large fire pit and a sizable number shuffled off, "and if you are here to provide child assistance, step forward."

I recognized a coral-skinned young woman, Leilani, and remembered seeing her with my children on occasion. Two others, also young women, stood beside her, looking as nervous as I felt. I nodded to Leilani, "Can you oversee organizing the children's care?"

She nodded, obviously timid but trying to stand strong through this. "Yes, Cory Human. I help."

"That is not my—Good," I corrected my habitual reply with a grateful smile instead. "Good. I will let you speak with the parents, then, and if you could see to my own? Kate and I have left them in our hut while we help."

Leilani returned the smile, clearly lost on some of my words although she seemed to understand enough. "Yes. I help babies."

Broken Orbit

I left the group to see what the hunting party had to offer, not that I had intimate knowledge of any form of hunting, in groups or otherwise. My quick headcount gave me eleven members, of eight men and three women. I saw Yagin among them, his lighter lavender tone easy to spot amidst the deep reds and vivid oranges.

Where on earth would I start with this task?

"Everyone, split into groups of three, you know the rules." Braxen's strong voice boomed behind me just as I opened my mouth to speak. I had never been happier to hear his cadence as he managed to purr despite the command in his words, "Yagin, your group can have two, you're experienced enough. I'll take Cory. Find your partners and start tracking!"

They all broke into groups so fluidly I nearly missed their departure, leaving Braxen and me alone.

I turned to him in relief, nearly ready to collapse from the startling effort of the last few minutes. "Thank you, Braxen. Did you get enough rest?"

He nodded, expression energetic and alight with...pride? "Thank you, it helped. And you did well, it seems I had little to worry over."

I let out a shaky breath. With it, a monstrous weight fell from my shoulders. "You were not the only one worried. Now, what is next?"

Braxen looked out over the productive change in the atmosphere, though the underlying tension and horror were still apparent. "I believe you and I now have time to assist in the hunts." He appraised me hesitantly. "Or perhaps foraging? Some berries could help see us through until the hunters return."

Karma Rose

I nodded gratefully. Harvesting I could do.

~~ * ~ * ~ * ~~

    It must have been hours we scoured the forestry outside of our haven. The baskets slung over our backs were now filled to the brim with a variety of berries, roots, and nuts. I knew we must have been another hour's walk from the village, only now turning around to make the return trek.

    Braxen glanced at the sky shining through the canopy, the changing colors beginning to cast an orange hue. "It's almost sundown. We should hurry; the hunters could take until dawn."

    "Who knew hunting for wild game would have proven more entertaining than stationary plant life?" I commented idly, although I enjoyed the thrill of picking fruits once more. Even after all this time, it still held such satisfaction to see my efforts rewarded with a full container. It stirred in me a wistful longing for my old farm work.

    Braxen stifled his laughter behind a smirk, torn between admonishing me and humor. "Don't tell the hunting parties you said that. The last thing they need is the village finding out their work is play."

    I chuckled. "It certainly sounds more delightful than negotiating with thorns."

    "Speaking of which," muttered Braxen, picking up the pace. I saw where he was looking, and the massive berry bush we had somehow neglected. He gently removed his basket, setting it against the nearest tree and stretching his wings. "They won't fit in the basket, but they'll fit in our stomachs."

He began plucking the ripe berries from their perches, fingers dodging their thorns deftly. I followed suit, setting my basket beside his and finding a relatively undefended group of fruit. When our hands were overflowing, we took our seats beside the bush, famished.

"How did we miss this one?" I wondered, tossing a berry in my mouth and savoring the tart flavor. My stomach turned, hunger clawing up into my throat. It was everything I could do to not devour the entire handful at once.

Braxen shrugged, more excited by the berries than discourse as he threw back his entire handful. He gulped them down before reaching for the bush again. "Must have been distracted by another bush."

He took his second handful more calmly, although the mess was already made. I could not help a chuckle, seeing his normally dignified disposition covered in juices like a child. He fixed me with an impatient scowl. I held my tongue and kept at my berries, wishing the flavor could tame itself enough for me to eat them more swiftly. As it was, the acidic bite of it burnt my mouth, but I was too ravenous to care. One way or another, I would finish them.

We continued in silence for a time, the sky's orange tone slowly turning red. The forestry around us began to cast long, twisting shadows, yet I found myself as calm as ever. My thoughts wandered lazily, straying through various topics before they finally settled, seeing Braxen before me with new eyes.

"Do you have any siblings?" I wondered aloud, picking at my pile of berries.

Braxen, on the other hand, seemed to be swallowing them by the dozen still. "Hm? Oh! My parents had two other children, twins, but I honestly only had an older brother, from...somewhere else."

Finally, something I could relate to more easily! I grasped at the topic, refusing to lose the opportunity to truly connect with him. "What was he like? What did you do together? Is he here?"

He laughed awkwardly, shifting with obvious discomfort. "Hm."

"My apologies," I said hurriedly, "I allowed my excitement—"

"No, it's okay," he interrupted, holding up a hand to silence me. He tossed another clump of berries in his mouth, swallowing quickly before he continued, "We never did much. I'm not sure he knew I existed, but I watched him a lot. He was so graceful and calm, it was hard not to idolize him. After I stopped hating him, of course."

We both laughed and at last, I could understand something of this world. I clung to the familiarity as he continued, "He was kind, generous, but just a little dense. I felt like sometimes he would need you to all but beat him with your words for him to accept when you meant something. And he was strong."

His admiration was touching; I could not help but smile. "He sounds lucky to have had you as a brother, as well."

That stopped him for a moment and he nodded,

wistful. "I suppose. I regret not knowing him better."

My heart turned to stone in my chest. "Braxen, you have my condolences..."

"Don't," he replied in a strained tone, quiet voice nearly begging me. He searched my face for a moment, growing more distressed the longer he took. "H-He's here, he just...Something happened. It shouldn't have, but it did, and I couldn't—I watched him being stripped down to nothing, and they just—

"They broke him," he told me, wounded deeply by the memory. For the first time, I saw a crack in his composure, listening to his impassioned words while they ran across his face as tears. He rubbed at a faded scar on his chest, the motion like an old habit when he faced this duress. His movements grew more agitated, voice angry, "It should have been me. I should have been there when it all happened, I should have helped him, not watched from—"

He cut himself off, turning his glare on the pile of berries I picked at. I leaned forward to set a hand on his shoulder for comfort. Doing my best to keep my voice calm and steady for him, "Braxen, I am certain you did everything you could, and your brother knows it, too. You should not blame yourself for things you could not control."

Braxen stared at me like he was a wounded child, confused before he nodded slowly. "Thank you, Cory. I wish I could tell you what those words mean to me."

I smiled, returning my attention to my berries shyly. "There is no need."

He nodded slowly. A strange, hopeful nostalgia

cast his face with shadows. "Cory?"

"Hm?" I savored another morsel, glad he used my given name in favor of his crude pet name.

"Did you?" he asked, then fumbled, "Have any siblings, I mean."

I nodded. "They were human. Two older brothers and a younger sister. It was a shock, finding out I was adopted," I joked, making Braxen smirk. "The eldest grew into a good man, I remember. My sister raised a family, and she was always very kind despite her ambition."

He watched me for a moment, keen eyes guarded. "And the third?"

A cold pit settled in my stomach, ruining my appetite as I choked on my most recent bite. I looked away, too overwhelmed to meet his gaze. "The best thing he did in his life was also the worst. I could never understand if he was simply in the wrong company for too long, or if he truly was so cruel, but...As far as I could care, he is better off dead."

"I'm sorry," he murmured abashedly. He was quiet for a long time, finishing what he had picked before he spoke again. "What was it like, living with the humans?"

"Stressful." The first word which came to mind made us both laugh, and I continued, "Oh, it was... different, very different. There is so much more restraint and humility involved, but the satisfaction of a hard day's work and lying down with..." I smiled wistfully, a strange pain wringing in my chest as I found myself missing my life before captivity. "It was no easier than living here, at least. I don't seem to fit well in either place if I am honest."

Braxen's face twisted with guilt and shame. "I'm sorry for what fault I have in that. I—You remind me of my brother," he admitted sheepishly, eyes downcast. "It's hard to treat you differently, and I-I only want to help you become the great character I can see that you are, just fragmented. For all the times I couldn't help my brother, I want to help you now. If you'll let me," he added awkwardly.

The pain in my chest eased, finally feeling something I could connect with and hold to in this place. "Thank you, Braxen. I would be honored to have someone as passionate as you help me, with anything."

He could not seem to help the childish grin which split across his face, showing his youth in the dying light. By comparison, he looked younger than Robert. He nodded to himself, looking around and sighing, "I suppose we've had enough. It's time to get these baskets home."

He leaped up lithely, his basket on his back before I could shamble to my feet more awkwardly, stiff with scars. I lifted my basket, careful of my shoulder as the weight of it pressed on me. I motioned ahead of us for him to lead, following behind and keeping pace.

Finally, I thought with a smile, comforted by his company. *Finally, I feel like I could belong, if only with this one friend.*

~~ * ~ * ~ * ~~

The moment we returned, the village surrounded us with excited chatter. We were swept up, our baskets all but pulled from us to be passed around, feeding both new faces and old. Braxen was whisked off to his endless responsibilities. He spared me a wave farewell as he allowed me to fade to the background and rest at last.

It was not long before I felt eyes boring into me, turning around to find Katelyn's relieved smile. I hurried through the bustling crowds, hugging her close and breathing her in.

I sighed, safety sweeping over me. "Oh, I missed you today."

Her tiny arms held me tighter. "I'm so glad you came home okay."

I kissed her hair, pulling back enough to smile for her. "Of course, my dear. You could never be rid of me so easily."

She laughed quietly, simply overjoyed now it seemed the hardest parts of the day had passed. "I wouldn't have it any other way, mister."

A familiar shriek of excitement caught us both off-guard, turning to see the children's elated grins as they sprinted towards us. I knelt, catching them both in my arms and hugging them tightly as I lifted them. They each held onto me, Kyle bracing with my wing and Sarah with my neck.

I gave them each a peck on the cheek. "I've missed you both. Where did you run off to, hm?"

"Leilani took us swimming, and I got to leave the shallow parts," boasted Sarah gleefully. Kyle nodded enthusiastically.

"Oh, is that why your hair is wet as a mop?" I teased, grinning at their giggles. "If you were swimming, did you catch any fish to eat?"

"Ew, no." They both wrinkled their faces, Kyle piping up, "Leilani gave us some berries and meat."

"And was this your dinner or supper?" I asked, skeptical.

They stared at each other, trying to decide on the wisest option.

"Lunch."

"Dinner."

"Very well, I will make you a deal." They both turned to me with rapt attention. "You may each go get one handful of berries, and then we will go back to the hut for bed, agreed?"

Kyle was instantly distracted by the immediate promise of fruits, while Sarah bore a look of quiet disappointment, no doubt at the prospect of sitting still after such an energetic day. I gave them one last squeeze before setting them down. They sprinted off toward the berries being handed out.

Kate's smile radiated through her entire being, black eyes dancing with it. "I love watching you with them, you know."

I stretched my shoulder, tender from both the basket and the weight of Sarah. "Truth be told, I am especially grateful for their distractions after today. I only hope they did not see what we did."

She nodded slowly. "The stories they told were worse than their condition, Cory, believe me. Did you know that these people are at war?"

I hesitated, nodding sheepishly. "I never realized the war-front was so close, or their enemy could be so cruel. Kate, I...I want to help them."

"They're fighting *angels*, Cory!" she hissed at me, earning a few wary glances from the demons around us. She was torn between heartbreak and fury. "I need you, the *kids* need you, and we need to know that you'll be home at the end of the day. Please."

I nodded, wanting to explain myself but getting cut off by the bouncing children as they snacked on the fruits they held. As agreed, they followed with us to the hut, its cozy space suddenly inviting and welcome after the world had seemed so vast today. The children sat on the furs and licked their fingers clean, already yawning and rubbing their tired eyes.

Kate and I each knelt to strip off shoes and jeans, settling them into nightclothes and tucking them in. Within moments, they were each slumbering soundly, tiny faces exhausted from their adventures. I smiled, undoing the buttons of my shirt so I may follow their example.

"I know we're not done with what we were discussing earlier," came Kate's quiet voice behind me. My heart stopped, waiting for her next words. "But please, remember that we still have a home outside of this place. I can't lose you again, and the children... Just, think about it?"

I sighed quietly, turning to meet her eyes. Their endless depths seemed to engulf me. "I will, Kate. I love you, and I love them. I've yet to decide on how to help, by any means. All I know is, after today, I cannot sit by as a burden any longer. They've yet to establish proper agriculture in the village, perhaps I could help there," I offered her. She seemed pleased to hear I was not so foolhardy as to rush off into the night with a war-band.

Kate saw me working to remove my shirt gingerly from my aggravated shoulder. She came to my aid, helping me out of the garment with a smile. "Thank you. I don't know what I would ever do without you, mister."

I stopped her from turning away, brushing her cheek with my thumb as I cradled her face. Oh, that I could stare at her face for eternity! I ducked in for a kiss, lingering on her lips long enough to savor her taste before I pressed my lips to her forehead.

Without a word, I turned from her blush to finish changing into my nightclothes, settling in beside the children. At the first sign of my presence, they snuggled into me, latching onto my arm and tail. Kate had lain down on my other side, resting her head on my chest, one arm wrapped over my torso. I heard her quiet breath, listening to it slow and soften as she, too, drifted off.

I was not far behind, settled in with our little family as sleep finally claimed me.

~~ * ~ * ~ * ~~

"What are you doing here, Half-Child?" spat a voice I knew too well. Vishar approached with Kayhali close behind, naturally. The two of them shared the same hateful glare, tails whipping back and forth angrily.

I sighed quietly, feeling hollow at the thought of dealing with this again. "I'm here to train, like every time you ask."

Vishar, as always, didn't like my answer, coming over to shove me. "You should know better by now. We don't want you here. Not even your Master wants you, didn't you know?"

The thought bit me. As if it wouldn't be enough to be despised by my village, it would only make sense that he wouldn't want me, wouldn't it? The uncertainty caught me off-guard, the flames I balanced falling to cinders in my hands. I threw them to the ground with a hiss, grabbing my staff to leave when Kayhali blocked my path.

"I'm leaving, like you wanted," I told her firmly, gasping at the fist she shoved in my gut when I made to step around.

"Great. Now I want my mother back, you half-bred monster," she spat, adding a knee to the growing bruise for good measure. I fell to the ground, breathless.

"I... I didn't..." I struggled to speak, the words lost as I continued to gasp.

I could feel it, my skull splitting open as a vision approached, and I screamed at the pain as my entire being was shoved away to make room for my Master. I fought as hard as I could, all of my hate welling up in my chest, but it wasn't enough. My vision changed from my dirty hands clinging to the earth to a face—his face.

I gasped in surprise, but it was masked with horror, his horror, as we stared at our reflection in a flat crystal—mirror.

Shame. I felt it well up and devour us whole as we stared at our face, and then came the loathing. The unearthly beauty of our face brought an acute awareness of how different we were from our family, our friends, and we longed for normalcy and humanity. The tears burned our face, loneliness all-consuming.

Broken Orbit

"This is fine," he whispered to us with a sniffle, nodding eagerly. "It is nothing I have not adapted to before, I can do it again. It will be all right."

Lies. We both knew that to be lies, the pain of it sharp. We took another shaky breath, gaining confidence with it. And the longer we stared, the more I gained my awareness in this muddled mixture of thoughts—like I was the one staring at him, and he at me. His expression changed, softening, nothing but open generosity and kindness left despite the drying tears.

"I have to do this. They deserve a perfect wedding," he told us both, smiling with such genuine happiness at our face. I wanted to reach out, indignantly at first. That quickly faded to something stronger, a need to know I could be okay, too. I wanted to feel that acceptance, the forgiveness he gave us—himself. But as the vision began to fade, I thought I saw a flash of my face in the mirror. Did he see it, too? Did he know me as I knew him? Could he spare me any of the same generosity?

My mind reeled in time with my stomach, making me cough until—

"Disgusting! Who knew you really were such a maggot?"

I groaned, looking up dizzily and tiredly at the hateful faces of my siblings. The sorrow I felt was so abrupt it hurt. I wanted to go back, to find his face again and beg to know if I could receive the same kindness while wearing my skin. I found myself yearning to speak to him now, to know him out of admiration instead of hate.

I wanted him to be a brother, not my Master.

61

Karma Rose

~~ * ~ * ~ * ~~

I groaned as the images faded, blinking my eyes open to the dim light of our hut. The children were still asleep, contorted on the other side of the bedding now. I was unsurprised, exhausted as they had been after everything last night.

Kate had shifted on my other side, turned away now and still sleeping. I moved slowly to disentangle myself from all of their sleeping bodies, managing to get myself propped onto one arm with surprising ease. I kissed Kate's bare shoulder before I made the final hurdle, climbing over her while taking every care not to disturb her rest.

Finally free of the bed, I stretched hesitantly and grabbed at clothes to wear for the day. Dressed, I left the hut as I was finishing with my buttons, trying to orient myself with the new day.

It was early morning, the sun barely rising, and the just-waking village reflected such. With a yawn and final stretch, I made my way toward the fires where food was usually cooked, glad to find something was already on the spit. I took a seat, enjoying the feeling of the embers' heat before I ate and started the day.

A weary Braxen trudged into the circle, taking a seat next to me. His face was drawn, eyes bloodshot. Had he even slept?

As if he could hear my thoughts of concern, he grumbled tiredly, "Nightmares. Couldn't sleep."

I nodded slowly. While I had most certainly slept

better than he had, my dreams were so vivid it was more like restfully watching a show than sleeping. "I had the strangest dreams, as well."

He stared at the fire. "Tell me."

"You interpret dreams, too?" I attempted to tease, the jibe falling short.

"I'm a Shaman. It's my job." He shrugged, in no mood for any humor this morning.

I mimicked his shrug, holding a hand near the fire to feel its heat against my palm. "There was a boy, and I do not know how but I knew him as I knew myself. Two others were harassing him, being cruel. And then...he saw someone—me, he saw me. In a vision in my dream, and I was talking to myself in my old home, about my brother Dustin's wedding. When the vision ended, he was so distraught. It was vivid like my dreams have been before, but it was different, somehow.

"Not quite a vision, more like a memory," I murmured to myself, laughing at the idiocy. How would I have a memory which was so distinctly...foreign? I shook my head, laughing at myself. "I must have eaten too many berries."

Braxen looked numb, eyes glassy. "Must have."

"Are you all right?" I asked him, quiet to avoid anyone else hearing.

In an instant, his fatigue was whisked away, the energetic man I had come to know smiling back at me. "Of course! I couldn't miss your first day of training."

I stopped short. "Training?"

"Of course," he laughed again through his exhaustion. "You were, how did you say, drafted?"

"Well, yes," I admitted, pausing at his choice of words. "But I never told y—"

"Then I recommend starting in on your meal now," he warned me, standing to grab himself some of last night's hunt. "When I'm ready, we go train."

~~ * ~ * ~ * ~~

Braxen's idea of combat training was far from what I imagined. For one thing, half of it took place in the sky. His primary focus was on endurance, particularly with flying. His secondary concerns were with deflecting blows, dodging, and fleeing.

Needless to say, his confidence in my ability to genuinely hold my own was far from inspiring.

I groaned as I finished our morning meal, exhausted by the prospect of another day of endless physical rigors and arduous labor. It had been two weeks now, non-stop. Did the man have *nothing* better to do? "Braxen, as much as I love to fly, I am sore. My wings feel as if they might fall off."

His eyes went wide, horrified. "What?!"

"An expression," I sighed, waving it away idly. A human expression alone, it seemed.

"Oh. Then get up, it's time to go," he barked, all but dragging me to my feet.

"What is it today?" I grumbled tiredly, giving my family quick hugs before I left for the day.

"Flight. I want to see how well you maneuver after all the endurance practice. Most bulls are clumsy, especially compared to women," he explained with a shrug. "It gives the angels an advantage. They're smaller, faster, and more agile."

"Very well, then," I sighed. At my begrudging resignation, he took a few quick strides and was airborne in an instant, his wiry frame doing little to weigh him down. With this rigorous work, my former bulk was returning, adding some difficulty to my less practiced abilities. I made the charge, leaping up as I brought my wings down and felt the burn in my membranes.

I followed him as he climbed up and out of the crevice serving as the village's sky, the world bursting forth below us as we escaped the cavern's confines. I gawked in awe. The expansive emerald forests and endless blue skies dulled little in their splendor no matter how many hours I spent staring at it all. Braxen was still above me, climbing higher as I followed, although I seemed to be gaining on him quickly.

Too quickly, I realized with a rush of horror.

A split second later, he was plummeting out of the sky. I panicked, correcting myself to dodge the massive demon as he fell past me in a rush of air. I adjusted again, racing after him in a flurry of concern before I saw how he was grinning at me. I pulled up, moments from the canopy, and corrected course for the higher currents. My irritated growl was lost in the wind.

Braxen was right behind me, banking too close across my right wing. I corrected again, dropping down to avoid the collision. Again, he wore a mischievous grin which was all too proud of his antics. Oh, he was being cute, all right.

Before he could make another pass, I surged

upward with a quick series of strokes, dropping down over him. He dodged the bulk of me, but the slap I felt when my tail flat came across his face was all too satisfying despite the sting. If it was acrobatics he wanted, I would oblige. I may have been out of practice, but I had spent endless hours perfecting aerial tricks when I was younger.

He kept at his uncomfortable proximity, trying his best to knock me off my balance and faltering as I was always able to catch myself or soar away. He was faster, there was no debate, and my decades of neglect added to his being more nimble. Yet for versatility with tricks, it seemed I had the upper hand. Odd, given he must have had much more opportunity to fly. Then again, I supposed he lacked my younger sister to keep entertained with aerial shows.

After some time we traded places, and where I bore his grin he wore my disgruntled glower. I laughed loudly, the sound catching in the wind and falling away from me. I dove low, throwing my wings in Braxen's path and following with a forceful downstroke to throw his balance. I clipped his back, turning to flit away in the direction of the sun, using it to add difficulty to his chasing after me. My plan backfired, however, the light searing in my eyes and sending daggers through my skull.

I cried out, clutching my head and unable to see as I felt myself losing altitude. Above me, I heard frantic wingbeats and Braxen's yelling, even over the rush of air as I failed to catch myself. The pain was barely fading when I felt a change in temperature, only a second before I crashed through the canopy below. I tucked my wings over myself, hoping to avoid any serious injury. The branches and their leaves felt like whips against my membranes, and then I was on the ground, the breath knocked from my lungs.

I groaned, unfurling my wings from my body and righting them behind myself. I pushed myself to stand slowly and blinked the blinding light from my eyes, vision returning slowly. I heard Braxen's wings shuffling nearby. Meaning to walk toward the sound I slipped, barely catching myself before I plummeted again, this time from the edge of the crevice and into the village below.

With some difficulty, I was able to pull myself back onto solid ground, exhausted from the flight and now sore from the crash. My vision cleared and I saw Braxen stalking toward me. His expression was torn between worry and disappointment.

"It seems someone put a cliff there," I commented nervously, plucking leaves and stray twigs from my clothes.

"What was that?!" he demanded harshly.

"That was me landing with all of the grace of a wet sack of rocks," I retorted with a sigh, shrugging away my embarrassment. I winced, shoulders and wings alike aching in protest. "The sun hurt my eyes, is all. It happens from time to time."

His hand whipped out to latch onto one of my horns, forcing my neck to arch uncomfortably as he turned it this way and that. "Your horns aren't right."

"Let go!" I growled, baring my fangs with a hiss when he tossed me away and sent me reeling. I caught myself before I fell into the crevice again. My horn felt violated where he had gripped it, a primal humiliation pooling in my chest. "What is *wrong* with you?!"

"You're sick," he spat, frustrated. His tail lashed behind him, destroying some of the underbrush.

"So are you, grabbing my horn!" I snapped, rubbing the odd stiffness from my neck with the way he had pulled at me. At least the feeling of molestation was easing quickly enough. "Damn you, Braxen, how is that not considered rude?!"

"No, you're *sick*," he stressed the word, irritation calming some. "You've no *euliyah*. Your horns aren't colored right; you need to fly more."

"I saw a doctor, he said it was some vitamin deficiency," I grumbled, glaring at him still. "Why did you—?"

"To check your color," he interrupted, raising one brow as if to challenge me to keep at my petulant spite. "Your horns should be black. Fly more—they'll turn the right color, and the pain stops. How did this happen, though? It's usually elders or cripples with this problem."

"I am an elder, and crippled in the shoulder," I muttered, pursing my lips when he cleared his throat in warning. "Fine! Perhaps my cautious upbringing? If not, then would forty years in a stone box do the trick?"

He paled, chagrined. "Cory, I—"

"It is no matter," I cut him off sharply, sighing and dropping my hand as my neck finally relaxed. "An inconvenience, if anything. Just—Please, refrain from grabbing my horns again?"

"Right." He nodded, wings shuffling awkwardly. "Anyway. You do well flying. All things considered.

We'll focus on that until your *euliyah* returns, then. There are places we could fly to, even. Nearby temples from the time of the Ancient Races, and the like..."

He trailed off, still nervous. "I suppose we should be done today, though. You're tired, and after that fall... Go relax. I have work to see to, anyway."

Braxen's dismissal was abrupt as he jumped into the crevice, gliding to the village below. I followed after him, fumbling my landing with how sore my wings were still. I grinned sheepishly as nearby demons found my mistake entertaining. Yet their revelry was not derisive in the slightest, reminding me instead of laughing at simple mistakes back home.

With such in mind, I set off to find my family and enjoy the remaining hours of the day with them.

~~ * ~ * ~ * ~~

The medical huts were surprisingly uncrowded given the recent influx of injured demons. The lack of other people only made me stand out all the more, between my size and way of dress. I linked my hands behind my back before approaching a nearby Healer.

"I beg your pardon, I was hoping to lend a hand if you needed the help?" I offered, to which I received a wide-eyed stare. The brick-red man pointed across the room nervously, muttering a word in a language I did not understand. Nevertheless, it was clear he meant to direct me to someone I could speak to. "Thank you."

My next attempt was greeted by an older woman as I stepped nearer. She addressed me before I had a chance to speak, "I heard you. Are you not comfortable with Len's dialect?"

"I lack the language entirely, never mind the dialect," I explained sheepishly, smiling politely. She turned to face me, and I saw then her brilliant blue eyes. They stared through me blindly. "My apologies if I was rude. I can scarcely manage the customs, although I am learning what I can."

Her smile was patient, almost motherly, as her deep blue lips turned up at the corners. "There's no need for apologies, I was only curious. We have enough help here, thank you, but if you've energy and time, there's work to be done with the builders. They're making new huts."

"Thank you, I'll investigate that lead," I thanked her readily, pausing when I realized my ease with this particular woman. It was not quite the same as the curiously little demoness from the other day. This was different, deeper, as though I felt to my very core I should trust this woman. I shook it from my mind, although it would not leave my chest entirely. "I suppose I will be on my way, then, madam."

"Oexis," she corrected me lightly.

"A pleasure, Oexis." I hesitated only a moment before I replied, "My name is Cory Charles Lawrence. I hope to see you again soon."

Oexis nodded, her smile broadening to a fanged grin. "Fly safe, Cory."

The traditional farewell left a lingering warmth in my core as I excused myself. Queer as it was, I could not shake a feeling of familiarity. Although were I honest, everything about this world held an aura about it which was both mortifying and comforting. As strange as I was, I was still not the stranger here. That, in itself, was enough.

~~ * ~ * ~ * ~~

I ducked my head into our hut, spotting Katelyn as she finished changing into her nightclothes. I smiled, taking a moment to appreciate her allure. We had been here weeks now, and I found with every passing day my absolute adoration of her in this wild place only ripened.

"Kate," I called to her in a whisper, glancing at the pile of furs to make certain I did not disturb the children sleeping there. She looked over to me, a knowing smirk on her lips as she met me at the entrance.

"How long have you been there, mister?" She raised one eyebrow, crossing her arms over her chest and cocking her hip. Damn it all, but I *loved* her!

I grinned mischievously. "Long enough. You are as gorgeous as ever, Miss Katelyn."

Oh, how her blush could set my heart racing! "Are you coming to bed, Cory?"

"Not quite yet. Truthfully, I've come to abduct you, my dear," I confessed, grinning wider. I pulled her from the hut gently, guiding her with my tail. She followed along, laughing excitedly when I swept her up in my arms.

"What's the occasion?" she asked gleefully, black eyes dancing with all of the love I had ever known. Kate settled in my embrace, leaning into my chest. My arms had been barren of her weight for too long, and I felt so perfectly whole with her held against me now.

"Grace is going to sing, and *we* are going to take advantage of the empty lake."

"Skinny dipping? Really?"

I laughed, keeping hidden the best of the news. I had seen Grace just earlier in the day, singing near a pile of ashes and compelling flowers to bloom from it. Her unique brand of magic, she had explained, granted to her as a Choir angel.

Fireworks, I thought wryly. *And I have just the perfect show for you, Kate.*

The scene had given me an idea, and Grace had agreed quite happily. So, while the demons gathered at the fires to listen to her slowly rising aria, I hurried along the river bank to the lake.

The water was still, a velvety mirror of stars shimmering in the night. Katelyn's gentle gasp of wonder warmed my chest with passion. I set her down carefully, keeping one hand on her waist as she collected her balance.

Grace's flawless soprano reached us even here, echoing across the cavern as an unearthly hymn. Vaguely, I could recall hearing such angelic singing, as if in a distant memory from another lifetime. I set the thought aside, eyes only for Kate as I took her hand in my free one.

"Dance with me, my dear?" I asked, breathless as she agreed with a wordless nod. She placed her spare hand on my shoulder, smiling with all of the vibrancy I remembered of her youth as we swayed slowly. I ducked my head to kiss her, lingering to savor the feel of her lips. Around us, the night began to glow as the world yielded to Grace's peculiar talent. "I love you, Katelyn. Now and always."

Just then, the world around us bloomed to life. Flowers emerged and spread their petals wide, from trees and vines alike. The earth beneath our feet grew into a carpet of delicate foliage. I plucked a blossom from a nearby branch and tucked it behind her ear, kissing her again.

Grace's angelic voice rang out as we danced with the stars at our side, flowers continuing to bloom. Still, it all paled in comparison to the woman in my arms as she captured me with her depthless eyes. She never needed to say a word, and I felt so completely how much she requited my declaration.

My Kate.

Chapter Three:
Of Monsters and Men

The next several weeks passed by in a blur. Most of my days were spent at Braxen's side, following him through his daily routine, or fending him off in aerial sparring matches. Kate and the children had settled into favored activities of their own, namely crafting or running about with the other demon children, respectively. Despite such active days, I still saw them frequently, glad for every minute of it.

Even with the laborious regime Braxen was forcing me through, I found myself waking every morning in better conditions than I had gone to sleep. Bruised, perhaps, or scraped although always feeling I had more energy to take with me through the day.

This morning was no different. The sound of Sarah's shrieking laughter stirred me from my slumber, drowning out the usual birdsong at this time in the early morning. I smiled, basking in it for a moment before I began my day.

When I left the warmth of the furs, I dressed and made for the lake to bathe and tidy up. No one stared at me anymore. No one was astonished by my countless

74

scars. Here, I was as physically normal as could be. Everyone had scars, everyone was red-based in color, every man had horns and every woman had spur-like bone ridges.

Still to my wonder, Kate and her grandchildren were physically alien here, even more so than Vladimir and Grace. After the first week, however, they were treated as breakable but still individuals—breathing, living, thinking people. The irony would never escape me how demons were being more kind and respectful than humans.

After bathing, I meant to brush my hair back, as it was still too short to tie up. I paused in front of the still water, however, confused at what I saw. I frowned, smiled, winked. Every movement matched mine perfectly, which meant it was genuinely my reflection.

"How could that be?" I murmured to myself, frowning again. The scars on my face were thinner, the purple lighter. I rubbed my eyes and blinked rapidly to clear my vision, inspecting again.

Still, the scars appeared to have healed some. I looked at my arms and chest. Lo and behold, even there the scars seemed to have changed. What was this? An illusion? An actuality? A bored deity jesting? I shook my head slowly and brushed my hair back, ready to be gone from the trick of the water.

It was then that I realized I was not alone, nearly falling into the lake at the sound of a shocked cry. When I looked, I saw Braxen crouching by the lakeside, shivering. For a moment I wondered what could be wrong, then put it from my mind. There was no use guessing with the whimsical Shaman's mood.

While I had seen Braxen, it seemed he had not noticed me, giving me hope to buy precious time before he found a new wringer to put me through. I took to the woods without thinking, knowing Kate would not worry for some while yet. I slipped past the guards at the edge of the village, beyond the tunnel and into the calm, still canopy cover which finally spoke of my peaceful solitude.

It had been too long since the last time I had found a moment for my mind to collapse, so I might piece my world back together again. Demons, oh, *demons*! Still, I could scarcely believe it. After decades, they finally remembered there was one of us left with the humans. Yet I was beginning to worry it was not for my benefit they had come for me.

I kept hearing curious whispers behind my back. Everyone was careful to speak a tongue I did not understand, although I had gleaned enough to catch snippets of a conversation here or a comment there. I was attracting attention, and it was not simply my human behaviors which had done it.

Perhaps this was simply a strange world, though. After all, everyone seemed to be wired with the same knowledge, the same beliefs. I had seen every demon of every color, dialect, and size kneel to pray in the morning, and raise their hands in thanks at night. Strange, but I supposed I would be the pot calling the kettle black if I were to criticize.

Oh, but my mind could go on and on in endless circles with this! How had this world been created, who was it they prayed to and thanked, what language had birthed theirs?   Where did humanity end and their demonic natures begin?

Endless circles, I chided myself, finally pausing to look at where I had wandered to. I frowned, finding myself much farther than I could remember having gone before with Braxen. *Perhaps I should turn back...*

From behind me, I heard the heavy footfalls of someone following me. Recalling my encounters with the demons, I wondered why they were being so uncharacteristically loud now. When I turned to confront my follower, however, I froze with a stab of shock.

"Who...?" I managed to choke out as I collected myself, staring at the man not ten feet from me. He was dressed in armor, polished and shining in the sun. His skin was nearly paler than the moon, with golden hair and the bluest eyes I had seen in what must have been decades. An uncanny shiver of recognition shuddered through me, and I felt I should know this man. I should trust him.

The smile he gave me was kind. When he replied, I thought such a creature should never have been wandering unprotected and alone near the demons. "I'm sorry to have startled you. My name is Bravery; I'm an angel."

I continued to stare, dumbfounded. "An angel?"

I should run, I noted blankly. I knew something was wrong about this man. I knew the horrors he must be capable of, and yet an eerie calm kept me from feeling proper panic. How curious.

"Yes, an angel. I've been sent for you, Cory, and I am immensely ashamed that the demons reached you first. Have they hurt you?" he asked concernedly, taking a step toward me with an outstretched hand. I jumped back, horrified by the thought of anything so heavenly touching the unholy thing I was.

In the distance, I heard my other shadow calling for me, "Cory! Cory, Kate is looking for you, and you're not getting out of flight practice!"

Bravery's expression changed suddenly, hardening to that of a vengeful beauty which could have killed, it was so devastatingly breathtaking. A groan of frustration escaped him, yet all I could find myself desiring was a way to please him, to make his anger vanish.

A second longer and Braxen broke through the forestry, freezing when he saw the angel. Terror overtook him, a feral bellow echoing back from the trees. Bravery drew a dagger from his hip, holding it idly.

"Cory, you need to run!" cried Braxen, baring his fangs at Bravery fiercely. How was I was supposed to run when I was still so utterly hypnotized? How was he able to retain any control over himself, to resist such an enticing pull?

"Stay there, boy, this will take but an instant," commanded Bravery, moving towards Braxen with his dagger brandished in front of him.

"Run, Cory, RUN!" The demon gave a mortified bellow, eyes wide as he strove for a way to fight or flee from the enrapturing calm.

There was a second longer where I could hesitate before Bravery lunged. All I could do was stare in shock as he sheathed the dagger in Braxen's side. The demon screamed and, just like myself, could not find the will to move. He gaped at Bravery, betrayal etched clearly on the

Shaman's face as tears came to his eyes. I felt the burn of it in my veins, that cold blade as good as stabbing into my gut instead.

"You're no better than the humans are," I realized in horror, crying too as Bravery turned a serene smile back to me. He left the dagger where it was lodged into Braxen's side.

"I'm sorry you had to see that, but I suppose it's better than when they fight back, right?" apologized Bravery cruelly. All I could see was every crime committed out of hate rather than need, of pleasure as opposed to desperation. Bravery tried to put a hand on my shoulder.

I remembered Kate and her countless bruises when we were younger. Richard and his cohorts always had some heinous act planned. Then there was just this last year when I had been lured into a trap.

I smacked him away with an infuriated yell, "Get back! You lying cur, GET BACK!"

Without glancing back, I hurried to where Braxen was struggling to pull out the dagger. I stopped him, trying to urge him back toward the village. He shook his head, staring behind me.

"Run...I-I'll hold him off," he argued weakly, materializing fire from his wound.

"What? You're saving a *demon*? A futile gesture, I assure you. They're like vermin, multiplying by the thousands to pervert and corrupt this world!" laughed Bravery behind me. I glanced at Braxen, an innocent man, and made to leave with him. "You'll be crawling back when you realize their faults, Prince, this I promise you."

I ignored Bravery, half-dragging Braxen away. After a few moments, it seemed he caught a second wind, trying to walk without my assistance. He kept faltering, his wings dragging half-limp behind him, tail utterly lifeless. I thought of how far we were and the hundred-some yards we had already come.

"Here, Braxen, you need to rest," I sighed, leaning him against the nearest tree. He slumped against it and stared at me, heartbroken, shaking his head slowly.

"You should run," he told me, still faint. "Bravery—He's burnt forests to the ground and poisoned seas to bring the end of us. You...Just run."

"No. I refuse to leave you out here to die, least of all by the likes of Bravery," I retorted more sharply than I would have liked. I glanced around, my eyes always finding their ways back to the dagger protruding from Braxen's side. I wished I knew how to treat the wound, thinking back over my time at the NSISD. "We need water and something to stop the bleeding. Is there a creek or river anywhere nearby?"

"A creek, it leads from the lake. You may as well leave me to the angel, Cory. I'll slow you down, and they—they can't take you. Not you. Please, just run." He started crying again.

"No, you are going to lead me to the creek. Are you ready?" I asked, holding out an arm for him to brace against. He made to move toward me, collapsing to the ground instead. I cried out in shock, kneeling beside him but dumbfounded in the face of so much blood. What could I recall from Paul? What did one do with the blood?

Broken Orbit

What happened when there was blood?!

Knives.

"Braxen, get up, we need to get to the creek!" I begged urgently, terrified of what my eyes deceived me with more than the angel who was sure to find us soon. Shards of glittering, shimmering metal were strewn throughout the leaves above us. The sure horror which scalpels promised me shone in the sunlight there.

He was falling out of consciousness, leaving me alone to drown in the midnight blood—filled with blades for stars. No, no, NO! He could not abandon me to their merciless hands, they could never take me back! Without thinking, I hoisted Braxen up and slung him across my back. Pain shot through my shoulder, urging me on as I hobbled toward where he had said the creek was.

There was a flutter of blue to my right, startling me. I whirled around, nearly losing my balance as I searched for the icy eyes of the man who had sold me out. I could hear his gentle laughter, the trees whispering with the words of the kind doctor as he gave his sermons.

"You're better off dead!" I yelled at the forest, whirling again when I saw the blue flitter away. "I'm free now, you whore! The last forty years were for nothing! NOTHING!"

I laughed insanely, continuing on my way even as the masked faces lined up on either side of my path to watch. Just like their exams, their *tests*. Wind tunnels and machines, with their monitors and wires attached to my skin. White walls and tiles, sterile and sanitized rooms smelling of latex and bleach.

"No, you can't haunt me if you're not ghosts, not if

81

you never left!" I laughed hysterically, trudging along shakily. I looked over and saw my parents walking with me, the irony slamming home. "Oh, that makes me the ghost now, doesn't it...?"

I stopped there, gawking at my feet and the water running nearly halfway up my calf. I forgot to move for a moment, confused as I struggled to recall the crick's significance. Once I did, however, I had Braxen off of my back and in the water as quickly and gently as I could manage.

Then I was staring again, realizing this is where my plan ended.

"Well, now, this was a poorly thought idea," I muttered with a defeated sigh, looking up and down the sparkling creek. My attention was drawn to the inky black as it swirled down the current, too thick to mix with the water immediately.

"Cory. Cory, what have you done to yourself?" demanded Mother worriedly. She came to examine my bloodied hands and the deep cuts and bruises there.

I pulled away quickly, remorseful of the pain I had caused myself by acting an animal in the clearing. "Nothing to worry over, Mother. I was just about to tidy myself for supper."

"Cory Charles, you answer me this instant!" she snapped, but the strain in her voice was from fear and not anger—fear for her child, for me. "Where have you been running off to? Why would you do this to yourself?!"

Tears of frustration welled up to burn my eyes, and I whirled in a fit of anger. "Nothing you would be proud of! What else could come from a demon? Or did you honestly think you could pray it from my blackened horror of a soul?!"

"Don't you speak to your mother like that!" yelled Father, stepping up to reprimand me. We both stared down his empty threat in the face. I snarled in disappointment and turned away to climb the stairs. "You will turn around and apologize right now, boy!"

"What did *you* do, Braxen, to be killed by an angel?" I wondered, watching the blood being swept away from his wound. "Or are you just as innocent as the children of your home, back in the desert before your water was poisoned?"

"I...I'm sorry," I said again as Paul pulled another stitch through the gouge on Kate's arm. They both gave me a stern look which silenced me in my guilt.

Kate smiled through a wince. "It's okay, Cory. I know it was an accident."

"An accident," I muttered bitterly, ashamed.

"Accidents don't kill," I murmured, scowling to hear my mad ramblings. "But perhaps that makes me the accident? Unless I did not kill you, and I may yet save you...? Braxen? Braxen, why won't you answer me?"

The blood on my hands was still too thick to wash away completely, feeling like hot sap between my fingers. As I stared at it, I slowly began to understand something, some curious notion which was far saner than any other thoughts I could have possessed right then. I had seen Braxen use his blood for things he called magic. He had healed wounds before, all with a whim; he claimed only intent was needed. Could it matter who's intent it was, who's blood?

Did it matter when there was no pulse at his throat?

Pulling the dagger from his side, I laughed at myself for thinking it possible. Smearing the blood from his wound across his torso for good measure felt like some morbid interpretation of finger painting. All I could do was pray this could work, that all of Braxen's fantasies could be right. I felt helpless, handing so much power over to this fading demon and his fireworks. Still, it was this or his dying over my stubbornness. I could not bear the thought of living with such guilt, however absurd it may seem.

I stared in despair, the weight of it all heavy on my shoulders. "Tell me, Braxen, tell me what to do. Is there some secret way to save you from this, one only living here would teach me? Please..."

The blood continued to flow and swirl in the stream as if it were oil. I felt like I was the one dying, as though the dagger had been stuck in my gut instead. The sensation was cold, the world losing warmth with every passing second. I choked, fighting to stay calm and failing.

"Braxen, please. Braxen? Braxen!"

"Braxen, stop ignoring your grandmother and listen." A familiar face scolded me, the insult to yet another injury. Jeckat's Avatar. He smiled placidly. *"That's better."*

I focused on what my grandmother was trying to say, the satisfaction apparent on her face. "This is healing magic, Braxen. You need to learn it well and master it if you hope to become a memorable Half-Child."

Broken Orbit

I felt the fear before I could stop myself. "But I'm a Shaman, not a Healer! What if I can't—"

The hard slap across my face was so loud it hurt my ears nearly as much as it hurt my cheek. "You can and you will, Braxen! I guarantee you that. Your life depends on it. If you fail to heal your Master, all you do is doom yourself. Now, watch."

"I know this." The memories seemed so clear to me, things I had never lived before coming as naturally to me as breathing.

The soft glow of another healed wound enveloped the small hut, giving me a faint twinge of pride. What little they hadn't beaten out of me already, that is. The small girl sighed softly, blinking her amber eyes open tiredly.

"Mara?" she whimpered, the demoness beside me answering the call for her mother. I stepped back, averting my gaze from such a private moment.

"Very good, Braxen," praised Jeckat's Avatar mildly, leaving the hut for me to follow.

My excitement started to build as it occurred to me what these memories meant. "I know this!"

"Run! The angels are here, RUN!"

The screams outside were haunting, but I had to focus. This was the village leader before me, the strongest bull-demon for days' worth of flight. If I couldn't save him, who would defend this village?

"My people..." he groaned, the gash splitting his cheek open gushing blood as he spoke. I could see his teeth glinting through the blood coursing through his mouth and into his hair. "Save...my people..."

"I'll get to that, but first they need their Cretan," I replied firmly, if routinely. None of this felt dire. I was in the middle of a battle, and calm as ever. Not that I wasn't afraid—I was terrified. I had just long since lost my ability to care.

"Save...them..."

The damage was extensive—the laceration on his face and a chunk of flesh missing from his right shoulder, down his abdomen. Had they tried to skin him? That thought was irrelevant. Now, focus! I placed my hands over the first wound, feeling the light building inside my chest.

"Hold on, Braxen, please!"

A third flash of light and the lead-bull groaned as his final wound knitted itself together into an ugly scar. I gasped, shaking from the effort it took me to pull him back from his near-death. His eyes snapped open and he sat up in one swift motion, staring me down coldly.

"Coward," he spat at me. I hated how he was right, how I would rob his death of such honor and hide from battle in doing so. He stood smoothly and brushed past me, back out into the fray. The only comfort I had was knowing that, if I could bring him back from the brink of death, I could protect my Master's life, too.

Before I knew what had happened, the water around us took on a glow before flashing bright blue. Braxen's body arched sharply, a choked gasp forcing his mouth open and his chest to expand. I felt relief when his eyes opened. He seemed as shocked as I was exhausted.

The cool water climbed up my body as I began to collapse, feeling as though I had sacrificed my own life to heal his near-dead flesh. A clawed hand caught me before the water overtook me, and I fell beneath the sweet bliss of sleep.

~~ * ~ * ~ * ~~

Lucidity felt at the edge of my fingertips, just barely out of reach despite how desperately I grasped for it. My last waking memories were vivid and haunting, torn between a near-psychotic episode and remembering a life which was not my own. I needed to feel my feet on solid ground, metaphorical or literal, so long as it gave me the relief of orienting myself once more.

I forced my eyes open, the images I found blurred and distorted, like peering through silty water. Sounds came to me in the same way, warped by the distance from their source to my ears.

I saw a demoness I did not recognize working over me, older and brick red. A blue light kept flashing, blinding me enough I could scarcely understand what was happening around me. I glimpsed Katelyn at the edge of the hut, with Braxen. He stood proudly, uninjured, looking so healthy I had to wonder if everything I remembered was simply a dream.

The demoness gave me little time to mull this over, her words the only distinguishable sounds I heard at all, "Rest now, warrior. You've fought enough for today. Dream of the peace you've earned."

As my world went dark again, I could have sworn that despite my understanding of her words, they were not the human language I knew so well.

Karma Rose

~~ * ~ * ~ * ~~

Start with the facts, with what you know.

It had been quite some time since I had needed to steady myself like this, and the use of it felt inadequate for this mess.

My name—My name is Cory Charles Lawrence. I am sixty-nine years old, and Katelyn Ann Smith is my fiancée. We are raising her two grandchildren, Kyle and Sarah. They are six and eight and playing somewhere with Leilani...

I kept on listing simple truths in my mind, eyes glazed over as I focused on the fire in our hut.

"Cory, are you okay?" asked Kate, placing a gentle hand on my shoulder. I continued to stare into the embers listlessly, another tear streaking my face. "Cory?"

I sniffled and shook my head, dragging myself from my forced apathy reluctantly. As I pulled away from it, I realized more deeply the injustice of what had happened.

"Braxen had done nothing wrong. He may be obnoxious at times, but...I watched an angel stab him, Kate, speaking like he was managing a pest," I admitted in a strained whisper. I looked at Katelyn, losing control. "He was terrified, Kate! He was innocent, and Bravery tried to kill him."

The anguish on her face did nothing to help. I wished she could say the angel was justified. I wished we were still in the city, that none of this was real, that angels and demons were nothing more than fairy tales. Even if it cost my sanity, I would pay the price to have this be a lie.

"I'm sorry," whispered Kate brokenly, holding me as best she could. Such a tiny woman, trying to comfort the innocent monster. Still, her small frame felt lacking somehow, my body craving something more for proper comfort. When had she never been enough? "I'm so sorry, Cory."

I held on to her care and warmth, desperate to seek consolation while this cruelty could find no way to be untrue. Finally, I understood a scrap of the pain my brethren struggled on with every day. I could grasp the horror of this war, knowing what helplessness the presence of angels could induce. It was nothing like Grace's delicate and subtle calm, so much more hypnotic in its all-consuming embrace. With naught to say of the ensuing betrayal, nor the absolute terror there was little to be done against it.

Like cattle for the slaughter, and the angels wanted my help in it.

"Are you okay?" she asked warily as I pulled away, all too soon given the circumstances.

"I'm fine," I brushed her off, lifting the dagger I was now required to wear, according to Braxen and Vladimir. Could I use it? Against a demon, let alone an angel?

"You don't sound—"

"I'm just fine!" I snapped irritably, hating how she flinched from me. I turned my face away to hide my fangs. The demons did not need me to be so meticulously in control! The thought only served to confuse me further, distraught by the weight of it all pressing down on me.

"Please, Kate, let it lie!"

When I glanced back, she was rubbing at her chest idly, frowning as she considered something. "I think we should go home, Cory."

I faced her again, shocked. "You would ask me to abandon these people? Turn tail now?"

"What difference could you possibly make?!" she demanded sharply, the motion of her hand growing more agitated.

"What difference did you make on my behalf, Katelyn?!" I retaliated sharply, an unintended growl escaping with my words. "Would you have sat by—"

"That's different, Charles, and you damn well know it!"

"How is it different, then?" I challenged angrily. I had to stand, tossing the dagger to the ground and pacing across the small space of the hut with little relief. It must have been my aggravated senses playing tricks on me, how wrong the air smelled now. It was sickening. "I watched you day after day, feeling as if you marched to war. How was your fight any safer?!"

"It's too dangerous here, Charles," she pleaded, sounding breathless in her distress. Still, she kept at her attempts to soothe herself by rubbing at her shoulders now. "Think about the kids! They're not safe here!"

"Neither are the demon children!" I cried out in desperation. "No one here is safe! Just the same as it was when we were children, Katelyn, and inaction then would have damned us both! It feels so much like a cage, I can't stand it, and then the knives—Kate, *the knives*! Angels and humans both, just cutting until there's nothing left!"

Broken Orbit

It took me a moment to return to myself from my crazed ranting. For the guilt to settle in and, as I turned to apologize to Kate, realize how she was not breathing.

Time stopped in that instant, every word I had been digging into her cutting me a thousand times over. I could not move, frozen as I waited for the breath, the movement, the flicker or blink of her eyes to tell me she was fine. She should be scolding me, she should be upset, she should be anything but so terribly still.

"Kate?" I managed to choke on her name, the full force of what I saw blinsiding me like a crash landing. The world blurred as my eyes burned; I made my way over to lift her from the furs gently. Her breath had ceased, yet her heart struggled on, weakly and softly, on and on. Stubborn as she, it refused to stop.

I hurried from the hut, turning to the first face I found and begging, "Help. Please, help her!"

They could not understand, torn as they shook their head and replied in a language I could scarcely comprehend. I turned to the next face. Then the next. Each time more desperately than the last, all I could do was beg for mercy where I had shown none.

"Here. Here, this way! This way!" Finally, a voice broke through to me, shattering the panic-stricken daze I had quickly slipped into. "Follow me!"

They ran and I followed, sprinting as fast as I could. I could not feel the fire in my legs, nor the torture in my shoulder as her heart continued to slow. Every frail beat was counting down the seconds at a pace I could understand, and which I could not bear.

The next few moments blurred by haphazardly:

My relinquishing her to another pair of arms, words in another tongue, then hands. Gentle at first, guiding me. Then they were pulling me from the hut. Screams, like the night I had been taken, and I was fighting harder than ever—to stay close, to never let her go—harder than I had ever fought before.

As they successfully hauled me from the hut, I wondered if this was her nightmare of the last forty years.

"NO!" I bellowed, tearing against those who restrained me. I felt their claws dig in and gouge me yet I could not care, could not see anything besides that damned woman who owned me so completely! It seemed as though my own heart should stop with hers. "Kate! KATELYN!"

A hard fist came across my face, forcing me to focus. "She will be fine. Jeckat will watch over her."

"*Hogwash*!" I growled, spitting blood from my mouth as I struggled against the hands, strength faltering to submission. "No one's ever watched over her."

Suddenly, the face came into focus. Braxen was pale and visibly weak with fear, but the intensity of his expression made me stop fighting. "I swear to you on my freedom, she will live, Charles."

I stared at him, grief crashing against me with such force I felt it echo inside me. The hands holding me transformed from restraints to supports. "I wish she'd never met me, Braxen."

As abruptly as I had been detained, I was being embraced, without question or criticism. Arms wrapped around me, so many pairs that I had to wonder how anyone else could find a way to reach me. Still, they did, over and over, all of them murmuring their comforts in countless languages that I did not speak. Yet I understood every utterance, every condolence, every wish for wellness and promise that she would be fine.

One word I became all too familiar with was "Jeckat." Always, Jeckat.

~~ * ~ * ~ * ~~

"Dear child, are you still here?"

I started from my forced calm, looking to find the voice's owner. I recognized the older woman with a smile, honestly glad of her company. "While Katelyn is here, I should be, as well."

Oexis sighed softly, making her way over to me in her gradual, cautious way. It took me a moment of watching, admiring the piercing blue of her eyes before I realized she had never looked *at* me. Only ever in my direction, and slowly I understood she truly was blind.

It took her some time, but she reached me at the hut's entrance all the same. Her hand found my shoulder, fingers feather-light as they glided down my arm to rest atop my hand. She sat beside me, gripping my hand firmly. It was a familiar gesture, and one which felt all the more reassuring as the odd comfort of her presence surrounded me again.

"Sweet boy, you need your rest, and time with your children," she told me softly, squeezing my hand.

"Oh, no, they, ah—They are not mine," I corrected her awkwardly.

Oexis smiled knowingly, the gentle expression

accentuating her age and the laugh-lines she had collected over her years. "Even I can see they're yours. I can also see that you're tired, sweet boy."

My replying smile felt lost on her. "No, I will stay where I am needed. Thank you for your concern."

She nodded slowly, smile saddening with forlorn wisdom which reached her voice, "Remember to save enough for yourself, when you're feeding others first."

I nodded out of habit. "Thank you, Oexis, but I will be just fine. I only need to see her through this, and then we will return home."

She patted my hand before returning to her gripping. "It's an old piece of wisdom, from my village in the Great Forests. All Healers are taught to care for themselves the same way they care for others, even if they're last."

"I am far from a healer," I replied a bit more bitterly than I expected. I pulled my hand from her hold as I felt a fresh wave of shame for my actions. Was it not my sharp tongue which had resulted in Kate's condition now? "My apologies, madam, my patience seems to be thin today."

"I'm fine, sweet boy, don't worry about that," she replied softly. Her smile was kind, expression gentle despite her proud features. "What work do you do? Your hands are...rough," she decided on the word carefully. For the first time, I realized she would feel the scars on my skin as clearly as others could see them.

"I used to be a farmer, but now, I...I don't know," I admitted with an odd twist of regret in my chest. I missed an honest day's work if I were truthful. There was no accounting for the ache of hard labor, nor the satisfaction of a job well done. "I suppose I tend to my family if it could be considered work."

"Some of the most difficult work, I'd say," laughed Oexis quietly, mindful of the quiet needed in the hut behind us. I could feel her curiosity regarding the unanswered question of my scars, all the more grateful when she let it lie. "There's nothing wrong with taking pride in tending the home the same as you would any other work."

I felt uneasy at her insistence in trying to comfort me, as well as her subtle attempts to see me off to get rest for myself. "And you? I would guess your family is grown and raising their own children by now?"

Sorrow cut across her features. It reached her voice just as deeply as it forced tears from her eyes, "I don't know. We were separated by the angels some time ago; my bull died defending us."

I choked on her grief. I could not begin to imagine if the Institute had made good on their threats against my family to gain my more submissive cooperation. What if I lost the children now? There was no accounting for such heartbreak.

"My apologies, Oexis, I never meant to bring up anything so painful," I offered weakly.

"It's in the past. The important thing now is that others like you are raising their own families," she recovered with a sad smile, a hint of genuine happiness bleeding through. She found my hand again and gave it a solid squeeze. "Remember to hold on to the people who enjoy every bit of who you are. They're not often, and they make it all worthwhile."

I nodded, again out of habit, before I managed to reply, "I know. Another reason I cannot leave just yet."

There was a knowing gleam in her blind eyes which she left unspoken. Giving my hand a gentle pat, she dropped her grip entirely and shifted to stand.

"Everything will work out, sweet boy. Just remember to save enough for yourself," she reminded me kindly. Sparing me one last smile, she left me to my waiting.

~~ * ~ * ~ * ~~

It was not until sundown when I was finally permitted to enter the hut where they were caring for Kate. Even so, my permission was tentatively granted, with the stipulation I must remain at the farthest ends of the hut, by the exit should anything...happen.

Someone had awkwardly explained to me the situation. "She ill, need rest and no excite. Yes?"

I nodded, the rough message more understandable than their choppy attempts with human words. I was still frozen and speechless, staring at the pale, drawn face I had so carelessly attacked. The children knew she was not well, although I had neglected the details of how serious this was. Woe and worry were the last things these children needed. If it came to it, then I would ease them into this reality gently, not a moment sooner.

As it was, they were allowed to say hello, bring her flowers, hugs, and all of the love they so willingly had to spare. Calmly, of course, but it still wrenched my heart

96

to see them loving her so completely and knowing I could be the one to take her from them. I sighed quietly to myself, doing my best to ignore both the sight of her frailty and the sickly-sweet scent pervading the hut.

Katelyn was, as always, a mortal embodiment of grace and endurance in the face of adversity. Not once while the children visited did she ever falter in her smiles, her voice holding strong no matter the subject. As often and as long as she could stand, those little ones were at her side. At times, Leilani would join in silently, helping the children to demonstrate what new knot or weave they were learning.

As the days dragged on, those moments grew shorter and fewer. Leilani's aid was invaluable as she gradually urged them to new locations with a slew of distractions which never seemed to cease. Always, with her calm beckoning of "Come, babies," and they would follow without question.

My own unbearably endless days were endured in an insufferably different fashion.

Exercises with Braxen were forgotten entirely. In their stead, I held a vigil at Katelyn's bedside. I counted her breaths when she slept and listened to every word she uttered when she favored me with a lucid moment. I let her save the bulk of her strength for Kyle and Sarah, scraping by with what little of her attentions I could manage with otherwise.

In the evenings, I would leave to tuck in the children and muddle my way through keeping enough clean laundry ready so at least Kyle and Sarah would not go without. Kate could barely stand to be moved without her poor heart shuddering; her clothes sat neatly folded in our hut after their first washing. Most days, I only changed shirts to put on the front of normalcy for the children's sake.

If I was fortunate, I could carve out a moment or two of sleep before morning came. I had to be there to help dress Kyle, the boy who forever insisted on wearing his shirts inside out and backward. Leilani had taken to braiding Sarah's hair, sparing me a precious few minutes more to spare with Kate. After breakfast was our visiting Katelyn as a family before the little demoness came by for her charges, and my vigil began anew.

This evening was like any other, save the smallest of changes in the company I was being granted.

Braxen stood silently at the edge of the hut, watching me watch Kate. Her quiet breathing was all I heard, ears trained for it as I awaited her next inhale, my heart stopping on every exhale. My every breath hinged on hers, delayed by the smallest second. I could hear Braxen mimicking me, somehow timed perfectly to match.

Why was he here?

"I have a confession to make," he answered my thought quietly, the declaration sounding abrupt. He left the solitude of the hut's edge, joining me in sitting beside Kate. He looked her over with fear and concern, his expression a mirror of my own. "I would rather make it now, if that's all right."

My gaze never left Katelyn's face, but I nodded numbly. "Very well."

"I...I'm the reason for your coming here," he told

me quietly, violet eyes guilty. "The reason she's here, but...I never wanted her to be. Please, believe that I never wanted your family in harm's way."

Slowly, I turned my gaze on him, tired and bitter with it. "What do you *want*, Braxen?"

He hesitated a moment, cat-like eyes fixed on his hands. He took a deep breath in time with Kate, nervousness out of character as he explained, "I-I'm not just a Shaman, Cory. I've been trained as long as I can remember for a reason—because I have visions. Glimpses, into another demon, just the one. Our legends call me a Half-Child, that I have half a soul to make room for the one I share with the demon I see into."

"Braxen, I am in no mood for your stories," I sighed, turning back to Kate and my tempered guardianship, patiently waiting for the next breath. In, out...in...out...

"Do you remember, when you used to meet her in the orchard at night?" he asked, invoking the memory of the warm evenings and the smell of ripening apples that came with it. He chuckled, hands fidgeting tirelessly. "She always loved seeing you at sunset. She said it made it look like your skin was on fire. The way she would blush..."

"What else did she tell you?" I asked quietly, unsure if I was grateful for the memory or angered that he would dare intrude upon it.

"What about Dustin's wedding?" he offered. "Grandfather Charles was so angry that you were involved at all, let alone attached to, well...And the way he pushed you to seclude yourself again! Even so, there was Kate at the end, stubborn as ever."

"Stop this," I whispered, sharply.

"And then you were sold you to that Institute," he murmured, scowling at his hands the same way I stared down my violent scars. I saw them there, etched across his skin, the faintest markings which looked so very much like my own. With the ritual mutilations they practiced, why should this perturb me? "It was so long in those walls. There was so much white. And that *smell*—"

"Stop!" I hissed angrily, fixing him with a glare. "I don't care how you learned any of this, just stop!"

"I know about the acid," he added, finally looking up at me again. I felt myself paling, panic-struck as he continued, "I know about the humans forgetting it. I know you went back to the place where it happened, but you couldn't make it happen again."

"There is no way you could know..." I said slowly, keeping myself as quiet as possible for Kate beside me. "How do you know that?"

"I told you, I have visions. In our legends, the one the Half-Child shares a Bond with is heralded as a hero, born for greatness," he explained, smiling apologetically. "I had my first vision when I was ten years old. Of you and her, beneath the old tree that summer. A picnic which went so right it was wrong. I remember everything so vividly, it still feels like I was there. But I was on the ground, screaming for my grandmother to get the people out of my head."

"You're lying," I muttered, shaking my head slowly.

"I'm not," he insisted, then pointed to the cut from

just months ago when I had my mental lapse. "That was me. I'm sorry for the scare, I never meant for it to cause alarm."

Slowly, recognition dawned in my mind as I recalled the face I had worn in my hallucination some time ago, my deep familiarity with it when we first met. It had to be a lie, some elaborately planned ruse. How could it be anything else? Why tell me now?

"I wanted you to know that you're not alone," he replied to my thoughts again. The eerie sense of an emotional echo akin to the one when we first met overtook me again. I felt insecurity and anxiety not my own, intensified by my fear that he was trying to trick me somehow while I was vulnerable worrying over Kate. "I remember so much of you; I feel what you feel. I even wear your wounds for you, look!"

He held out his hand to present the faded scarring there, an exact match to my own. I fixed him with a skeptical frown. Impatient, he grabbed my hand and cut the palm with a claw quickly, holding up his matching hand. Slowly, his skin split open even as mine sealed itself shut.

I started, scowling at his bloodied palm with a new realization. "In the water, when there was that magic... what I saw was you? The memories which led me to..."

"Yes, those are mine," he told me excitedly, catching himself with a furtive glance at Kate to make sure he had not disturbed her. "The magic was yours, but the memories were mine. I know about you the same way, except my visions don't show me memories, just current events."

"Why now, then?" I asked, finding myself insulted and frustrated. "Nearly seventy years I was left alone, isolated, and over half of which was spent in confinement being tortured while you...*watched*? And you chose to wait, not only decades but until now, when Kate is ill?"

"I wanted to wait until the right time, but with Kate...Now I just want you to know that you're not alone in this," he pleaded, desperation taking hold. "And I never watched them do those things to you: I lived it. When it became too much I was there, suffering alongside you. Once, for three years, after Paul passed away. I returned to a body that was barely alive anymore. But I remember, that's when they ruined your shoulder," he pointed to my right side, a hint of anger in his tone.

How could he know any of this? Unless what he claimed was true, he would have to be informed by too many people to count—neglecting to mention the acid blood, of course. Yet what was there to gain from such an elaborate lie? The demons did not value possessions, so robbery was no longer an option. Perhaps a long ploy to turn me against the angels? Why, when I had already witnessed firsthand their wanton, ritualistic violence?

"You are not lying...are you?" I asked, but I knew the answer. I had seen his eyes as mine, his hands moving for me. Even now, I felt an eerie echo of emotions not mine, just as I had periodically since our first encounter. Most recently was Bravery's dagger in his abdomen—I had felt it in mine.

He shook his head slowly. "No. I even left you a note, remember? In that book?"

I let out a deep breath, listening to Kate's steady

intake and exhale as I mulled this over, considering our conversations until now. "So, then...your brother, who may not know you exist...?"

"He knows now," he confirmed guiltily. He stared at the cut on his palm for a moment before it flashed with blue light, the blood there dissipating as the magic consumed it. "I'm sorry that I couldn't wait until you were more comfortable with this world. I wanted to wait."

"I almost wish you had told me sooner," I admitted, suddenly understanding some of the curious occurrences of late. "So many things are explained now. The dreams?"

"My nightmares," he confessed with an awkward shrug. "But enough of me. I told you for your sake, to comfort you."

"You know so much of me, it seems only fair," I pressed further, oddly happy and at ease as I accepted this new piece of reality. My world had already been turned over so many times in the last several weeks, what was one more tumble?

Braxen smiled, relieved and grateful. "Fine, but please don't tell anyone else. I would rather keep this secret."

I nodded. "I understand."

So we sat together as he reminisced with me and I learned more of him. The arrangement was a welcome reprieve from my demanding schedule. The longer we spoke, the more I felt at ease, finally smiling despite the circumstances. I could see him as a brother, much more easy-going than the two I had already known—*we* had known. He remembered them with me, mulling over how

Dustin had at least warmed to me with age.

Meanwhile, I learned more about him. The two children from my nightmare were his siblings, older twins who still tormented him when given the chance. He told me about the Avatars of his gods and how they trained him so harshly he came to despise himself and me, both.

"You hated me that much?" I asked, startled though amused.

He grinned sheepishly. "I did. It was awhile before the visions had enough detail of you that I learned you weren't anything like the person they painted you to be. You were kind, forgiving, thoughtful—and still so incredibly dense," he added with a laugh. His jibe caught me off guard and made me chuckle.

There was a soft moan which had us holding our breaths, looking at Kate anxiously. She blinked her eyes open slowly, our unified exhale one of relief. She looked between us both tiredly as she smiled.

"Am I missing the party?" she mumbled, her hand fumbling for mine weakly. I took it gently, hating how cold her fingers felt against my palm.

"Only a bit of poor humor," I told her with a smile, glad to hear her voice. "You missed very little."

She returned my smile, still exhausted. "I missed you laughing, mister. That's too much."

"You'll hear plenty more of it just as soon as you get out of this bed," I told her softly. Reaching my free hand to cradle her face, I stroked her cheek with my thumb. "The children's, too."

"Will you sing to me?" she asked, breath growing heavy the more she spoke. She struggled to keep her eyes open, my heart twisting with panic.

"What would you like to hear, my dear?" I asked her, hoping to keep her awake with me even a moment longer. I could not resist my momentary greed for any time I could have with her right then.

She sighed heavily, frowning thoughtfully. "I always loved hearing you sing hymns. It used to be my favorite part of Sunday."

"Very well, my dear," I whispered, hoping to hide the tears in my voice. I began to hum, struggling to remember the tune I sought. My voice fell short when I realized she had already fallen asleep again. "Another time, then, Kate."

Braxen stared at me for a long minute, sighing, "You should get some sleep before the little ones wake up. I'll stay with her."

I looked up from Kate's pale face. I wanted to protest, although I knew he was right. They needed me, too, and very soon. I searched his face, its preternatural features familiar to me now. I knew I could trust him to see her through the night.

"Thank you," I murmured with a nod, leaning forward and kissing Kate's cheek. She smiled at the touch, still too deeply asleep to wake. It felt like severing my flesh, leaving her there, but I stood and allowed Braxen to continue the vigil in my place. "Take care of her."

"Of course." He fixed his eyes on her; I could see him awaiting her next breath as I had been. I nodded, tearing my eyes away with a ragged sigh and forcing myself to leave the hut.

Outside, the village was quiet, the only demons awake any longer standing at their guard posts. I made my way toward my family's hut, feet heavy as I considered what to say to the little ones when they woke in the morning. I could not stand their questions nor their anxious pleas to see their grandmother. They were convinced now of the next visit being their last.

I sniffled, resisting any tears as I approached our hut slowly. I saw Leilani sitting just outside, asleep as she leaned against the structure. How long had she been waiting for me? Kneeling, I set a hand on her shoulder gently to wake her.

She stirred, looking up at me tiredly. "Kate? Is okay?"

"For now," I replied quietly, smiling as I glanced at the hut behind her. "You should get home, Leilani. This is no place to sleep."

"Babies safe," she yawned in reply, gifting me a weary smile. "I help soon."

With that, she stood in a single fluid motion, making my stiff mimicry seem clumsy by comparison. I watched her head off, a smile on her lips and a dance in her step. I stared, amused, before ducking inside to see myself to bed.

Smoldering embers were all which lit the hut, just warm enough to keep the space comfortably warm against the cooling evening air. I slipped through the main area, too tired to change into sleepwear now that I was so close to the bed of furs. I knelt carefully, reaching out to find where the children were before I searched for a way to lay myself down. As it was, I had to shift one of them. Kyle, judging by the size.

He moaned sleepily, shifting as I nudged him toward his sister. "Daddy?"

"No, Kyle, just me," I told him, humored by his tired confusion.

"Oh." He rolled over, allowing me the space I sought. "Good night, Grampa."

"Good night, my boy," I whispered, nestling into the furs and grateful for the comfort they provided. I was not down more than a moment before they sensed my presence, both children finding a way to snuggle up to me. I smiled at their efforts, chest swelling to know they were still comfortable with me. The thought gave me some hope in this bleak mess. "Sleep well, you two."

Chapter Four:
Now and Always

First Week After Paradise

Tuesday (October 4th)

The next morning when I woke, the children were just stirring, affording me little time to delay waking.

I groaned and sat up stiffly, removing myself from the mess of a bed to gather up outfits for the day. My shoulder burned, the wear of the last several days aggravating my damaged nerves. With an awkward stretch and tired sigh, I put the matter aside to worry over later. Right now, Kyle needed help with that shirt of his, already dressing all wrong after only a moment of my back being turned.

"Here now, Kyle," I murmured, pulling it back over his head correctly and tucking the tag beneath his collar. I smiled for him, too exhausted for the action to feel much more than hollow. "Now, get your shoes on. Would you like help to tie those today?"

He nodded, yawning widely as he stretched his arms to their fullest. My, but that looked painful. "Yes, please."

108

Broken Orbit

I nodded, kneeling once he had slipped his feet in. My fingers made quick work of the knots, well-practiced with this by now. I pat his feet, making him grin and wiggle, waking up quickly.

"There you are, my boy. Go on ahead now to breakfast, your sister and I will be along shortly," I told him, barely finished with my sentence before he was gone. I turned, expecting to find Sarah ready and needing assistance with her morning hair routine, only to find the hut appearing empty. "Sarah?"

A tiny flutter from the furs caught my eye.

I went back to the bed, crouching down and saying quietly, "Sarah, it's time to wake up."

"No," came her muffled protest as she shifted again. "I'm not coming out."

"You're not?" I frowned, lying back down gingerly. "Well now, would you mind if I joined you, then? This hut seems to be a bit too big for my tastes just now."

There was a long pause, but she finally held up the large fur she was huddled under, inviting me to join her. I pulled it over my face, thinking it might pull too much of her precious coverings if I sought much more than that. The light was dim, the air warm.

"Good morning, Sarah," I offered after a moment of silence. She glanced up at me before fixing her eyes on her hands, picking at her stuffed rabbit's button eye with a frown. "Are you hungry?"

She shook her head, scowl turning her face to an all-out grimace. "No. I don't want to get up."

"Why not, sweetheart?" She kept at her picking,

109

the action growing more urgent with her worsening upset.

"Because I want to see Grandma, and you're just going to get rid of us with Leilani again," she grumbled bitterly, the accusation far more accurate than I liked to admit. I pursed my lips, biting back a sigh. "You can't just pretend we don't exist!"

Her last protest seemed deeper, more personal than any rapport we had built upon over the last year. I nodded slowly. "You're right, I can't."

Her fingers froze while I took a breath to steady myself before continuing, "And I have no intention of it. Your grandmother is simply tired right now; she needs my company. Otherwise, I would be right with you in learning whatever new things we can find."

Sarah started her picking again, more thoughtful now. "Really?"

"Of course. Mind you, while I'm sure Leilani is a good teacher, I would honestly rather have you and your brother's company," I whispered with a mischievous glance behind myself, pretending to keep outside ears from hearing. She smirked as I tweaked her nose with a grin. "And as soon as your grandmother is better, I say we are overdue for spending some time as a family, hm?"

She nodded, pulling from her sour mood gradually. "But can it just be us? Without Kyle?"

"Well, at some point Kyle will need to be involved in family time," I explained, watching her face pinch in a pout. I smiled for her. "But, I suppose I shall put in a good word and find a way you can have your grandmother and me to yourself for a while. If Kyle may have his turn, as well."

"No, just you," she corrected, fidgeting nervously. "I mean, I still want to see Grandma, but I also want to see you, too."

I felt my chest fill to the brim with a startlingly overpowering joy. "Of course, Sarah. We can do that."

She nodded, hiding her exuberant glee behind her businesslike mask and curt gesture. "Good."

"But first..." I narrowed my eyes to punctuate my stern reasoning, "We do need to get out of bed."

She sighed but agreed, "Yeah, I guess."

"We'll visit your grandmother after breakfast, Sarah, for as long as she can before she needs her rest to get better," I bargained. Her mood brightened considerably. "Are you ready?"

Sarah nodded and I pulled the furs back slowly, breathing in the cooler, crisp air outside of them. She gasped for air dramatically, grinning. She clambered over me and out of bed, jarring my shoulder along the way. I kept quiet, simply glad I had managed the one task of getting her out of bed for the day.

"Close your eyes, I'm changing!" she announced, and I obeyed while I waited for her announcement when I could open them again. "Okay, I just need help with my zipper, Grampa."

I pushed myself up with a groan, barely even registering my actions as I did up her dress and pulled her hair from catching in her collar. I brushed at a bit of dirt on her shoulder, wiping a smudge from her face. She glowered at me, and I realized I had begun to get carried away.

"Is Leilani braiding your hair today, or am I?" I

asked, doing my best to hide my fatigue.

"Leilani, she does it better," she replied matter-of-factly. I nodded.

"She's had more practice," I agreed, finally realizing what she was wearing. "It's a bit cold for just a dress, Sarah. Be sure to put on leggings and bring your jacket."

She groaned and rolled her eyes. "But it'll be fine once the sun's up!"

"Yes, but before and after it will be too cold, and I don't want you catching anything," I explained patiently with a nod to the clothes. "Leggings and jacket, please. Then breakfast."

"Then Grandma's?" she checked skeptically, appeased by my nod. She grumbled but obeyed, slipping her shoes on a moment later with a disgruntled frown. "There. I'm ready."

"Thank you, sweetheart. Now, let's go find your brother, hm?"

Breakfast passed swiftly. The two of them kept talking at me, speaking too much for me to catch everything before they were on to their next thrilling topic. I listened as best I could, having to force any scraps of a meal into my exhausted body. As soon as they were done, I gave up on my endeavors. I stared at their faces, already smudged and dirty.

I pulled my long sleeve over the heel of my palm for ease, wiping at the mess quickly to not wear their patience too thin. I kept a smile on my face, standing to follow their enthused skipping toward the hut where Kate was still no doubt asleep.

Broken Orbit

We made it there in a blur, the habit barely registering to my numb mind. I scarcely even noticed Braxen excusing himself from the hut as we approached.

The children were already inside by the time I reached the hut; I entered after them silently. Lo and behold, there they were at Kate's side, excited but quiet as they murmured with her. I knew she had woken just for this, the wear of these last few days apparent on her face in my eyes. I forced the panic the thought invoked to silence itself, focusing instead on my little family.

I listened to their conversations, remaining at the edge of the hut. I felt out of place, a stranger invading this private moment of a grandmother and her grandchildren. The hushed tones were heartfelt, making me smile when it seemed as though my chest was being steadily constricted with each of their words.

"Hey, babies," crooned Katelyn, smiling broadly as they hugged her gently. "How have you been?"

"Okay, I guess," mumbled Sarah with a frown. "I miss you, Grandma."

Kyle nodded. "Me, too. It's no fun without you."

"Oh, it isn't?" she asked, still smiling for them. I would forever admire the strength she was able to project no matter how dire the situation seemed. "What about Cory? I thought you really liked him?"

They both nodded slowly.

"I mean, yeah," admitted Kyle reluctantly. "He is a lot of fun."

"And he makes sure to do stuff like you do," added Sarah with a shrug. "Like breakfast and bedtime."

Kate glanced at me conspiratorially, face serious.

"Well, you remember how I talked to you both last year about that man who was going to audition to be a dad, right?" They nodded slowly. "Cory's the one who auditioned. What do you think, did he get the part? Is he a good dad?"

Kyle jumped and grinned, nodding with unerring enthusiasm. "Yeah! He's good. He tells stories at night if we can't fall asleep."

"Sarah?" Kate smiled gently for her more skeptical granddaughter. "What do you think?"

"He's not like *our* dad...right?" she said slowly, glancing my way nervously. Oh, child. How is it a girl so young learned to speak with such cynicism?

"No, baby, he's nothing like your dad, I promise," Kate reassured the young girl with a smile, tucking a stray lock behind her ear. "He won't ever hurt you or leave you."

"If you say so, Grandma," she mumbled, tone still painfully mistrusting of the notion despite our earlier progress.

"I do." Kate hid a wince behind a quick and strained smile, whisper breaking despite her greater efforts, "What's Leilani going to teach you today?"

"Weaving, I think," replied Sarah with renewed vigor. "Like baskets!"

"Oh, baskets?" My heart was pained for my dear Kate as she struggled to keep her composure. It was more than I could bear, watching the woman I loved shattering apart as it sounded like she was making final farewells. "Will you go make me one, then? A pretty wicker one with a handle."

They nodded, giving final hugs and kisses with murmurs of their love. I took a deep breath, bracing for my turn to smile as they ran to me. They each grabbed for my hands, holding on tightly despite how small they were.

I led them outside, grateful to find Leilani was already making her way over. Her hair was disheveled, face drawn from sleep and adding to the effect of her barely waking up now. Any trace of fatigue left her when she saw the children, however, as she ducked down and held her arms wide with an excited grin.

"Babies!" she cried, giggling with joy when they ran to her and fell into her waiting embrace. "How you?"

They chattered at her with all of the enthusiasm of puppies to their mother as she led them off, the demoness hanging on their every word no matter if she understood. I exhaled a sigh of relief, glad they could have at least one more day where everything was right in their world. They would have countless more if I had my way.

I turned back to the hut, bracing myself for another long day filled with tallied breaths.

Entering quietly, I stared across at the pale Katelyn, forcing myself to believe what I saw, how weak she was. She stared back, the strength in her black eyes slowly crumbling and melting into terrified tears which streaked across her face quickly. I crossed the hut in two strides, taking her in my arms in an instant.

"Hush, Kate, I'm here. I'm here, you're all right, the children are safe," I murmured, holding her tenderly. She clung to me tightly, her aged fingers digging into me powerfully, as if she held on for dear life.

My heart stopped for a moment.

"I'm dying, Cory, I can feel it," she sobbed brokenly. The desperation in her words knocked the wind from me. I simply held her, unable to move and unable to breathe as I slowly recovered from the confirmation of all of my fears.

"I..." I choked, kissing her hair, stroking her cheek, anything to prove she was alive, here and now. If she ever... "I love you. Kate, my Kate, I love you, my dear, I love you."

After that, neither of us could speak for a time, each too trapped in the other's embrace. Her slowing heart was like a clock, ticking down the time until we would finally let go with no way to grab hold again. The thought of losing her completely after all we had been through—after finding her again—was nearly enough to cripple me.

"Somewhere out there..." Her voice trailed off. She laughed quietly and continued, "The luckiest girl in the world is out there and she doesn't know it, but you'll be the best husband she could hope for. Someday."

"Oh, Kate, I'm sorry," I sobbed, eyes burning with tears I refused to shed. Had I not yelled at her, she would be fine. If I knew to control my temper—if only my sanity were in my grasp. If only I had listened to her first pleas to leave. "I'm sorry."

"It's not your fault, Cory, I'm just getting old," she whispered, sounding utterly defeated at the fact. "It's been a long time coming, just...Just promise me that you'll take care of our babies, please. It's about time you got to be a real father, and they've already lost so much, I can't—"

"Of course, Kate, but that's years away," I interrupted her, hating how her words tore at my heart and made my lungs burn between stifled sobs. "So many years, you'll see."

"Promise me," she said more firmly, and I thought she must surely have drawn blood by now with how tightly she continued to grip me.

"I promise, Kate. I'll take care of them. They're Lawrences, after all," I tried joking lamely; she sighed in relief, relaxing her fingers. "...Kate?"

It felt as though she had fallen asleep in my arms, and when I looked to see her peaceful smile I could have been fooled by it. But the hut was too quiet, the air too stale.

"Oh, no, Kate, please," I begged brokenly, unable to fight my tears any longer. "Katelyn, I need you to wake up, my dear, please. Kate? Katelyn!"

A heavy hand rested on my shoulder, and I found no solace in its inhumanity. I hated it. I despised what this world meant, what I was and how she suffered so deeply because of it.

Had we only stayed home, had we no reason to leave...

"Cory, she's gone," came the gentle murmur of Braxen, remorseful.

"No. No, no, no you have to help her. Please, help her. She needs help waking up, Braxen, *help her*!" I cried, unable to let her go. My grief sounded too loud in my ears. As if it must have been someone else who mourned and screamed, "Braxen, you promised me that she would live, now help her!"

He shook his head, helpless. "We already used all of the magic we know. Something was broken, Cory."

I buried my face in the curls of her hair, the sensation all wrong when she did not react. "Please, Kate, wake up. I can't lose you again, I can't do this alone. We need you, my dear, please."

Braxen said nothing, staying with me while I denied this injustice as long as I could bear. My throat grew raw, eyes burning from the tears, yet my chest was hollow as ever. Even as I finally found a way to cease my wails, I felt something continuing to chisel away at the flesh and bone inside me, emptying me.

Finally, it occurred to my deadened mind what I held was no longer my Kate, and I set her down gently despite how heavy every inch of my body felt. I stared at her smile, tranquil and grateful, knowing I was the one who had done this. I had yelled; I had led us to this world. Even back to the little girl and her basket in my room—I had damned her then, too.

"I've already talked to Leilani. She's watching the children for you for as long as you grieve," came Braxen's mournful murmur. His usual cadence was lost in his grief.

It took me a moment to hear what he told me, and another moment longer to realize he must have spoken to Leilani before he had come to comfort me. "You knew."

"Kate told me to prepare," he confessed guiltily, voice heavy in the stifling air of this place. "I only did as she requested."

"And did she request you tell the children?" I asked monotonously, the slightest bitter note cutting into my words.

"No. She wanted you to have time to grieve first," he replied. "Whatever you need, Cory—"

118

"I need my fiancée," I whispered, eyes seeing nothing as they burned with fresh tears. "I need to give her the life she deserved. I need to apologize. I need more time—just one more day," I choked on the lie for what it was, knowing it would never stop this feeling of drowning in an empty pit.

"If I could give it, I would," he replied, and when I finally looked to him I found him torn apart by this. Why? What attachment could he have beyond echoes of my memories? "But all I have to offer is a day to mourn, what little that does. We can bury her, whenever you're ready."

"No." My voice was too strong for how weak I felt. "No, she deserves to be buried by her family."

Braxen nodded in agreement. "I can take you to the Hrexis Tree."

"Thank you." I looked back at the woman I had known my entire life, my best friend, our childhood finally lying dead beside her. I steeled myself, lifting her carefully and cradling her close for the final journey home.

The trek blurred by as a numb, haphazard mixture of grief and the start of chilly rain. Braxen was true to his word, guiding me with a quick and sure pace to the tree we had first stepped through to come to this place. I stared at it, regret washing over me that I had ever let her come with me.

"It's not your fault." His bright eyes were piercing

as if he could see my thoughts as clearly as I heard them. "She wanted you to know that."

"Her perception is always distorted where I am concerned," I replied quietly, eyeing the gateway. "Keep the children safe. I will return...soon."

Braxen nodded. "I'll guard them like my own. Fly safe, Cory."

Without another word, I stepped through, finding myself alone in a clearing on the other side. The trees were shorter, the forestry so much more mild than the wild and untamed world behind me. It took me a moment to recognize this as the place I had come to in my youth after the disaster which was Kate and I's exploration of physical affections. With a jolt, I righted myself, recalling which way the church must have been from there.

Perhaps someone would still know the Smith family.

~~ * ~ * ~ * ~~

The church still stood where I remembered, its paint peeling and porch in a sorry state of disrepair. The lights inside were on, visible through the grungy front windows. As I approached, I could hear someone in the church, sounding like a sermon. Perhaps practicing? I climbed the porch steps all the same, too tired now to turn back.

I knocked tentatively, hoping anyone might hear me from inside. The door opened not a moment later, a ghost from my past smiling in welcome.

The young man beamed up at me, familiar blue

eyes alight with curiosity. "I was hoping I would get to meet you. Come on in, out of the rain."

I followed him inside at his behest, glad when it seemed I was welcome here. My mind was far too exhausted to wonder how or why he seemed to know me so cordially, however. "Please, I need help."

"Most people do when they come here," he chuckled, the laughter dying on his lips when his eyes fell on what I held, the body clutched tight to my chest as if I may still protect her. "Oh. Oh, is she...?"

"Please," I said again, begging now. "Please, her family deserves to know what happened to her. They used to own the orchard on the outskirts of town, the Smiths. Please. Help me."

Without a word, he led me to the front and sat me in a pew. He made to take her from me, hesitating when my arms turned to stone. "It's okay. I'll set her next to you, but you need some rest. Okay? All right, thank you. See? There, just right there. I'll be right back, don't move, just rest, all right?"

I nodded numbly, my eyes burning yet again as I stared at the body where he had set her next to me on the pew. She was so pale, so tired, but she still looked as if she could have fallen asleep, smile ever-present on her lips. Before I knew it the man was back, crouching in front of me with a cup of water and a small package of crackers.

He smiled apologetically, shrugging. "Aside from communion, it's all we have on hand, courtesy of the kids' room. Anyway, it's better than nothing until we can get you something more solid."

I accepted the water with a grateful nod, my stomach still too nauseated to begin thinking of food. "Her family?"

He nodded. "I called them. Jeff still lives there, with some of Kate's cousins, if I'm not mistaken. They'll be here in a little while."

I took a sip of the cool water, all at once relieved and feeling I should vomit. "Thank you."

"Of course," he replied with his kind smile; I knew I recognized him. He must have seen my puzzling stare, introducing himself, "I'm the pastor here, by the way. Corey Ericson, with an 'e'. You're Mr.Lawrence, aren't you?"

I nodded, appreciative of the small talk. "My father was, I was just his son."

"I thought so. I wish we could have met under better circumstances. Paul was my father; he told me all about you," he said, trying to keep me distracted. He had the same way of speaking as his father, calm and collected, keeping their patients focused on anything other than the pain.

"You look like him," I told him quietly, and suddenly I could see so much of Paul staring back at me. This man's hair was dark brown, and his face was rounder but the expressions were uncanny, as were his eyes. I felt as though Paul may be staring back at me through those eyes.

"I get that a lot," he agreed. "You look like your photos, give or take a few years of wear."

"I do not have photos," I argued weakly, shaking my head. "No one was supposed to know..."

122

He frowned. "Well, we have pictures of you here, on the prayer wall. My dad insisted they stay up, right until he passed away. I've kept them up to honor his wishes."

My eyes drifted to the wall he pointed to, covered in notes and photos, then back to him. "My condolences."

"Do you miss him? I was told you were good friends," he continued trying to keep me talking.

I nodded, distracted. "Yes, for years I missed him. Then I remembered...something. It's difficult to miss him now."

He winced, ashamed, but nodded in understanding. "He told me he'd made a mistake, but I never knew what. I'm sorry, for whatever he did."

"I can accept he would do it to me. I have had to accept plenty which would be done to something like me," I mumbled, fighting to construct my thoughts through my fatigue. "But how he could do it to my mother, my father, my—my Kate. That he could rob them of anything—Oh, damn these eyes..."

He offered me a tissue as my tears fell over, though I missed from where he pulled it. "There's a lot of people who've missed you here in town. The Smiths, for one, and your sister refused to sell the farm no matter what anyone's offered, despite how much she talks about wanting to."

"She did not seem to have missed me too terribly when I visited," I replied numbly, wiping my face with the tissue. My cheeks burned with tears again, and I could not bother to dry them anymore. "She seemed rather horrified by the whole ordeal."

123

My namesake smiled. "Well, it was supposed to be a secret, but we got some advanced notice to be careful with you. Something about amnesia, we weren't supposed to discuss anything until you mentioned it first. Kate wanted to make sure nothing would set you back."

"Kate? Even then...?" My thought was cut off by the doors opening, the sound of the storm outside rushing in with a small band of people in drenched coats. I turned to get a better look, confused. "Who...?"

I recognized Jeff as soon as he threw back his hood, despite the years on his face and the hunch in his posture. I could not help a small smile at the familiar sight as he made his way over, gait remarkably brisk for his age.

"Where is she? What happened? You weren't very—Oh, no." Jeff faltered. A younger man appeared beside him to comfort him, the devastation I saw rending my exhausted calm anew.

"I'm sorry." How I was able to speak was beyond me, but I knew that the words needed to escape me. "I couldn't—She just...Jeff, I'm so sorry."

I watched her family weep, feeling even more deeply like the villain I had always appeared to be. It stabbed at me, the sensation which her passing and the ensuing grief was my fault. How could it be anything else? At every turn, I had been the demon in her life, the reason for her pains and sorrows.

Slowly, their mourning quieted and they made their way closer. No doubt they sought closure, to know this was undeniably irreversible. Even as they seemed to be accepting her smile, I denied the truth and listened for the next breath which meant this was a lie.

Jeff wiped his tears away. "Well. We all knew it was coming."

"What?" His words blindsided me, as much as the initial shock of it all. "How?"

"Doctors," he replied sadly. "I guess she got it from her mother. Heart problems, you know."

"She knew?" I whispered, and I could not understand if this angered me. "She knew."

"Yeah, she knew," he agreed, subdued. He sighed, so much life leaving him with the exhale he barely looked himself a ghost of the man I once knew. "Thank you for bringing her home, Cory. You always did right by her where you could."

I shook my head slowly, scoffing bitterly, "I feel like I caused this. Had we stayed home, not gone off on some mad expedition..."

"She was given six months, last year. Right before Robert reached out to her about you," explained Jeff, taking a seat on my empty side. He smiled. "She showed that doctor."

The timeline he gave me was terrifyingly short, punctuating Kate and I's constant trials and near-misses together. "I was almost too late."

"You made her so happy," he told me, crying again as he stared at his hands in front of him. "I'm glad I got to see my little girl smiling like she was on top of the world again."

"She deserved the world," I murmured, still waiting for her breath. "She deserved everything."

He sniffled and nodded. "Yeah. She did."

Karma Rose

We sat together in silence for a moment, the sounds of hushed conversations coming from the back of the church, from the other family members and Corey. The voices were filled with sympathy, no doubt unfamiliar enough with Katelyn they were not moved as Jeff and I were.

"How would you tell a child about this?" I asked Jeff quietly, thinking of the two little ones back at the village. How could I leave them alone there? Was this dour church truly so much worse for them? Leilani's happy face and dedication to her charges came to me then, my worries fading.

"It depends on the kid," he replied, a new sadness touching him at the thought. "But it's never easy."

"Her grandchildren, Kyle and Sarah." I could barely stand to say their names with the somber atmosphere hanging thickly around us. "They are so young..."

"Charlie's kids?" he choked, pained.

I nodded numbly. "The same. They have been so happy lately, I cannot bear to tell them."

"Be gentle with them?" he asked of me, eyes thoughtful.

"As best I can be, of course," I agreed, sighing and fighting back even more tears. He stiffened at my subdued tone.

"You take care of those kids, understand?" he said sternly, wizened features giving his expression a unique severity which chilled me. "I mean, really fight for them."

"Of course, Jeff. They're my children, in a way," I told him honestly, my tears nearing the surface again.

"I've waited so long for them."

He smiled slowly, relaxing some. "I always thought you'd make a good father, you know. Just don't prove me wrong, huh?"

I returned the smile tiredly. "Tempting as it is, I wouldn't risk it."

Just as we had found some shred of light in this dark, dreary day the church doors opened again. Uniformed men and women entered this time, a team of four with one pair carrying bags of equipment.

"Come on, Cory, let's get out of their way," muttered Jeff. I stood with a groan, offering him an arm to brace with as he stood more slowly. "Thanks."

I nodded, helping him to leave the area and shuffle toward the front of the building. His family and the young pastor were still congregated near the door, ceasing in their murmurs and watching both of us carefully as we approached. I had the distinct impression they were waiting to catch us if we shattered apart again.

The sounds of the storm outside grew louder as we neared the door. It was befitting of the world to weep at its loss of such a perfect woman. Oh, and she was perfection made mortal, so much more beauty than I had ever deserved to touch in this lifetime.

The stab of pain I felt was mercifully interrupted as the door creaked open, a wild-eyed and befuddled Robert peering in tentatively. He was soaked through, even as the rain began to ease up behind him.

His brown eyes spotted me, relief spreading across his features as easily as his grin. He made his way over to give me a quick hug. "Cory! You have no idea how

worried we've been, I'm so glad you're all right! What—
Where is everyone? The kids, Kate?"

There it was, the spear of anguish resuming its
demented path through my lungs and into my heart.
"Kate...She's...Robert, she—I can't. I'm sorry, I can't."

Robert searched for answers quickly, eyes darting
from the somber faces beside us to the uniformed group at
the front of the church. They unfurled a long black bag,
the realization hitting home for him. He looked like I felt
after a crash landing.

"Oh, shit," he gasped, flustered and wounded as he
scowled at the other end of the church. "Cory, I'm so
sorry, I didn't know. We got a call that you were here, and
I didn't...I'm so sorry," he added brokenly, embracing me
again.

I returned the gesture, feeling too hollow to garner
any relief from it. My words failed me, lost for how to
continue my day anymore. I had completed my task, with
no immediate indication of what to do next. Had this day
been like the others, I would have been sitting in a hut,
listening.

Still, the breath I strained to hear did not come, the
silence of it paining me deeply.

Robert cleared his throat abruptly and broke away,
leaving one hand to rest on my arm. I knew it should have
provided comfort, but it simply felt too alien. It was as
though he was touching someone else, not me.

"I was visiting with your sister, Cory, she's pretty
worried," he told me with a sniffle, drying his cheeks with
the back of his free hand. "What do you say we get you
cleaned up, maybe have a bite of something while we're at

it?"

"I'm not hungry," I protested quietly, the world feeling so disorientingly far away from me as it spun slowly.

Jeff chimed in then, tone fatherly, "Come on, Cory, you look just terrible. We'll finish up here and keep in touch, you go get some rest and take care of your kids, okay?"

"Yes, I—The children," I agreed in a murmur. The fatigue I had fought off so vehemently these last few days was finally catching up with me. My shock was wearing off, reality inching painfully closer with every second.

"Where are the kids, Cory? Are they safe?" asked Robert gently.

I nodded. "Yes, with Leilani for the night. They're making baskets today."

He smiled bravely through his tears. "Okay, then. Rest first, then we can go talk to Leilani in the morning, all right?"

As desperately as I wanted to return to the children, I understood the wisdom of resting before making the return trek. I nodded with a tired sigh. "Very well, Robert. We shall see if Lisa would mind terribly if we imposed."

He smiled in relief. "I don't think she'll mind at all. She's probably already got dinner on the table."

I knew I should be amused, yet the pit in my gut turned over and chilled my blood to ice. I stopped where I was, staring at the doors and the world beyond them. My arms felt painfully empty, every fiber of my being all too aware of what was missing. My first step outside, knowing beyond a doubt she would never again be there with me.

I took it, feeling as though I had left behind my flesh, my wings, unable to live the same again. My nerves burned with it, but I pushed through the painful wrongness. The children needed me, and I needed to be capable of caring for them. The certainty of the thought was the only strength which kept me standing.

Robert must have seen my distress, putting a hand on my arm again for comfort as he guided me toward his vehicle. "It's all right. You're not alone in this, Cory."

He was right. Decades away, and yet there were so many kind faces still living here. It felt welcoming, in spite of the circumstances. I stopped where I was, dazed.

"Robert, I...I think I would like to fly. The car—" The words were choked off with a rush of anxiety.

He smiled at me. "Whatever you feel helps. I'll meet you there, okay?"

I nodded, stepping away before making my head start, leaping into the air, anticipating a rush of relief to escape the ground below. Its stifling reality seemed to still press in on me with the rush of air against my skin. I fought against it, pushing my wings harder as I tried to race away from the truth I wished so desperately to be lies.

Why could I not stop waiting for that inhale?

The farm appeared below me before I could escape the suffocating weight of how empty the world was now. I circled once, dropping out of the air and stumbling as the soil beneath me slipped away. I saw Lisa on the porch, waving at me, the ghosts of everyone I loved standing beside her. Kate was among them now.

My legs collapsed beneath me, my exhaustion finally overtaking me. I heard someone yelling to me as I struggled to right myself, shaking uncontrollably. Before I knew it, Lisa was helping me to stand, giving me a firm hand to hold. She led me to the porch where I fell once more, the stairs getting the best of me.

"Cory, are you okay?" Robert came from behind us, going to my other side to help me up again with all of the delicate care one used when handling fractured glass. To Lisa, his words were hushed, "What happened?"

"I don't know, he landed and just fell over," she replied, worry marring her voice.

"I...I can't feel..." My words escaped me again, voice shaky and weak as we climbed the porch steps. My gut churned, and before I could think to brace myself what little water I had managed to drink at the church was spilling from me, burning my throat. "I'm sorry, I—I just need to lie down."

"You can rest in the living room while I finish getting dinner on the table," replied Lisa with all of the gentle commanding of Mother.

I nodded weakly, knowing full well I was in no state to argue. "Very well."

They helped me up again and into the house, the last few feet into the living room blurring by. Next I knew, Robert was helping wipe the mud off of me, no doubt at Lisa's behest.

"Thank you," I mumbled awkwardly.

He gave me a smile. "Don't make a habit of it, but you're welcome, Cory. Any chance you'll tell me where you've been?"

I spared him a cynical chuckle. "You would never believe me. Magic trees and hidden worlds with demons."

"Sounds about as believable as me being your therapist," he joked, finally finishing with his muddy rag and the bowl of what once was water. His humor fell away, an odd seriousness about him. "We missed you, Cory, all of us. The manhunt seems to have blown over, too. We'd love it if you would come home."

Just as swiftly, the heavy expression vanished with a smile, and he shrugged as he stood with the bowl and rag. "Maybe that's a better topic for tomorrow. For now, you just get some rest, and I'll help Lisa."

Suddenly, I was alone, feeling it completely. For the first time since before meeting the demons, and I found myself unsure of how to feel about the solitude.

The old house was just as I remembered. I glanced around, seeing too many memories in this one room. My eyes fell on a dusty bottle of whiskey, still half-full, with two tumblers sitting beside it. Just as Father always left it, despite so many years since his last drink.

I smiled sadly, lifting one of the dusty glasses to inspect it, seeing my father sitting down to an evening drink after a long day of hard work. Such a carefully practiced ritual, and yet my own experiences with the liquor were vastly different.

"What are you doing, Cory?" I was lucid enough to realize Paul was disappointed, yet blissfully drunk enough not to care.

"The only thing I can in this hell, didn't you know?" I smiled bitterly at the bottle in my hand, its

amber liquid still so very beautiful in this world of polished steel and bleached white. "The only choice I have is pain or this, and I'm tired of hurting."

He glared at me angrily. "Don't you realize what you're doing? Do you know how disappointed people would be? Your parents?"

"The same parents I'll never see again?" I snapped sharply, taking another sip as the pain of reality slipped too close. "I'm sure they're proud enough of their monster son, the science experiment!"

"Don't you dare talk like that!" he yelled, lunging for the bottle.

I batted him away and stood with a groan, towering over him despite my wavering balance. "Or what? You'll release me to their disappointed faces and a stern talking to? Hm? What else could you possibly do to me, Paul? You people already have my freedom, my dignity, my home! What more could you want?!"

"Please, don't think ill of me, Father," I whispered brokenly, setting aside the tumbler and trading it for the bottle to stare at it numbly. One night. Could it hurt so terribly, to dull the pain for just one night?

"Cory, dinner is ready," came Lisa's voice from the hall. I could feel her staring at me. "It won't help, you know."

"Not forever, no," I agreed, still so very tempted by the promise of even temporary relief. "It always brought relief, for a little while."

"I never knew you drank," she confessed, the discomfort apparent in her voice. I felt ashamed, never wanting my sister to know the darker sides of me.

"I didn't, before the Institute," I told her, the bottle in my hand burning my skin. "Still, it helped me leave that place, no matter how badly it hurt. Over forty years, and it was the only thing which helped me escape."

"Don't you dare talk like that," she snapped sharply, echoing Paul's words from so many years ago. I looked at her then, seeing how pained and defiant she was, ever my willful little sister. "Kate fought for you. Her entire life, she fought so that you and people like you could have a voice, and *that's* why you escaped. Not some bottle. And you should be ashamed of yourself for even *thinking* of doing that to yourself again after everything she sacrificed for you," she added, turning on her heel and leaving for the kitchen.

My words caught in my throat, eyes turning back to the bottle in my hand with newfound guilt and shame. I knew I was weak and despicable for wanting it, and she was right. Kate had given so much for me, it would be nothing but disrespectful to throw it away to the bottom of a bottle now.

I replaced the whiskey by its tumblers, forcing myself to leave the room for supper instead. I sat at the table, unable to meet Lisa's eye after her scolding. She gave me a bowl of steaming stew all the same, as Mother would have, no matter how much trouble we could get into. I looked at her then, finding, despite her disappointment in me, she still wore a concerned frown just as Mother used to, still alive in her.

"Thank you," I mumbled awkwardly, accepting the bowl gratefully.

"What was all that about?" asked Robert quietly,

curious but wary to intrude. I wondered why it was I had not realized sooner he was sitting there, although my guilt was heavy enough I assumed it to be the culprit.

"Nothing, as long as it's settled now," replied Lisa with a pointed look at me. I nodded wordlessly, and she finally gave me a forgiving smile which touched her eyes. "Good. That's the last I'll hear of it, then. Now eat up, you need it," she added as she took her seat at the table.

I sipped at the hot stew, my appetite reviving with a ravenous clawing in my stomach. Before I could suppress the impulse, I was slurping down the last of my bowl, chunks and all. I gasped for air, my mouth seared from the hot broth. The pain of it did nothing to diminish how desperately I needed more.

Robert was staring at me in shock. "I guess you were hungry?"

Lisa was laughing, already taking the dish to refill it. "Just like you used to eat when we were kids, huh?"

"I happen to be more civilized now, thank you," I muttered, appreciative of the fresh bowl. I set it down, allowing it to cool for a moment before risking another bout of burning broth.

"I know, it's just because you haven't eaten, don't worry," she reassured me, sitting at the table with me. It felt like no time had passed, with my little sister teasing me so easily. Mother should have appeared at any moment with a stern word for us both. "To be honest, I kind of missed it. Just another thing that only you do, you know?"

I stared at her, confused. "I thought you were only tolerating me, my last visit. It felt so reserved."

She nodded guiltily. "I was told to be careful with what I said. Everyone was. A lot of people were excited when the news happened and we saw you everywhere. Magazines, TV, you name it. I couldn't wait for you to come home," she added with a smile, words echoing those of Paul's son.

Robert was deliberately silent, eyes anywhere but on the conversation at hand. I shook my head, looking back at Lisa with a tentative smile. "I wanted to come home, but...It feels so different, almost haunted. There is so much I miss."

"It was like that for me for a while, too," she admitted. "First, you disappeared, then the funeral, and Mom never got better after that. Then Kate left with Charlie, and Mom and Dad passed away. It's lonely sometimes, but it gets better. I just wish I had more help to run the place. Maybe if I could get a few more of you," she joked, sipping at her spoonful of stew.

I laughed dryly at the thought, the sound still weak and bitter. "There seems to be plenty more of me these days. Perhaps I could introduce you."

Lisa smiled at me. "I've missed you, Cory. It's good to hear your laugh again."

My eyes dropped to my bowl, embarrassed. "Truth be told, I am still uncertain how I can anymore, no matter how polluted it may be."

"Well, you're strong, and you always look for the good in things," replied Robert thoughtfully, finally joining in. "And you're always trying to make other people smile. I know my family changed for the better when we met you."

"Thank you, for bringing him back to us." I glanced up to see Lisa had turned her smile on my friend, her eyes watering. She sniffed, dabbing at her face like Mother used to and gave us both a cheery smile. "Anyway, that's enough being sad at the table. Can I get you boys anything else to eat?"

I sipped my stew, finding my ravenous appetite had subsided considerably. "No, thank you, Lisa, this is perfect."

"Just a tiny bit for me, thanks," replied Robert eagerly, passing her his bowl.

The remainder of supper passed quietly, for which I was grateful. My grief-stricken exhaustion had turned slap-happy by the time I was able to excuse myself, Lisa insisting I go straight to bed while she and Robert cleared the table. I obeyed after a stern glare which could have cut through stone, hunching to fit as I trudged up the stairs tiredly.

I found my room, habitually closing the door behind myself before taking a seat at the end of the bed. I sighed, lying down slowly. The bed was still comfortable, if dusty, despite what I suspected was fresh bedding. Something felt wrong, and as I turned to the side to discuss the day out of such a deeply ingrained habit I was reminded of what it was that bothered me. The empty pillow I found brought with it a fresh reminder.

I reached out to where I knew she had once slept, wondering if there had been a time when she had done the same for me. If we might be able to defy the years, could we surmount the distance, for one last night of stolen whispers against cool linens? Could she feel me here, all those years ago, as clearly as I could feel where she belonged beside me?

Finally, I began to accept I would never hear her intake of breath, my vigil having finally ended.

I knew all there was left was vacant space and silent nights. I felt it so deeply I thought I might shatter from the pain. I curled in on myself, hoping I could protect myself from the seemingly endless space around me. Too weak to fight for composure any longer, tears began falling to soak my pillow as I told myself, again and again, there was no more dreaming of one more day—just one—if I could only escape this nightmare. This was it, and I waited in quiet desperation for sleep to take me.

~~ * ~ * ~ * ~~

Wednesday

When I woke in the morning, the light was dreary and cold, the patter of rain still falling against the windowpane. My body was stiff, having slept in the same fetal position all night. I curbed my expectation of her hand on my membranes or playing with my tail flat. It felt wrong to be in this bed, my usual morning greeting choking me as it burned to leave my tongue.

With a groan, I pushed myself from the bed, looking around at the room I used to know so well. It felt so painfully empty, and I hurried to stand and escape it. As soon as I opened the door, I could smell breakfast, unable to help the start of a smile as it all rushed back to me how happy it always was to see my family in the mornings—or evenings, depending upon the season.

I ducked across the hall into the bathroom to wash my face before going downstairs, unsure of what I would find in the kitchen. The habit was old, and one I never thought I would practice again.

My smile broadened, chest feeling hollow. "Good morning."

"Good morning, Cory," greeted Lisa from the stove. "Sit down, it's almost ready."

Robert and my new acquaintance, Corey, were both at the table, looking up to greet me simultaneously. I found a seat, taking it silently.

"So, I wanted to get to know you under better circumstances, and," Corey motioned to a bundle on the table, "I brought pie. Courtesy of the Smiths, but I was hoping I could get points for delivery."

"Is it the same recipe, I wonder?" I murmured, knowing better than to sneak anything from the dessert with breakfast so close to done and a spatula in Lisa's hand. If she truly was so much like Mother, I would not risk the injury to my pride.

"That's what I'm told," he replied with a smile that made his blue eyes dance. "Anyway, they sent plenty."

"I will have to wait for mine. I need to retrieve the children today," I said, the words feeling awkward. "A friend is watching them."

"Are you going back to the city after?" asked Robert, his tone one of a concerned friend.

I sighed quietly. "I have yet to decide. I feel... compelled, to return the children to someplace more familiar, more human, yet I cannot say I would like to forget what I have seen of...our adventures. And I cannot say I find returning to our...Well, the notion is unappealing, at best."

"Well, you're welcome to stay here," offered Lisa as she set several plates of food on the table, from eggs to hashed browns. "If you need more time before going through Kate's effects. I haven't put the farm up for sale yet, so you can take as long as you need."

Corey shot me a knowing smirk at my sister's words, making certain no one else saw.

Robert must have observed I had yet to consider this, agreeing cheerily, "That's a great idea! I can help handle some of the paperwork, so you can focus on the kids."

"We'll help you get back on your feet before you know it." Lisa took a seat at the table, pouring herself a glass of water from the pitcher. She reached over to give my hand a reassuring squeeze. "Everything will work out."

"Thank you, Lisa." I returned the simple gesture carefully, giving her a grateful smile. I felt the atmosphere growing heavy, adding jokingly, "Don't tell Ethan, but you always were my favorite sister."

She giggled, smacking my arm playfully. "Oh, just eat!"

I held on to the momentary feeling of belonging, the scraps of happiness untouched by time. Our meal blurred by, my appetite still recovering. As we finished, I was met yet again by Lisa's refusal to allow me to assist in the cleanup.

"Go get the kids, you can help later!" She silenced

my protests, pointing to the front door. "I want to see kids with you when you come back, too."

I held up my hands in defeat, going to the front door. "Very well. I will be home by tomorrow."

"Tomorrow?!" Her surprised cry followed me outside, my feet taking the steps in a habitual rhythm. I hit the wet soil running, rain misting against my skin as I flew into it, glad it was lighter than yesterday's downpour.

My flight was swift, and I recognized the forestry beneath me at last, landing in the overgrowth. Decades had gone by, yet I could still make out the scars on trees where I had clawed them. The memories were still vivid, the guilt and grief I had felt then renewed now. Although, I now had the presence of mind to restrain myself and focus on my responsibilities.

Shaking the recognition from my clouded mind, I turned to the tree I sought and the eerie archway it formed, stepping through. I glanced around, the forest I found myself in quiet but for the rain falling on the canopy above. I listened for a moment for the creatures I had heard the first time, pausing. I knew myself well enough to realize I was delaying. With a final, quiet sigh of defeat, I forced myself to walk towards where I knew the children to be.

The trek was remarkably short, knowing now where to go. Before long, the tunnel to the village was in sight and devouring me whole. The darkness was welcome this time, a visual reminder I still had at least one more breath before I broke the hearts of those two little ones I was responsible for now.

"Cory?!" I heard the call ahead of me, a figure

standing at the edge of the darkness where the tunnel broke into the massive cavern. I recognized the silhouette with a weary smile.

"Braxen!" I called back, quickening my pace to meet him sooner. He laughed when he was able to see me clearly, giving me a firm hug. The familiarity of it was easy, the first hint I might feel any relief soon. "I never thought I would miss you, Braxen."

"Bah," he laughed, waving away the notion. His eyes were bright, curious as he watched me. "How are you?"

What momentary distraction I had relished in collapsed under the weight of what I knew was coming. "Lonely. Terrified."

"You wish it had been you," he added, voicing the thing I dared not even think to myself. "I know."

"Of course," I murmured, nodding slowly. Even so, knowing how I was not alone did little to comfort me when I knew what was to come had to be handled by me and no one else. "How have they been?"

"Happy, getting into more trouble than usual for offspring," he joked, but the words fell flat. I wanted to know all of their mischief and grins, regretting how they would be gone for an immeasurable time after this. He spared me a sympathetic smile. "I'll tell you another time. No more distractions. They've been asking for you."

It was uncanny as always how he seemed a step ahead of my next thought, but I nodded. "Very well. Can you take me to them?"

He nodded sadly. "Yes, of course. Leilani has been taking good care of them, this way."

Broken Orbit

It was difficult to follow him, my feet heavy and dragging against what was to come. There must have been chains weighing me down, growing heavier the closer we came, so that by the time we crossed the cavern it felt as though I might have been drug through the earth itself. Braxen stopped and gestured toward an open glen, sharing a wearied glance.

"If you need me, I'll come," he said before retreating, no doubt fleeing what was to follow.

I saw the children with Leilani long before they noticed me. Delaying the moment when I broke their hearts, I watched them play instead, excited and happy as she showed them how to weave a basket. I supposed they must have gotten distracted yesterday, then. I could not bear to disrupt them. Still, Sarah caught sight of me, lighting up even more with her glee as she sprinted toward me.

I knelt and she charged into my waiting arms, with Kyle close behind. They collapsed against me, a mess of mad giggling which twisted in my chest, despite how I cherished the sound.

"Hello, you two. What have you been up to?" I asked, trying to prolong the inevitable.

Kyle bounced in his excitement, pointing behind him. "We're making things! Leilani is so much fun, and sleeping over was fun, too! She told us stories all night long."

Sarah nodded with a grin, Kate's eyes staring up at me. "And she did voices, too."

I tried to laugh for their sake, never wanting their happiness to end. "That sounds like a lot of fun. What did you make?"

They shared a glance, Sarah admitting somewhat bashfully, "Well, Leilani was the one making things. We were watching 'cause we kept messing up."

I gave her a gentle smile. "That is perfectly fine, Sarah. Observing can be just as important as doing at times."

"Yeah, I guess." She shrugged, lighting up again. "Is Grandma back with you? Braxen said you'd left with her. Does that mean she's feeling better?!"

The feeling of my heart breaking was far from over, my words cutting me as I spoke, "No, children. She's not coming back."

Kyle's confusion hurt me. "Is she mad?"

"No, Kyle, no, she loves you both more than you could know," I told him quietly. Understanding dawned across Sarah's face.

"You're lying." The apology I wore only angered her and she threw her fists against me, screaming, "You're lying! You're a liar! Liar!"

Then Kyle understood, tears hitting his cheeks as he sobbed brokenly, "Grandma? I want to see Grandma!"

"Oh, little ones, I know," I murmured, hugging them both close. They only fought a moment before they caved to their need for comfort, clinging to me tightly. Just as Kate had done. "Hush now, I'm here. Everything will be all right, I have you. Sh, hush, it's all right."

Even in their need, there was so much anger and indignation, but I took it all. If only to help them smile again, however much sooner, I could bear their screams and their blame. This was my job now. Whatever they needed, however I could build them to be their happy selves, I had to do it. Even playing a momentary villain they could abuse, to make sense of this senselessness, was an easy burden to bear.

"Everything will work out."

Although they lacked their previous magic, I would do everything in my power to make those words true for them, however long it took.

Karma Rose

<u>The End of an Era</u>

After going missing eight weeks ago, along with the former N.S.I.S.D. specimen released late last year, Katelyn Smith has been reported as deceased. Her family is declining interviews at this time, and details of the cause of death are being withheld from the media. According to sources, the funeral will be private, with an undisclosed time and location.

The former demon rights activist pioneered the modern recognition of demons as potentially sentient animals. While she advocated for demons being sentient as a whole, scientists are still studying whether that can be said or if the development is unique to select individuals. Due to the limited availability of live specimens, there has been little progress on this front in recent years.

It is with sad hearts that supporters of her work say farewell now. The flurry of responses has been peaceful, but not quiet. Although Miss Smith is gone, her legacy is not forgotten.

Karma Rose

Chapter Five: Breathless

The children slept soundly as I packed everything, ignoring the sharp pain which came with each piece of her I stuffed into the bags we had brought. I grit my teeth, biting back any more tears. I was tired of crying, tired of this empty grief. Without thinking, my hands fell still, an overwhelming weight crushing me from within.

Breathe.

I glanced over at the children, taking a deep breath to clear my mind. A break, that was all I needed. A quick moment to stretch and rest, then I could return to packing. I stood with a quiet groan, focusing on the single task which would lead to the care of the two sleeping children who were suddenly mine to raise.

As I stepped from the hut, I felt a rush of anxiety, recalling just days ago when I had carried Katelyn to the Healer huts. I should have taken her to the humans. Had I known, I never would have pursued this place if it risked her health further.

Breathe.

The wave of emotion was disorienting, the world spinning before I caught myself. I looked around for anything else to focus on, catching sight of Leilani as she made her way to our hut. Her cheeks flushed when she realized I was watching her approach, fresh rose blooming against her sunset coral. I spared her a weary smile.

"Hello, Leilani. Was there something I may help you with?" I asked, calling on practiced greetings even as it failed to feel sincere.

She stopped where she was, fidgeting shyly. Her accent was heavy, and it seemed as though her words had been practiced as she recited, "I have sorry. Kate is nice, very sad. I help?"

The laugh which escaped me startled us both, and I found myself happy about her broken speech and the effort she had put into it. "Thank you, Leilani. Just your visiting helps."

She smiled awkwardly, embarrassed. "I...I has no words. Ah...I help?" she repeated, struggling with herself. "Babies. I help? I help...food?"

"You...would like to help me with Kyle and Sarah?" I wondered, at a loss if this was not the case. She perked up excitedly at the names, nodding. I chuckled, enjoying her enthusiasm. "Very well. Now, food? Do you have food? No, you said help—help food. Help give food, help make food? Cook?"

The confusion and elation blended evenly on her face, resulting in my stabbing sympathy for her and the barrier we were struggling with. The sweet young demoness was deeply torn, frustrated at how we could not communicate but certainly glad for what we had already accomplished.

"No words," she eventually sighed, disappointed.

"Well, that will not do," I murmured, wanting to see more of her avid excitement and enthusiasm. I knew it could be a very long time before I saw anyone else with her kind of glee, and I wanted so desperately to see plenty more before I endured through the coming weeks for the children. "Ah, perhaps Braxen could translate?"

At the mention of Braxen, she lit up anew, grinning at me with glinting white fangs. "Braxen has words!"

"Yes, so he does," I chuckled. Without a word, she darted forward to grab my hand and drag me away, running through the village. I stumbled before I caught myself, correcting pace to keep even with her smaller stride.

She did not lead me far, just to the first community fire where supper was being had. "Braxen!"

He looked up from where he was speaking with an elderly pair of demons. He was startled at first, then concerned when he saw it was me she had in tow. He stood and hurried over, but before he had time to ask she began to babble in their exotic language. She never dropped my hand, motioning to me with her free one every so often. I stood there awkwardly. The only thing I had to return to was painful. With the children asleep, this incomprehensible exchange was far more preferable.

Without my realizing, she had finished her eager rambling, and Braxen was looking at me with an odd expression. "She wants to go with you, to help with the children and, what is it? Ah...caretake? Feed you, help you, tend to needs."

I blinked in surprise, glancing from her to Braxen

151

awkwardly. "Ah. I gathered she meant the children, but I...That is to say—"

"She doesn't mean to replace Katelyn," interrupted Braxen, eyes knowing. "She sees you grieve and wants to help you. Leilani thinks of you as a friend, and she loves the children. She would be sad to see you go knowing she would be more useful with you."

She looked between the two of us, growing uneasy. She settled on Braxen, speaking quickly to him before turning to me, "I help?"

Her eager and honest expression left my numb mind feeling as though she may be able to bring me to smile, if only because of her enthusiasm. It was hard not to join in her humor when she was so inviting with it.

"The house is small, and I..." I sighed heavily, honestly glad for the relief which came when I thought of having such happy help with Kyle and Sarah in the coming days. "I am sure we can find a bed. Yes, Leilani, I would love your help."

The little woman's initial excitement was curbed, looking to Braxen for confirmation. He gave her a short answer which made her grin, squeezing my hand before finally dropping it. She gave him a quick, excited reply before racing off again. I assumed she was going to pack what belongings she had. My smile was small, but it was genuine, content to have such happy company.

"You need to sleep."

"Hm?" I looked back to find Braxen fixing me with a knowing glare, stern.

"Before you go anywhere, you need to sleep," he repeated firmly. "I feel your grief, Cory, and I see your fear but you are no good to them if you are not taking the same care of yourself. The work can wait until after you've met your own needs."

"I cannot sleep, Braxen," I replied quietly, terrified of what I may find awaiting me in dreams. Worse yet, I dreaded waking to expectations which would forevermore go unmet.

His eyes tightened, worry bleeding through to me with the curious sensation of being split between our two bodies. "Perhaps with magic? We can give you a dreamless sleep if it would help. You can't keep going like this."

"No, no magic," I protested hurriedly. Oh, how tempted I was by the promise of sweet nothingness. My mouth burned with the desire to partake of an old habit, going dry in anticipation of the whiskey. I best not entice myself to find a new crutch. "I have gotten along perfectly fine until now without it, I can manage however long I have left."

Braxen's expression changed to an odd mixture of confusion and pity. "A good meal, then. We have, what's the word, *pog*?"

I caught sight of the large animal roasting, amused briefly by his butchering of words. "A pig, Braxen. Or a hog, I suppose, since it was wild."

His face lit up at my speaking to him in any casual capacity. "Then you'll stay?"

The hopeful expression he wore was painful to me, so much more than my prior tasks had been. It reminded me how the world could see my broken dreams. My scars burned with a new shame, demanding I cover more completely these emotional fractures which felt like they may never heal.

I did not want anyone to see this. It felt too deeply personal, the private moments Katelyn and I had shared sitting too close to the surface of my skin to remain secret.

"I need to return to my packing," I muttered, excusing myself awkwardly. I felt Braxen's watchful eyes follow me as I left the fire, trudging back to the wretched task of admitting the end of this era. I only hoped the next one could include these people more—if only to fight back the loneliness I could feel on the edge of my sanity.

I reached the hut more swiftly than I desired, staring at its exterior reluctantly. Inside, there were tasks and responsibilities which brought me nothing but grief. I wanted to turn and walk away, ignore it just a little while longer.

A small sniffle from within shattered my plan.

I slipped inside silently, eyes adjusting quickly to the dim light of the fire's embers. There was a quiet gasp from the furs and they went deathly still. I crossed the hut in two easy strides, watching the bundles of fur where the children slept while I listened carefully.

A long, stressed moment later, the little bundle nearest me sniffled and shifted.

"Whatever's the matter?" I asked in a whisper, easing myself onto the furs and careful to make sure I did not harm either of the children.

There was a tiny, startled gasp. "Um..."

"Sarah?" I found enough room to settle down, joining her under the furs as I had done just the other morning. "What is it, sweetheart? You sounded upset."

154

Another sniffle and she shook her head. "No..."

"Hm." Why would she lie? It was so very unlike her usual, pointedly honest self. "Well, I'm a bit sad."

"You are?" Another tiny shudder, her voice growing more distressed despite her attempts to hide it. "Do you want a hug?"

"That would help," I agreed, sitting up and leaning against the hut's wall. She wriggled out of her hiding place, hugging my arm awkwardly. I hugged her back with my free arm, rubbing her back for comfort. "Thank you. That helps."

She nodded, refusing to let go as she began to tremble. "Yeah."

"Would you like a better hug?" I offered, not needing to wait for her answer as she all but jumped into my lap, clutching her stuffed rabbit tight. I found a spare fur and bundled her up, hugging her gently. "There you are. Does that help?"

She nodded, still obviously upset but calming down now. "Yeah."

"Were you sad?" I asked, worried for why she had been crying and trying to hide it. How long had she been awake? Should I have returned sooner?

Sarah nodded again. Her reply was muffled through both the fur and her rabbit, "I was afraid you wouldn't come back now that Grandma's gone."

My heart was torn anew. "I'm sorry you thought that, Sarah. I will always come back for you two."

"Really?" She peeked up at me, hopeful and surprised. "You won't take us back to our dad's?"

"Not unless you want to go," I told her. "And only

155

if I could know you're safe."

"I don't wanna go there," she gasped hurriedly, frightened by the idea. "But...I was just scared, since Grandma was the only one who wanted us anymore."

"Oh, sweetheart," I sighed softly. I gave her a smile, hoping to hide how deeply her sincerity in those words hurt. Who could ever not want them? "I want you. My sister wants you, Robert and his family, too. Especially Bailey, she adores you and your brother."

"Even Leilani?" she asked, the name surprising me. I supposed they had been seeing more of her of late, and they always enjoyed their time with the demoness.

"Yes, sweetheart, even Leilani," I confirmed, Sarah's immediate glee reminding me of Leilani's excitement to join us on our return trek.

Her face fell just as suddenly, although the worst of her mood seemed to have passed. "I wish she could come with us."

"She *is* coming, Sarah." The way her eyes lit up made my heart warm, my smile coming more easily. "She wants to keep seeing you and Kyle."

Sarah seemed to force back tears as the news sank in. She yawned widely, nodding slowly and fighting sleep. "I'm glad. I like her."

"I do, too," I agreed quietly, brushing a stray hair from tickling her nose. She relaxed slowly, breaths changing as she fell asleep in my arms. In spite of my empty aches, I felt my heart swell.

For all of the despair of the days which did not seem to end, the children still brought forth anything aside from heartache. Like Leilani's infectious smiles, yet their presence wielded the force of a hurricane in my growing apathy. I looked between the two little ones, holding fast to this feeling of strength as it rooted itself too deeply to ever be cut out.

~~ * ~ * ~ * ~~

<u>Thursday</u>

The morning was difficult.

There was no excusing it for any sort of silver linings: there were none. From the start, Kyle and Sarah both took turns at being heart-wrenchingly upset, neither of them wanting to speak to me. Whatever need they had of me yesterday seemed to have vanished, this infuriating defiance taking its place. It blocked my usual ways to speak to them, leaving me helpless to mend their broken smiles.

Relief came only when Leilani arrived. She carried a small basket across her back, entering our hut without any announcement. Where I had yielded no results with this foul morning, she was able to turn it around in a matter of minutes. I bit back the feeling of rejection crawling beneath my skin. There was a reason for their spite.

If this is what it takes, I reminded myself feebly.

While Leilani led the children off for breakfast, I kept at my unfinished packing in solitude. Alone, it was difficult to keep back my tears, and it was beside me how I managed to cease their flow time and time again. My hands burned with every article I touched, and before long

157

I had nothing left to reach for.

I stared at the hut dumbly. We were leaving no trace of our having lived here for weeks outside of the few bags sitting beside the entrance. Leilani had taken her basket with her, leaving little else to wait for in this overdue departure.

On the trek here, I had carried most of the bags, and I loaded myself down again in much the same fashion now. They felt so much heavier now, weighed down by memories and guilt while I trudged toward the fires. As I approached, I could hear Leilani's animated voice speaking in her native language, the children's laughter ringing out alongside it.

The moment I was in sight, however, both Kyle and Sarah lost any trace of humor, expressions flat. Leilani followed their spiteful stares, smiling more kindly at my approach. She stood fluidly, gliding over to meet me.

"You food?" she asked. I shook my head slowly. The smell of it all was sickening again. I was too stressed to want for anything, nor feel the need for it.

"No, thank you. Are you ready to go?"

Concern flashed in her eyes but she smiled and nodded. With the quietest murmurs, she called the children to her. They were at her side in an instant. Grasping her hands tightly, the trio followed me toward the main tunnel. I had the distinct impression the only reason Kyle and Sarah stayed behind me was because of that demoness.

There were whispers. I heard them, I felt the stares, and I wondered if rumors had spread of Katelyn's passing. Could they care? She was human. Everything I had envied, everything I had yearned to be, and everything these people considered an insult. Could they understand why my heart had stopped with hers? Why I still waited to hear her next breath, why my intake felt so tasteless without hers to match?

Along the way, I was aware of Braxen stepping up alongside me, matching my stride easily. There was a comfort to his presence, something which had gradually developed over weeks of companionship. If only we could have been off to another day of flying, of fighting, of his endless berating. Anything else.

Then we were there, my feet halting at the edge of this world I had so long wished into existence. I could have been happy with humanity. Had I simply stopped chasing dreams, stopped seeking answers about blood, stopped wanting for more.

Had I stopped then, she might have woken with me today.

The sense of purpose which had quieted over these last weeks flared indignantly as I stared down the dark tunnel. I ignored it and the brutal feeling of betrayal rearing with its neglect. Whatever they had meant, their reasons for driving me toward the demons, it no longer mattered. Katelyn was gone because I had pursued this; the children beside me deserved better.

"Cory." I looked back to see Braxen's hesitance, feeling the regret etched into his features. He sighed. "You're always welcome here."

I smiled dryly and nodded. "The same for you back home, Braxen."

Karma Rose

Feeling as if I were tearing whole new pieces from my flesh, I led our odd group back to the suffocatingly domesticated world of humans.

~~ * ~ * ~ * ~~

What had taken an entire night once before now took a matter of a few hours, with Leilani and I. The children had tired out shortly after stepping through the archway, leaving the demoness and me to carry them. Burdened as I was, Kyle was all I could bear to manage, slumped across my shoulder and drooling in his sleep. Leilani carried Sarah in a very similar fashion as the young girl fell asleep quickly.

Lulled by the rhythm of walking and watching Leilani's lithe, dancing strides, my own had lengthened to match. Without realizing—and barely possessing the presence of mind to notice—I had taken up a pace I never used in the company of others. As easily as she kept up with me, I found myself unable to care much about this slip in self-control, impatient as I was to reach our destination.

So we kept on until we reached the old church, and I steered us toward the road in the direction of my childhood home. Traffic was mercifully non-existent given the time of day, making the trip pass all the more swiftly. Before I realized it, we were stepping up onto the porch. My gait was thunderous as hers was silent; exactly what I expected of a demon by now.

My sister must have been waiting on the other side for me, the front door flying open as we drew near.

"Cory, you're ba...ck. Oh. Hello," greeted Lisa, no doubt startled by the demoness with me. She gaped at the two of us, looking like she might cry. "I-I'm sorry, I just...You're really not alone, Cory. She looks like you."

"I apologize for not telling you sooner, but she insisted on coming with me to help with the children," I explained abashedly.

Lisa laughed at my bashfulness, waving away the notion of it being troublesome. "I don't mind, but...May I?" she asked Leilani, holding out one hand in question.

The demoness looked to me for answers, copper eyes wide.

"It is all right, Leilani." Bracing Kyle with one arm, I reached out to accept Lisa's hand as an example, then motioned her to do the same. "It is how we greet each other here."

She relaxed, obviously eased more by my general tone than my words. Mimicking my actions with a smile, she echoed my sister's greeting, "Oh, hello."

"Oh, you're actually real!" cried Lisa with another laugh. She dropped Leilani's hand and took her up in a motherly embrace which startled the poor woman. It was made all the more awkward by Sarah, still cradled against Leilani's shoulder. She looked at me pleadingly, realizing a moment later what Lisa was doing and returning the gesture with one arm. My sister stepped back, wearing a teary-eyed smile. "I'm sorry, I've never met anyone like him. I'm Lisa, Cory's sister."

"Lisa, she, ah..." I glanced at Leilani's confused curiosity, still watching me for any indication of how to proceed. "She does not speak English, I am afraid. Not very fluently, at least."

Before Lisa could make much of her guest's limitations, the children began to stir in our arms. Their quiet yawns and moans of protest gradually cleared as they peered around, alert. I set Kyle down, anticipating his distaste of me before he had the opportunity to voice it. He gravitated toward Leilani without a word.

As if just now seeing the bags I carried, my sister stepped back to allow us inside, waving me up the stairs to the second floor.

"Dustin and Ethan's room is set up for the kids," she called after me as I struggled through the confining space to the landing. Without worrying myself with our brothers' old room, I disencumbered myself in my room, bags landing clumsily. I stretched awkwardly in the small space.

When I returned downstairs, the children were with Leilani in the living room, chattering with her quietly. Sarah watched me warily as I made my way to the kitchen across the entryway, finding my sister there. She had the pot of stew reheating on the stove as she sat at the table to a steaming cup of what I could only assume was tea.

I joined her with a tired groan, done with this day already when I spied the clock on the wall. How was it barely past noon? My sister did not seem to notice my fatigue, absorbed entirely by Leilani's presence.

"She's gorgeous, Cory," whispered Lisa excitedly, glancing again at where the demoness was engaging with the children in the living room. "Smaller than I would've thought, given *your* size, but just as stunning. And that color!"

I chuckled at her enthusiastic ramblings. "She is just small, is all. The others are considerably larger. As odd as it sounds, her color is bland compared to some others I saw, as well."

"Really?" she gasped, sipping her tea thoughtfully. "Do they all get along with humans? Or is she just special, like you?"

"They are...different. Their customs and social norms, at least, but they were all very kind to us and mindful of how much more fragile humans are," I replied, thinking over how quickly they had adapted their understanding of humans not being as durable as themselves. "They are tribal, even primal, but still so very kind with one another."

"That sounds a lot like you," she giggled, sparing another glance. She sighed quietly, a more grounded worry overcoming her. "The kids seem okay, considering. How are you holding up?"

At the reminder, I found myself suddenly hollow, but I nodded slowly. "As well as I can be, I suppose. There is so much to be planned and done, yet I have trouble thinking beyond a few minutes from now."

She nodded knowingly. "You'll get tired of hearing this, but it does get easier."

"I almost feel as if I should wake up in the Institute again," I confessed quietly, scowling at the table. Lisa reached over to squeeze my hand reassuringly. "It is all I know of not having her with me. Even living with Robert, I knew she was out there somewhere, but now—It's so final."

"I'm sorry, Cory," she whispered. "I can say for sure that you're not there, and you're not going back, ever. We just have to take it slow and keep you occupied."

I nodded numbly. "I know. I have them to worry over now, and they need someone, only..."

"What if you're not good enough?" she asked, echoing my fears. She smiled at me when I looked up from the table. "I'm a mom, I remember thinking that. I wanted to give my babies the world, I just didn't know how, and I thought I had to be a terrible mom because of it. Our mom always made it look so easy and natural. It's like she just existed to be a mom, but me..."

I laughed awkwardly at her confession. "She always had a way of making you feel loved, even if you knew you were in trouble. I see a lot of her in you, Lisa," I told her, returning her smile habitually.

"Thank you." She sipped her tea. "So. Are you going to adopt them?"

The thought was all at once elating and horrifying. "I-I hadn't considered it."

"Robert was talking after you left, he's going to handle as much as he can to help you," she told me with another sip of her tea. "He's a good friend."

I nodded. "Yes, he is."

"You know...you could always ask the kids what they want," she offered, no doubt recognizing my hesitance at the whole notion. She shrugged. "If you really think you're not right for them, I mean. But I've always thought you'd make a good father, for what it's worth. Kate, too. I mean, that's why she put your name on Charlie's birth certificate."

Those words stopped me cold, my heart skipping and breath hitching. "She did?"

Lisa nodded, eyeing me hesitantly. "Are you okay?"

"Yes, just fine," I replied numbly. Such a small detail, one which mattered very little in the end, and yet it blindsided my guard entirely. Katelyn had never let me fade, she had never once relented to the hopeless ideas I might never return home. The stubborn woman I loved so completely had always been planning for the day we would be reunited.

"Well. Just think about it, okay, Cory?"

I nodded, so accustomed to life without being a legal person. It was odd to think of, adoption. I thought of the certificate I had been given upon my release, with my parents' names listed in such neat print. They had given of themselves by taking me in. Had I not already considered some sort of long-term with Kyle and Sarah, as well? It was the least I could do, then, to give them the option.

Of all the things which could have unnerved me these last several weeks, however, the brief consideration of legally becoming a father won out.

～～ * ～ * ～ * ～～

October 7th, 2011

This day has done nothing but drag on endlessly. I have a new appreciation for Leilani already. I would be utterly lost if she were not here to occupy the children while...

Jeff insisted I be involved.

Flowers. We discussed <u>flowers</u>. We perused caskets. Cold, lifeless, unnecessarily decorated things. None of them seemed suitable for her. Nothing is suitable for this.

None of it matters. Not now that she is gone.

~~ * ~ * ~ * ~~

This is not me.

The realization was brief, staring at the bright orange hands in this dream. The relief was lasting, however, every part of me grateful for any reprieve from the life which was mine.

"Braxen!"

"Yes, Grandmother?" I straightened reflexively, gripping my staff tightly as she approached. Behind her, two creatures I didn't recognize followed closely. It only took a second longer before I saw the feathered wings, one pair white as clouds and the other blacker than my blood.

My eyes widened.

Why was the Drinker here? Didn't Grandmother know better? He was an animal, a murderer that drained us dry if given the chance. And an angel, too? What if she was working for Bliss?

"We have guests, Braxen. This is the Drinker, Vladimir, and his companion, Grace. They've decided to take up arms against Bliss." My grandmother sounded amused under that scathing tone she always spoke with.

I crossed my wrists and bared my throat as I had been trained to do. Submit early, establish my undeserving place. "It's an honor."

The sentiment was empty. My voice and eyes were flat, angry. I wanted to end them now, prevent the inevitable destruction these two were sure to bring to our home.

Vladimir grinned, fangs making me shudder. "I like him. He's spirited."

I hated that look, being appraised like little more than meat. My eyes tightened, grip nearly painful on my staff. I could show him spirited.

~~ * ~ * ~ * ~~

Saturday

My eyes opened to the dark living room of the old farmhouse, body aching in protest of my not moving from this odd half-sprawled position on the couch.

I had not slept. Again.

What scant few moments of rest I had stolen on the couch could barely be called sleep. My eyes had closed, my body had slowed itself, but my mind was as awake as ever as it wandered through countless memories. Just the same as every night since—

The quiet creak on the stair was a mercy, and I stood stiffly to investigate. I expected children, out of bed in the middle of the night for treats or nightmares. What I found was still too new to adjust to entirely, the bright copper eyes startling me at first.

Leilani smiled sheepishly, face worn as she yawned. I fought a shudder seeing those fangs bared wide, so much like my own. I recalled Bailey's questions last year about my smile frightening me. While my own was certainly just fine, the wild demoness in my tame family home was another matter entirely. My two worlds were colliding in a messy heap.

"No sleep," she whispered with a shrug. She tapped her ear with a frustrated scowl. "No sleep, is..."

"You have an earache?" I wondered. Although, she did not seem to be in pain. I sighed quietly, too tired to be playing at this translation game we both seemed to fail at. "No, not that. You are listening? You hear something?"

She huffed quietly, slinking down the stairs silently in the dark. "No words."

"I know, Leilani," I muttered, retreating to where I had been struggling for any respite. The demoness followed me, sitting daintily on what little of the small couch I did not dominate while lounging. I glanced at the plethora of alternative seating options, putting it out of my mind. I did not have the patience for puzzling over anything now.

Still, I could not help my curious glances, fatigued or not. She was still so foreign, and her presence here—in this house which once marked my isolated existence— made the last several weeks feel tangible, real.

I was not alone, however different our cultures may have been. Nearly seventy years, and I was no longer a solitary creature while this tiny woman flitted about in the old trappings my life had worn. All I could do was hide my stares, worried that should I look away for too long the evidence of my ended isolation might vanish.

It was odd, seeing my old flannel shirts on her. I could so clearly remember how unbearably tight the seams had been last time I wore it. Despite this, there was nearly enough fabric to make a second shirt for her, she was so minuscule by comparison. She was Robert's height, of course, but such a slim build she seemed average by human standards.

How could such a little thing possibly be the same species as myself?

If the shirts had not been painful enough, the poor woman then had to make do with my old pants. A problem Lisa quickly helped me remedy by turning the baggy, worn garments into skirts. Leilani seemed much more pleased with the articles then, and had I not known better I could have been fooled she had been raised a simple farmer, the same as myself.

Until she caught a claw on the carpet and tripped herself, or began tasting soaps and candles because of the appealing smells.

The reminders of her unfamiliarity with the human world were never slight, always ending with a grand flourish befitting of the Stooges themselves. It was everything I had in me to resist the humor of these situations, act the gentleman, and help her through.

My particular favorite was introducing her to new technologies, the television and radio especially. For hours, she was convinced someone had trapped little people within the screen, or stolen voices were caught inside the radio. At least, I suspected as much from her panicked, half-broken cries which could not settle on a language to protest these injustices in.

It had taken a single word to calm her, however: magic.

If only she knew how much I cherished these distractions, perhaps she might understand why I smiled at her mishaps.

Now, however, it was a simple fascination I held as I watched her fall asleep. Her wings relaxed, falling away from her slowly to splay out across the floor and furniture. Her tail twitched, reminding me of a cat as it dreamed. It was oddly mesmerizing, seeing someone else sleep with a body so much like mine. I would have watched for hours had I not followed suit, drifting off into another half-waking slumber.

~~ * ~ * ~ * ~~

Breakfast the coming morning was an odd affair. The somber atmosphere aside, it was an awkward attempt at normalcy—two demons, an elderly woman, and the two young children. Between the five of us, we had four separate skin colors, three different cultures and too many social barriers to count.

I cleared my throat toward the end of the meal, startling us all after the silence and scraping of forks on plates. I took a deep breath and tried again, "So, children, what would you say to a stroll after this, hm?"

They shared a glance which spoke volumes of their immediate dislike of me. As if I had not already been monstrous enough as the bearer of ill news, I could not

170

seem to find a way to approach them since then.

"Um. Can we play video games?" asked Kyle shyly, making a visible attempt not to insult me. I bit back a sigh, completely lost already. I was still learning about more modern technologies; Kate had always handled what I could not.

"I'm sorry, Kyle, we don't have any here," said Lisa gently. I smiled gratefully.

"Perhaps we could read something?" I offered instead. Another glance, this time with a hint of a distasteful cringe.

"Can we just play with Leilani?" suggested Sarah hopefully, nodding to the woman who was still struggling with her grip on her utensil.

Hiding my disappointment, I nodded. "If Leilani is wanting to, I see no reason why not."

They were satisfied with my answer, all but inhaling their remaining breakfast before fleeing the table with all of the calm of evacuating a house fire. I made to call them back to clean the dishes, knowing it was my responsibility now. By the time I found the words the children were gone, leaving the back door hanging open. The moment they were out of sight, Leilani forgot her fork. In an instant her eggs and hashbrowns were being treated as finger food.

Lisa was forgiving of the poor woman, having never used these manners or tools before. The same patience was not spared for the children or my lack of experience with them.

"You're going to have to be strict with those two," she commented, glancing between their dirty dishes and the open door. I sighed with a subdued nod, collecting their plates into the sink and filling it with hot water for a quick soak. "We were doing dishes by Kyle's age, remember?"

"Yes, and darning by Sarah's, but—" My thought was disrupted at the back door, knob in hand to close it when a distinct scent caught my attention on the morning breeze. An involuntary growl escaped me as I stepped outside, door slamming behind me more forcefully than I intended.

I looked for the children quickly, panic spiking in my chest when I found the animal I had scented first. Near the edge of the back field, a small family of wild hogs were snuffling, looking to be finishing their routine for the night as the sun was beginning to rise. A playful shriek startled them as much as myself. The children were dancing about like madmen, with no notice of the danger they frolicked towards.

Without waiting for the beasts to react, I dashed out to put myself between them and the little ones playing so carelessly. The children skittered when they saw me running, turning to escape and screaming when they spied the large boar charging out to meet me. I only just made it to the children in time, fanning my wings wide and bellowing deeply. The beast barely slowed, screaming at me in return.

I managed to put a few feet between myself and the children behind me before the boar made it to me. Oh, how I wished for my claws then, staring down those ugly tusks. As it was, I scarcely managed to time a solid blow to its shoulder, following it with a slap from my tail.

While I felt the creature budge, I knew I would have better luck against a stone wall if it came to much more than this.

Startled, it finally stopped, backing up to give me a small area to breathe. I bared my fangs and snarled, sounding more like a rabid bear than anything resembling civilized. It snorted at me, gave one last shriek, and sauntered back to where the others had retreated into the brush at the end of the field.

It took a moment before my sigh of relief escaped me faintly. My thundering heart had me tasting my pulse in my throat, hands shaking as I realized we had scraped by without being gored. I turned to the children then, gaping at me and a good bit farther away than I had left them. At least they had the common sense to flee when they finally *saw* danger!

"Are you two all right?" I asked breathlessly, tucking my wings and going to where they stood, frozen in their gawking. They both nodded, Kyle's face breaking into a broad grin.

"That was so cool!" he crowed gleefully.

"No, it was not!" I snapped, finally able to breathe and see how close they had come to such a threat. They jumped, chagrined and nervous. "Do you have any idea how dangerous those animals are?! You could have been severely injured, or worse!"

"We didn't know," protested Sarah, flinching at my frustrated scowl.

"Now you do," I retorted harshly, terror clouding my better judgment. What if I had been too late? What if I had waited for a second longer to close the door, or not caught the scent? "I expect more caution from both of you in the future. I already lost your grandmother, I will *not* be burying either of you next. Is that understood?"

They nodded, eyes downcast. Sarah grabbed Kyle's hand and held it tight. Guilt settled in atop my calming trepidation. I breathed deeply, heart slowing in its race, allowing me clarity enough to regret every word which had stumbled so drunkenly off my tongue.

"Now, go to your room, please, until I can do a proper check for any more dangers," I said quietly. Oh, if there were any gods with mercy, they would have struck me dumb. The children shuffled off into the house, my eyes trained on them the entire way. I saw then both Lisa and Leilani were just outside the back door, witnesses to the entire exchange. Despite the differences between species and culture, they both wore the same shocked and appalled expression which reprimanded as much as it demanded.

Damn it all, but I had made myself quite the bed to lie in with my brash reaction.

Leilani followed the children back into the house, nothing but concern on her face as she turned away from me. Lisa, on the other hand, strode out as I made my way back. I could all but hear the opinions in her eyes as she stared me down, accusations etched into her wizened features.

"I heard every word, Charles," she informed me, quite impressively keeping pace with me as she crossed her arms sternly. She seemed set to keep me such unpleasant company.

"And your point?" I demanded, ashamed enough

without her assistance. She stepped in my path, refusing to let me pass. I sighed sharply. "What, Lisa?!"

"How the hell could you say that to kids that just lost their grandmother?!" she cried out, expression demanding how I could be so dense not to realize the obviousness of the question.

"They nearly ran into a mauling by wild animals, Lisa, I—I was terrified! I should have cut out my tongue before I spoke, but they need to learn," I tried to defend myself, failing miserably. Regret and guilt pooled in my chest and turned to self-loathing, the result of some forsaken emotional alchemy. "They need to know it is dangerous out here at times."

"They're from the city, Charles, they don't know any better. That's what *you're* here for," she explained sharply. My sister relaxed some when she saw the change in my expression, my acceptance of her reprimand and admittance of my wrongs. "Besides, you don't want to ruin whatever rapport you already have with them right now. I know you were scared, but they're alone. They need to know that they can trust you."

"Why, Lisa? They already dislike me," I sighed, shrugging hopelessly. "They have done nothing but avoid me if they can help it since I told them about Kate. If it keeps them safe, what harm is a bit more distaste for me?"

"Did you ever hate Dad?" she retorted, raising one brow skeptically. She had spent far too much time with Katelyn growing up.

"No, Lisa, but this is not—"

"Were you ever scared of him?"

"No, but he—"

"Then you can do better," she concluded with a nod.

"I've barely been at this a week, Lisa!" I cried out, at a loss for how else I was supposed to handle this. "I scarcely made the cut as a grandfather playing second fiddle to Katelyn. I haven't the faintest idea of what to do here and they likely despise me entirely now! How do I fix this?!"

"Figure it out," she suggested, and I sighed sharply at her steadfast insistence on tough love to help me. Mother had never been so infuriatingly unhelpful. I had been too generous to Lisa's likeness of her. "You're an adult, and those kids need you. I suggest you start there. And don't you ever talk to them like that again, Charles," she added sternly, all of the conviction of both of our parents in her final warning.

My sister left me to flounder, wading through this flood of mistakes and all of its damages. I let my feet carry me along the boundary of the fields as I struggled to compose my thoughts into anything resembling the coherent, responsible figure those children deserved. There was little use to my insistence on checking for dangers, barely more than an excuse to ponder in solitude now.

The most obvious thing I should do was apologize, explain my piece and hope we could settle on a compromise for future safety. How was I supposed to manage such a thing? As Lisa had said, the children needed an adult, a guardian, not some commonplace companion. What options did that leave me with? How could Katelyn always make this look so simple?

Broken Orbit

Before I realized it, I had made a full round. I stopped and stared at the back door dumbly. My heart began to race again as I worried over how best to proceed. With more caution and self-control, that much was apparent. What else? Was there anything more I could do to prepare myself for this?

Deciding there was little more to do for delays, I took a deep breath and braced myself as I returned indoors. I saw the dishes still undone, tempted by the allure of any sort of distraction to keep me from facing those children. Linking my hands behind my back, I made for the stairs.

When I reached the second floor, I found their door closed. The sounds of subdued chatter and Leilani's tender murmurs escaped all the same. I had made those voices so shy. I had acted the fool, and it was my job now to clean the mess.

My knock was tentative, silencing the voices on the other side. I hesitated a moment before calling through the door, "It's safe to return outdoors."

Silence. I nodded to myself. It was only fair. I had not expected much, and their sparing me continuing our already strained interaction was a comfort. Without another word, I returned downstairs for the kitchen. I needed to busy myself with something. Anything to stave off this mounting remorse which called out all too clearly to everything I had managed to avoid this morning.

All the same, as I cleaned it came crashing around me—grief, longing, desperation. I fought to keep my hands steady and my breathing even as I allowed myself silent tears. This was it. This was life now, without her.

Karma Rose

Tomorrow, I would have to begin letting go at last.
If only I could bury my ravaged heart with her.

Broken Orbit

October 8th, 2011

My dearest Katelyn,

I hope you are able to read this. Wherever you are, in the heaven you so rightly deserve, I hope they allow letters so I might have one last chance to give you my love. It would be a merciful relief, to think I can still make you smile.

I must confess, my dear, I have had trouble with the children these last several days. They want little to do with me, and when they think I cannot hear they conspire in fervent whispers. I long to hear some secret of yours which might help me to connect with them, to ease whatever spite they may harbor towards me for my part in your passing.

How had I garnered their trust and admiration before? Whatever minute detail it was, I fear I have forgotten it, my dear. All I do is flounder in my failures, falling towards extremes in my attempts to be any sort of guardian to them. Like sharks, I know they smell my novice blood in the water.

Forgive me, my dear, if I cannot fulfill my promise completely. I will try.

All my love,
Cory

Karma Rose

Chapter Six:
As I Love You

Second Week After Paradise

Sunday (October 9th)

"Are you ready for today, mister?"

The excited whisper made me grin, opening my eyes to the beautiful face I loved so much. Kate's eyes shone brightly with her glee. Oh, she had wanted this for so long, to be anywhere else in the world with me.

"You haven't the faintest, my dear," I replied softly, heart racing when I thought of what I had planned. Soon, all too soon, I would ask the question which had been burning in the back of my mind for years now.

"You've never been that far, have you?" she wondered, although she knew the answer before I shook my head. She flopped across my chest, an absolute wreck of jitters and giggles. "I'm so excited! You're going to love it! There's even a lake by the campgrounds, so we can go swimming!"

I chuckled, basking in the brilliant glow of her joy. "I might sink, Kate."

"I won't let you," she protested stubbornly, face

set with her adorable determination.

"Oh, and I suppose you'll carry me out of the lake, then?" I teased playfully. Before she could answer, I swept her up, wrapping my wings over us both. The weight of her in my arms was a comfort I never thought I could live without. I sighed quietly, hoping she did not see my nervousness, and my pounding heart did not give me away. "I love you, Kate."

Her fingers traced over my face, lingering on every detail I hated and she loved. How had I ever earned her affections? She was too good, an angel in my lacking world of hiding away. My Kate.

Should fortune allow, soon to be my fiancée.

"I love you, mister."

~~ * ~ * ~ * ~~

There was a somber weight in the air when I entered the kitchen in the morning. Whether from my lingering dreams or the coming day, I could only guess. The sky through the window was dark, the rest of my family still asleep. I set the kettle on, readying some tea for a fresh pot to go with Lisa's breakfast.

As the water was heating, I started on making the meal, focusing on each task individually to stave off this encroaching despair. I found the pots and pans exactly as Mother had left them, not an item out of place even after all these years. I worked quickly, my hands recalling easily the rhythm of this kitchen.

I pulled the kettle off as it began to whistle, pouring the water into its teapot and allowing it to steep.

182

The smell of cooking food slowly wafted through the room as I set the table, making certain to have both water and milk on the table for the children. This was how Kate had done it, was it not?

Gradually, one task bled into the next. The meal came and went, the cleanup passing too quickly while Leilani saw to soothing the stressed children. Lisa helped to get them dressed in something appropriate. Not the easiest effort, given what little we had with us. I did everything I could to keep my hands occupied, mind dulled to the onslaught I knew was coming.

"Are you ready for today, mister?"

The words from my dreams—my memories—echoed in my empty room as I dressed for the day. My fingers froze on my buttons, eyes drifting to the bed I had been avoiding using the last several nights. My breath left me, chest going cold. I forced myself to continue dressing, for the first time noticing the shirt I wore. The black and white floral print taunted me with more echoes.

"And I think you're handsome...in spite of the tourist shirt."

I stripped myself of the shirt, finding anything else and settling on a deep blue with full-length sleeves. Kate deserved to be spared the brunt of me. It was the least I could do today.

Next I knew, I was on the porch, while Lisa was busy herding the children into her vehicle. I stared at Leilani, swimming in an old shirt of mine and a makeshift skirt. Her enthusiastic smile was kind, copper eyes watchful as she made to follow us.

"No!"

We were both startled by the severity of my declaration, and it took me a moment to recall why I had said it. I thought of the dozens of human faces who would no doubt be at the church, of outsiders and gossips, and how quickly rumors could spread. I looked her over and saw myself decades ago, unsafe at the hands of humans, forced to lurk in my own home.

"Leilani, you...stay here," I explained quietly, leading her back inside. I brought her into the living room, sitting her on the couch. I stared at her coral skin, the inhuman face which was so like mine. Kate had suffered for the opportunity for me to not be alone. It was only right I should protect Leilani in turn.

The demoness watched me as I found Mother's old box of needlework crafts. It was dusty, with no promises of being undamaged by time as much as varmints. Hopefully, it would be enough to keep her busy, given her constant need for crafting.

"Here you are." I set the box at her feet, gesturing for her to help herself. "Stay here, away from the windows and...make something. Anything. Just stay. Wait."

Leilani was confused, understanding so little of my words it was painfully aggravating for us both. Yet she seemed to gather enough from my actions how I wanted her inside, busy and distracted. She nodded once, eyes drifting to the box and lighting up when she recognized the threads and yarns. I drew the curtains before I left, locking the door behind myself.

Lisa was already gone, the children with her, leaving me with the unenviable task of being alone. I breathed deeply to steady my shaking hands, stepping off the porch and looking to the sky.

It was time to say goodbye.

~~ * ~ * ~ * ~~

Heart failure.

I stared at my hands, lost as the world moved on around me. So many faces I did not recognize passed me by, others still which I could not care to greet. I had been told to sit in the front pew with Katelyn's closest family. Every fiber of my being told me to hide in the back, in a corner, where the light might struggle to reach me. Had it not been for the young children at my side, I would have.

Stubbornly, my mind refused to believe the words. *Heart failure*. Jeff had told me they had been expecting problems. For so long, they had been expecting this. The stress of our youth had left its mark on the precious organ, with two prior attacks since the turn of the century.

How had I not noticed? How had I missed such an important detail, no matter how stealthily she worked to hide it?

Robert glanced at me nervously at my question. When he spoke, it was with all of the care he had used when I had first become his patient. "Cory, you've been...sick. You're getting better—a lot better, and very quickly—but... you're still sick."

"I'm perfectly fine, Robert," I snapped bitterly, but he was right. I could feel it, could feel those doctors with me now, as though their gloved fingers still probed me beneath my skin. I was sick. It had eased considerably with the comforting habits of living with Kate. Now,

however...

My sister was less gentle. "Cory, you lost a few screws there for awhile. It happens."

"I love her! Loved her," I corrected myself, catching my rising volume before the children could overhear from their beds. "How could I love her and still miss this?"

At some point, the people around me had finally settled into their pews. The lights dimmed, any remaining chatter quieting with them. My attention was brought to a projection on the far wall ahead of us, counting down to the start of a film.

Three.

Two.

One.

My heart must have collapsed in on itself, the pain was so sharp.

Kate stared out at us, twenty-three and breathtakingly lovely. Her smile was patient, eyes verging on the depthless black which could have swayed gods.

I remembered this photo. I remembered wanting to step in and join her, I remembered sneaking to watch the church picnic like some peeping Tom. I remembered strangers were visiting in town, and how I had to hide. I remembered how utterly amused she was by my antics, the glimmer in her eyes, the ring of her laughter, the blush of her cheeks.

All I had anymore was this faulty memory of mine, and like the shameful coward I knew I must be I wished these moments might slip from me again. I yearned the agonizing work of the last year in pursuit of sanity might be mercifully undone.

Music began to play, a new photo showing on the wall. Her, exhausted and soaked in sweat, a bundle in her arms and a loving smile of complete adoration on her face. Stolen moments which I should have been there for, which I had criminally been absent during.

Again the image changed, and again I felt the stab of loss chip away just a piece more from inside my chest. So much deeper than it should have been, this pain lanced through me.

I saw so many things I had missed, so many things it hurt to know I would never remember. News clippings of her political success for demons, small films of her and Charlie, Katelyn at the births of her two grandchildren. I heard a sniffle from Kyle, and my hand reached out instinctively to rub his back for comfort.

Then the palette of the photos changed, too much red distorting them while my eyes adjusted.

There we were. What few photographs of she and I which existed played by, finishing on a very recent image. It was the four of us: Katelyn, the children, and me. In the background, I recognized Robert's couch as we sat together. Katelyn was tucked under my arm and the children were sitting in our laps. We had been talking, I could recall, but this moment was so calm, so candid, I found it difficult to pick out the exact second.

I never knew anyone even had a camera then. I found myself glad for it, cherishing the precious moment in time when we were simply a happy family.

My meticulous self-control was slipping, eyes burning with tears. Had it not been for the trembling boy beneath my palm, I knew I would have shattered to the countless pieces of a man she had helped build up once. The day was not even nearly over.

It was almost time to return her to the farm for the burial.

~~ * ~ * ~ * ~~

There was something utterly wrong with the music playing, too tinny in my ears. I knew the song as one of our favorites—hers out of sentimentality, mine because she adored it so. Now, however, it seemed the music had died with her, gone from the sound of the instruments and their futile attempts to soothe us as the pallbearers lifted her coffin from its perch.

This was it.

Their every step was too short, drawing out the precious few seconds before there would never be any denying of this truth. Before I knew it, I had Kyle in my lap, Sarah still sitting beside me. I set my hand on her back for comfort, which she did not shy from. Still, those criminally short and slow steps shuffled on to the sound of a butchered hymn.

Corey was speaking then, with all of the passionate fervor his father had always mustered. I did not care for the words, precious things claiming her life had been a fulfilling one, and her work had done great things for the world. The only things he had right were how much she would be missed and how dearly all those present had loved her. The girl who had helped me from my prison, time and time again, my best friend for as long as I could remember, Katelyn. My Kate.

The rest was simply hogwash.

The world did not care for its loss, beyond our gathered peoples. It raged on, oblivious to the egregious mistake. No one had kept her safe, and no one was waiting to embrace her with safety in whatever precious heaven she deserved. She had always been so criminally neglected by the guardian angels my mother had once promised existed. Kate had received the opposite in me and paid all too dearly for it.

My love. My Katelyn. Simply forgotten by the world's mercy.

At last and all too soon, the procession made it to their destination, resting her coffin on the mechanism waiting there. It settled with a quiet groan which made my heart protest painfully.

Around me, the congregation had begun to dissolve into grief-ridden hysterics. Beneath my palm, Sarah was trembling as she fought back her tears, failing quickly. She relented, leaning into my side for me to hold while her brother was an absolute mess bundled in my other arm. He was latched onto my neck, sobs ringing in my ear with agonizing clarity.

I could not breathe deeply enough to brace myself for this. I wanted to grieve, needed to feel this loss, but feeling the children in my arms demanded otherwise. I could remember the value of having strong parents. Certainly, I could give them such a comfort, at least, even if I felt so completely out of my element otherwise? I could bite back tears. I could provide comforts.

There was a startling clack, followed by a quiet

hum of machinery. The coffin was slowly lowered into the ground, vanishing from my view. I felt I should have been buried with her, barely alive in my body and numb from it. The air in my lungs did not taste right, like a synthetic mockery, almost as stale as the bleach-soaked air my former prison had held.

Tiny hands gripped and pulled at my shirt like steel clamps, reminding me to breathe. People were standing, forming a queue to say their final farewells and drop a rose for her. The color of the flower was all wrong, a red deeper than my skin. It was too vain, too much of some hollow trope for what she deserved. I wished then I had had the presence of mind to make the one suggestion to use yellow, to bury her with sunshine.

"Come now, children," I murmured, hoping to hide the tears in my voice and the hollow ache I felt so deeply I wondered if my heart had vanished. Kyle clambered out of my lap, the both of them following me to the edge of the grave, now littered with gaudy blossoms like empty promises of remembrance.

I watched the children select their roses, each of them taking a second before dropping their flowers in. Kyle was a mess, while Sarah was brave and grabbed his hand, fixing it with a tight grip which seemed to help steady her brother some. I grabbed myself a rose, uncaring of the thorns biting at my skin as I took the final step to where it all ended, completely and wholly.

I wished I could have had a moment alone, to release these animalistic outcries I could feel built up and locked in my chest. I yearned to speak freely of all of our secrets and promises without the sacrilege of spying ears hearing. I needed her to know so many things, and all I had to cling to was the stem of a rose, my palm cut and bleeding from it. She had known only a fraction of the love I had wanted to give, of the neglected years I had intended to make up for.

"Katelyn, I...I have no words, my dear," I whispered brokenly as I stared at the petals of the flower I held tight. I kissed the cool surface of the rose, its rich aroma too much for the woman I knew, too narcissistically pungent. "I love you."

Stem stained black, the rose fell from my fingers and hit the casket's gleaming surface with a painful finality. I may as well have cut my wings from my back to bury them with her, the weight of the rose was so great. Again, I had to force myself to breathe, no amount of air giving me the relief I needed.

Katelyn's grandchildren followed me back to our seats. Kyle was in my lap once more, Sarah at my side as they refused to release their grip on each other. Before I realized it, my sister had taken up my hand, dabbing at my bloody palm with a damp napkin from her purse. I glanced over, seeing her motherly look of concern as she cleaned the mess of blood from my skin, keeping at it until she was satisfied.

Corey approached moving slowly, the same way I acted with humans. He was trying not to startle us. His tone was soft when he spoke, "If you would like, the close friends and family are going to the diner. We've got all of the cleanup handled here."

I had not noticed sooner how Kate's family members had all left after their turns at the grave, the congregation now thinned and sadly lacking. My sister was waiting for my reply as much as the pastor. I was ready to decline the offer—words already on my lips— when I remembered with a shocking abruptness that mine were no longer the only needs I had to consider.

With a glance at the children, I nodded slowly. "Very well, then."

~~ * ~ * ~ * ~~

"You should've said something, Cory." Lisa materialized at my side, her antagonistic tone that of the obnoxious terror I remembered. "At the service, you should've said something."

I took a deep breath to brace myself, biting back against the torment which came with it. "What is there to say, Lisa?"

"You loved her, Cory, you of all people should have said goodbye," she choked on the words. When I looked down she was fighting back her tears.

"Here now." I pulled her into my side and gave a gentle squeeze. Even as a 60-some-old grandmother, she was the same little sister I knew so well. "Hush now, it's all right."

We were six and ten again, the familiarity of acting her older brother more than welcome. She hugged me tight, fingers gripping my shirt. I rubbed her arm where I held her, able to focus on this task over my deepening turmoil.

"There now, Lisa, you're all right."

"She was my sister," she sobbed into my side

brokenly. Everyone looked away at hearing her distress, an odd detail which was so very different from the village.

"I know, Lisa, I know."

Beneath her jaded bravado, she was still sensitive. Despite the pointed lack of stares, I used a wing to allow her some measure of privacy while she mourned.

Minutes or hours later, my sister finally sniffled and nodded. The side of my shirt was soaked, the air cold against it when she pulled back to stand on her own. I tucked my wing back into place behind me.

"Better?"

Lisa nodded with a heavy sigh. "Thank you."

"Good." I faked a smile, teasing gently, "You look disgusting."

"Joke's on you." She tugged at where she had turned my shirt to a mop. With a glance behind me, she gave my arm a quick pat. "Looks like you've got a line of visitors, Cory. I'll leave you to it."

I nodded nervously, watching her slip off and away through the crowd. My eyes searched for the children before I could be distracted again, finding them in a booth toward the fringe of it all. They were minding themselves, talking quietly to each other and picking at plates of food. It only took me a moment to recognize how their collections of treats were void of anything close to, well, *food*.

"There's Prince Charming!"

I stiffened at the declaration, knowing I should recognize those words. It had been too many decades since I had heard them last. They were the favored nickname of only one person I knew, and one I was little more than an acquaintance with.

When I looked for the culprit, I only identified her by the mischievous and flirty smile she always wore so proudly. She was still the same deep walnut tone which had always contrasted beside Katelyn's caramel, yet it was as far as I could recall for similarities. She was much heavier set now, aging far less gracefully than the woman we were here to remember. All the same, I smiled politely, unappreciative of the oxymoronic title.

Better than Braxen's 'human' nonsense, I reminded myself patiently.

"Jeanine," I half-laughed, startled and feigning any sort of feeling outside of this emptiness. "Oh, it has been ages since I saw you last!"

"Dustin's wedding, I think," she replied, leaning in to give me a quick hug in greeting. "It's weird, seeing you again. Especially without...well..."

"Yes, it certainly is." I nodded, awkward. "Have you been well, all things considered?"

"All things considered, yeah," she agreed.

We sat in silence for a moment before I gathered my courage. "Jeanine, how was she? The last few years, was she happy?"

"Oh, shit," she scoffed, shaking her head. There were tears she fought back, the question taking its toll on her. "I mean, better than she had been in a while, I guess. She was making it work, at first. But after she buried the empty coffin, she just...shut down. Moved in with my family with her daughter, took a few years to recover, but she wasn't the same. Until she got that call from Robert last year. I hadn't seen her smile like that in so long,

194

especially after Charlie's accident. But, I mean, I still think she was better off...*without*, you know? At least she took care of herself."

Without me, she took care of herself. It was natural, of course. With me, however... We had always had a way of falling so completely into the company of each other the world ceased to matter at times. We cared for one another as best we could in such a space, but I had always known my being a demon demanded more of her than was right. This last year, in particular, I had been in no state to bear the brunt of any burdens for her.

She would have been better off had I remained imprisoned.

"I always could count on you for the harsher truth of things," I commented, voice thick. I gave her a grateful smile. I preferred this to honeyed words and dolled-up sentiments. "Thank you, Jeanine. I wish we could have reconnected under better circumstances."

"Me, too. Speaking of harsh truth, though..." She cleared her throat and her smile turned sarcastically inviting. "The Lawrence who shouldn't have been born is here."

I frowned, glancing over my shoulder at where she was glaring icily. I groaned, turning back and hoping with a ridiculous stupidity that perhaps I could go unrecognized for once and hide in the crowd. Even old and ragged, I recognized my brother Ethan as he shuffled along like the undeserving cur he was.

"I have no patience for this," I muttered tiredly, eyes drifting to where the children were still in their seats. I found some comfort in it, watching them briefly before my concentration was broken by a stiff pat on my shoulder.

"Hey, it's my little brother!" Ethan's voice was frail now, as withered and battered as his face when I turned my cool stare on him. He smelled foul, like festered sweat and alcohol.

"Ethan." My reply was barely above a growl.

"Ethan, *honey*, who invited you?" asked Jeanine with a sickly-sweet inflection.

He was trembling, and it seemed he was unable to control the slight shake of his hands as he wrung them anxiously. "Oh. I-I-I just heard about it. Wanted to pay my respects, see the kids. Yeah."

"Honey, when Kate said over her dead body, I think she meant a little bit longer than that." My brother and I flinched at Jeanine's words. "What are you really doing here, asking for handouts?"

His eyes darted around the room nervously before landing on me. "I-I'm here for Cory. To talk about the kids."

I stiffened, a glare hardening my features more than I liked in such a somber, crowded setting. Moving with forced precision, I clasped my hands behind my back. "You would do well to speak quickly and cautiously."

"Oh. Yeah. Right." He cleared his throat and smiled, the smile which was nearly a grin. The very same one I had grown to love seeing on Kyle's face, and I despised it so entirely on Ethan's. "Well, I figured, with everything, they'd need someplace to go. I know their dad, so I gave him a call—"

"Get out." I had to whisper the words, too many sounds so much worse than I had felt before clawing at my throat to escape. Had I been at the village, I could have caved to these cravings. "Don't you dare talk to me about taking my children, Ethan, now *get out*."

"Cory, I'll be doing you a favor," he protested sheepishly. "Their dad's willing to—"

"No." Not here. I could not let my self-control slip here. My eyes darted to the children and back, their messy faces helping to remind me why I fought for composure as I kept my tail close. There were too many people. "No, Ethan. They are mine. Just like Charlie should have been—*mine*. He has shown no interest in them in a year—*a year*!"

"He wants them now, and it's not like you could raise them." He was growing meek as he persisted. He had to be drunk as well as stupid to have taken this long to realize the line he had crossed.

"And why not?"

He hesitated before gesturing to me. "I mean, look at you. Don't you think they should be with, you know, their own kind?"

I traded my reactionary growl for a deep and deliberate sigh. Ethan flinched. Behind my back, my hands curled to fists, filed claws itching to be buried in something. "*Their own kind*."

"Ooh, Ethan, honey." Jeanine shook her head slowly, and what desperate part of me was clinging to civility noticed how thoroughly she was enjoying this exchange.

"Because being raised by me is so much worse

than the alternative?" I thought of Sarah begging me not to return to their father's custody. "They are mine, you worthless swine, and I will not send them off for the sake of convenience! I will see to it I do what it takes to ensure their safety and happiness, however. Their own kind or not, at least I can claim to be family."

"Look, Cory, I didn't mean—"

"I've said my piece, Ethan," I ground out, savoring the sharp reek of his fear. After my brief time with demons and a more relaxed hold on my primal needs, I found the scent of it intoxicating. Another glance at the children, and I found Sarah's eyes locked on me. "Now get out, before I *help* you out."

He scurried off and toward the exit then, ever the coward. I breathed deeply, sighing shakily. I took in the faces around me, hoping no one had witnessed the exchange or my less admirable reactions. There were a few faces scattered in the crowd who seemed startled. They must have caught sight of me when I had a lapse in control, wearing expressions far too severe for polite company.

"Damn, I was really hoping you'd kick his ass," sighed Jeanine longingly. She shrugged. "Probably best you didn't, but it's something I've fantasized about for a while."

"My apologies, Jeanine, I should not have lost my temper so publicly," I said quietly, ignoring her comment and how very much I had wanted to beat him senseless. How he could even *suggest*...

She rolled her eyes, scoffing, "Because *that* was an offensive display. Yeah, sure, offensively disappointing."

I nodded once. "Regardless, it was good to see you again. I should, ah..."

My excusing myself was less than graceful as I slipped away tactlessly. I found myself drawn to where the children were growing restless, appreciative of the calm and quiet pervading the area. I took a seat with a tired sigh just a few feet away, giving Kyle and Sarah a wide enough berth so they would not need to ignore me so quite pointedly.

To my surprise, Sarah approached me. She was wary, appraising me with a critical and fearful gaze. "Why's Uncle Ethan here?"

I smiled patiently to hide how deeply I found myself loathing the title she gave him. "He wanted to talk to me."

"Our dad isn't here, is he?" She was forthright as ever.

"Not that I know of, Sarah," I reassured her gently, and I found myself reaching out to offer comfort. She took a step back, waiting for me to pull my hand away before we continued.

"Okay. I know they're friends, so I was scared," she confessed shyly. She hesitated just a moment longer, voice dropping to a whisper so no one else might hear, "You still won't take us back to our dad's, right?"

"Never, sweetheart."

Sarah nodded once, returning to her brother before I could recover enough to speak anymore. Her line of inquiry was worrisome, to say the least. Yet despite that, I felt confident in my answering I would not send them away. My telling Ethan they were mine felt right, as well.

They were, no matter how little they liked me currently. Lisa had mentioned adoption, and I finally felt myself considering the option more seriously, to make them mine.

The thought helped me through the remainder of the day, one small light amidst all of this darkness.

~~ * ~ * ~ * ~~

The loneliness of my empty room pressed in on me, all the more suffocating after the funeral. There was no denying this any longer: Katelyn was gone, lost to me forever and yet so poetically close it was agonizing—buried on the farm she loved so dearly, alongside my own empty grave.

My heart twisted in my chest although I kept my grief quiet, painfully aware of the children in the next room who could all too easily hear. Before it could overtake me, I heard sounds in their room, rustling and shuffling of little feet on the wood floor. I sat slowly, my door's handle rattling noisily preceding the door creaking open.

"Grampa Cory?" The tentative whisper had me out of the blankets and on the edge of the bed in an instant. Even fatigued, I found I was excited to finally be sought out again.

"I'm awake," I replied just as quietly, welcoming Sarah into my arms when she shuffled over. I cradled her close, feeling tears on her face. "Whatever's the matter, sweetheart?"

"I miss Grandma," she choked with a sniffle,

trying her best to silence her sobs. She curled into me, shaking so forcefully for such a tiny thing.

My voice caught in my throat. "I know. I miss her, too, Sarah."

"You do?" she asked, forcing herself to look up at me. The moonlight was the only glow in the otherwise dark room, but it was enough to see her face torn apart with heartbreak.

I nodded, trying to dry her cheeks futilely. "Of course, I do. I loved your grandmother so very much since we were young."

"But I haven't seen you cry," she argued, voice still thick with tears. "I thought we weren't supposed to cry."

"Oh, hush now, you can cry as much as you need," I told her softly, kissing her forehead. "I cry, too. I simply do it away from you and your brother, that's all."

"But why?" she sniffled, still undecided on if she would break down completely.

Trust me, Sarah, let me do my job, please.

"Because I want to be brave for you, in case you need to cry," I whispered, fighting back my tears even then. "It's my job. I'm here to keep you safe and make sure you two are all right. I can't do that if I'm busy crying, now, can I?"

"It's okay, Grampa, you don't have to be brave," she whimpered, trembling as more sobs tore from her. Oh, my sweet girl. "I know you'll still do your job. You always did it at Grandma's house, no matter how sad you got."

I smiled dolefully. She had been watching me so much more closely than I had thought. "I'll keep that in mind, thank you. In the meantime, I think you need me more, hm? No need to be brave, little one, I have you, you're safe," I added, the poor girl's bravado falling to pieces.

I rocked her slowly, murmuring comforts I knew would do little to ease the ache. There were no words to soothe the grief of this loss, especially for her. She had been so brave for her brother, looking to Kate for guidance through the loss of their mother. Now, she looked to me, and already I felt I may have failed her. Had she needed to see me grieve more openly? Or was it simply her nature, this kind, thoughtful child?

Whatever the reason, it seemed she had neglected this outburst long enough, sobs growing louder as she wept. I rubbed her back, hoping I might provide at least some solace. She only curled up tighter, burying herself in my arms as she trembled.

"I know, Sarah," I hushed her, finally losing control of a few of my tears. "It's all right, darling, it's all right. Everything will work out."

"I miss Grandma, and Mommy," she keened into me; I could hardly stand to hear her so distraught. What more could I do for her? What had I not done yet?

I hummed clumsily, my voice tired and strained. It was all I could think to do anymore, the only thing I had not yet tried. Slowly, Sarah's sobs quieted to sniffles and whimpers, finally settling down. I kept up my tune, glad for its success no matter the wear on my throat.

"Mom used to sing to us," she whispered tiredly, hand grabbing hold of my fingers and clutching them tightly. "But it always made Grandma too sad."

"Would you like me to sing for you?" I asked her, and she nodded, the movement fatigued. I smiled, recalling the lullabies Mother used to sing when I was Sarah's age. Keeping my voice low so as to not disturb the household, I sang the old songs for her, feeling her falling asleep quickly in my arms. Well after I knew she had slipped into dreams, I kept singing in the hopes I could stave off any nightmares which may torment her now.

Just as I was ready to put her back to bed, however, I heard more shuffling. The small shadow of Kyle appeared in the doorway.

"Dad? Can I sleep with you?" he mumbled tiredly, sounding still-asleep. He must have been, given his slip of names. He rubbed his eyes with one hand, his bear clutched tightly in the other.

I sighed quietly, torn between amusement and exhaustion. "Yes, come here."

He hurried over, clambering up onto the expansive mattress eagerly. He found my pillow with no trouble, asleep before I could protest. I settled for the other pillow, pulling myself back into bed with one arm as I kept Sarah balanced in the other. As I lay down, I pulled the blanket back over the three of us, Sarah tucked into one side of me while Kyle rested against the other.

It took me a moment to settle in, somehow still tormented by the grief of the day despite the swell of joy in my chest. I took a deep breath, releasing it slowly and quietly as the tears fell silently. I still felt so lost, as if there was no possible way I could do this on my own. Yet...I already was, the role feeling so natural to me at the moment I wondered how I had ever not been their father.

No matter how desperately I missed Kate or how my heart felt it should shatter from the loss, somehow I knew I would hold together. Just for the simple fact, someone would need to clean their faces after breakfast or help Sarah pick out her barrette, or ensure Kyle's shirt was worn correctly. Every little task was one I looked forward to eagerly, if only for the single moment in each one which meant I was there for them.

Finally, my eyes grew heavy and I could rest easier knowing, come morning, I would have their mishaps, messes, and grins. Even if this moment of reliance was short, and those grins were not for me, it was something to hope for.

~~ * ~ * ~ * ~~

Monday

I knelt at Katelyn's grave, the movements feeling stiff and wrong as if someone else moved my limbs for me. With how weak I felt, it must have been the case, certainly. I was hollow, unable to recover without her smile, her reassurances of, whatever we faced, we would be together.

No longer.

The thought was heart-wrenching, but I saved my tears. I would need what scant few emotions I could bear in a day for the children who would be waking up soon. They needed me in some sort of an unbroken whole, no matter how fractured I felt as I fought to hold the pieces together.

"I miss you, my dear," I whispered brokenly. My hand longed to reach out at her pet name—only ever hers. My skin burned, body aching to find her and feel her. I dared not touch the overly-smooth stone, anticipating the disappointment its cool, hard surface would no doubt supply. It was still just before dawn, winter settling in preemptively now she was not here to stave it off with her stubbornness and warmth.

It was apt the world was so dark now when the woman who had acted as the moon to light my sky was dimmed and gone. I could scarcely make out the color of my skin or the inhumanity of my body, my scars. Everything she had always taken time to pointedly appreciate in an attempt to ease my self-hatred.

Who would stand between me and my inevitable self-destruction now? Who would be at my side to help fight back the thoughts which tore me down, or the screaming voices echoing them all too clearly? Who was left to see me beyond this demonic visage—*me*, the monster who fought and clung so desperately to act like the man I felt I was? Who would I whisper secrets to in the still of night against pillow casings and bedsheets?

All of our laughter and promises had gone with her, buried too deeply out of reach to grasp at. I was left with nothing as she dragged it all away with her.

"Damn it, Katelyn, I miss you," I choked. I would have gladly gone back to the Institute's stale white rooms if it meant I could only hear her voice on the phone when I arrived there.

Karma Rose

The light of the morning was changing, growing brighter and casting the world into its odd, gradating shadows. I sniffled, wiping at my dry cheeks and the tears I refused to shed there, before standing to return to the house. I had to get breakfast on before the children had time to go mad with hunger and terrorize the kitchen.

I thought of the grand mess they had made just the other morning—while I had been searching for the will to get out of bed—and I could not help a small smile despite the hollow ache in my chest. Even as Lisa's oddly selective patience seemed ready to snap, I simply adored the opportunity to propose a communal meal schedule. They were excited enough by it, as well, agreeing easily.

As the sun broke over the horizon with those first sharply beautiful rays, I blinked into it. I felt the start of a stab of pain in my skull which dulled quickly, nothing at all like the searing blades I had grown accustomed to over my lifetime. A change, and one I would take as a sign for the better.

~~ * ~ * ~ * ~~

Tuesday

"I want to go home," whimpered Kyle pitifully. I offered him my arms and he shook his head, sobbing, "I want Grandma!"

I sat helplessly, wanting to join in his grieving, comfort him, anything but being so uselessly idle. He needed for something, and I doubted I was anywhere near experienced enough to supply it. All I had were the few times I had seen Katelyn comforting them over their mother. So I took a deep breath and braced myself to give what little I could.

"Kyle, your grandmother, she..." I stared at his terrified, sad little face and hated how I could not fix this. "We won't see her for a long while."

"Like Mom?" he sniffled.

I nodded, replying quietly, "Yes, like your mother."

"But why not now?" he cried tearfully, tiny shoulders shaking.

Oh, Kyle, why must you ask things I have no answers for?!

"Kyle..."

"It's like Grandma said, Kyle, they've gotta get everything ready," chimed in Sarah mercifully. I would have to thank her somehow, directly or discreetly. "But it's supposed to take a long time, remember?"

Kyle's face relaxed and he nodded, sad but accepting now. "Oh, yeah. I remember now."

I smiled for his sake, glad when he returned it. Although I loathed the lie, it was better for the moment he believed in happier places, rather than the cold finality of a grave. Right on cue, Leilani rushed in, worried at hearing their distress. Her hair was soaked and dripping from her shower.

"Babies?" She took in their sad faces, gathering them up with her tail to guide them back to their room. I glanced at the clock. Her punctuality with their scheduled nap was astonishing.

Just as I thought of her praises, however, she

gathered up her hair and wrung it out across the entryway floor. I covered my face with one hand, torn between frustration and laughter. As soon as she knew the language well enough, she and I would have a few words about this.

In the meantime, before my sister could see the mess, I hurried off to find spare towels.

~~ * ~ * ~ * ~~

Wednesday

Katelyn had been prepared.

Little else could be said, if not that. I had been free just over a year now, legally sane for very little of that, and yet she had set everything in place as if we had never been separated. Those were Robert's musings, at least, after we had met in the city about her will.

She had left me nearly everything, with the utmost trust I would know her wishes with how to proceed. Everything, that is, save a scant few family heirlooms which were to be returned to the orchard home, or the accounts she had for Kyle and Sarah's college funds. Scarce as those funds were, I had to wonder if she had been intending to keep her heart beating through stubborn determination alone if only to see these children off better.

I now owned her city home. Her little yellow vehicle, as well, once I retrieved it from where it had been parked when we left. I had also inherited the debts and taxes associated with this nightmare. It was not as though I minded greatly the opportunity to tend to her affairs. It was far overdue, and it put my time spent "earning a living" at the Institute to good use. I could spare the rest of her family the financial weight of this burden.

In spite of it all, I had no desire to return to the city, least of all to the house which held so many precious moments. Now I was back in the old farmhouse, I found I preferred these ghosts to distract me. I enjoyed the nostalgia of waking in the room which had always been mine, of watching the sun lighting the kitchen table at dawn. The children had acres to run wild; Leilani had space to spread her wings. Perhaps my sister would consider a trade, if not allow me to purchase the farm outright.

In the meantime, however, we had to make space for the belongings we intended to bring back from the city. If only for temporary storage, while we sorted through it all. Lisa had recommended the study, saying it had been used for just the same purpose for years already.

So we set about cleaning and organizing boxes. I had cleared a path to the window, opening it and allowing the cool autumn air to help us bear through the decades of dust. There were just as many treasures as there were outlandishly superfluous keepsakes. The sound of the children playing outside with Leilani wafted in with the breeze.

"It figures that when you come back, it means I have to clean," sighed Lisa over another box, pawing through it.

"I thought you wanted me home?" I pointed out, smirking at her half-hearted glare. "You're to blame for this predicament as much as I am."

"I wouldn't be in this room right now if it weren't for you," she muttered, pulling out an old quilt. Her fingers brushed along one tattered edge, worn with age. "I wonder if we could send it off to be fixed...?"

I reached out to inspect the damage. "That, or we could teach Leilani how to quilt and then let her have at it."

Lisa giggled, folding the article and replacing it in its box. "I've been meaning to ask about her. How does she know about so many crafts, even though I caught her *licking* the kitchen *sponge* this morning? You don't talk about her much."

I shrugged, grimacing at the box of photos I had stumbled upon. At the top, Dustin's youthful face smiled out, awkward and lanky. "There's little to tell. She has a passion and knack for crafting things, particularly if any sort of string is involved. She likes the children. You know as much as I do."

"But where's she from? Where'd you go to find her?" wondered Lisa, coming to inspect the photos I was sifting through. She found one of herself and winced. "Oh, burn that box."

I chuckled and set it aside with the boxes to keep and sort again. "She's not local. It is not for me to share any more than such."

My sister pouted. "You're no fun. Shouldn't you be a gossiping old man by now?"

"Oh, certainly! I could go on for hours about your school crushes," I teased, earning a firm smack to the arm. She hissed, rubbing her hip as the action jostled her wrongly. I frowned in concern. "Perhaps once this room is finished with, we can move you downstairs."

"I'm not admitting my age just yet," she argued bluntly. I nodded once, drawing my attention back to the stacks of things to organize. One, in particular, caught my eye.

"What is this?" I asked Lisa, lifting a larger box onto the space we had cleared on the desk. The top had an odd scrawl, reminiscent of Mother's writing yet too chaotic and uneven for what I recalled. Inside, there was a mess of media, dusty from storage.

Lisa looked over, paling when she saw the box. "Oh. That...That's from Mom. She meant to give them to someone."

"To whom? Perhaps we should—"

"You, Cory." My sister's voice was thick abruptly, heartbreak twisting her features. "The tapes—they're for you."

The box held a new weight, and I stared at the contents with a curious shiver of grief. "What are they?"

Lisa cleared her throat, banishing the distress from her features. "Messages. Home recordings. She used to do letters, but she got arthritis pretty bad starting around '89, so she couldn't write you anymore. Dustin got a camcorder, so she could make you recordings instead. It helped, for a little while."

"Why? Why would she do this to herself, Lisa?" I could not stand to think of her as being so broken. Not our mother. "Everyone else grieved and moved on, so why...?!"

"She was convinced you were still alive and coming home." Lisa shrugged, at a loss for anything more. "Turns out, you really were, huh? That's what she kept saying, and it just broke her that everyone thought you were gone. I mean, she was already pretty done in by you being taken, but..."

"I'm not even human, Lisa, this never should have happened." It was my fault. For trying to free Kate, and damning whatever consequences my family would have to suffer through. My poor mother...

"Your kids aren't demons," she pointed out sharply. "You were Mom's son and you broke her heart by not calling, Cory. Demon or not, with everything that happened...You were her baby, just as much as you're my brother."

We had trouble continuing afterward, calling the work done for the day. I was grateful, taking just a moment to rest before Leilani returned inside with her two hungry wards. Without much thought, I was up again to feed them, still struggling to put what Lisa had told me out of my mind. Watching Kyle and Sarah at the table, it was difficult. I kept imagining if I lost them, should Ethan come again to argue their returning to their father. I would have so little left in this world.

Mother had deserved better, certainly, but I found myself unable to fault the devastation she had endured. I had been her son, just as surely as I was coming to think of those little ones as my own, as well.

~~ * ~ * ~ * ~~

Friday

"Now, Robert, Anne, please remain calm," I instructed gently, glancing between them and where I knew Leilani was, safely hidden in the living area. I took a deep breath, calling, "Leilani, it's all right now, you can come out."

The startled gasps were expected, I knew, but Leilani's eyes went wide as she looked at me for instructions. I nodded, keeping calm as I reached my hand out if she needed it when she took the next step forward and toward my human friends. By their murmurs and hushed whispers, I knew they saw the natural, almost primal grace all of the demons walked with. Oh, if only they could have seen her in the sun, how wonderful it was to not be the only one to glow at its touch!

Robert managed to collect himself first, marveling breathlessly, "She's...she's like you, Cory. Well, different—different shade, gorgeous, I mean—"

"I know," I agreed with a chuckle, sparing him his continued bumbling. Leilani smiled tentatively at the sound, gaining her confidence despite the strangers present. "She is fantastic, and such a natural with the children. It is uncanny how easily she is settling into this world, for their sake."

She gave a tiny wave of her hand, her tail flat mirroring the gesture behind her. "Hello. I is Leilani."

"That accent!" gasped Anne, still too stunned to compose herself. "It's so...exotic. Where's she from?"

"Ah...Nowhere local," I hedged at my inability to disclose anything more, smiling apologetically at the Smiths. "There are others. She requested to come with me to help with the children and general work, after..."

They both nodded, saddened by the reminder. Robert refused to let the moment be stained, for which I was grateful. "She speaks English, then?"

"Very little." She kept watching me for social cues, and I realized it must have been easier to read my demon features than the humans I preferred for the sake of familiarity. "However, she learns more every day. I look forward to having conversations with her in the future."

"Does she fly?" he asked, cringing as he realized the absurdity of the inquiry.

"It's all right, Robert, she is just as alien to me as she is to you," I reassured him. He gave me a grateful smile. "She does fly. Spare my pride the demonstration, but she may be better than I am."

"Fly?" The quiet, curious tone was familiar by now, and I found it second nature to think of how to explain the word to her.

"Fly." I shuffled my wings in a mock stroke without unfolding them, and she understood the gesture quickly.

Leilani smiled her infectiously cheery smile, copper eyes glistening with excitement. "Fly!"

"Oh, Leilani, no!" She was already out the front door and running, her slight frame taking off like an arrow through the air in two strokes too quick to catch. I laughed, Robert and Anne both watching with gaping stares. "Well, now. I suppose she has plenty to learn where her manners are concerned, but she's nothing if not eager."

Leilani was airborne not a second longer before she was landing again, staring at me quizzically. She shuffled her wings with the same mock motion I had, calling timidly from the front yard, "Fly?"

"She's asking you to fly with her?" Robert was fascinated, and I knew it must have been thoroughly enjoyable for him to have more than one demon to observe, socially. "So, social flying, is that a thing? I mean, as an activity. And how does it work?"

"Come inside," I called back to her, waving the demoness over before I grinned at Robert's endless questions. He resisted flinching, reminding me to be more mindful now I was in the company of humans. "It is magnificent, Robert, like a game I never knew existed until now. I fly with her in the evenings, after the children are into bed, so I suppose she got a bit overexcited just now for an early start."

"Naturally," murmured Robert, a shiver running through his frame. I glanced back at Leilani's dancing predatory gait. It had disturbed me at first, as well, although I was the same species. What kind of terror could it illicit in a human, then? Based on the tang in the air, I presumed the effect was quite a bit more perturbing. "It's so...*odd*. I knew you put work into being more approachable, but I guess I just never realized how much. Do you restrain yourself a lot?"

I shrugged, allowing Leilani to pass by me into the house as I closed the door behind her. As always, she gravitated naturally toward the sound of the children, stirring late this morning. The demoness wandered upstairs. "Truth be told, I never think much of it anymore. It has become second nature."

"And the kids?" asked Anne. I caught sight of her

pallor and frowned in concern. She would look herself the part of a ghost if she lost any more color! "They're not scared of her?"

I shook my head, mindful of my horns near the ceiling. "No, not at all. They adore her like they adore Bailey. Perhaps more, if their nonsensical babbling is any indication."

"You're really not scared that she'll hurt them?" she continued to question in her worry. I felt a pang of indignation, stifling it as best I could.

"Nonsense, Anne," I replied, keeping my voice even and gentle. It seemed to soothe her some, hearing my confidence and ease. "Leilani would never harm them, even by accident. Perhaps if you saw her with them, it would help you to understand?"

As if on cue, the tiny demoness appeared at the top of the stairs, one child on her hip and the elder being tenderly herded in front of her. The tender murmurs and coos were clear over our sudden silence.

"Come, babies, food." She gave Kyle a quick nudge as he fell asleep on her shoulder. "No, Kyle, is eat now."

They arrived safely downstairs, if slowly, and she continued toward the kitchen without much care for us. The children were awake, and her attention was absorbed entirely by their every need and movement. Anne visibly relaxed, color returning to her cheeks.

"Oh. I guess that's a lot better than I imagined," she confessed, smiling at the sight.

"I'll take a stab and say that she's watching the kids for you today?" asked Robert dryly. I nodded. "Great.

Broken Orbit

Are you ready, then?"

No.

"As ready as I will ever be for this."

~~ * ~ * ~ * ~~

I entered our old home, finding its quiet interior eerie. Robert stood beside me, face drawn already despite our day barely beginning. It smelled stale, almost dry, small signs of disuse and neglect scattered here and there in the form of undisturbed dust.

"Just as we left it, if a bit...musty," I murmured thoughtfully, breath hitching and shuddering abruptly as my chest constricted tightly. "My apologies, Robert, I...I could never be ready for this."

He gave my shoulder a reassuring pat. "It's all right. That's what we're here for, moral support as much as anything."

I nodded, grateful. "Thank you. Now, I suppose starting with the children's room would be best? Then, the Old Thing Room..."

There was a commotion as Anne entered behind us, shuffling flattened packing boxes noisily along the way. "Sorry I'm late, I picked up some lunch on the way from the truck rental, in case you boys get hungry."

"Thanks, honey," whispered Robert, leaning over to peck her on the cheek before she passed by to place her bags in the kitchen. My heart twisted wistfully.

I took a deep breath to steady myself, forcing my feet to move toward the back rooms. The door to the children's room was open, and when I switched on the light I found two neatly made beds; the room was tidy save for a handful of toys scattered beside their toy box. My eyes fell on the rocking chair positioned between the beds, a book still sitting in it.

"It was Katelyn's turn to read next," I recalled weakly, the small detail hitting me with more force than I expected. I sniffled, lifting the book from its seat to stare at it. One more small tether to break in this seemingly endless endeavor of grieving and letting go.

Robert came up beside me, glancing at the book I held. He smiled. "I used to read to my girls every night, too. Do you do voices?"

"It's their favorite part," I chuckled, disoriented by how bittersweet this sensation was. I smiled sadly. "Sometimes, I would have to read the voices while Kate read the rest."

My friend gave me a kind smile and nodded, his wife following us into the room with boxes in hand. She did her best the remain chipper. "Right. We're starting here?"

I nodded, avoiding looking at my surroundings too closely. I could still smell Kate, everywhere. Her phantom danced around us, and all I had left to do was take our life and pack it away neatly.

~~ * ~ * ~ * ~~

"What is this?" I had barely been home from the city a minute before Lisa was shoving a stack of envelopes in my hands.

"They're for you. Mostly bills," she explained

with a bored shrug. She made to return to the kitchen, the smell of supper saturating the air.

"And how do I handle them?" I followed her numbly, too exhausted from the day to think clearly.

"Really, Cory?" My sister sighed and turned an exasperated scowl on me. "Do you have a card or something? I know Robert mentioned the Institute having to compensate you."

When was this now? "Yes, I do."

"Then you can pay over the phone. Most places have instructions when you call, so just go over each bill one at a time."

"Thank you." Of course, how could I have been so dense? I felt a pang of shame, at how the simplest of things gave me such trouble. "I will be in my room for the moment, then."

"Be down in an hour to set the table!" she called after me as I trudged upstairs tiredly.

My card. As I entered my room, I already knew where it was, and it was something I dreaded fetching. It was in my closet, among the belongings of two bags I had yet to unpack since leaving the village. *Hers*. They were hers.

Taking advantage of the protective numb my fatigue granted, I reached for the purse I knew was in the pile, finding it easily. It was a practical thing, nothing commanding of attention with its simple design. I sighed quietly, fingers burning as I rifled through its contents and found the little pocketbook Kate had kept in it. I remembered giving the card to her, insisting she permit me some way to care for her, even if I was otherwise unable.

I found the card, eyes falling on the photo of her license across from it. I scowled, stabs of grief making it through this apathetic calm. Snatching out the card I needed, I snapped the pocketbook shut and stuffed it back in its purse. I returned the article to its space in the closet, fighting against my trembling hands.

"Come now, enough is enough," I muttered, taking a deep breath to steady myself. I did not have time for this yet. There was work to be done, children to feed. My grieving could wait.

Chapter Seven: Amends

Fourth Week After Paradise

Monday

Another morning, and with it another day to wade through as easily as wet clay. Being so blatantly avoided by the children gave me more time alone than I liked to busy myself with my unending list of work. Today, I had my attention focused on better settling Kyle and Sarah into their room.

It had been my brothers', with two well-worn beds and a derelict wardrobe that half-blocked the doorless closet. The wardrobe would be simple enough to remove, although I would have to be certain to mount a new door soon. It looked to have been converted into a neglected guest room over the years, with sheets and bedding which had been freshly lain out at least a decade ago, if the dusty scent of them was any indication.

In all, it had done its job well over the past few weeks. Now I had the moment to spare and presence of mind, though, it was well past time Kyle and Sarah had something more suited to them.

Karma Rose

The better half of my morning was spent breaking down the dying furniture and taking it downstairs, just off the back porch. I would discard it properly later. Weather permitting, perhaps a bonfire would be in order.

Cleaning was another matter entirely, and I found myself crouching with a butter knife in hand to scrape old gum from the walls the mattresses had hidden. The result of Dustin's habits, no doubt, and his appallingly lacking sense of cleanliness. Had we a proper barn, he may as well have been raised there instead.

I broke just before midday to prepare lunch for the children, Leilani, and me. My efforts were deterred as I checked the various cupboards, sighing when I realized the kitchen was criminally barren. Oh, of course, I was supposed to have gone to the grocery market today, not...

"Damn," I muttered, scraping together what I could in the meantime with the meager odds and ends I found in the pantry. I would have to run to the market after I finished with the room.

Lisa already had a roast in the oven for supper, and I could wait until then to eat so as to spare a heartier portion for the others. As if by some magic call, the trio of mischief tumbled into the kitchen as I was finishing preparations. They were a bundle of laughter I had learned not to disrupt with my fruitless attempts at participation. I set the table silently, ensuring they had their drinks and meals before returning to my work. I could clean up the dishes later, between tasks. My sister could forgive the delay, certainly.

It was as I sat to construct the bed frames from Katelyn's home when I heard a quiet shuffle in the doorway, a series of small clatters following it. I glanced over to find Kyle had followed me with his plate and glass, sitting with wide eyes and a full mouth as he watched me.

I smiled tentatively, despite how I knew it would chafe my sister's adoration of household order. I knew I should send him back to the table. Still, I bit back the comment in favor of what I hoped might be him warming to me. I could nitpick on the less harmful rules later.

"What are you doing?" he piped up after a moment. I stood the first frame up and slid it into its place, tucked into the corner along the far wall.

"I'm making your room up properly," I replied, minding my voice to keep it tame. When I checked his reaction, it was still wide-eyed and watching, face messy with his meal.

"Oh. But, I mean, we already had beds." He shrugged as if those would have been good enough. No matter the beds he referred to had been new before his mother was born.

I nodded, starting on the second frame. "Yes, that's true, but this was my brothers' old room, and I imagine you would like it to be made your own, hm? With your own toys and books?"

He perked up at the mention of toys, eyes going impossibly wider. He bobbed his head in an urgent nod which threw his tightly curled hair about messily, reminding me of a limp sponge. Oh, I had not considered I would have to add their grooming to my endlessly expanding list of responsibilities.

"Yes, please! I didn't know our toys were here!"

"Not at first, but I made certain to bring them back with me when I was packing," I told him, enjoying the familiar rhythm of working with a tool in hand. It eased the aches, helping me to fall into a more natural flow of conversation with the young boy eating in the hall.

"Really?" His gasp was incredulous and hopeful. When I looked, I guessed he thought I may have made pigs fly as well.

"Of course, Kyle." *There, now.* I set aside my tools with a satisfied smile.

With both frames built and set in place, I stood with a fatigued groan and went for the mattresses propped against the closet's wall. Even to my crippled shoulder, they were easy enough to move. I begrudgingly noted I would have to thank Braxen for helping me return my body to a stronger state.

As the beds settled into their frames, I grabbed their fresh linens from the top shelf of the closet and busied myself with making the beds up. When I finally finished, I looked back to find Kyle staring at his empty plate with a guilty scowl.

"Whatever's the matter, my boy?"

He huffed a sigh and shrugged. "I dunno. I guess I'm just confused."

"What about?" I asked, worried by his twisting frown. I leaned forward over the bed in front of me, drawn in by his upset.

"Why are you being so nice?" he grumbled, baffling me. Why would it frustrate and disappoint him when I worked toward improving our relationship? When I sought ways to provide them with better care and circumstances? "Sarah said you weren't going to be very nice anymore now that Grandma's gone, especially after we got in trouble outside. And I know we haven't been nice, either, and Grandma always said people are only nice if you are."

I nodded slowly as he laid out his reasoning, simplistic though it was. I should have known Sarah was the mastermind behind my apparent exile. She truly was like her grandmother in so many ways, such a stubborn little skeptic. Yet I found it endearing how she sought to keep herself and her brother safe with such efforts, no matter the imagined dangers.

"Nonsense, Kyle. I certainly have my faults, and I'm sorry you two had to see them, but..." I debated how to continue, scowling at my idle hands as they rested on the freshly made bed. *Oh, please, let me not make an ass of myself now.* "I do love you both, and no matter my failures I hope I can do my best for you and your sister. If that proves unsatisfactory, then I suppose I will strive to learn better until...Kyle, why are you crying?"

"I'm not!" he muttered, sniffling and wiping his face. He stared at me, eyes red and face puckered with the effort it took him to hide his upsets. He squared his shoulders bravely. "Can I help with our room?"

"Certainly, Kyle." Did he need me now? Was I supposed to let him be? What little intuition I had managed to draw on for this was well past spent. "In fact, I have a toy which makes the whole box just a mite too heavy for me to lift. Would you carry it up for me while I get the box? After you put your dishes in the sink, please," I added, my wavering conviction all too apparent in my voice.

He glanced down at his small mess, doing his best to pick up his crumbs before dashing downstairs, plate and glass in hand. I let out a breath I had not realized I had been holding. At last, I felt I had taken the smallest step towards an understanding, at least with Kyle.

"Hurry, Grampa, come on!" The excited call from downstairs had me smiling, the start of quiet happiness warming my chest.

At last.

~~ * ~ * ~ * ~~

Wednesday

I am not prepared for this.

It was nothing overly dramatic—certainly not life-threatening—and yet I felt a flash of panicky failure all the same that this was happening: growth spurts. Struggling for any way to make do with what was on hand, I found a new appreciation for how Mother had managed mine so gracefully. If only I could find a scrap of the same miraculous ability now.

"Perhaps this will do," I offered Kyle a larger shirt, still only barely fitting his taller frame. I would have to remedy this, and soon.

Sarah was sitting on her bed, watching us with wary scrutiny. "Mine aren't fitting, either."

If I suspected her of cruelty, I would have thought she was enjoying the opportunity to be spiteful. She was shrewdly devious, yes, but the girl was still kind at heart.

So long as I was not involved. I stifled a sigh. Her imagined enjoyment of my floundering did no one any good now.

"Very well, then."

~~ * ~ * ~ * ~~

Friday

Eyeing Kate's little yellow car, I sighed heavily and bit the bullet as I clambered into the driver's side. Robert hesitated a moment longer before accepting his fate as a passenger, wincing nervously as I did my best to adjust everything so that I might fit better. In the end, I had scarcely any room, feeling like a laughable cross of a medieval horror and a modern contortionist.

"Have you ever driven before?" asked Robert warily, cringing when my horns scraped the roof.

"It may have been a few years," I confessed, staring at the dashboard in confusion. Were there always so many dials?! What was the use of having buttons on the steering wheel!

He strapped himself in and tested the belt. He settled with one hand gripping his seat while the other was tight on the handle above his door. "Do I want to know exactly how long?"

I sighed thoughtfully, fumbling with the keys before managing to insert them into the ignition. "Oh, since I could no longer fit in the farm truck, so I was...ah, twenty or so? Where did they put the blasted clutch?" I muttered with a scowl, feeling about with my foot.

"Um. No, it-it's an automatic," replied Robert tentatively. He released his grip on the seat and gestured to the gear shift between us. With a glance at my expression, he winced again. "I miss driving with Bailey already."

I groaned, thinking of the test I had scheduled already. Had I not needed for a way to transport the children, I would have called this endeavor forfeit now. "Oh, dear. This is going to be a long day."

~~ * ~ * ~ * ~~

Fifth Week After Paradise

Tuesday

Nearly seventy years of experience, over half of which was best forgotten, and none of it could have prepared me for this—shopping. It was a ceaselessly awkward endeavor. The few other patrons stared at me without the faintest attempt to hide it. Even one of the shop's staff stayed close to me, hovering not ten feet away at all times. She was tensed, eyes trained on my every movement. As if searching for clothing for Leilani and the children had not already mounted to be a trying enough task on its own.

Kyle and Sarah had blatantly refused to leave for anywhere today. Although it would have made little difference, given I had yet to receive licensing to drive, and could not fly with them. So I took measurements for the trio, jotted down preferences of color next to their numbers and had made for the small downtown Littleton had developed. The stores were small and selections limited, but it would certainly do the trick in a pinch.

At least I was not needing to find anything for my impossible size.

"Can I *help* you?" The clerk asked this yet again, despite my repeated attempts to decline any more attention than I had already garnered.

"No, thank you, madam." It took more effort than I liked to remain polite with her now. I pulled out the measuring tape I had borrowed from the sewing station at home, earning a wary stare from the clerk as I measured an outfit. I checked for the listed size of it, glad to have finally sorted out Kyle, at least. Working quickly, I was able to settle on a handful of outfits which should fit the young boy and tossed them in the cart.

I made my way for the bright pink area I presumed to be for young girls, my ever-faithful shadow of a clerk trailing close behind. I recalled then how closely Braxen had always kept to me, finding myself missing his aggravating pet names compared to this enterprise. The clerk's caution had turned to borderline disgust as I did the same measuring to various sized clothes, having a bit more difficulty finding the proper fit here. Still, the patrons gawked.

"Can I help you?"

I fought a sigh, replying patiently, "No, thank you, madam, I need only find things for my children."

Finally, I was able to guess properly, if on the larger end for safety. I did my best to select for simpler patterns, recalling Sarah's distaste for frills. Save for a dress I grabbed on impulse, reminiscent of a garment one of her dolls wore. Perhaps she could find some enjoyment in it.

Finished again with the small selection, I went next to the women's department for Leilani. This was where I had anticipated having the most hardship, given she was on the taller end for human women, despite her lean figure. She was nowhere near where I fell on the comparison scale, thankfully, though still large enough to possibly pose a problem.

The clerk cleared her throat sharply. "Can I help you find anything for kids?"

I glanced at the shelf I was next to, embarrassed to spy a small selection of laced undergarments. "Ah, no, just dresses. For their nanny?"

She glared at me skeptically, eyes flicking to my ringless left hand pointedly. "Uh-huh. Over there."

"Thank you," I muttered shyly, giving a nod and hurrying away from the display toward the much more generous variety of dresses. Leilani certainly had a strong preference for anything more flowing, and it was simply easier on my time to only worry about modifying a single article to fit.

Again, I pulled out my tape, this time to even less abashed murmurings and spiteful stares. It was then I realized the majority of the other patrons were women, dominantly looking to be young mothers. Perhaps my measuring was far less appropriate than I had previously considered.

"Really?"

"That's just sick."

"Can you believe this guy?"

"Jackass."

I scowled at the dress I was measuring. Where had their protests been before now, when I had done the same for children's clothing? Setting those thoughts aside, I settled on one of the larger options hanging in front of me.

"What all do you have in this size?" I asked the seething stalker of a clerk, eager for an additional pair of hands to help me collect what I needed to leave.

She saw the tag and seemed to relax warily. "What kind of style are you looking for?"

"Anything which matches a pale red."

The clerk nodded, helping me find several options. The instant I knew I had more than enough to suffice for now, I made my way to the counter to pay and leave. I had little care of how cumbersome the flight home would be, glad to have the torment over and done with.

~~ * ~ * ~ * ~~

Thursday

"Sarah, would you mind assisting me with something?" I asked, noticing her reluctant envy as Kyle and I finished with our garden tools. He was admittedly more of an interactive observer, hitting at the ground with a small trowel while I did what I could to prepare the beds for next season's planting.

His sister refused to participate in activities with me, equally stubborn with the notion of leaving Kyle alone in my care where she could help it. This made for quite the odd company as she sat beside Leilani. Two spectators: one curious and one judgmental.

The young girl was skeptical and cautious. "With what?"

I brushed any dirt from my hands. "Oh, I need to set to work on fixing up a dress for Leilani. I could use your help picking which one to start with?"

I had piqued her interest, if only begrudgingly. She nodded, hopping up and allowing Kyle to start his excited babbling at Leilani, as he was prone to do after our activities now. Sarah was perfectly content to leave him alone with the demoness, while I toiled away at earning her trust. If that was the arrangement they felt best with currently, I supposed I had little room to argue.

I led her to the living area and the small corner which had always been prepared for sewing. I lifted a wooden box filled with the dresses I had purchased for Leilani, bringing it to the couch where Sarah sat. I took a seat beside her, gesturing to the box invitingly.

Her hands dug in and in an instant, she was displeased with my choices. She fixed me with a glare, a critical inquiry in her eyes while she brandished a fistful of fabric at me.

"It's green," she stated flatly as if the very idea was criminal enough to have me seen off to a penitentiary immediately.

"It matches her color," I offered, the spring green vibrant enough to complement her naturally bright coral.

"Leilani *hates* green, it reminds her of home and makes her sad," sighed Sarah, rolling her eyes and shaking her head, disappointed.

"Not green, then," I agreed, terribly guilty for not knowing better with the choice of color.

"This one is okay," relented Sarah, beginning to enjoy herself as she lifted a salmon tone with plaid print. Her eyes lit up as she spotted a deep navy blue, nearly black it was so dark. "This one is really pretty."

"I was worried it may be a bit too dark for her," I confessed, and she debated if for a split second before nodding in agreement. I reached for a soft violet number, offering it up. "How about this?"

"That, or..." She pulled out a gentle cream dress that glittered faintly in the light. We shared a glance, nodded, and she handed it to me to begin my work. Her hands went back to the navy blue piece quickly. "Then this one, okay?"

"Very well, then," I chuckled, watching her stuff the remaining dresses into the box before replacing it in its corner for me. She flitted off humming a tune, and I smiled hopefully. Perhaps there was a chance for us to make a family out of this mess after all.

~~ * ~ * ~ * ~~

Sixth Week After Paradise

<u>Thursday</u>

"CORY!"

The shrill cry came from inside the house. I dropped the tools I was organizing, sprinting for the back door from the crumbling shed behind the garden. In my

233

rush, I forgot to duck quite as low as I needed, horns knocking against the doorframe and throwing my head back.

"Agh! Lisa, is everything all right?!" I called, righting myself and scrambling inside.

My sister stood with an envelope in hand, a lunatic grin plastered across her face. "It's for you! From the Department of Transportation. Open it, open it!"

"Very well, Lisa, calm down," I sighed, taking the envelope and sliding a dulled claw down the seam. I dumped the contents into my free hand, something clattering to the floor as it fell through my fingers. "Ah, well now—"

"Look! It's a license!" she cheered, snatching up the piece of plastic before I could bend to reach for it. She held it up for me to inspect. I stared at the terrible photo, cringing.

"Did they intentionally mean to make me look so...disgruntled and bored?" I wondered, oddly impressed that they had found a way to make me appear even more aggressively unappealing to the eye.

"Mom would go crazy if she got to see this! Look at that!" She continued to brandish the despicable photo on the card, mocking me with it. She looked it over, for the first time taking in my appearance with a flinch. "Ew, Cory, were you about to sneeze yourself to sleep or something?"

"Very funny, Lisa, hand it over," I sighed, holding out one hand patiently. She skipped away stiffly, holding the card behind her back.

"Oh, no, I'm showing this off!" she laughed,

looking at it again. "Oh, I'm so glad we're not related."

"Did you finally figure it out about the milkman, then?" I retorted, reaching out to snatch for the card. She dodged me again, the obnoxious little gnat of a sibling.

She giggled madly. "Well, you're adopted!"

I gasped in mock horror. "How could our parents hide such a thing, Lisa?! Of course, it was so obvious, between my having manners and you being raised in the sty!"

"Your comebacks are rusty, old man," she teased with a snicker, relinquishing the card at last.

I pocketed it, unwilling to risk her making off with it again. "And you are still a hugely aggravating terror for such a little sister."

Lisa grinned and curtsied theatrically. "I try."

I laughed in spite of myself, pulling her into my side for a quick hug. She accepted the gesture, and it felt like the years had done little to diminish the affectionate rivalry we had nurtured as children. Before she could pick the card from my pocket, I excused myself to return to my work outside.

～ * ～ * ～ * ～

<u>Saturday</u>

Tucking Kyle in carefully, I smiled at his tired expression as he fought to stay awake. "Good night, Kyle. Sleep well."

Turning to Sarah, I found her still sitting up atop her bedding, wringing her hands with more worry than a child her age ought to have. I took a seat on the bed beside her, setting a hand on her shoulder for comfort. With our recent efforts at making peace, she did not seem to mind the gesture.

"What seems to be the matter, Sarah?" I asked quietly, hoping the world had yet to catch up with her. She deserved to sleep easy, at least one more night. Always, at least one more night.

"I've been thinking a lot about what Grandma told us," she confessed, picking at her rabbit's eye nervously.

"What about it?" And perhaps, what specifically? I imagined there must have been countless conversations to choose from.

"Um, well, the last time I saw her, she said..." She took a deep breath, tensing her shoulders as she steeled herself. "I've never really had a dad before, but I think what you do is what it's supposed to be like, and I've always wanted one, so I was wondering if maybe you'd be mine? I mean, if you want to," she added meekly, as though there could ever be any answer besides yes.

I felt my heart sink even as my chest swelled, but Kyle beat me to a reply as he shot up from his pillow eagerly. "Me, too! I want that, too."

A laugh escaped me. "Children..."

"But only if you *want* to," interrupted Sarah, stressing the point. "I mean, our dad didn't want us, so I won't be mad if you don't."

"Don't ever think that I wouldn't want you," I corrected her firmly, startled by the forceful conviction in my tone. They started, giving me shy glances which wondered if they were in trouble. I sighed, softening my voice, "I've wanted you both for a very long time, and I would never trade either of you for the world. I would be honored to raise you in any capacity, but especially as a father. In fact...I want to adopt you both," I told them, receiving tear-filled grins from them both; Sarah's tears fell over onto her cheeks.

"Really?" she asked, sincere and hopeful with her wide, dark eyes. "Really, you want us?"

I nodded, her words cutting me despite the joy I could hear in them. I dried her face with my free hand, pulling her into a hug. "Of course I do, sweetheart; I always will."

Kyle scrambled from his bed, running over and clambering up into my lap. "I always wanted a dad."

I hugged them both, pulling Sarah onto my lap to rock the two children gently. "And I always wanted a son named Kyle and a daughter named Sarah."

Despite their earlier protests against sleep, they drifted off quickly in my arms. I sighed quietly, too happy to want to move them just yet. Remembering their elated little faces made my heart swell, excited to see them so joyful.

A gentle knock behind me caught my attention before Lisa entered quietly, whispering, "Would you like help tucking them in?"

Had I been at it so long now she felt a need to check on me? I glanced down at my otherwise occupied arms and grinned. "I suppose I am lacking in enough hands."

She returned my grin, going to prepare Kyle's bedding with practiced hands. She turned back to me, scooping him up with ease before she settled him in. One arm now free, I stood to arrange Sarah's bedding. Careful not to wake her, I placed her in bed, tucking the blanket around her just so.

I made to brush the hair from her face, stopping short when she reached up to grab hold of my hand. I smiled, spotting her stuffed rabbit and switching my hand with it easily. "Sleep well, darling."

I checked on Kyle, making certain he had his bear before I was satisfied to turn out the lamp. "Sweet dreams, my boy."

I snuck out, finding it startlingly difficult to leave. Lisa was waiting for me in the hall as I pulled the door shut behind myself, wishing I could peek in again and feeling silly for the urge.

"How'd it go?" she asked in a hushed tone, no doubt asking after any more antagonistic behavior.

"Sarah asked me to be their dad," I told her, the words catching in my throat with joyful tears. "They were so happy to hear I want to adopt them."

My sister smiled. "Come on, you giant softy, it's downstairs with you before you wake them up."

I nodded, following her to the living room. Leilani was huddled up on the couch with a bundle of string, a web of intricate knots laced around her fingers. I sat beside her, careful not to disturb the delicate process she was engrossed in. The demoness chirped once quietly in greeting, refusing to look up, and earning a raised brow from Lisa as she settled into her favored chair.

"So, they beat you to it, huh?" asked Lisa, calling my attention away from the mesmerizing work Leilani continued with.

I smiled and nodded. "It seems so. Kate, she told them I had auditioned for the part before she...I suppose they took her words to heart."

My sister's smile was doleful. "I'm not surprised—about Kate *or* the kids. I know I give you a tough time, but you're doing great with them, Cory. Even Sarah won't stop talking about the dresses you make Leilani," she added with a giggle.

"Oh, I never thought she would warm to me," I confessed, chest still overflowing with this elation. My broad grin could not be held back any longer, although Lisa did not seem to mind it. "She asked me to fill this role, Lisa. Perhaps she was only testing me with these last few weeks. Oh, but...A father, Lisa. No longer the awkward, barely defined relationship we have been struggling with."

"Stop crying, I don't want to start," she laughed at me teasingly. "I'm happy for you, though. I know it's something you always wanted."

"If only I had been more specific about the terms," I joked weakly, shrugging. "Still...I find I would not trade this moment for anything."

~~ * ~ * ~ * ~~

Eighth Week After Paradise

Sunday

Lisa stopped me on my way outside, grabbing my

hand and looking to make certain the children were too busy with their coloring to notice us.

"Cory, can I talk to you?" she asked in a hushed whisper that worried me.

I frowned at her insistence on discretion. "Of course, Lisa. Is something the matter?"

She scowled, obviously concerned. "That's what I've been wondering, Cory. You've been having a lot of nightmares lately."

"Have I?" Truth be told, I could scarcely recall dreaming since everything that had happened in the village. When I could sleep, that is.

Lisa nodded with another furtive glance toward the children. "The kids probably think it's an animal outside, but it sounds bad, Cory. I'm worried about you."

"I'm perfectly fine, Lisa," I assured her, hoping she did not hear the lie in my voice. I knew I had been stressed, certainly, and my frayed nerves had been playing tricks on me. It was nothing I had not endured before, nor could not wrest into submission again. After all, I could still stand to use the kitchen knives to prepare meals, no matter how nervously.

"Don't be mad, but I contacted Robert," she confessed, still too quiet for the children to hear. "I told you, I'm worried, Cory."

I sighed heavily. "Lisa, there is no reason to bother him with this. Nightmares are simply expected for me. Aftermath from the Institute, Robert said as much."

The hurt on her face stabbed at me. Had she not noticed their tests had cut deeper than these surface scars? "Oh. I'm sorry, I didn't realize...Can I help at all?"

"It's alright, Lisa, I know you meant well." I hesitated, thinking back over the last year wistfully. "Kate used to help me on bad nights. I...I fear little else will help but time."

My sister let me to my work afterward, although her words lingered with me. Now my attention was drawn to my worsening nights, it seemed my blissful ignorance had been wrenched away from me. My peaceful nights of timeless sleep were gone.

In their stead, I saw every second of every horror of a memory playing while I slept, helpless to stop them and unable to wake.

~~ * ~ * ~ * ~~

Thursday

The enticing aroma of a cooking turkey and baked dishes filled the house. Even the pungent smell of dust from the box of home videos was drowning in it. Lisa had insisted on some light organizing of the study despite the holiday, taking the form of sorting through memorabilia. She claimed it would serve as a good activity as a family. I would have been more satisfied with a radio show.

Still, I had little reason to protest, tolerating the foray into the past with a patient smile. It was startling just how many movies there were of our family, even more so when she had found a select few featuring brief cameos of myself. I was commonly in the background, avoiding the camera for safety, although what she had found now seemed to be a compilation of Kate harassing

241

me with the recorder. I vaguely recalled the time, when she had insisted on surprising me day in and out for two weeks straight.

"Is that you?" asked Kyle, pointing to my laughing face on the screen.

I nodded, still baffled to see any evidence of my existence at all, let alone from such happy times. "Yes, that's me."

"How old were you?" he asked next, leaving his place by the screen and clambering up into my lap instead.

I wrapped my arm around him without thinking, scowling at the scene as it continued to play out. "Oh, this was...1965?"

"No, '64. Your least favorite sister is there." Lisa pointed to Ethan in the background, acting his usual disgruntled self. She wiped her hands on her apron, taking her seat to rest a moment while the meal she insisted on cooking alone allowed her the break.

"Yes, I see him now," I chuckled, nodding. "So, 1964, I would have been twenty-one at the time, turning twenty-two that year."

"Wow," breathed Kyle, eyes wide as he grinned. "That's so old!"

"Oh, your definition of old is biased," I laughed, ruffling his hair.

"Why? How old are you now? Like, thirty?" He kept his grin, tipping me off that he knew better.

"Let me see, that would have been forty-eight years ago, plus twenty-two, which makes me...twenty," I replied matter-of-factly, nodding. Lisa snickered.

Kyle made a face, skeptical. "No, but then you'd

be younger, and you can only get older."

"Are you certain?" I asked, feigning confused amazement at the notion.

He nodded. "Yeah, I'm sure! I've only gotten older, so you must be older, too."

"Ah, you caught me," I confessed with a grin. His beaming pride made me laugh. "I'm sixty-nine, Kyle. Next August, I will be seventy."

His mouth popped open in disbelief. "That's a big number."

I chuckled. "Yes, it is, and if I have any say in the matter, you will be even older someday."

"How much older?" he asked with an excited bob, absolutely fascinated. Yet, he always had trouble with his math, the odd little boy.

"Oh, let me think," I muttered, frowning as I kept up the playful tone. "Somewhere around two or three thousand, I believe."

"Dad, people don't live that long," he giggled. The title he used so casually made me feel as though my heart might burst.

"Then you'll be the first, won't you?" I tweaked his nose, loving the grin he gave me. From the kitchen, I heard the chime of the timer.

"Turkey's done," announced Lisa, easing herself from her chair tenderly. She needed to be mindful of herself, no matter how much she wanted to tend the home as our mother had. I made a mental note to teach Leilani more household tasks. No doubt, Lisa would never have a chore again, the demoness was ever such a helpful little thing.

"Very well. Go on upstairs and wash up, Kyle, and bring your sister and Leilani back with you," I sighed, removing him from my lap so I could stand.

"'Kay!" he chirped, rushing upstairs in a thunder of footfalls and calling to his sister as he went.

I laughed and made my way to set the table for supper, leaving my unscarred face to fade from the screen. The past could stay where it belonged today; I had better things to indulge in.

~~ * ~ * ~ * ~~

November 25ᵗʰ, 2011

Every second I can without her noticing, I find myself staring at Leilani. Since returning to the farm, I have been missing demon faces, and do my best to satisfy the craving by watching her. I am certain she has noticed by now, and I cannot shake the distinct feeling I am flirting with rudely inappropriate behaviors.

It is utterly fascinating, the plethora of ways she emotes with a flick of the tail or twitch of her wing. She uses them so naturally and easily, incorporating them seamlessly into so many countless tasks I now wonder how detestably crude I must appear, limited by my human upbringing.

The thumbs on her wings she uses to grip with just as easily and deftly as the digits on her hands. Her tail is undeniably prehensile, skilled in her use of it and shaming my clumsier, far less creative incorporation of my same appendage. Where I had thought myself inventive in hugging others, she will humble me by all but juggling her tools when she helps me with preparing the garden beds.

My eyes are nearly always glued to her, I have discovered. I am taken in by her natural grace, the very one the other demons all move with. The same one I feel I lack. Again, due to my unorthodox upbringing. I do my best to avoid dwelling on such sad musings, sorely discouraged to consider what manner of creature I might have been, if only...

Just as I watch her, I have noticed her doing the same to me when she thinks me too busy to notice. She is certainly much more subtle, even discreet compared to my near-blatant gawking. It most often occurs when I am engaged with more human tasks—farm work and household chores, the careful handling of the children, even reading.

She had been intrigued by cooking briefly, but as the tools became familiar to her she lost her obsessive interest in the endeavor. While she still works to learn the finer points of the kitchen—and has since surpassed me in operating the more sophisticated appliances I detest so keenly—she often prioritizes her efforts toward learning other things.

Leilani also listens. While her copper eyes take in every sight with intense curiosity, she always wears a look of maddening focus when any of us speak. Her efforts have not gone unrewarded, yielding results much more swiftly than I would have anticipated otherwise. She wants to learn, repeating and practicing words endlessly. She asks as best she can what they mean and what certain objects are called.

Karma Rose

She has even taken to practicing human habits, as well, from her way of dressing to her hygiene. She is even learning household tasks from Lisa or me as we have the time. While she has a knack for laundry, she has an apparent preference for dusting and sweeping. I imagine she finds the rather immediate results gratifying, smiling that infectious smile of hers which makes my lips curve no matter the day I have had.

I also find myself favoring her company over humans now, so much more at ease with her coral skin and fanged grin. It is so much less isolating, having this one companion to face the world with, even if we have barriers to overcome in our communication. I am not alone, and she is more than happy to make it clear for me with her sunny smile and pandemic-like enthusiasm.

It is especially comforting and enlightening when she treats me as she does my children, giving hugs and affection freely simply to make us smile. Where she is large enough to embrace the little ones, however, she has to improvise with me. Her arms are able to embrace my front alone, the difference in our sizes is so great. So, to produce the effect she so desires, she must encase me in her wings and hold tight.

The feel of her membranes was alien when I first felt it, but not unlikable. There is a part of me which feels it is right, so much more fulfilling than the embraces I have shared with humans over the years. I knew the first time without realizing this was what it should have felt like all along, such a different method of expression which satisfied me so wholly.

Still, it had startled me all the same.

I was frozen solid. Even my tail locked into place from the shock of her membranes pressed against me, surrounding me. I held my breath against my startled hiss, allowing myself to calm down slowly. Then, nearly as quickly as it had felt so unnatural, it could not have been more...right.

And why would it not be? She is the same as I, and—even if I had not known who or what I was all these years—my body had always been brutally aware of the instincts I must restrain with such meticulous care and practice. This is simply one more innate behavior I have never encountered, and one I will not be filing away like the rest. This is pleasant, subtle. Far from the dangerous urges I have chained previously.

It is my hope to, one day, be able to express to her more completely my growing appreciation of her companionship.

~~ * ~ * ~ * ~~

Ninth Week After Paradise

Tuesday

There was a loud knock on the front door.

"Come in!" I called, refusing to look up from my papers at the kitchen table. I was too tired to be bothered by polite formalities, worn to the bone after comforting the children through nightmares last night.

"I have a surprise," announced Robert, grinning as he entered. He held up a thick envelope. "I called in a

247

favor."

I looked up from the stack of legal papers and bills, neither of which seemed to cease. "If you've come to add anything to this mountain of work, I insist you turn around now."

He laughed cordially. "The opposite, actually. This eliminates some of those papers."

"You have my attention, sir," I sighed, leaning back to stretch the stiffness from my shoulders.

"You should stay sitting," he warned, handing me the envelope to open. I broke the seal, sliding the papers out to stare at them. My exhausted mind was painfully uncomprehending at first.

"Birth certificates? But how does this—?" I stopped short, reading the names printed there. The certificates were for Kyle and Sarah: I was listed as their father. I looked up at Robert, waiting for him to laugh at the joke he must be playing. "Truly?"

He nodded. "Yeah. Like I said, favors. Lots of favors and I may have sold my soul, but..." He shrugged. "It's worth it."

I stood, still clutching the papers as I stumbled around the table to give him an awkward embrace. "Thank you, Robert, you have outdone yourself."

He hugged me back, patting my shoulder as Father used to before breaking away. "It's the least I could do, to make up for how I used to act about you."

"Thank you." I sniffled, sighing and smiling despite the tears I felt. I stared at the papers a moment longer before slipping them back into their envelope. "Excuse me, I need to tell my children."

Broken Orbit

The words made me giddy as I went upstairs, taking them two at a time. I knocked on the children's bedroom door, silencing the playing I heard inside. I nudged it open gently, grinning at the curious faces I saw. I was even too excited to notice entirely Leilani's being absent.

I stepped in, setting the envelope on Sarah's bed and sitting beside them on the floor. "Kyle, Sarah, about the adoption..."

They shared a look of horror at my abrupt mention of it.

"Oh, no," cried Kyle, terrified.

"You still want us, right?" Sarah was pleading with me with those black eyes.

"Of course, I want you," I laughed, although I was sad her first thought could be I would not want her. Yet this news was too happy to dwell on doleful things. "Children, the paperwork just came in: I'm your father."

The news registered slowly, as though they expected anything but what they had wanted so much. When it sank in, they shrieked and jumped me, all hugs and smiles and giggles. I hugged them back, kissing their faces, simply glad to know they were not going to be stolen away anytime soon. They were mine. Legally, with the print to declare it, *I* was their father. My tears escaped me, chest ready to burst from joy.

So little had changed from how we had been for so long now. They had already considered me differently, since before we had left for the village. Over the last year, I had gone from a stranger to their grandfather, and somewhere in between our dynamic had settled with me as their father figure, even with the brief and trying bout Sarah had instigated. This only sealed it all together, so neatly and perfectly nothing could go wrong with it.

"Oh, I love you both, so very much," I told them, relaxing my grip. They still clung to me tightly, refusing to go anywhere else.

"You're really our dad now?" asked Sarah quietly, face buried in my arm.

"Yes, sweetheart, and I always will be," I told her. How was it possible my mood only grew lighter, when I already felt the happiest I had been in decades? There were no undertones of grief or confusion, only pure joy. I was their father, now and always.

"Really? Promise?" asked Kyle, finally pulling away just enough to hold his little finger up.

"I promise," I chuckled, amused and confounded by the gesture.

"No, you have to pinky swear!" he cried, shaking his tiny hand at me.

"What is that?" I asked, smiling at his antics. Whatever reassurance he needed, I would give it.

Sarah gasped, horrified. "You don't know what a pinky swear is?"

I shook my head, stifling a laugh as she leaned back to fix me with a stare, wide-eyed and aghast. "No, I've never made one. You'll have to show me how."

"Never?" Kyle was skeptical.

"Never," I repeated dramatically. They shared a glance, but Sarah held up her pinky to mimic Kyle.

"First, you have to hold your hand like this, one for each of us," she instructed, and I had the weighted feeling of being prepared for an ominous responsibility.

I did as instructed, letting them go completely so they were braced solely on my lap. "Like this?"

Kyle nodded, then wrapped his pinky around mine. "Yeah, then you go like this."

"And you have to say 'pinky swear', and shake," said Sarah solemnly, doing the same.

I entwined my little fingers around theirs, the drastic difference between my fingers and their tiny hands nothing but humorous. I kept my composure, sensing how this was an immensely meaningful ordeal for them. I shook their hands.

"Very well. I pinky swear, I will always be your father," I agreed, and they finally seemed satisfied with the vow. I dropped my hands to my lap, looking between the two conspiratorially. "Do you know what that means?"

They shook their heads, Kyle piping up, "No, what?"

"Well, I've been reading the special guide fathers get and I found this thing called tickling..." I watched their faces with a grin, amused by the mixture of glee and horror that settled there. They squealed and jumped up, running from the room with their shrieking laughter. I clambered up, moving more slowly as I kept my head ducked under the ceiling. "I'll catch you!"

Robert was waiting at the bottom of the stairs, content to watch our shenanigans. I stopped long enough to give him a sincere smile. "How could I ever thank you?"

"I already got what I sold my soul for," he replied with a shrug, then pointed toward the back door nonchalantly. "They went out that way, by the way."

My grin returned, mischievous when I heard their continued shrieks and giggles out the back door, still hanging open. I hurried to follow, catching Kyle just outside the door and scooping him up with a dramatic cry.

"I've got you now, Kyle!" He screamed with laughter as I tickled him, sprinting off madly when I released him to run about more. I glanced around, spying my daughter giggling as she half-ran toward the other side of the house. "Sarah, it's your turn."

She screeched a laugh and ran. I followed after, enjoying simply playing with them as the game turned from running from me to pulling me to the ground and pinning me. I went along with it, overjoyed by their proud grins, all of us having a moment to forget the worries of the world and enjoy our little family.

My family, with *my* children.

~~ * ~ * ~ * ~~

Friday

I settled into my seat at the table with a stiff groan, right shoulder sore from a day of tilling in fresh material for the garden beds next season. It marked the last of the garden work, opening my time to the countless other tasks left to breathe new life into this place. I did my best to remind myself of today's success through the sharp throbbing which made it difficult to lift my utensil.

"Thank you for supper, Lisa." I settled for using my left hand, my right too weak and trembling fiercely.

"Perhaps I could give you a day off soon?"

My sister laughed, shaking her head slowly. "Oh, no. It's one of the things I'm still good for while you're running around outside, and your cooking is...ehh."

While I could not deny she was better than me through my bite of supper, I was still able to narrow my eyes in protest. "Come now, when was the last time you had a meal I helped with?"

"A long time ago, and it was still too soon," she teased, sipping her evening glass of tea. "Mm, on a less traumatizing subject, are you ready to enroll the kids in school next semester?"

Her question was answered by groans of protest from Kyle and Sarah both. Their faces were miserable in an instant, as though they had been told the truth about Christmas. I fought a smirk, finding it oddly adorable.

"What might it entail?" I asked, ignoring the mumbled indignation that was half-muted by their unfaltering interest in their meals.

"Getting school supplies, doctor visits to keep vaccinations up to date, a bit of paperwork. Nothing too much." At my incredulous gawking, she added, "I helped with my granddaughters last year, I can give you a hand, too. But just this once, then you're on your own."

"You are such a generous soul, Lisa," I said sarcastically. She only grinned, unashamed.

"Dad, do we *have* to go to school?" asked Sarah pitifully. The title she used warmed my heart.

Kyle nodded, eyes pleading. "Yeah, can't we just help with work like we have? We're good helpers, aren't we?"

"Of course, Kyle, you are both wonderful helpers. However, you deserve an education and I am ill-equipped to supply much more than what I know from farm work and reading," I explained, to more upset grumblings. I caught sight of their empty plates. "Are you two finished with supper?"

"Yeah," sighed Kyle sadly. He looked at his sister. "It's your turn."

She nodded, collecting their dishes and taking them to the sink to wash. I fixed my boy with a stern look, questioning his continued presence at the table when there was a bed to ready himself for.

"I'm waiting for Sarah," he explained without my asking, knowing well what he should have been doing.

"Very well," I relented patiently. "But when she is done, it's upstairs to ready yourselves for bed, teeth brushed and all. I will be up shortly for tucking in and a bit of reading."

Sarah returned, wiping her hands on her pants clumsily. "Can we have two chapters tonight?"

"If you're in bed before I get there, I can agree to it."

They took in the mostly-empty plate in front of me, sharing a wide-eyed stare before rushing off to the stairs.

"Teeth brushed and clothes in the hamper, please!" I called after them, grinning at their enthusiastic replies lost to the thunder of their footsteps. Lisa sighed pointedly at me, but I could not care. Even with my pained shoulder and pain of a sister, at the end of the day, I was beyond noticing.

Broken Orbit

I had monsters to check for, a book to read and my two little ones with dreams in need of guarding.

~~ * ~ * ~ * ~~

December 8th, 2011

Finding a doctor who will accept us is proving to be trying, to say the least. My first attempt at an appointment had been simple enough. The next town over has an office which serves children, with an availability just earlier this week. I should have trusted my instinct which told me it was too good to be true, however.

Upon arrival, we were refused service.

"May I ask why?" The question was irrelevant; I knew why.

"Look, we just don't help demons here," the receptionist all but hissed through a tight smile.

"The children are human," I persisted. Why, when I knew the effort would be fruitless? "Surely, you can see them?"

Her smile tightened, so much so I wondered if her skin should split from the strain of her expression. "Yeah, but you're not. We don't take demon patients, only human families, okay?"

I forced back a growl of frustration, fighting to keep my features tame. I sighed quietly and nodded. "Very well. We will be on our way, then. Children?"

They flitted over as I opened the door, a panicked cry coming from the woman I had spoken to. "Excuse me?! What are you doing with those kids?!"

Karma Rose

I closed my eyes and breathed deeply, preparing for the worst. "I am taking my children home, madam."

"No, you're not, those aren't yours!"

When I opened my eyes, I saw people outside the open office door had heard her declaration, stepping forward to block my way while the receptionist called for the police. I took a seat in the far corner of the office to wait since the human blockade showed no signs of moving for me. It was everything I could do to distract the children, keeping them engaged and away from the hateful glares and murmurings at the exit.

"What are we waiting for, Dad?" asked Sarah, suspicious.

If only she could be as blissfully unobservant as her brother as he chased my tail. I fumbled for any sort of explanation, "We need to speak with someone before we go home."

Ah, sweet ineptitude and its wasted struggles. Needless to say, Sarah was unconvinced but did not continue, much to my relief. The police arrived shortly thereafter, one officer thankfully taking my place in entertaining the little ones while I clarified the situation with the other. After several calls, they were able to verify my honesty and sent us on our way.

In light of the mishap, I have now learned to carry a satchel with copies of my legal relationship, for ease as much as safety.

~~ * ~ * ~ * ~~

Tenth Week After Paradise

Broken Orbit

Saturday

This day had not gone as planned.

It began with breakfast. What was supposed to be a simple meal had turned into a catastrophic mess when Leilani gave up with her utensils early—while both children still had food on their plates, no less. Where the demoness caved out of necessity for her waning patience, the children each found an exuberant glee in using their hands.

The cleanup was disastrous, delaying the day by hours. An already busy day, as well, in which I had planned to address Kyle and Sarah's need for hair trims. A topic for which I was utterly lost, as Mother had always helped with mine and Katelyn had always helped with the little ones'.

So I asked my sister, given her history as a mother, to which she replied with a firm, "Figure it out."

Lisa seemed fond of learning on the job, this exhausting trial by fire. Overly so, with her refusal to help me with the most simple of tasks. Despite this, I knew she was trying to help me in the long-term. However much I detested her methods, I begrudgingly had to thank her somehow. I felt more competent as a parent for it.

In this instance, however, I would not have the children suffer for any inexperience on my part. Luckily, I had an idea of how to salvage the day, dressing the children and herding them into the little yellow car with Leilani following overhead.

Karma Rose

~~ * ~ * ~ * ~~

"Jeff, I sincerely hope I am not intruding."

"Not at all! Any excuse to see these guys," he laughed, opening the front door further and allowing our odd medley of a group into his home. He eyed Leilani with restrained curiosity. "I'm glad you called. Today was looking like it was going to be just one long nap."

"Oh, one would be a welcome relief after this morning," I chuckled, watching the children run to visit their older cousins where they were relaxing in the living area.

"Trouble waking them up?" he guessed, eyes glued to the demoness as she shadowed her charges.

"Messy breakfast."

"I remember those," laughed Jeff with a nod. He sighed thoughtfully. "Well. You said you needed a hand with something for them, right?"

"Hair trims," I confessed sheepishly. "I would rather not have them endure whatever botched job I could do, and my sister refuses to assist under the pretense I must learn."

"Sounds like a doozy," he agreed. He gave me a fatherly smile, patting my arm. "Come on. We'll start with Kyle."

~~ * ~ * ~ * ~~

Leilani had watched intently through both Kyle and Sarah's grooming, taking in every action even as the instructions Jeff gave me were lost on her. When both

258

Kyle and Sarah were finished with their practical torment, the demoness began sniffing the different oils lain out. Her face was inquisitive, eyes alight with glee. I winced as she made to lick one, the gagging whimper she gave making me smirk in spite of myself. Jeff raised one brow at the scene.

"She's a curious one," he said slowly, clearing his throat awkwardly. "A little special, maybe?"

"She...lived a secluded life," I hedged cautiously, unable to fully explain Paradise for fear of the village's safety. "She often makes up for it by being an exceptionally quick learner."

"Right," he laughed, shaking his head slowly as he gathered up the tools we had been using. "How about you? Feel like you learned anything today?"

"Certainly." I accepted the broom he offered me to sweep the floor. "I can manage their hair through force of will, but I should leave the rest of the populace to trained professionals."

~~ * ~ * ~ * ~~

Eleventh Week After Paradise

<u>Thursday</u>

"Do we *have* to get shots?" Kyle's timid plea tore at my heart. I had luckily found an office that would accept us, so I steeled myself against his pitiful whimper. We had to make the most of this opportunity.

"Yes, Kyle. Robert and Aunt Lisa both say they

are necessary for you to attend school in January," I explained gently, watching as the nurse entered carrying a tray. He set it on the counter, pulling out a pair of blue gloves. The smell of latex was sickening; I forced it back to focus on Kyle now.

"Okay, big guy, I need your arm. Don't worry, it won't hurt a bit," the nurse told him, sterilizing Kyle's arm with alcohol.

I frowned at the unnecessary lie, recalling my years of experience with needles which contradicted his statement. "It may pinch, Kyle, but nothing terrible. Remember when you got this scar?" I pointed to the faded bite mark from the little demon girl. He nodded. "This will be nothing compared to that. And you were very brave with that, weren't you?"

My son nodded, taking a deep breath and staring at me as he had when I cleaned the bite wound. I smiled, chest swelling with pride. That was my boy.

~~ * ~ * ~ * ~~

The ordeal of both children receiving their care was mercifully swift. The nurse had been interactive with the children, ignoring me for the bulk of his time in the room with us. Once he had finished with their imagined torture, he rewarded their patience with a small sheet of stickers each. Then came a long wait for the doctor to greet us at last. There was a small corner in the room with a collection of items to entertain children, at least.

When the doctor finally entered, his greeting was brief, explaining in short what the nurse had already done.

"Is there anything else I should know?" I asked, straining to keep my words polite and remain mindful of my voice. Short as the day was, it had already been more than enough to tire me completely. I glanced at the children to help steady myself. Kyle busied himself with the small selection of toys in the room, Sarah with a pamphlet. "Some manual or guide for raising children, perhaps?"

The doctor smiled. "New to the gig, huh?"

I nodded. "Exceptionally so."

"I can get some print-outs together on the basics," he offered kindly. "Growth spurts, uh, recommended vaccination schedule, nutrition, stuff like that. I know it sounds like a lot, but it's really not too tricky. Be right back."

With a nod, he excused himself to collect the information he had offered. I sighed shakily, watching the two children entertaining themselves for something to focus my nervousness on. I did not have long to distract myself, the door opening after a light knock only minutes later.

"Okay, so I've got a lot of the basics here for you, but if you feel like it's too bare-bones you can always go to the website listed on the bottom of each page. They usually have good links to more thorough information," he explained, handing me a stack of papers and taking in my baffled expression all too patiently. What did he have to gain from being so polite? "Where did I lose you?"

"Websites?" I echoed, the word odd in my mouth, alien.

"It's a place you can look up on the Internet."

Oh, dear. "What is an Internet?"

"Wow. Um, I've never had to explain that one before," he laughed uncertainly. "I mean, it's been around for a while now..."

"I admit, I have been somewhat...preoccupied," I explained awkwardly, feeling myself floundering in this.

He smiled sympathetically. "Do you have anyone tech-savvy who could help you?"

I nodded, grateful for the suggestion. A trip to visit Robert's family was already overdue, and his daughters would no doubt delight in teaching me more about the modern world. "Yes."

"Good. They can give you the grand tour online. Oh, I also put down the office information for a friend of mine. He's a dentist, great with kids, and he's just down the street. I figured you could use it, being new to the job and all."

I was moved by his consideration, if hesitant to accept such kindness at face value. "That is very gracious of you, sir, thank you."

"I'm here to help," he replied with an easy smile.

"It certainly seems so," I chuckled nervously. I glanced down at the papers I held, my vibrant crimson hands contrasting with the bright white of the room. "Do you think he might accept, ah..."

For the first time since meeting the young man, I felt him appraise me as something else, the inhuman thing I was. "I don't see why he wouldn't take care of the kids. He's professional about his practice."

It was none of my business about outside of the practice, so long as the children received the care they needed. "That is a relief. Thank you, again."

"Sure thing. It was nice meeting your family, Mr.Lawrence. Merry Christmas." He held out his hand to me. I accepted the gesture with a smile. He waved farewell to the children and left.

I took a deep breath, glad to be finished with the ordeal. Gathering the children, I led them out of the room. Near the exit was a plump older woman sitting behind a large counter, looking to be only a few years my junior. She waved me over with a smile.

"Checkout's right here," she chimed, manner welcoming as I approached. When we arrived at the counter, Kyle tugged at my hand and gestured to have me pick him up. I obliged, the woman's smile twisting strangely. "You handled the general office fee already, but we'll need to settle the account for services rendered during the visit."

"Very well. Sarah?" She looked up and handed me the satchel she insisted on wearing for me. I set it on the counter and fumbled for a moment before finding the card which had turned into such an invaluable help with managing the children of late. I was glad for my fortunate ability to focus my time on getting our little family adjusted. Despite how unfortunately the opportunity had come about. "Here we are."

"Thank you." The woman glanced at Kyle, cheeks flushing and eyes going wide as she smirked. She focused back on her task, biting back laughter. "Give me just a moment, Mr.Lawrence."

"Of course." I noticed Kyle's hushed giggles then, catching sight of him in the corner of my eye peeling stickers from his sheet, reaching up and... "Kyle, what are you doing?"

He grinned and snickered, reaching to adhere another image to my horn. "Sarah dared me to."

"Snitch," she muttered, crossing her arms.

I sighed patiently. What attention would a few stickers on my horns draw which the rest of my visage would not? "Please, ask next time, you two."

They caught my implication of this being a recurring event, and I regretted my wording immediately. Oh, today was already long enough, but I knew they would need feeding soon. Not to start on the drive home...

"Okay, if you can sign here for me, and this is your copy." I obeyed, the woman's smirk unable to hide her absolute delight as Kyle continued with his task.

"Sarah, I'm out of stickers, give me yours," he whispered noisily. I silently accepted my fate, ignoring how they were carrying on so blatantly. This was a battle not worth fighting today. "Thank you!"

"Okay, and that's everything! You have a good day and a Merry Christmas now!" she said cheerily. I smiled and nodded politely, too tired to muster much more than such a weary effort. She gave me a sympathetic expression as I gathered everything together to leave. "Good luck."

"Thank you," I mumbled, feeling like sheer luck would be far from able to make the cut for our little family. Perhaps divine intervention could do the trick if there were any godly beings patient enough for Kyle and Sarah's antics.

Yet once they were settled into the car and I had

cleared the town line, I felt my energy returning. The radio played quietly, the even hum of voices chattering and music playing lulling the two children to sleep. Their day must have been as exhausting as mine, being dragged hours from home with such an unfamiliar guardian. Stickers aside, they had handled it with more grace than I could claim, certainly. I felt a swell of pride and adoration then, as I glanced at the mirror to sneak a look of their sleeping faces.

Today was not an easy one, and I would do it over again just the same.

Chapter Eight:
On Solid Ground

Saturday

Lisa dropped a large box on the coffee table in front of where I was hanging stockings for the season. It hit the worn wooden surface with a heavy thud, startling me. Had she packed bricks inside?!

"Shoes."

"I beg your pardon?"

"They're required when you go out places," explained Lisa with a sly smirk. I rolled my eyes, turning my attention back to the box of Christmas decorations I had found in the old office. "Seriously, Cory, you're out and about in the world more, you need to start wearing real shoes! Not just those sandals. Especially if you're wanting to do anything with the kids at school, or make it easier to go out, maybe improve your general image—"

"My image is perfectly fine, thank you," I snapped irritably, although I knew she was right. If I was going to play at this imitation game for my children's sake, I would have to take further steps to...adapt. "Besides which, my claws destroy shoes, if you recall. Mother always tried to

266

dress me properly, but this damned anatomy conspired against her better efforts. Mine as well."

Lisa glanced at my hands, now clutching at a mass of tinsel, and gave a pointed nod. "You file the ones on your hands, don't you?"

"How did—?"

"Two things: you're being a lot less careful with a lot less damage, and the sink is *white*, Cory," she sighed heavily. I frowned. Well, now.

I sighed quietly, inspecting my claws idly through the shimmering decorations I held. "I suppose I could improve upon my grooming routines, then. At least to try your suggestion."

"I can't believe that wasn't the next thing you did after your hands," she laughed incredulously, shaking her head slowly. Finally, she seemed to realize what I had been doing and joined in with decorating the living room.

I gave her an exasperated look. "I never claimed to be the smart one, dear sister. You, at least, went to college."

"College has got absolutely nothing to do with personal grooming, you're just being a Negative Nancy that you didn't think of it first!" she teased, but I smiled to hear the humor in her voice. Her expression softened, wrinkles crinkling at her eyes as she smiled in return. She set a small cluster of seasonal figurines on an otherwise undecorated shelf. "Sometimes, it almost feels like you never left. You know?"

I nodded slowly, glad she felt that way no matter how I still wrestled with my past. I kept my composure, joking half-heartedly, "With the added benefit of dodging holidays with Grandfather Charles. I wonder how I got to be so lucky?"

Her smile fell, hands stopping in their task. "Dad didn't let him around anymore, after... Mom couldn't take the comments. Or, honestly, the lack of them. She said he was being too nice."

"A bit late to the game for the development," I muttered bitterly, shaking my head as I fought to keep back the memories of our dreadful grandfather. "But I'm glad Father finally did act, for Mother's sake."

"We missed you, though," she said earnestly, voice thick despite her smile. "Mom hung your stocking up every year, and you wouldn't believe how long it took for her to stop with the extra place setting and start cooking less."

I laughed at that, feeling my own grief welling up. "That's odd to imagine. So much of what I remember, she was working in that kitchen. Whatever did she do with herself?"

My failed attempt at humor made my sister weep. "Nothing good. She usually just sat in your room, at your window. She said it was the place she could feel you best. Eventually, she started taking her needlework up there with her, but..."

"I see." It was impossible to visualize our strong mother so crippled by anything. She had always been such a solid figure in my mind, soft enough to comfort her children yet unflinching in the face of adversity. She had helped me cultivate my quiet tones and gentle demeanor, giving me hope by seeing the fear in others' hateful actions towards me and the opportunity to ease their aggression with kindness.

Yet I had been the worthless cretin that had broken her spirit, all the more villainous that I had ceased contact.

I cleared my throat sharply, letting out a shaky sigh. "Well, now. I suppose we should get a tree up, then? Celebrate properly on her behalf."

Lisa followed my lead in providing a distraction from the painful past. Her eyes lit up. "It's in the study, actually, and I *think* I can find—Hold on."

My sister hurried off excitedly, leaving me with a now-empty box and a handful of tinsel. There were muted sounds from the study down the hall, a triumphant cry, and Lisa rushed back into the room. She looked herself a mad crone, silvered hair flying in every which direction while she bore an insane, proud grin. She carried a small box in her arms, a dusty red garment balanced on top.

I recognized the article immediately. "No, Lisa."

"Do it for the kids, Cory!"

"No, I am not wearing the suit! Besides which, I've grown nearly half a foot since I wore it last, it won't fit," I reasoned sternly. The mad gleam in her eyes told me there was no getting out of this effort in humiliation. "Lisa, *no*."

"Mom made it big, remember? I've got all the pieces here, and—" She flipped open the box she had presented earlier, revealing an impressively large pair of black boots. I glared at her. "These will go perfectly with the Santa outfit!"

I pursed my lips, knowing one way or another I was going to be bribed into the embarrassing thing. "You're getting nothing but coal."

Karma Rose

~~ * ~ * ~ * ~~

Twelfth Week After Paradise

Sunday

Not much longer, and the day is done.

The thought was a boon I clung to for dear life. After the day we had endured, it was all I had left to look forward to this evening. It had begun with the children waking far earlier than their normal hours. Tired and refusing to rest at all today, what had started as minor issues quickly turned to world-ending fits. The children missed their mother, to which my consolations meant little, escalating their yearning for Katelyn's comforts.

I was useless but for my ability to feed them. Leilani did not know their history, nor did she have the language to learn it in time to tend to their growing needs appropriately. To her credit, the sweet woman did her best, which certainly helped much more than I could claim for my wasted efforts.

Lisa was beyond taxing on my patience, as well. While she refused to aid me in the slightest, my sister had no shortage of opinions regarding my painfully lacking parenting experience. Where I was inclined to give the children the space they insisted on needing—sparing us both the trying endeavor of forced affections—Lisa had other ideas. She insisted they had no right to be disrespectful, and their time for leniency had well since passed for a healthy grieving period. I should put my foot down, tighten the reigns and remind them which of us was the adult. She also offered repeatedly to fetch the wooden spoon she favored so heavily.

It all led here, to the kitchen table and a more than tense atmosphere.

I set the plates as supper was finishing in the oven. By now, Leilani regarded the sound of setting the table as a call to seat herself and her charges. Ordinarily, this was a welcome habit to expedite the evening meal. Tonight, however, it was a damnably egregious offense to the remaining scraps of patience I had managed to keep hold of.

With one quick look at the children, I took in their dirty state tiredly. "Go wash up before supper, please, both hands and faces. There's no need to be at the table like that."

Kyle grumbled and made to move, but his sister stopped him. Sarah glared at me petulantly. "We already did."

I set the last of the utensils in their places, crossing my arms with a patient sigh. "Then you need to wash again. Between the both of you, you're wearing the entire front yard."

"We don't have to listen to you," she muttered, glaring at her place setting. "Besides, we have to wash up after dinner anyway, so what's the point?"

"The point is to be clean when you eat supper at the table, Sarah," I explained, struggling to maintain any semblance of composure as my frustration added a biting edge to my tone.

"Grandma wouldn't make us," she retorted bluntly.

271

Kyle agreed timidly with a wordless nod, the gesture only encouraging his sister while I did what I could to ignore how this hurt me. "She could do things right."

I took a deep breath, the attempt to calm myself worthless at best. Lisa was watching the exchange from her chair in the living room, embroidery hoop in hand and a cool skepticism on her face. Even Leilani's eyes were trained on me, waiting to see how I would respond. She may not have known the words, but she recognized the defiance in Sarah's tone.

"If you won't wash up for supper, then you may wash up for bed," I decided, forcing my tone to remain quiet and tame. I felt my nerves winding tightly, a growl building in my chest which I refused to grant freedom.

"I want Grandma," sniffled Kyle sadly, too tired to keep up with this day any longer.

"Me, too, Kyle. At least Grandma was nice!" Sarah's glare turned spiteful, tears of neglect and anger welling up in her black eyes. "Grandma wouldn't make us go to bed without dinner!"

"These may be bitter pills, young lady, but I am *not* your grandmother!" I snapped, wishing desperately that Kate could have been here now to help me through this. I missed her, the pain of it all the more cutting with how the children seemed to despise me today. "Now, if I have to help either of you upstairs to bed, you won't have your stories, either."

Sarah clung to her tears, shaking with the effort of it. "You can't do that."

Please, Sarah, enough of this!

"I can, and if you two aren't upstairs immediately I

272

will," I warned her, regretting the threat the instant it left my lips. There was no need to punish them having a terrible day, certainly, but what else could be done? I was beyond spent, with nothing left of myself to give. What else could I do after a day like this? *"Upstairs.* Now!"

Kyle sniffled and nodded, sliding out of his seat and shuffling off looking like a guilty criminal. My heart twisted at the sight. What had he done wrong? Missing his mother, or his grandmother? Their behavior was unpleasant, but was it deserving of this retaliation on my part? Did I have it in me to find any other solution?

"Sarah?"

"I hate you!" she spat angrily, standing sharply and stalking to the stairs.

"I expect you both to be washed up properly and in bed before I'm up there!" I called after them as they climbed the stairs. My chest was heavy, loathing my behavior. Leilani watched me warily, glancing back to the stairs worriedly. She was no doubt confused about why the children were not eating.

"Babies have food?" she asked timidly.

"Not tonight, Leilani," I muttered, as much in answer to her question as it was a plea for her to spare what little sanity I had left. She whimpered nervously, excusing herself awkwardly to go to her room.

Well now, I had made a perfect mess of the evening, then.

"Oh, I am an ass," I sighed as my sister came to join me in the kitchen. I closed my eyes against the world for a moment, hoping to find any scraps of reprieve and seeing only Sarah's angry, grieving face. When I opened them again, Lisa was watching me expectantly. "I take it you have something to add?"

"You're really going to let Sarah talk to you like that?   And you're still reading to them," she sighed, disappointed.   I scowled, unable to stomach the idea of reprimanding them any further for being in pain already.

"She's eight, Lisa, and today hasn't been easy for her, either." Yet I had neglected to find a way to reach out to her properly, favoring instead the easier route of punishment. This heavy guilt was well-earned and just as sickening in my system. "Besides which, she was right. Katelyn was much better at this than I am, on all fronts."

"You can't be such a pushover, though, Cory," she scolded me. "They'll take advantage of it."

"Why? How, Lisa?" I sighed heavily. "They are children! When you and I were their age, we were not malicious, even if we set out to break rules! They've been forced into this mishap of a family, and I punished them for their inability to act an adult."

I shook my head slowly, scowling at the empty table. My appetite was gone now, buried beneath my doubts. It was my job to protect them, help them through times just like these, and I had failed miserably. As tempting as it was, I could not waste my energy with self-pity or resentment now. I had a mess to clean with this.

"Uh, Cory, do you smell that?" What was no doubt intended to be some continued criticism on her part turned to confusion, and I realized too late what the smell of burnt charcoal must mean.

"Blast it," I muttered, removing the blackened mass of supper from the oven. I set it aside with a sigh of defeat, shutting off the appliance and tossing aside the potholders.

"Um..." The tiny voice I heard startled me, and I turned around to see Kyle on the bottom stair clutching his stuffed bear tight. His eyes were wide, pleading.

"What are you doing downstairs?" I wondered. His eyes fell to his feet, his reply mumbled too quietly to hear at first. "Speak up, Kyle."

"Oh, um, please don't be mad but I can't get the toothpaste out," he muttered shyly. His cheeks were still damp, a sight I could hardly stand to see no matter how stressed I was. "I still want the story, but you said...so..."

I nodded. "Very well. Head on up, I'll be right behind you."

"But we're not ready," he squeaked, the conundrum posing a problem for him.

"I'm aware of that, Kyle," I told him gently, finding a new well of patience to draw from. Too late, of course, but better to have it now while I made amends. "I need to apologize, I spoke without thinking earlier. If you need help, you've no need to fear punishment for it. I will read to you afterward."

His optimism was cautious, but he nodded all the same and sprinted back upstairs. I could feel the daggers in my sister's gaze, still far more pleasant than the foolish behavior I had been partaking in. For the first time this evening, I felt a spark of hope my actions may be right.

"Really, Cory?"

"I'm their father, Lisa, not their warden." The words were so very right, reminding me of how best to steel myself for the sake of my children. "If they need help, I will give it."

They did need me. First, it was Kyle and his teeth. Next, the instant I was tucking them into bed Sarah was clinging to me for dear life. She was begging me to keep her and her brother, to not send them away. No amount of reassurances would calm her, so I simply cradled her close and hummed lullabies. They both fell asleep quickly then, exhausted from the day we had all endured.

There was still plenty to do, I knew, and a wasted supper to clean up, but for the life of me I could not move. With Sarah tucked in my arms and Kyle nestled into his bed, I took a moment to be grateful I had them at all. As the slightest hollow ache started in my chest, I was glad I was here to suffer through the worst with them.

Even if I had failed tonight, I would simply have to be a better father in the morning.

~~ * ~ * ~ * ~~

Tuesday

The air was dryly chilled today, the wind biting even through the long coat I had found in my belongings when unpacking. We had dropped to freezing temperatures twice now, although we had yet to get snow. Taking in the mind-numbing gray clouds in the sky, however, I knew that was soon to change.

Lisa's steadfast insistence on shoes was admittedly beneficial with this bitter weather. The city had not gotten so aggressively cold last year, and I was still not entirely accustomed to the severity of winter or summer just yet.

Broken Orbit

Too many years living in only stagnant temperatures had arrested my tolerance to the more extreme seasons.

The soil crunched beneath my boots as I walked the fence lines, the ground already beginning to freeze. If I wanted a clear look at these fences, it would have to be today, before they were half-buried for the next several months. It was not a consuming task, counting broken or leaning posts and what sections may need sorting out come spring. The old, smaller animal pens seemed to have taken the brunt of the damage over the years, giving me plenty of time to think even as I mulled over my options for repair.

My thoughts did not wander far, wondering instead just how long it would take for the old farm to be legally mine. Could I own land? I could own a vehicle and a home, so I supposed it would be ridiculous to draw the line at land.

Lisa had been all too happy to hear my desire to buy the derelict farm from her, I recalled with a sigh. My breath hit the air in a puff of smoke. She claimed she had only held onto the farm so long to honor a request from Father. He had wanted me to inherit it, and in the event Mother was correct and I ever came home...

"Stubborn old goat," I muttered to myself, glad for it all the same. Their refusal to let me fade away silently was a comfort I had not anticipated enjoying so wholly. It gave me the opportunity to act myself a proper son now, to keep on with my parents' work and home. Perhaps my children might even have the desire to inherit it after me. It would only be right to keep it within the Lawrence family, after all.

Karma Rose

A blast of bitter wind cut through my thoughts, biting to the bone and painfully cold across my wings. I would need to find my cloak if winter settled in with more weather like this! With a quiet shudder, I finished with my counting of posts. Not too many broken, but plenty I would need to straighten out when the ground thawed in spring. Another gust of icy air breaking against me had me hurrying for the house. How had I endured these days when I was younger?!

When I scrambled indoors, the air burned hotly against my skin. I sighed in relief, stripping my jacket and boots by the back door. Once I finished, I found the rooms of the house to be conspicuously quiet. At this time of day, Leilani commonly had the two little ones engaged in some sort of activity, often resulting in shrieking laughter. Instead, I heard tamed voices speaking in the living room. I made my way toward the front entryway, peering into the room in question and smiling at the sight I found.

Kyle and Sarah both sat on the sofa, while Leilani was cross-legged on the floor in front of them. Kyle clutched a stack of large rectangular cards while his sister held one up at a time for Leilani to see. Flashcards? I realized then what they were doing.

"Okay, now what's this one, Leilani?" asked Sarah patiently, holding up a new card.

Leilani frowned deeply at the image, moaning in confusion as she forced out awkwardly, "Dock."

"Dog. D-og. Dog."

"D-awe-gck," she repeated tensely, straining for the correct pronunciation. The last consonant was giving her more trouble than was fair for how hard she worked at it. Still, I felt a spark of pride, for her and my children both.

Kyle shrugged. "That's close. Right, Sarah?"

"Yeah, I guess. We'll work on it later," agreed Sarah with a shrug, trading with her brother for a new card. "What about this one, Leilani?"

"Is cat?"

The children cheered for her, making Leilani laugh excitedly. I chuckled, smiling at the scene. It was heartwarming and bittersweet, watching them having such a wonderful time together. I only hoped they did not feel as I did, how there was someone wrongfully missing this season.

Before they could notice my presence, I slipped upstairs to shower after my long day of work.

~~ * ~ * ~ * ~~

Thursday

"Hold still so I can get you ready!" I chuckled as Kyle squirmed with excitement. I checked his hat and scarf before slipping his hands into mittens.

"*Now* can I go?" he whined anxiously. I smiled patiently and did up the laces of his boots. "Sarah got to go outside already!"

"Sarah was completely dressed," I pointed out. I gave his shoulder a quick pat. "There you are, Kyle, you may—"

"Thanks, Dad!" He was out the door and off the

porch in nearly the same second, screaming far too enthusiastically to be healthy.

I closed the door to finish readying myself. As much as I loathed the boots Lisa had initially surprised me with, I had to admit there was an element of practicality to them in this weather. Certainly more than the open sandals I had been making do with, at least. I slipped on my gloves and long coat, throwing a scarf around my neck as I made for the door.

Leilani was watching me intently, eyes wide and curious. "Where?"

"Just outside, Leilani," I reassured her. "Kyle and Sarah insist on playing in the snow."

"S-no?" She peered out the open door anxiously. "No good. White. Like fire dust."

"Ash. Hold on, now. Have you never seen snow?" I wondered, more to myself than asking it of her. By her puzzled look of terror, I assumed not. "It is perfectly safe, Leilani. Wait here." I stepped out and collected a handful of fresh powder from the porch railing, offering it to her for inspection. "See now? Perfectlyly sa—Leilani, wait!"

The demoness tore across the porch in much the same fashion my son had, a wide grin on her face. She wore nothing more than the light summer dress she favored, navy blue cloth nowhere near thick enough to keep her warm in this weather. I closed the door hurriedly, knowing she would need the house as warm as possible when I finally caught her to return inside.

"Leilani! Get back inside, it's too cold for this!" I called worriedly as she ran about barefoot, mad with laughter. She appeared gloriously feral as she flitted about in the falling snow, wings spread wide to catch the flakes on her membranes. "Leilani, please, you could catch cold!"

Arrogance against the seasons was how I had fallen ill in my youth, after all, was it not? Yet she seemed completely unbothered, looking like she had danced from the pages of a fairytale. Her coral skin contrasted brightly against the gray and white of winter, like a living embodiment of spring. Behind her, the children did their best to follow along, giggling and twirling in the snow.

I stopped where I was, my boots becoming too cumbersome to move quickly. Not that I could have kept pace with my bulk, compared to her lithe frame. I scowled at the scene, all at once frustrated and enthralled. They made their way to where I stood, my children breathless, all three of them grinning.

"I take it you've had your fun, then?" They nodded. I held my gloved hand out to Leilani. "Good. I need to take Leilani inside, and I will be back out in a moment."

"But why? We want to play with Leilani, too," protested Sarah sadly. Kyle nodded silently, wide eyes pleading.

"She's not dressed for this weather, children," I explained, glad when the demoness accepted my hand without complaint. "Come now, Leilani."

As soon as she saw I was guiding her to the porch, however, she halted. Her hand stayed in mine, but she refused to budge her bare feet. The abrupt stop caught me off-guard, as much surprised by the defiance as I was by the weighted strength she threw into the gesture. She was tiny compared to me, how was she so strong? Leilani cocked her head to one side, upset by something.

"No inside. S-no like home, my home." She forced the words out, struggling with their pronunciations desperately. "Home no Bravery? No good, no words."

"Leilani..." I sighed, breath turning to a puffed cloud of white. She was begging me to understand, I knew, but I felt as if I had only half of the words she wanted to speak. It was the least I could do to try to communicate, was it not? "Your home had snow?"

She pondered for a moment before shaking her head slowly. "No. Like s-no."

"Like snow? It was...white? No, green reminds you of home. Ah...cold? Your home was cold?" I offered, at a loss otherwise.

"Cold." She tried the word with a frown. She held out a hand to catch snow in her palm, offering it to me. "Is cold?"

"Yes, snow is cold."

"Is cold inside?" she asked, doing what she could to explore the words she was learning.

"No, inside is warm."

Her eyes lit up. "Cold is good. Home is cold."

"Your home was green and cold." The details were bare, but it made her smile to hear I knew something of the place. "Before Bravery."

Leilani nodded, copper eyes sparkling with her elation. I sighed again, relenting. I released her hand with a nod, trusting her to know better what she was familiar with. Her replying grin was nothing short of ecstatic, fangs glinting with the same white as the dancing snow.

The moment was interrupted as a snowball broke against my horn. Snow scattered in my hair and fell on my face, catching in the grooves in my bone. Leilani giggled, the sound nearly a chirp as it caught in her throat. I turned my head slowly to look at my daughter, her arm still tensed from her throw. The two children pointed to each other as they realized the mistake. I raised one brow, grinning.

"Uh-oh. Sarah, run!" screeched Kyle, tearing off. Not quickly enough, as I had him slung over one shoulder in a fit of laughter only seconds later. Another snowball caught me in the leg, barely more than a tap.

I took a knee, crying out playfully, "Whatever shall I do?! I've been hit!"

There was a weight falling across my wings, little hands clutching at my coat to hold on. I allowed Kyle to slide from my shoulder, waiting for him to run off before I fell forward to land in the snow dramatically. Sarah landed on my back between my wings, giggling at her triumph.

"Alas, I've been vanquished!" I choked and groaned theatrically, resulting in even more laughter from the girl on my back. The snow was cold beneath me, but still bearable for the moment. Despite my overdone act of defeat, I grimaced as a mound of powdered snow fell across my horns and settled in my hair. "All right, now, who's the culprit?!"

I looked up to find Leilani grinning at me, unashamed for attacking an unarmed man pinned to the ground. From behind my head, a snowball flew and hit the demoness across her exposed chest, flakes catching in the folds of her dress. She laughed, outnumbered now as my children came to my aid.

For just a moment, I felt perfectly content. There were no demands to pursue greater things, no wants for missing times and people. I laughed as Leilani joined me in the snow, Kyle hopping between her wings with a grin. I felt this, warm and happy to the core even in the chill of winter.

~~ * ~ * ~ * ~~

Friday

My sigh was tired, worn after another day tending the children and getting this house settled into. My evening habits were passing by in a blur, Leilani following me closer than my own shadow. Not unusual for her when the children were asleep, although this evening she was more vocal and curious than her norm.

She watched from the hall as I combed out my hair and checked my claws to determine if they needed filing. All the while, she was whispering at me in her native language. It sounded as though she had opinions of my habits, not all of them positive, many of them inquisitive. Her fingers found the streak of silver I often forgot was there, a disbelieving scowl on her face before she tucked it back with the rest of my hair.

I paid her no mind, far too accustomed to this by now. Between her and the children, my personal boundaries had turned into optional guidelines rather than, well, boundaries.

Leilani was distracted at last when I readied my toothbrush. She grabbed the paste from where I had set it on the counter, sniffing at it. "What is?"

How had she not noticed this routine ritual by now? "Toothpaste."

Perhaps she has been too preoccupied tasting the bathroom soaps, I thought with a shrug, keeping on and minding myself.

She watched me brushing, sniffing the tube again. It was too late for me to stop her before—

"ACK!" The look of utter disgust on her face had me choking on my laughter and toothbrush alike, struggling to keep quiet for the sleeping children across the hall.

"Leilani, no," I hissed as I fought a grin. "It—It's like soap for your teeth, not—Oh, heavens, you are such a helpless thing!"

Her whimper only made me chuckle. I found a spare toothbrush in one of the drawers, lost for how we had gone so long already without encountering this particular habit. I suppose I had been too busy to notice sooner, but with half the tube already nearly consumed by her adventurous curiosity, now was as good a time as any to teach her.

~~ * ~ * ~ * ~~

Thirteenth Week After Paradise

Karma Rose

Sunday

December 25th, 2011

I wish I could say today, of all days, was free of strife. Overall, I know it has gone splendidly. Dustin was able to join us, and Jeff even made a brief appearance.

These are the things I must focus on, the happy moments. Like Kyle and Sarah at the tree this morning, and the absolute joy of watching their excitement while unwrapping gifts. It was only small trinkets, given how little time I have had to spare in any direction, but they were overjoyed all the same.

I need to keep my attention on the good of it all, but it feels like an insurmountable endeavor in light of what else I have learned today. Ethan came by, unannounced, apparently thinking himself included when he heard from Lisa we had a holiday gathering planned. He never was the brightest of us, but I at least hoped he may not have been quite so dense as to...

He was touting nonsense. It must have been. I thought it was, at least. Although the details he shared seem to make more and more sense the longer I have to mull them over. Little things, honestly. Why was the ranger out in the rain that night? How did he know to look for me in the storm, to listen for the boom of my wings, even over the crashing thunder?

We had been careful. My entire life, we had all been meticulous in the exposure the outside world had of me. Such paranoia had served us well for so many years. Why should it have failed then, of all times, when the

286

Broken Orbit

campgrounds should have been empty?

Ethan sold me out; he confessed as much today. Which then meant Paul was only ever trying to keep me safe through all of the ensuing mishaps. My brother admitted today to informing officials of my existence then later paying off the ranger who shot me. He broke our family for a place in our grandfather's will and an opportunity to romance Katelyn.

"She was better off heartbroken than with you," he had said.

I am not proud to say I very literally threw him from the porch once I had collected myself well enough to react. Even now, I find it difficult to manage this feeling of betrayal. I suppose I should not be surprised by his villainy at this point in life. Still, criminal behavior aside, I had always considered us to be family until now. It was his treachery which led to our mother's ill health, my imprisonment, his opportunity to rape Katelyn.

There is good to be found. I have to remember there is good here. Paul had not been my undoing. I have rights now. Leilani has rights, as well, no matter the news of possible changes. I have Kyle and Sarah. None of these would exist if not for Ethan. There is good here.

Why do I feel this heavy fatigue in my chest, then? It is a tar-like sensation of hopelessness that seems to devour my lungs if I think on it too long. He betrayed not just me but our entire family. He broke our mother. He continues to use our sister, neglecting to tell her the truth. I suppose it is for the best by now; she deserves the rest of her life to remain intact, or as much as she can manage.

It was a good day. I know it was a good day, but

for those brief few minutes when I meant to tell him to leave. It was a good day. Just months ago, I was able to move past it all when I thought Paul had been the culprit.

Why can I not push on now, then? Why do I feel trapped and hollow? It was a good day. I want to feel it. Outside of this aching numb, I want to feel today was good.

~~ * ~ * ~ * ~~

Wednesday

There was a hearty thump as the box I held landed on the cluttered desk. Its contents let loose a cloud of dust, choking me for a moment. The air cleared quickly enough, my cough feeling delayed as a result.

"This room's looking better," commented Robert, setting a smaller box beside my own. He was more careful about dust after seeing my fit.

"With still plenty more work to be done," I sighed tiredly. I peeked inside my box, finding it stuffed full of yellowed old paper scraps. Shuffling through the top papers, I discovered countless drawings and scribbles, recognizing my unpracticed penmanship from when I was much younger. Mother had kept my attempts at learning on my own? I moved the box to the stack of unnecessary items. "I have a suspicion someone keeps slipping more things in here when I look away. It seems the only explanation for this unending chore."

"Maybe we'll find the stash of socks that get lost in the dryer," he laughed as he pushed the smaller box toward me for inspection. I chuckled at the thought.

"Perhaps the missing kitchen towels, as well?" Another box of photographs, this one seeming to be dominated by Dustin's wedding. Goodness, how many photographers had his wife needed for one event? I set the box with the others which would need to be sorted further.

We continued to work in silence. No matter how many musty boxes we went through, it felt as though they were simply multiplying. I worked to remain patient with the task, finding the precious resource criminally deficient as boredom began to set in. My companion must have sensed the atmosphere's utter lacking, clearing his throat quietly.

"So, with there being female demons and all..." Robert's words trailed off, a sly glance my way eliciting a heavy sigh from me. Not this nonsense again. If he mentioned Leilani... "Well, maybe one day you'll meet a pretty girl with nice horns and have some kids of your own."

I set my paper stack down and fixed him with a stare which told him everything wrong with what he had said. He blanched, stumbling over his words to correct himself.

"I-I mean—Not that Kyle and Sarah—I am so sorry," he finally settled on what to say.

"They are my children, Robert," I told him, startled by the hostility I heard in my voice. My tail emphasized it, smacking against the floor sharply. "I teach them, I feed them, I tuck them in at night and check their room for monsters after a nightmare. They call me Dad.

They are mine."

He kept his gaze on his hands, fidgeting with the desk's edge anxiously. It took me a moment to smooth my features, realizing I had nearly bared my fangs in my upset. "I'm sorry, Cory, that was—That was insensitive of me."

"It certainly was," I agreed more calmly. My attention wandered back to the papers I had been sifting through. There was no focusing back on this dull task, not after such an abrupt rush of indignation. "You have my apologies, however, for my harsh reaction."

"No need to apologize." Robert was quick to assure me of this, his smile contrite. "I was rude, and you've every right to be assertive about your family. It's honestly good to see, even if I wasn't on the preferable end of things," he admitted.

I shrugged, feeling awkward now. "I never thought much of it, but...they *are* my children, Robert. No matter how our little family came about, they are *mine*."

"I know, bud." His smile broadened and he nodded. "It's not hard to see it. The kids have settled in pretty well, all things considered. You're doing great, Cory."

"Thank you." I nodded, managing a small smile in reply. It had been far from easy, and there was still endless room for improvement, but it was reassuring to hear from him I was at least competent. He was a father himself, with a profession that provided a unique insight into the situation, as well. Even if I felt his praise was somewhat overstated, it was a small relief from my usual anxieties.

Broken Orbit

~~ * ~ * ~ * ~~

Saturday

This is what loss looks like.

The thought was clear in my mind, detached as I observed at a distance. The way the Avatars had taught me to be, neutral. Impartial. As the grief-struck cries rang out, I found that strict disconnect difficult to maintain.

The bull I watched threw back his head, a strangled bellow tearing from him. His voice was mangled, his grip on the broken body of his son still tight. I couldn't ignore the stirring remorse in my chest. Following instructions, I hadn't acted when I should have. I'd stayed out of the fray, to keep myself alive until my Master could make use of me. I had effectively allowed this to happen.

This wasn't right.

I stepped forward toward the bull, listening to his pitiful growls that built to another deep cry. His tears caught in the grooves of his face, body shaking with sobs. He clutched his son closer. For the first time, I truly saw the boy. He was younger than me, still obviously immature based on his face and how thin his horns were. Certainly younger than twenty, even. Barely more than a child.

"I'm sorry."

The bull snarled at me, the sound rolling off into a sob. He bared his fangs, grip tightening on his son as he

demanded brokenly, "Where were your horns?!
Worthless Shaman, where were you?!"

Waiting for my Master, I thought bitterly. Where
was he? He wasn't here to stop this, and I had allowed it
to happen by sitting to the side assuming he would save
us. I was tired of waiting. I was done watching these
things happen when we needed a hero.

~~ * ~ * ~ * ~~

Again last night, my dreams had bled into
memories not my own. While I found it to be a welcome
reprieve at times, what I had seen felt far too personal to
excuse knowing it without permission. Even an unusually
hectic morning had not been able to shake my guilt, and I
knew I must find a way to apologize.

So I stared at the bathroom mirror, sighing deeply.
I must have been mad, thinking this might work, but doing
nothing seemed to be a poor choice, as well. It felt nearly
criminal, to have seen things so private, knowing now
who's memories I had witnessed. Clearing my throat
nervously, I kept my voice quiet in the hopes my sister
would not hear me downstairs, nor Leilani or the children
playing across the hall.

"I...I imagine you think this foolish, Braxen,
speaking to a mirror, but...I hope you might be listening,"
I began awkwardly. I scowled at my reflection, monstrous
and monstrously scarred. Still, it was the face my children
begged to check the closet for sinister shadows and read
them to sleep. "I saw something last night. A memory, I
think, one of yours.

"You have my apologies, Braxen, I do not intend to intrude upon your privacy," I told the glass hurriedly. Oh, this was foolish! "Yet, I also feel that...that you were attempting to speak to me, in your own way. I find it comforting to know, in any case. It helps with this feeling of isolation, knowing that somewhere, at least, there is someone who knows some parts of me too...savage, to show the world I live in."

The memories played again in my mind, the sounds and images of what a grieving demon was. It was brutal, instinctive, so much more than anything I had allowed or done. Perhaps in my time with the humans, I had learned to tame my primal nature, to allow it to leave through speech and intentions toward a better future.

Idiot Human.

I started, surprised as I stared at the mirror. I thought I had heard him reply, perhaps seen a flash of orange and violet in the reflection. Of course, it was all the more likely I was losing my mind in the wake of all of this loss.

"I suppose I should finish this by thanking you, Braxen. Deliberately or not, you have brought to my attention that I still need to grieve. I will, in time. However, at this moment there is no opportunity. It can wait a while longer, once it numbs over a bit," I muttered with a frown. Perhaps it was not the most ideal option, but it was the only one I saw available to me. "I should also say, no matter what the Avatars have told you, I am proud of you, Braxen. You are a good man, with good intentions. I...I should return to my day, and I imagine you need to stop laughing at my lunacy. Until next time, then?"

     With no better idea of how to end this one-sided conversation, I nodded at the mirror and left.

<u>Chapter Nine:</u>
<u>Relapse</u>

Fourteenth Week After Paradise

<u>Monday</u>

"Kyle, I'm afraid I need to tie those today." I knelt to confiscate the laces from my son's slow-working fingers. He pouted at me but cooperated, allowing me to tie his shoes quickly. "We're running late. *How* are we late?"

How are we late?!

I had woken two hours before the bus would arrive to start breakfast. The children were up thirty minutes after me, eating. I had triple checked everything the evening before to ensure eating and dressing were all we needed to be ready. Thirty minutes for breakfast, twenty for dressing, ten to help Sarah with her hair, five more for a final inspection on backpacks and supplies...

Where had the remaining time gone?!

"You both have your backpacks?" I asked, staring at the straps over their shoulders. "Shoes, pants, coats, heads firmly attached? Yes? Good, we need to get outside. Go on now!"

Karma Rose

I opened the front door, hearing the rumble of a large vehicle down the road. Kyle and Sarah seemed to be taking the porch steps a fraction at a time, judging by how slowly they moved, and I scooped them both up in a hurry. Sprinting to the roadside, I barely arrived before the bus as it groaned to a halt. At least there would be little time waiting in this cold weather.

Setting the children back on their own feet, I did one last look-over, finding myself surprisingly anxious to send them off for the day. They let me fuss, too tired to protest. The door to the bus opened noisily, my breath catching in my throat and creating a cloud of smoke in the brisk air.

"You two be safe, all right? Mind your teachers, eat your vegetables."

"We'll be okay, Dad," sighed Sarah, rolling her eyes even as she smiled. I knew she enjoyed how I worried. A beneficial thing, as I felt I might go mad with it. "It's just school."

"Yeah, Dad." Kyle followed her example, and I could not help but smile.

"All right, I know," I muttered, giving them each a quick peck on the forehead. "I love you both. Have a good day, hm?"

The driver cleared their throat nervously, annoyed by my delays but appearing too intimidated to say much else otherwise. My smile turned apologetic and I steered my children toward the vehicle. I stepped back as they climbed in, the door slamming shut behind them. My eyes followed them through the windows, the bus lurching forward well before they had found seats. I bit back my protests, linking my hands behind my back. My chest felt hollow from missing them already, worry settling in about their first day away from Leilani or me since leaving the village.

How was I supposed to do this again tomorrow?

~~ * ~ * ~ * ~~

No amount of work could distract me. Even glaring at the hen house and its sorry state of disrepair did little to ease my worry. Oh, there were days' worth of things to be done with the one affair alone. Were the children settling in? I would need to make a trip out for tools, parts for repair, and hinges, by the look of how the door hung so precariously. Had they found their classes? Then there was the covered yard, looking like the wire netting had been the plaything of a bear. What if they got scared while they were away? Nervous? If the other children tormented them?

A shrill scream like a banshee ripped me away from my worries and distractions alike.

I whirled around, heart racing in panic, as I saw Leilani darting out the back door without a care for the biting chill in the air, still in her nightclothes. Her head was twisting this way and that, looking for something. She found me, sprinting over quickly. Her face was torn apart with fear and heartbreak, tears streaming down her cheeks.

"Leilani?! What happened?!" I looked her over for cuts or bruises as best I could with her panicked flailing.

"Babies!" she cried, copper eyes drowning in grief. My heart stopped. Had something happened?! "Babies no here!"

It took me an unbearably long moment to get a solid grasp on the situation, having to pause to understand why she was panicking. When I did, I breathed a sigh of relief, realizing she must have forgotten or misunderstood the conversation about school last week. I gripped her shoulders firmly, commanding her attention.

"Leilani, the babies are all right," I told her gently, and she perked up hopefully. "They went to school, is all. They will be home later today."

"School?" she echoed weakly, staring at me as she struggled for anything to compare the word to, anything to help her understand. "No words!"

"They are safe, Leilani," I persisted firmly. "They went to learn."

She knew that word, *learn*. Her eyes went wide and she nodded eagerly, taking a deep breath to steady herself. "I go."

"No, no, we stay here." Again, her heartbroken confusion. "They went to learn with other children. We do not go there unless there is an occasion for it."

The demoness was growing frustrated. She slapped my hands away, worried and angry from it. Leilani began to rant at me in her native language, voice strained. Despite the communication barrier, I had the distinct feeling of being reprimanded, scolded for my blind acceptance my children were safe anywhere but at my side. She was seething, lividly spitting profanities which I could not understand beyond basic intent. All I could do was stare, dumbfounded, and wait for her to calm down.

"No *euliyah!*" snapped Leilani at the end of her tirade. She gestured to my face, making me flinch. She bared her fangs with a rabid hiss, "No horns!"

No horns? What did horns have to do with my scolding? I stared at her hornless face, recalling then the distinct anatomical difference between men and women. The human equivalent played in my mind.

Ah.

"Leilani—"

"No words!" The declaration was more than her usual plea for assistance. It was a stern command, an exasperated outcry at my stupidity.

I held up my hands, a silent gesture to ask for a moment of calm. She relented, tail whipping behind her. She glared at me, an adorably petite thing looking more like a flustered fairy than a medieval monster. She bared her fangs and I had to resist a smirk in the face of her upset.

"Let me make you breakfast, and we can talk more about this. All right? Good. Good."

It had taken all of our collected patience to find a way to discuss the children being away at school. By the end of it, Leilani had begrudgingly accepted this practice was not all too different from the village, allowing children to find mentors and spend their days away with them. Had she not filled such a role herself for a time?

Karma Rose

Acceptance did not equate to the enjoyment of it, nor forgiveness of my blunders for sending them off without fully explaining it to Leilani. I wanted to be frustrated by her outlandish overreaction, but I found it comforting to know I was not the only one worried about the little ones being away from home. It was even amusing, watching her indulge in those instinctive reactions I kept so tightly restrained.

Leilani was angry with me. Hissing, growling, baring her fangs with the rare yowling snarl. It was fascinating, how I understood every minute detail of her displeasure. It was also humorous, the tiny thing she was being so brazenly upset with me. I knew in her own culture she was challenging me and my oafishness. It was all I could do not to laugh.

Overall, the distraction from my nagging concern was welcome.

"No horns," she grumbled, beginning at last to tire of her spite. Outside, I heard the rumble of the bus which had taken the children this morning.

I was out of my chair quickly, Leilani not a step behind as I hurried out to the front porch, too preoccupied to think of donning anything over my thin sweater. The bus was stopped along the roadside, two children disembarking. I grinned, restraining myself from running off the porch in my relief to see them returning home. Leilani was another matter, a blur of coral as she all but flew across the distance to see the charges she adored so entirely.

The three of them chattered excitedly with one another, and once they were inside the warm home I

300

listened. I hung on every word happily. I had not realized just how empty the house had been without my children here. The evening went on as usual, with the exception of my helping with homework. Namely, keeping the two of them company and hoping that if they had any questions to ask it might have been something I knew, with what little informal education I had managed to get along with.

Bedtime came and went, and before I knew it I was waking in the morning to do it all again. Leilani woke with my alarm to see Kyle and Sarah off, the start of a new habit for the four of us while my sister slept through it all.

~~ * ~ * ~ * ~~

Saturday

I stumbled into the kitchen through the back door, wincing as I had to duck inside. Going to the icebox, I searched for an ice pack, desperate for anything to relieve the ache in my shoulder. I found what I was after, taking it with me to the table. I stripped from my coat clumsily, shoulder burning as I pressed the pack to it with a sigh.

"Are you okay?" asked Lisa, concerned. I started, too distracted to notice her sooner, standing at the stove cooking.

I took a seat at the kitchen table, grunting as even something so simple jarred the joint angrily. "All things considered, yes."

She heard the strain in my voice, setting aside her wooden spoon and coming to check on me. "What's wrong?"

"I was patching up the old coop," I admitted with a groan, grimacing. I rolled my shoulder tenderly, hoping I could stretch it enough so the nerves might find some relief. "The roof needed work, although I was able to finish with it. Then the door needs new hinges, and not to start on the framework for the covered yard. I may as well be building *that* from scratch."

She giggled. "You haven't changed a bit. Not wasting a second to get started on fixing this old farm up, are you?"

"I have wasted more than enough time already," I grumbled, a hint of bitterness marring my tone. Damn, but this ache would not cease!

"So, did one of the support beams hit you or something?" she asked, eyeing my shoulder warily. "I mean, it looks pretty swollen..."

I shook my head, mindful of my horns in the small space. "No, my shoulder is just terrible these days."

"What happened to it?" she wondered, still worried but accepting my dismissal of the injury. She went back to her cooking, keeping a watchful eye on me.

"A routine surgery went awry," I replied, words distorted by a hiss of pain as my shoulder began to stab and throb in time with my pulse. "I was told it was an accident."

"Well, that's a fat sack of horse shit," she scoffed skeptically, startling me.

"Lisa!" I gasped, staring at her in shock. "You kissed our mother with that mouth?"

"Dad did first," she retorted quickly, making us

both laugh. I winced as the laughter shook my shoulder, unable to help my grin, at least. She glanced over her shoulder, guilty in her humor as she nodded to the entryway and my children standing there.

"Dad, what's—"

"*Lisa!*" I scolded again, sparing her a disapproving glare.

The two little ones shared a look, Sarah saying slowly, "We were wondering what's for dinner?"

They hopped up into chairs to join me at the table. Sarah leaned over with a conspiratorial glance at Kyle, whispering, "It's okay, Dad, I already know what a sack of poo is."

I joined in her cautious glance, whispering back, "Then you understand why such vulgarity is considered inappropriate?"

She watched as Kyle distracted himself, leaning in his chair in the hopes he might spy whatever Lisa was cooking for supper. "I don't know what a ver-gar is, but I know it's something not nice to say in public or with strangers. Kyle used to say that all the time, but don't worry I won't tell him that Aunt Lisa says it, too."

"Thank you, sweetheart," I murmured with a smile, reaching over to give her hand a quick squeeze. She grinned at me, proud of herself.

"Babies." Leilani's call came from upstairs, her quiet footsteps descending after it. She appeared in the entryway, a maternal smile on her face. "Babies, you have mess. Come clean."

As always, they obeyed with little protest, as if she spun her singular sort of magic into her words. With everything else demons seemed capable of, it would not surprise me. Despite that, I knew it was simply a matter in which they were far too comfortable defying me, whereas they adored Leilani too much to ever risk upsetting her. Watching her gentle smile, I could not fault their favoritism.

The little demoness looked to me then, eyes falling on how tenderly I was nursing my pained shoulder. "Hurts?"

I nodded, wincing as even that aggravated the old injury. "Yes, my shoulder, that blasted thing is utterly usele—What are you-?! *Ah*. That...helps, thank you," I sighed in relief.

"Father has Healer," she explained awkwardly. "I learn...small?"

Leilani's fingers moved with all of the precision she used with her crafts, finding the root of it all just below where my wing met my shoulder. With her gentle massaging, the pain was finally easing, the joint feeling better than it had in years. She pulled the ice pack from my hand carefully, setting it atop the area she had been working.

"Thank you, Leilani," I sighed again, turning my head to smile gratefully. Her replying smile was radiant, brimming with her glee that she had been helpful.

She held up the ice pack, my pain now nearly gone entirely. "Where?"

Lisa spoke up then, showing the demoness to the icebox and where to find the packs. While Leilani was busy memorizing it all, my sister shot me a mischievous look laced with implications. She nodded to Leilani pointedly, reminding me of how obnoxiously heavy-handed she had been with our brothers and me when we were younger. I replied with a stern glower and a shake of my head. Lisa rolled her eyes, and somehow we were both able to return to our nonchalant smiles as Leilani turned around completely with her proud grin.

Before there was any more to the exchanges, my children came tearing through the house, sounding like a stampede down the stairs. I reached out as they sprinted our way, catching Kyle carefully and slinging him over my good shoulder in the same motion. He screeched with laughter.

"I've got you now, my boy!" I chuckled, amused by his half-hearted struggle which indicated he did not quite want to escape. "Oh, but it seems I'm missing a daughter."

Sarah stopped, debating saving her brother, and took a wary step forward. Just within my reach, I scooped her up, as well, crowing, "Ah-ha! I've apprehended the criminals! And just where were you two off to in such a hurry, that you needed to run in the house?"

"Outside," giggled Sarah, and I could hear the grin in her voice.

"Outside? Whatever for?"

"We're gonna build a big snow fort!" cried Kyle excitedly.

"A secret fort," added Sarah boastfully.

"Well, now, that seems to be a task of the utmost importance," I agreed, lowering them one at a time to the floor. I took in their proper snow attire, proud they had managed on their own, if somewhat sloppily. I nodded gravely. "Continue, then."

"*Without* running in the house," reminded Lisa sternly. I shared a guilty smirk with my children as they shuffled off with pointedly slow steps. Leilani followed them out, ever-watchful and unflinchingly oblivious to the cold.

They were not outside but a moment before my sister started in.

"So, is she single?"

"*Lisa!*"

~~ * ~ * ~ * ~~

Seventeenth Week After Paradise

Sunday

January 22nd, 2012

Today, I held a celebration for Kyle and Sarah's birthdays. The two little monsters of mine are now seven and nine. Born just a week apart from one another, I opted for the simpler endeavor of a single party. Given how I have been increasingly fatigued of late, and to the point of utter disinterest in even the simplest of tasks, I did not want to risk one or the other having less of my efforts.

All things considered, I suppose the event went over well. Naturally, there was some sibling jealousy present over sharing the spotlight, but nothing I had not anticipated given their ages. Nor was it anything I could not easily dissuade their interest from.

Broken Orbit

Robert's family attended, as well as Jeff who, to my surprise, brought Jeanine and the cousins living with him at the orchard home. What I had initially guessed would be a small gathering quickly escalated to something much more boisterous. For the children, it was an absolute daydream of games and praises, their grins the biggest I have ever seen. For those more mature, it was a memorial of sorts, watching over our dear Katelyn's legacy appreciatively.

Bailey's presence was possibly the most excitable, by far. Even compared to my children's ecstasy with the day, she was so far beyond the moon I worried she may have trouble returning to Earth. Firstly, it was her simple joy at seeing the children she loved to play with. Then came Leilani, and the poor girl nearly fainted, forgetting to breathe in her excitement!

She was the only one to draw attention to Leilani's presence, however. Everyone else acted nonchalantly, as though an extra demon in the Lawrence home was of no consequence. I am grateful I was granted the small favor, allowing both the demoness and I to focus more wholly on the children we had gathered together for.

My only qualm with the day has been cleaning the aftermath. Namely, the pondering of how icing could have made its way to the ceiling, and how to wash the confection out of the finer dress I bought for Sarah some time ago. A perfectly good mess for a perfectly wonderful day.

~~ * ~ * ~ * ~~

Karma Rose

Wednesday

"It's been a while," commented Robert idly as he settled down into Father's old chair. "Are you sure you're okay?"

"Yes, Robert, I'm certain that I no longer require your professional services," I chuckled, although I was admittedly nervous. It was still odd how I could not hear Kyle or Sarah in the house during the day since they had been enrolled in classes. What was I supposed to do with myself? It seemed there would never be enough work in the day to get me through the hours between breakfast and when they returned home near supper. "I could use a friend, however."

"School, huh?" he guessed with a grin and a nod. "Every parent gets that, don't worry."

"They attended school in the city, and it never bothered me, but this is..." I sighed, shaking my head and ignoring the empty pit in my throat. "I had Kate then."

"I'm sorry, Cory."

"Please, Robert, I am tired of those words," I begged quietly, grief sneaking into my chest slowly. It was silenced easily enough, an oddly hollow ache left in its place. The children had given me much more than a lost opportunity. They presented a reason to pull through these last few months, helping me to find a well of strength I never knew I possessed. Enough to forget I had not grieved still, now numb where the aching loss had once been.

"I'm s—I can see why," he corrected himself in an

awkward mumble.

"I miss her, Robert," I admitted the words, for the first time truly allowing myself to feel them and everything they meant. My body yearned to see her, to hold her, and I was pained even more so knowing I never could. I was glad I had the numb in my system, dulling the pain better than whiskey in my veins.

My friend nodded slowly, remorseful. "I know, bud. I miss her, too."

There was little else to say then, a stifling silence overcoming us. I found myself preferring solitude and the powerfully blissful nothing which came with it. Surely, it was better than sitting and staring at the pain?

Robert stayed a short while longer, my evening playing out as it always did now. Before I knew it, the children were in bed and the household was settled for the evening, leaving me alone in the living room with my book. The hollow sensation of isolation crept over me slowly, dulling my ability to think concisely enough to read. I knew I should have been annoyed, at the least, and perhaps concerned.

Why was it, then, that I found a curious sense of gratification by entertaining this numbness?

~~ * ~ * ~ * ~~

Friday

It had been too long since I had last stepped foot in the old feed and seed store. The shelves had moved, now stocked with dozens of medicines and supplies I had trouble recognizing. The smell was the same, however, rich and comforting as it brought a smile to my lips.

"Welcome to Littleton Feed, how can I—" The younger man greeting me fell short as he turned to see his patron. Doing his best to recover, he continued weakly, "Um, help you...today?"

"It has been some time since I was here last," I admitted, taking it all in and simply glad that it still stood. "My family's farm needs some repair, and—"

"You're Cory," he blurted, still stunned. "William's son, right?"

I kept a polite smile, unnerved by how often I was recognized these days. This had never been a problem in the city, even with my face on every paper. "You have me at a disadvantage, sir."

"Oh, I'm Oliver, my family owns this store," he gushed with an awkward laugh.

It took me a moment, but I grinned when I recalled the name. I caught myself before he could be thoroughly unseated by the expression. "Oliver? Tim's grandson, Oliver?" He nodded with a grin in turn. "I last saw you when you were barely to my knee!"

"I don't remember much of meeting you, but I've heard stories," he confessed. "I go to the memorial every year at the diner, with the rest of my family. I guess it'll be more of a welcome back this year, though."

"A memorial at the diner?" I echoed with a disbelieving frown. He nodded. "Not the Montgomery family's diner?"

"The only diner we've got," he confirmed proudly, laughing at my confusion. "Yeah, Richard turned over a new leaf awhile back."

I laughed, lost at the thought of Richard changing for the better. "Well, congratulations to him, then."

"Yeah." Oliver nodded with a grin, jumping excitedly at a thought. He hurried back behind his counter to pull out some well-worn papers. "I know I have it here somew—Yep, an order from William Lawrence, and he requested it to be filled if you ever showed up. He placed it I think fourteen years ago when it was first up for consideration for demons to be granted rights," he added with a frown, thinking it over. "We all thought it was odd, given you were supposed to be, well...but we couldn't tell him otherwise. He wouldn't hear it, and the state Eleanor was in..."

There certainly was no accounting for small-town gossip and the tiniest details it continued to provide for me. I found myself having to force back the flood of emotions and the tears they brought, sniffling and asking, "What did he buy?"

"Uh..." Oliver looked over the list, whistling idly. "It looks like a complete restock for planting, some parts like door hinges, chicken wire and the like, some chicks, feed, equipment... And a note on the end that says, I knew you'd come home, we missed..."

He frowned, realizing that he had run out of his list to read. He handed me the sheet awkwardly. I scanned the paper, smiling to see Father had thought of repairing the coop already. My eyes strayed to the bottom and the carefully written note there:

I knew you'd come home. We missed you, son.

Karma Rose

I've always been proud of you. In case I don't see you, you should know your mom and I love you.

I turned the page over, hoping for more and finding it blank. I could hear my father's voice all too clearly in those words, blunt and to the point. It was just the sort of stubborn thing for him to do, as well, holding fast to the knowledge I would be home soon. I felt a fresh wave of guilt that I had stopped calling, sniffling again as I smiled for Oliver behind the counter.

"Thank you," I choked, clearing my throat quietly. I laughed awkwardly. "It seems he thought of everything, the stubborn old goat."

"Yeah, sounds like him," agreed Oliver with a sympathetic smile. "I'll start getting everything together. Might be a while for some of those things, since chicks are out of season, but I'll do what I can for you today."

"Well, Oliver, I originally came for the hinges," I admitted with a chuckle, still holding the paper. My tenuous grip on what was left of my father. "I may need to bring a vehicle for the rest."

"If it's all right with you, I wouldn't mind dropping it off myself," he offered, reaching out for the paper and its list. Reluctantly, I returned the scrap.

"If that is no inconvenience to you." I shrugged, accepting of the gesture. "How much would you ask?"

He waved away the question. "A cup of tea and a chance to pay my respects would be more than enough. But you're unloading."

"You would put an old man to work?" I asked, grinning in spite of myself. Again, I caught the action

312

before it startled him, taming myself.

Oliver laughed. "Yeah, when he's in better shape than I am!"

"Oh, very well, then," I agreed with a humored smirk. "I could use the activity."

He nodded with a smile. "Anyway, let me get those hinges for you. I'm sure you've got a busy day to get back to."

I nodded, simply glad to be back at work doing what I knew.

~~ * ~ * ~ * ~~

Eighteenth Week After Paradise

Thursday

"Have you ever wanted to not be tired, my dear?"

My tender whisper was nearly lost to the nighttime symphony of wildlife playing this time of year. In my arms, Katelyn swayed with me in time to the song on the radio. She tilted her head back to smile up at me, that gorgeous face of hers alight with humor.

"Every time I'm with you, mister." Her soft giggle was all I needed to hear, my replying grin wide and gleeful. She barely noticed the fangs that startled so many others, did not mind the claws I had to be unerringly careful with. In her eyes, I was just a man, the same as any other.

"I wish I could give you the world, Katelyn," I murmured, twirling her slowly. Her hand found my

313

shoulder once more, fingers sending shocks of wonderment through my skin. Even in the moonlight, she was simply breathtaking. I yearned for this same safety in the sunlight, to see her deeply colored skin shimmer in the light, to bask in the warmth which so easily mimicked the sensation she filled my chest with.

"I don't need the world when I have you," she replied easily, longing in her eyes. She motioned me closer for a kiss and I did one better, lifting her in my arms with ease. I kissed her, the world falling away from us. How it was that she could do this to me I would never know, granting me this feeling of being so completely human; breaking free of such a blissful kiss should have been criminal. "I love you, Cory."

I sighed softly, my breath a caress in the night. "As I love you, Kate."

Her depthless black eyes broke away to take in the world's range of greys, the sky growing light. "You have to let me go now."

"Stay," I begged softly. I set her feet back on the earth all the same. "I have to go inside, but stay with me, my dear."

"It's just the sun rising, Cory, not the end of the world," she whispered, expression tender. She kissed my palm, pressing her cheek to the calloused skin there. My hand warmed at her touch. "I have to go, mister."

~~ * ~ * ~ * ~~

The scene ended there, a blissful blending of dreams and memories. I opened my eyes to the dark

314

bedroom I had known so long. It was night still, the solitary window barely lit from the stars outside. Regardless, I could see the empty pillow where she had once slept. I thought I should still be able to hear the quiet breathing of her as she rested, see the quick flutter of her closed lids as she dreamed.

My arms ached. I still felt a hollow heat from the dream where she had been, lips pained as my body realized with me we had been lied to. Still, I cherished the gloriously detailed deception which had brought her so near to me, so much closer than she had been in too long now.

I reached my hand out for the empty pillow, imagining what it might be like to feel her once more. I took a shaky breath, stifling my tears to spare the children in the next room from hearing me. A thousand words were caught on my forked tongue, a thousand ways I should have shown her my love and could no longer. I closed my burning eyes shut against the barren space, hating this hollow need as it consumed my entire being from within.

My fingers curled around the empty linens, and all I had left to cling to faded from my mind as I yearned to sleep once more.

~~ * ~ * ~ * ~~

Saturday

"What are your plans for getting the kids through college?" asked Jeff idly as we listened to said little ones chattering at their older cousins.

I sipped at my glass of lemonade politely, ignoring the too-sweet taste. "I was fortunate enough to be compensated for my...cooperation, at the NSISD. I hope to see a financial advisor and plan from there on how best to use it."

"How much does *cooperation* cost these days?" he wondered with a dark hint of bitterness.

I shrugged apathetically. "One might say too much, for the purchaser and purchased alike."

Jeff nodded slowly. "That much?"

"More than Grandfather Charles ever boasted having," I offered, smirking at Jeff's vindictive cackle.

"Oh, what I wouldn't give to see that bastard rolling in his grave," he sighed. He turned to me, losing all humor. "You should bring your sister or Robert with you when you go see that advisor. Maybe Paul's boy, even. Make sure you don't get taken advantage of, you know."

I nodded slowly, glancing from my crimson hand to his ashen, mahogany face. The same black eyes as Kate's stared back at me meaningfully from behind his thick glasses. "Good advice."

He nodded once, glad to see I understood, before looking back at the children struggling to make the apple recipes at hand. The family business. "Good. How's that going for you, by the way? Better than the first time around?"

I sighed quietly. "I was still secluded for much of the first time, but I imagine better. If lonely, at times."

"Are you able to go places?" he asked, worried.

"Most places," I assured him, then smiled wryly. "So long as I do not mind sitting in the back on occasion."

"You're tall, you'd sit there anyway," he tried to comfort me, but the atmosphere of our conversation had grown heavier than we liked. He cleared his throat, lightening his tone, "I hear it's not so lonely these days, though. Word on the grapevine is your lady demon friend has been staying at the Lawrence house."

"Why must everyone stress her being a woman?" I laughed, glad for the change of topic. "But yes, there is another demon in the Lawrence home."

"I thought so." Jeff chuckled to himself. "Your mother would have had a fit."

"So would Father! Leilani can be a handful at times." Another sip and I was pleased by the more sour bite of the pulp. "Nothing terrible, simply excitable. Her English is still...lacking, despite the endless hours she asks to learn."

"Even if she does eat soap, you're loving it," sighed Jeff with a shake of his head.

"Every minute," I confessed with a grin, taming myself to a smile at Jeff's stifled recoil. "I finally have someone who understands the absolute suffering of a wing cramp."

Jeff made a face. "Yeah, I hate those. But you're both getting along well?"

"Of course. In all honesty, she is very pleasant as friends go, helps with the children, and always finds a way to busy herself." I shrugged. "Certainly an improvement over living with my brothers."

"She sounds like a nice girl," he noted, giving me

a pointed smile just as Father used to. "I'm not saying anything, just...sounds nice. You should bring her with you next time. I'll even put up the inedibles."

"I plan on focusing on my children, Jeff, I have no interest in romance," I replied sternly, hoping to nip that particular idea in the bud now. "With nothing to say on the matter of you being Kate's father, either."

"Hey now, I may as well be your father-in-law, young man," he retorted with all of the command I used when Kyle was in trouble. I fought a smirk. "And I owe your parents for everything they did for Kate. It's the least I can do to be a nosy dad. Not like I do much else these days, anyway."

"Then allow me to assure you, as your son-in-law, I have no interest in Leilani. Our relationship is purely platonic." I set my empty glass aside, glad for the pulp at the bottom. The bracing flavor added just enough of a sharp note to my tone to drive home my earnest declaration, "Good friends, mind you, but friends nonetheless."

"And that's perfectly fine." Jeff held his hands up in surrender on the topic, smiling at me. "Thank you for bringing the kids by. It's been good to see you all."

"I could never keep them from knowing where they come from," I replied easily, smiling to see them having such fun baking pies. Their older cousins were helping them place their crusts, my little ones' faces smeared with a mixture of flour and filling. "Even if it means an extra mess or two."

Sarah finished with her pie first, running over with her hands still covered in flour. "Dad, come look at what I made! Quick, before they cook it!"

"All right, all right, give me a moment to stand," I laughed. She grabbed my hand and pulled at it eagerly. I feigned weakness, "allowing" her to pull me to my feet and making a show of stumbling. "Oh, thank you! I never would have made it up without your help."

Sarah rolled her eyes at my overly dramatic antics, waving to her creation proudly. "See? I did the crust myself!"

I admired the work, smiling at the obvious mistakes of her less coordinated hands. Nonetheless, my chest swelled with pride. "I'm afraid I don't have any blue ribbons on me, darling, but it looks delicious."

"I want to make the lattice ones next time," she told me excitedly, grin reaching her eyes as she pointed to her cousins' skilled craftsmanship.

"That's going to take a lot of work," I told her, loving how it did nothing to intimidate her aspirations. "We can make some dough at home to practice with."

She nodded, chattering on with empowered enthusiasm about what she had made. All I could do was smile, fighting the grin which would have startled her relatives. After some time, Kyle joined in, his crust needing more assistance in being functional before the pies went in the oven to bake. They needed nothing from me to keep up their excitement; my perfect little monsters were finally back to their happier selves after last year's misfortunes.

Then they were off to their next task, leaving me in the wake of pride and admiration which came with watching them grow. I ignored the hollow knot in my throat and how manifested in every moment of solitude now. It could be dealt with later, while I focused on the perfection of the current moment.

~~ * ~ * ~ * ~~

Twentieth Week After Paradise

Tuesday

I stared at the phone anxiously, listening to the house settling as my family nestled in for sleep. I could not stand the thought of returning to that empty bedroom of mine, the mattress dressed with cold bedsheets which never warmed entirely. There was no more pain there, and I loathed the endless nothing which engulfed me when I was alone and idle.

Even the Institute was better than this.

The thought was brutal, yet I felt it was also profoundly true. At that moment, I would have taken their cuts, the stitches, the monotony of prison and isolation—if only I could feel *anything*.

Words burned in my mouth, some garbled mess I could scarcely make heads or tails of. Still, I needed to voice them. I knew no one would understand—certainly not if I was at a loss—but that was far from the point of it.

I wanted—*needed* someone to *listen* to them. What they did with them was irrelevant, so long as this inner turmoil could be heard by another, to be spoken aloud. For me to know it could no longer choke me once it was purged from my throat.

Broken Orbit

Briefly, I considered calling Robert. Surely, he would have some words of wisdom to console me with this predicament? It was his profession, after all, no matter how inept he may be at times.

The thought of speaking to him was still unsatisfactory, however. He was too human, and after all of my time spent with demons, I felt the chasm between our species even more acutely in my distressed state. My body ached to express itself in ways I could never hope to accurately portray to him, no matter how deeply I needed his friendship now. My wings were as good as broken, and he could not fly across this void to me.

My sister was not an option for similar reasons, and Leilani could barely manage a conversation as it was. This mishap of language on my forked tongue was much more than I could expect her to understand. She had found some buried part of me which could communicate outside of conventional means, certainly, but that was not what I needed now. I yearned for words, not nameless expressions.

Perhaps Braxen? I felt my heart nearly skip in a feeble attempt at hopeful excitement, thinking of speaking to what was as good as my brother. Without the pang fully blooming, I was mercifully unable to feel the crash of disappointment when I realized he was possibly the worst option. He knew me, yes, and it was an amazing thing he could remember so much with me, but his pride would blind him now. While he was not openly boastful, he possessed too much to justify my longing to find an end to this painful emptiness.

Even I had difficulty reasoning with it. I knew in

some part of me this could only pass. I knew my children held it at bay, the vibrant little ones I cherished so much. I knew that if anything were to happen to me, they...

Regardless, the mounting desire to not suffer another inescapable night gave me some small relief, to imagine anything beyond this. I wanted to act on it, to buy even the slightest sensation to fill my veins again, no matter how recklessly stupid I knew the impulse to be. I only wanted to feel.

With no better place to go and no one to speak to, I finally relented to my growing fatigue. Making my way upstairs to my bed—mine alone, no longer ours—I hoped I only had the strength to do this again tomorrow. For my children's sake, I needed to be able to surpass this.

~~ * ~ * ~ * ~~

Saturday

"What was Ethan here for, Lisa?" I asked, keeping my voice quiet. I feared to speak louder, should I lose my tight grip on this bestial rage. I stared at her, glad Leilani had taken the children to their room already. They should not hear us out here on the front porch, at least.

She shrugged nonchalantly, and I had the distinct impression she was hiding something more from me. "He just wanted to borrow some cash, say hi to the kids."

I took a deep breath, releasing it slowly. "He is not to see them—*ever*, Lisa. He has no right on his own, and especially not while he still openly fraternizes with their father."

"They're his—"

"They are not!" I snapped, gritting my teeth and reminding myself to remain calm. "He gave forfeit to all of those rights a long time ago, and in countless ways. I will not have him anywhere near them, nor anywhere on this property. I understand your desire to continue your association with him, although I do not share it. Can you respect that, at least?"

"Cory, he's our brother!" she protested, aghast. "He's done some stupid things—"

"Stupid doesn't begin to describe him, Lisa!" I cried out, wounded that she would defend him. "He is cruel, hateful, and possesses a level of bumbling idiocy I thought reserved for brainless invertebrates!"

"He's not that—"

"Enough!" I begged, feeling these nonexistent walls closing in slowly. "Lisa. I will not continue this argument with you. I've said my piece, and all I ask now is for you to honor my wishes. Please."

"Yeah, okay," she agreed, too easily. I had the suspicion she may work to find a way around my wording, but I could not be bothered to worry over that now. I was too stressed, the numb ache spreading through my veins to weigh me down.

I knew I wanted to fly, to release some of this anxiety, although my wings felt as though they were wrapped in a wet towel and chilled. Without saying another word, I shambled inside to sit in the living room, struggling to think of anything I might do to stave off this impending nothing. Where once it was a boon, I now felt it was a sinking anchor, my wrists caught in the chain.

Karma Rose

~~ * ~ * ~ * ~~

Twenty-second Week After Paradise

<u>Wednesday</u>

"What was that?!" shrieked Kate, cackling at me and my two left feet.

I smiled sheepishly. "I thought that was a waltz!"

She struggled to catch her breath, shaking her head fervently. "No, no, that—that was—painful. Just painful."

"What am I supposed to do with my tail, then? The steps are difficult to balance through without it." I narrowed my eyes as she stifled more laughter. "I know, simple box step, but you are so much littler, Kate. Without help, I fear I might topple over!"

She screeched with giggling mirth.

I snatched her up in my arms and tossed her over one shoulder easily. Katelyn's shrieking giggles ignited my rumbling guffaws. I had no doubts we looked quite the pair with our raucous tomfoolery.

"Put me down! I can't breathe!" she wheezed, body shaking with her humor.

"And subject myself to your continued mockery?" I adjusted her so that I was bearing the bulk of her weight off of her chest. I heard her breathe more deeply. "Never!"

"You can't dance!"

"Neither can you, my dear!"

324

Broken Orbit

"I have rhythm!"

"Not slung over my shoulder, you don't."

"You looked like a drunk spider!"

"A drunk spider who happens to be Dustin's best man." I grinned, dropping her from my shoulder to cradle her in my arms instead. I kissed her cheek, chuckling at her indignant huffing. "Shall we try again, Kate?"

"Are you going to keep treating me like a sack of potatoes?" she grumbled petulantly.

I laughed again. "Only as the most beautiful, adorable sack of potatoes in the world, you have my word."

~~ * ~ * ~ * ~~

At this hour in the morning, the household was fast asleep, awaiting me to begin the day for us all. One more day. Just one. How I had even woken for it was a mystery, let alone making it out of bed. My veins must have been filled with wet cement, my body felt so exhausted and heavy.

This morning was like any other, dressing for the day before tidying myself up in the bathroom. I could not look at myself in the mirror. From shame, from loathing, from the smallest fear that, perhaps, Braxen might be on the other side of the glass to see my weakness. He would not understand this hopelessness any more than I could.

I moved. I knew that much, I moved. Until my children were awake and in my presence, little else mattered. Work was done blindly, and breakfast was just the same: work. Agonizing, pain-staking work.

If only this morning *was* like the others. If only that nagging yearning for any feeling, any relief, did not consume me so entirely.

In spite of myself, my hands would not cease their quaking as I struggled to chop whatever it was I aimed to cook. The knife in my hand was too heavy, my scars burning. My eyes were fixated on the gleaming blade, too bright and clean to belong to this aged kitchen.

Why could I not stop this shaking?!

Then I realized it, the difference of the morning, the change in the burn of my skin. It was not fear or shame, but something far worse than either which had my hands trembling so fiercely. Anticipation, a longing for the familiarity of the sensation, if only to *have* sensation. Empty promises of the salvation that came with knowing my place.

The knife clattered to the countertop and I stepped back from it with a desperate gasp for air.

How had this happened? I looked around myself, for the first time seeing the room I was in—seeing at all since I had dragged myself from my bed. I knew I had been set to endure whatever passing grief had taken hold of me, but this? When had grief turned into *this*?

The burning desire in my skin was a shock, waking me completely from this excuse of living I had fallen into. I had the eerie sense that I had known my apathy had grown to a dire point; I had considered these idle musings before. Seeing promises of relief where I should have seen snakes reminded me that something was wrong. In every fraying fiber of my being, something was very wrong.

Shaking still, I went for the phone in the living room. I clung to the receiver as if it might stave off the demons clawing their way deeper into my core, these wayward thoughts threatening me. I was dialing before I could think, Robert's personal number ingrained into my mind.

It rang.

Damn that ringing, but it dragged on and *on* until I thought the murderous nothing might strike from there, too.

Still, this trembling would not leave me.

"Cory?" Robert's fatigued groan brought my attention to the fact that the ringing had stopped. "Do you have any idea what time it is?"

"Robert, I'm sorry, I—" My words failed me, guilt settling into the empty spaces in my veins. Guilt and the most convincing sense of inadequacy. It was very nearly enough to have me hang up then, but the thought of the knife in the other room bade me otherwise.

My children deserved better.

"What? Cory, did something happen?" Tired still, but his groggy irritation had given way to concern.

"Nearly," I confessed weakly. My cheeks burned, chest aching. Was I crying? "Robert, something is wrong with me."

"What happened?"

Nothing. Nothing at all.

"I was cooking, and I had a knife. Damn it, Robert, the things I felt, the things I thought—something is *wrong*!"

"Is it something from the Institute that's bothering you?" he asked, awake and alert now.

I knew he had good reason to assume that. So why was it so infuriatingly frustrating to me that he was incorrect, guessing at the obvious? I needed anyone to know, I needed my friend, yet I despised the idea of those words on my lips.

"No, Robert, not the Institute. You have my word, I never thought it would escalate like this."

When he spoke next, his commonly easygoing voice was strained, frightened, "Cory, what did you do with the knife?"

I could scarcely breathe anymore; my chest was too tight to expand quite right. "I dropped it."

"Did you do anything else?"

"I wanted to." Admitting it was agonizing, but I had let this go on long enough. "So badly, I want to."

"Okay, bud, can you stay on the phone with me?"

"I-I suppose. But breakfast for the children..." My voice trailed off confusedly, thinking of that villainous object on the counter. I shuddered. "They need something before school."

His voice was calm, manner soothing, "Do you have any leftovers?"

"Yes." I felt...not felt, and not quite solace, but there was an echo of gratitude for his efforts to keep me engaged. "Thank you."

"Can you come over? Today or tomorrow? I can come to you after that."

The thought of waiting for help was unpleasant, at best. I wanted to see this ended. "Yes, I can, I can make it today. During school hours."

"Perfect." I heard his sigh of relief, how he was nearly giddy with it. "That's perfect. It's supposed to be good weather today, too. How's the flying been where you are?"

He kept me talking with idle conversation and easy questions until I had calmed down, eased out of my self-destructive state. As the hour drew nearer when I needed to wake Kyle and Sarah, he made me promise not to act on my...urges.

"You have my word, Robert. Not today."

"I was fine, Robert," I whispered shakily, staring at my hands as the rabid nothing bit down and infected me to the core. "A little over a year, I was fine, with nothing but improvements. I fear I don't know how this happened. How could this happen?"

Robert hesitated, his careful expression growing too familiar for my comfort. How often had he worn such a mask when he was speaking to me nowadays? "Cory, it's not uncommon in trauma victims for relapses to happen. It's almost expected for something to set it off. It's called a trigger, and it can vary in severity depending on the trauma and how often you practice recuperating from it. You do well with knives most days, for example, but I think losing Kate..."

"You expected me to regress to this?" I asked, the slightest stab of betrayal reaching me through this apathy. Why? Surely, he only wanted to prevent added stress, in the event I did not reach this point? Ah, and there was the disappointment I felt so deeply in myself for my criminally weak will. "Does it get worse?"

"I've been hoping you'd surprise me like last year," he admitted gently. He was making an active effort to soothe me, using motions, expressions, and tones I recognized from my endless efforts to interact with humans. "I should've talked to you sooner, helped you prepare, but I didn't want to add anything to your plate if I didn't have to. I'm just glad you reached out when you did."

I nodded slowly, barely able to breathe. Even in the N.S.I.S.D., mad from the weight of captivity's chains, I always had something to hope for. Freedom, better treatment, those lingering false ideas that perhaps someday I might find myself home again. Even when I had wished for an end, never once had I ever considered...

"Then it does get worse?"

"It can. Yes."

I took a deep breath, for what little good it did me. "And why do I feel this now? Why not while caged in the Institute? I'm free now, I-I have children, Robert. I should be happy, shouldn't I? So why do I feel so damnably *alone*?!"

He shook his head helplessly. "Trauma can work that way sometimes, Cory. I'm sorry I don't have any better answers right now."

I nodded, more to myself than him. "No, it—I'm fine. Just fine. I can do another day."

"That's the best place to start," he agreed with a tentative smile. "I'm here for you, bud. We'll get you back on your feet. Maybe going back to a weekly meeting schedule again could help? Even just as friends?"

"Yes, yes, that sounds...acceptable." I scowled in spite of the futile spike of hope this might help. I knew it had before all of this happened, before the demons and Katelyn. "Informally, as friends. Just, please, don't tell anyone? My sister especially. She already has a difficult enough time coping with any knowledge of my, ah...condition. What is left after the Institute finished with me, in any case."

"Of course, Cory, as your therapist there's patient confidentiality that—"

"No, Robert, not as your patient, as a friend," I insisted, the difference so very important to me then. "I need a friend."

"Okay," he accepted quietly. "Okay, as your friend. You'll get through this, all right? Just take it one day at a time right now. And you can always call me if anything happens. Okay?"

Relief, however fleeting and small it was, felt like the coolest water in this forsaken desert of depression. "I can do that."

~~ * ~ * ~ * ~~

When at last I returned home, the children were already asleep by some merciful magic. Leilani was proud, grinning broadly when I joined her in the living area to read. I sat with a tired sigh, watching her fingers working with one of Mother's old hoops to embroider a delicate flower onto one of Sarah's dresses. Her expertise with all things needlework and woven was quite simply astounding.

"I read," she declared, boasting in the present tense. Somehow, she dragged a smile from me in spite of my ragged day. "Babies sleeping. Make things."

"What did you make today?" I asked politely. She set aside her project, gesturing for me to cover my eyes with my right hand. I obeyed hesitantly, feeling her grab my left wrist while I was blinded.

Her fingers worked deftly, barely ever coming near me with her claws. My, but I was woefully in need of improvement, even after all my years of practice. She patted my hand to signal she was done, and I pulled my hand away from my eyes to stare at my newly decorated wrist.

"What are these?"

"I have babies make, for you smile," she explained, confidence adorable with that broken speech and heavy accent. She smiled kindly, inviting the sunlight back into this dark and clouded day. "I see you sad. I help make smile."

I saw the woven bracelets with new eyes, wrist weighed down heavily with their good intentions. Worry made its way into my veins. "They know?"

Leilani shook her head urgently, eyes wide. "No. I see you sad. Babies have make for...lick? Good lick?"

"Luck," I corrected habitually, relieved at their ignorance and laughing at the misunderstanding. I most definitely needed to keep an eye on her in polite company. "They don't know, then? That I am...sad."

"No, only I." She pointed to herself, hesitating

before offering awkwardly and struggling with her words, "You have sad, I help? I make smile? Make smile, not sad, help-help—MMPH!" she huffed in defeat, the language failing her.

I considered one piece of Robert's advice earlier, regarding avoiding isolation where possible. Leilani certainly was not poor company. Contrarily, I looked forward to the day I could more easily converse with her, learn about her. I thought of her as quite a close companion, despite as little as we could properly communicate.

"That...Yes, Leilani, I would like your help," I agreed quietly, enjoying how she lit up at my answer, proud that she knew the words. "Well, ah, perhaps some night we could go someplace? As friends, of course, to— To the diner. Or, I heard that there is a drive-in theater the next town over, perhaps we could...hm. Just a thought, I suppose."

Leilani took my hand and gave it a squeeze, murmuring an apologetic "No words" before she picked up her project again. She glanced at me every so often to let me know I still had her attention. I scowled at the barrier we could not seem to overcome as easily as the children managed with it.

"I imagine these words mean little to you right now, Leilani, but...I feel that I owe you so much more than I can ever give back," I confessed quietly, overcome by the impulse to speak to her. Even if my words fell on her ears pointlessly, they deserved to be voiced. I held those new bracelets between my fingers, longing to feel that burst of pride and joy through this numb. "I hope you know your efforts are never unnoticed."

The smile I had come to enjoy broke out on her sky blue lips, copper eyes alight with it. For all of the brightness there, her features were tender and comforting. My words went without being understood, but it seemed that she made up for it with her ability to read my tone and expression. Her tail brushed against my leg, the simple gesture reassuring me that we were bridging this gap together, however tediously.

"Thank you," I murmured, my smile habitual and empty. Still, I felt the faintest spark of warmth in it, basking in the sunny radiance she shared all too willingly.

~~ * ~ * ~ * ~~

March 9th, 2012

I have been doing as Robert suggested recently, to fight back against this depression which has so suddenly gripped me. Perhaps the largest help has been Leilani. She knows me better than I know myself at times. She can predict when I might slip, at the ready to make me smile and engage my interest again.

Returning to my hobbies has also aided some. Lisa finds it both odd and entertaining that I have learned to play the piano, if poorly. I have made a point to do so every morning after the children are off to school, always before my usual work on repairs.

It is not pleasant, by any means, stirring in me echoes from what feels like another lifetime when Katelyn would listen. Robert is not discouraged by this in the slightest. In fact, he hopes I might, at last, begin to properly grieve now that I am committing time to myself every day.

I am not ready to let her leave, however. If I let her go, move past this, I fear I will be left utterly isolated. She alone has always seen <u>me</u> behind this face, forgiven my inhumanity and loved me in spite of it. Without her...Where do I stand? I know I am a father, of course, but I need something else beyond that. I need to feel the fulfillment I had at the village.

I need someone to speak to, who might hear me even if there are slips in self-control. Yet the only one I have ever been accepted by, animal and all, she...she is no longer here to listen.

<u>Family</u>

"What exactly are they *doing*?" laughed Robert incredulously, tilting his head back and squinting against the sun. Above them, he watched the two demons' aerial acrobatics in wonder as they darted and chased one another across the open sky.

"Teams tag, boys against girls," giggled Lisa with a shake of her head. "Sarah got Kyle first, so Cory has to win for a tie or the girls take this round."

A short distance away, Robert saw the children jumping about and screaming excitedly, cheering for their respective demon to win. The sound was nearly drowned out by the thunderous beat of wings overhead, crimson and coral blurring together against the sky's clear blue backdrop.

"What are the rules for a successful tag?" he asked with a grin.

"Wrestling style, pinned to the count of three. That's why Sarah won." Lisa shrugged with a laugh, obviously overjoyed to see so much vitality returning to the farm, no matter how rambunctious.

"Any spoils to the victor?"

The tumbling overhead was growing closer and

more frantic, two cats going wild with the chase.

"Loser does the dinner dishes." Lisa grinned. "Old family rule my brothers played by. My money's on Cory, but I really want to see Leilani win this one. He never had to do anything when we bet chores like this. It's Cory's turn to cook, too, so it would be twice as sweet."

The spectating was cut short as the demons fell out of the sky from some fifty feet overhead. They crashed into the ground, tumbling across the field as they lost momentum. What had been graceful blurs only seconds previously had turned into a mass of thrashing limbs and playful, although terrifying, growls and snarls. Eventually, the flailing ceased, and Robert could make out where Cory had ended up face down. Robert's heart stopped, unable to find the petite demoness and worried she had been crushed.

A coral hand shot up and waved from between Cory's wings, and they could make out where she had curled herself tightly to act as her pin. Lisa grinned, the crimson behemoth unable to unseat his opponent as his sister counted under her breath.

"That's three!" called Lisa, a frustrated outcry and gleeful cheer mingling together in reply.

Robert laughed and shook his head. "This is playing?!"

"That's *them* playing, anyway," giggled Lisa, rubbing her hands together. Robert thought he saw a flash of fear in the older woman's eyes, shaking it from his mind. "And this is a momentous day for the Lawrence household!"

The two demons disentangled and made their way

back, disheveled and gasping through their laughter.

"She cheated, Lisa, I demand a rematch!" Cory grinned, fangs bared and glinting in the sun. He brushed at the dirt on his pale blue shirt, ceasing quickly as he realized the futility of the gesture.

"I win!" Leilani stuck out her forked black tongue.

Cory guffawed, wheezing as he fought to catch his breath. "How rude!"

Her taunting expression fell back to her brilliant smile. "You clean. Ha!"

"Yes, yes, I clean," he sighed, all in good humor. He shook his head slowly, black hair falling messily around his face. His bright green eyes danced with amusement. "I'll rue the day I ever taught you anything, you little tyrant."

Leilani danced off cheerfully, calling out to the children as she went. Sarah was a mess of enthusiasm, while Kyle was making a dedicated effort to mimic Cory's every gesture in their humble defeat. His little hands were on his hips as he did a mock saunter up to his father, watching carefully as he crossed his arms. Robert chuckled.

Cory looked down, smiling broadly. "Well, my boy, it seems that we've made a bed for ourselves this evening."

Kyle nodded slowly, feigning understanding through his obvious confusion. "Yeah."

The demon laughed softly. "Come now, it's our turn to cook supper and clean. Let's get started, eh?"

The two wandered toward the house, Leilani and Sarah following behind, completing the unorthodox little family. Lisa smiled, crossing her arms against a chilly breeze and meandering after them more slowly.

"This is good to see," commented Robert quietly. "I was worried about him, after Kate and with the kids, you know?"

"He's always been one to rise to the occasion," replied Lisa with a shrug. "And he always wanted kids. As long as I can remember, he couldn't wait to start his own family."

"He fills the role well, that's for sure." As they drew closer, they could hear animated conversations from inside the home.

Robert breathed a sigh of relief, the last couple of weeks playing over in his mind. Cory had been calling regularly, in addition to weekly visits. It had sounded like the demon was getting at least a little better, but seeing the progress first-hand did more to ward off the worrisome imaginings that had been plaguing Robert. He smiled, listening to his friend's laughter as they entered the old home. It would be hard work, but he felt like Cory could get through this.

Karma Rose

Broken Orbit

My dearest Katelyn,

I dreamed of you last night.

It was vivid and surreal in its clarity. We were together again. These last months were nothing more than a nightmare.

I can't stop crying.

You smelled so perfect, just as you always have. Your smile was everything I have been needing, and the sound of your laugh could have been the song of angels. You have never felt so wonderful in my empty arms, my dear.

I miss you. More than you can imagine, more than I can stand, <u>I miss you</u>. Your grave holds nothing but false hopes anymore.

I need you.

My promise is being kept, my dear. I hope you rest well knowing that.

My enduring love,
Cory

Karma Rose

Chapter Ten: Countdown

25th Week After Paradise

Wednesday

"Robert, Anne..." I sighed quietly, eyes trained on my hands and the woven bracelets I now wore. "I know it may be too much to ask, especially considering how little time I've known you both, but I have very few people I trust as much as you and your family. Well, ah, I was hoping to ask—That is, would you two consider being Kyle and Sarah's guardians, should I be unable to care for them?

"I'm fit as a fiddle," I added hurriedly, not wanting to worry them given the nature of the request. I put the thought from my mind of any possibility of losing the battle to my hollow yearnings. "It would strictly be in the event of an accident, hopefully. Katelyn was prepared, and I would like to follow that example."

They shared a momentary look of concern, Robert clearing his throat to speak first. "Wow. Erm, I-I wasn't expecting that, Cory, honestly. Um..."

343

He trailed off, staring at his wife's enthusiastic nodding with mild alarm. It was easy to see where Bailey had inherited her excitable nature. Anne was laughing, overjoyed, "Yes, of course!"

Robert chortled awkwardly, "Well, I guess that settles it, huh?"

I breathed a sigh of relief. While I loved my sister, I trusted this younger couple to have a gentler hand, in the event I was ever unable to provide it myself. "Thank you."

"But wait, you flew all the way out here for just the one question?" asked Anne, confused.

I shrugged. "It seemed the sort of thing to discuss in person."

Robert nodded in agreement. "Who's with the kids today after school, then?"

"Leilani." I smiled. "She's come a long way with her learning. She knows more about these new technologies than I do!"

"Still losing arguments to the microwave, I see?" snickered Robert, and Anne smirked.

I scowled. "The blasted thing is spiteful, but only when no one is watching."

"Do you remember how to set the time and everything?"

"Yes, yes, and when I do *that* correctly the infernal contraption sets fire to its contents!" They laughed at my plight and I could not help but join in. "Oh, I am hopeless, I fear."

"Tinfoil," gasped Anne through a fit of giggles, gesturing with one hand. "Did you leave the tinfoil on it? Or a spoon?"

Broken Orbit

"Well, yes, I d—Is that not right?!"

We kept on in that fashion awhile longer, until I glanced at the clock and realized the time. I stood, body sore and aching from the initial flight. I stretched my wings carefully and as best I could in their roomy living area, joints cracking loudly. I sighed, glad to be rid of at least some of the ache.

"Well, now, I must get back. Leilani still has some trouble with cooking on occasion, and I need to get supper on the stove." I smiled, making my way to the front door.

Robert followed close behind, stopping at the threshold. "It was good to see you, Cory."

"And you." I pat his shoulder, mindful of our difference in size. "Thank you, Robert, for everything you have done."

He nodded with a smile, nothing more needing to be said. "We'll see you soon, okay? I'm only back to work part-time, so if you need me..."

"Of course. Good luck with your work." I ducked out of the home, closing the door behind me. Taking a deep breath to savor the spring air, I made my way to the sidewalk before sprinting to take off.

~~ * ~ * ~ * ~~

I landed at the front of the farmhouse, noticing immediately the deep tire marks in the gravel driveway. I scowled, eyes drifting to the front door that hung open, its screen door unlatched and clattering in the wind. My heart stopped, voice escaping me much more strongly than I thought was possible as I called for my children.

345

"Kyle?! Sarah!" My legs could not move fast enough as I bolted to the porch, barreling indoors and scanning the rooms urgently. "Where are you?!"

There was a clatter in the back room, down the hallway on the first story. I hurried through the cramped space, spotting Leilani sitting on the floor. She was panicked and sobbing as she curled in on herself. Black was spattered across the floor and wall, smeared across her skin. I knelt to see her better, too terrified to soothe her before demanding things of her.

"Leilani? Leilani, what happened?!" I saw that her arm was bleeding, horrified. Angels? How had they known where we were?! "Where are the children?"

She held one hand to her bloodied arm, trembling. "A-a man has thunder. Hurts, Cory."

"Thunder?" My heart faltered. Not angels, humans. "A gun. He had a gun, Leilani, what happened to the children?!"

"No babies, man has babies," she whimpered, the sound caught somewhere between pain and shame.

"He took them. He took them?!" My mind nearly stopped in its tracks, heart in my throat.

Lisa entered just behind me, seemingly returned from some errand, so much more collected than I was as she took in the scene. "I'll call the police. Cory, get her to Ericson's, now!"

"Leilani, can you fly?" She looked up at me with a frightened nod. "Good, follow me, I will take you to the doctor, all right?"

I helped her up and out of the house, taking the lead to sprint and jump into the air. She followed suit, the steady beat of her wings booming in time with mine. I climbed easily, checking behind me to find her just a few wing-beats back.

I aimed us toward where I remembered Paul used to live. Perhaps Corey had been taught by his father? Lisa seemed to think so, with her commanding me to take the wounded demoness there. At least Leilani could keep pace with me, both of us coming up on the old home quickly. Below, I saw a startled man staring up at us in shock, rushing back to his porch as we circled to land.

My feet touched down not a moment before I was hurrying over to my namesake, explaining breathlessly, "Please, she's been shot in the arm. Can you help her?"

Corey's bright blue eyes were wide, face pale. "Yes, I-I think so. My dad taught me a few things, especially about your anatomy, but—That, is that normal? That landing, I mean, that was spectacular!"

"Another time?" I asked tersely. Leilani came to my side, still clutching her arm.

He nodded, chagrined but determined. "Right. Yes, sorry. Inside, I have a place ready."

I nodded gratefully, ushering the demoness inside. It was a struggle to focus on even the smallest detail, confusion mingling with my shock. I should have been at home. It should have been a calm evening, one of the last few before the seasonal break. There should have been excitement now, gleeful little voices that could not cease themselves no matter their efforts. My wrist felt heavy, the woven strands there burning against my skin.

The sound of the screen door clattered loudly in my ears, a painful reminder that something had gone unbearably wrong.

Slowly, as the initial panic of Leilani's condition subsided, anxiety constricted around my lungs. I realized more swiftly how I had been keeping an important detail from myself—one I hoped Lisa had been able to rectify in my absence, however brief.

"I need to return home," I choked, excusing myself from the house. I felt the earth beneath my boots, the push and pull as I made my head-start and jumped into the air. Even the emotion that often drowned out my worries when I flew was a dim echo, silent next to the screaming terror that was on the verge of destroying what little sanity I clung to in the face of this.

My landing was a habit, my stride shortened and steps uneven. My heart was racing, breath stolen from my dry mouth. I saw Lisa run out to the porch, hopeful at first before her face fell to see me alone.

"Lisa, are they...?" I choked on the words, unable to complete the question. How would I finish it? To ask if they were or were not there? Knowing that they would be home when I stepped inside—that the police should have already apprehended the crook—was the singular thought that held me together.

She covered her mouth with her unsteady hands, heartbroken and crying as she shook her head. I stopped walking, only steps from the porch. My mind went blank, refusing to accept what she did not say. I stared at her numbly, uncomprehending.

"They're not here, Cory," she choked out, seeing my inability to understand her silence. It felt like I had been falling since first seeing Leilani's bloody arm; I was finally hitting the ground at those words. The air was knocked from my chest with such force that I dropped to my knees, wings falling limp at my side.

"No," I begged, gasping for air and finding none. My chest was on fire, face burning. Why could I not feel anything else? Why had I gone weak? I needed to stand, to be strong. They needed me. "No, they have to be hiding, Lisa. He had a gun—You heard her, he has a gun, they're not safe!"

"Cory, they're not home," she said again, coming to meet me where I had found myself on my knees. She reached out to hug me, the gesture lost on me in my fractured state. "They're gone, he took them. The police are looking, they'll be here soon, but—"

"No, their closet; they hide when they're scared," I realized hopefully. Desperate to deny this, I removed my sister and stood shakily. I stumbled and tripped my way into the house and upstairs, fumbling to open their door fast enough. I stopped there, staring at the mess.

Their bookshelf was tipped, its contents strewn across the floor. The beds were torn apart: one mattress was thrown off its frame. Toys were scattered from the wooden box they used as it sat on its side. My eyes fell on the closet door, hanging open and announcing its childless floor silently.

"NO!"

The outcry startled me, sounding to me as the voice of someone else, someone so angry and panicked and aggrieved. Surely, that could not be my voice? My chest was hollow, body numb. Certainly, I felt nowhere near enough emotion to cause such a scream of denial?

"Cory, I'm sorry." I felt a hand on my arm, heard a voice I recognized, but I could not care enough to see who it was.

My children were gone.

~~ * ~ * ~ * ~~

My hands moved, I knew. Slowly, ever so slowly, they pieced Kyle and Sarah's room back together. The officers had long since come and gone, unable to find anything to give them an immediate answer.

"Is there anyone you know who might want to hurt them? Or have a grudge against you, personally, even? It's usually another parent, but—"

"Their father," I replied numbly, the thought horrifying. *"Sarah was terrified that I-I would send them to him. She never told me why. My brother keeps asking for custody on his behalf."*

"Okay. Well, we'll get his name, it sounds like a good place to start."

I stared at the toys in my hands; the simple plastic figures were too heavy to hold for long. I dropped them into the box, the sound ringing empty as I strained for the next toys within my reach. The motion was a cold mockery of anything I had ever been.

"What do you mean, there is a time limit?" I echoed, a fresh wave of panic gripping me at the thought.

The detective spared me a look of sympathy. "If we don't find them in the first forty-eight hours, then the chances drop significantly that they'll come home."

Fresh tears burned my eyes, throat constricting

even more tightly. I shook my head slowly, barely able to breathe as I asked, "And what—What happens if we can't find them? What then?"

"We still have time," I whispered to myself faintly, finishing with their toys. I righted the unseated mattress before I stood. Tucking in sheets and bedding, I corrected them again and again as the cloth never seemed to sit just right. I ignored the tears that hit the blankets, sniffling and straightening myself. My hands reached for the other bed to do the same to its dressings.

"Cory, they'll bring them home soon, you'll see." I knew it was either Robert or Lisa who spoke, but their voices seemed to bleed together now. When had he arrived? Did it matter who it was? Could I care enough to know? They repeated the same lies, again and again, words that only served to chisel more and more from my already hollow chest.

"I never should have left today," I murmured, staring at nothing.

"Well, it sounds like we've got everything we need here, we'll keep in touch." The detective stood and left, abandoning us to our distraught confusion.

Sitting idly, even for a second, burned me from inside. I stood on impulse, scowling at my hands angrily. How had I not protected them from this? What kind of a father allowed his children to—?

"I-I'll go tidy the room. They'll need it. Soon." The words felt like knives in my mouth, ears burning from the strain to hear their play, their laughter, finding only a wrong silence that suffocated the rooms of the house.

"There we are." I stared at the books, all proper

and neat now on their shelves. I glanced around the lying room, nearly believing the falsehoods whispering to me nothing was wrong. All I had done was help clean after a particularly rambunctious day.

My eyes strayed to the closet, falling on a pair of items that broke my heart anew and shattered my desperate delusions. There in the corner were two stuffed toys, a bear and a rabbit, looking as if they had been tossed to the floor in a mad rush. They never treated these toys so carelessly.

The breath I gasped for caught in my throat, tearing from me raggedly. I retrieved the items carefully, precious and invaluable things that they were. My little ones needed them, the night encroaching slowly as it cast their room into a bloody light.

"You should rest," protested...*someone.*

I shook my head slowly, wondering why I had stopped on the stairs. My eyes had caught on a faint smear of black on the wall near where I had found Leilani. "No. I can't, they need me."

"Please, Cory."

"Where are they?" I choked, holding their stuffed toys to my face and longing for my children to be home. The animals smelled of mint and shampoo, their nightly routine everywhere I looked, more so as the room grew dark. Even the rocking chair I sat in felt wrong, this nightmare granted a lifeless form that I was not reading aloud now. I should have been reading.

My eyes burned staring at their neatly made beds, still empty. My heart twisted painfully, and I had to know that they were okay. I needed to know they were being

read to and their blankets were warm. Yet I knew they
would not sleep well, not when I was the one holding their
animals. Kyle could never get to sleep without his bear,
and Sarah would have trouble staying asleep without her
rabbit.

Who was going to read to them? Who would ease
their fears if they had a nightmare? Who was going to
make sure they ate more than pancakes and syrup at
breakfast? Would Sarah have help brushing her hair?
And Kyle still struggled with his shoes on occasion.
Would they have what they needed?

Or would they be in a frightening place? In
danger? Did they need me, now, when I had no way to
reach them?

The knock on the door frame startled me, and I
looked up to see Lisa standing there. "I'm just checking on
you. You haven't touched a plate all day."

"I'm not hungry," I replied numbly, staring at their
toys with fresh tears. Had they had their supper?

"You need to eat, Cory," she said, voice maternal
and soft despite being marred by worry. "At least come
downstairs? It's not good for you to sit up here by
yourself. Mom did it, and she...well..."

I sighed sharply, moving without feeling it. I
brought their toys with me, unable to bear the thought of
leaving them alone in the children's cold, empty beds as I
followed Lisa downstairs to the kitchen table. Robert and
Leilani were already waiting with food on the table, Lisa
taking her seat. I took a chair, too tired to stand, eyes only
for the toys I held. The food smelled unappetizing at best,
my stomach lurching uneasily.

"Can I fix you a plate?" asked Robert, barely waiting a moment before he started in on this nonsense.

I shook my head slowly. "I'm not hungry."

"Cory, please—"

"I'm not hungry," I repeated sharply, too stressed to make for safe company yet too apathetic to react to it. I stared at Sarah's rabbit and its loose button eye. She had been picking at it again. That would need fixing for her.

"Just a bite," he begged, distraught. "You'll feel better after—"

"Better?" I repeated disdainfully, fixing him with a glare. He flinched, but I could not care. "How am I supposed to feel better when I don't know where they are, but that their father has them and a gun?! He shot at Leilani, he could very well harm Kyle or Sarah! I don't know if they're safe, hungry, hurting—Robert, how does my eating help them?! How does anything I do now help *them*!"

He shrugged, dropping his gaze and the subject timidly. My eyes burned, staring at all I had left of my children. I could barely stand the sight anymore, covering my eyes and resting my head in my hand. Flirting dangerously with defeat, I set the toys on the table in front of me.

A small, clawed hand gripped mine with more strength than I expected. The feeling surprised me at first before I realized I was gripping the hand in return, as tightly as I would any lifeline while trying to escape this relentless current I had been swept up in. For the first time since returning to the bloody mess, I felt I might steady myself some, if only for a moment.

354

Broken Orbit

I pulled my hand away from my face to look at the demoness, grateful for her company now more than ever. Her oft infectious smile was gone, worry and grief taking hold where the sun had always resided.

"Leilani..." I spoke gently, unsure of what to say but knowing that I could not stand to see her this way. I spoke slowly for her out of habit, "Don't cry. It's not your fault."

She smiled kindly, eyes still sad. "I...am sorry."

"Well done, Leilani," I praised her, glad for what few slivers of goodness she provided in this nightmare.

She breathed deeply, nodding to herself even as she gripped my hand impossibly tighter. Her cat-like eyes met mine, and I knew that she would not let me fall victim to the raging sea my world had become. For as little as we understood each other at times, she was fast becoming my closest friend.

Leilani spoke in her native tongue, enunciating each word slowly with forced precision. It took me a moment, but I realized she was doing for me what I did for her, hoping that somehow the words might be easier to understand that way. I recognized my name among the exotic pronunciations, her accent making it sound so much more than it was.

What I was able to make out intuitively was the passion behind her words. Whatever she said, it was with heartfelt conviction that invoked confidence in me, however frail or fleeting.

I smiled apologetically, wishing that I could have understood even a fraction of the words she spoke. "Thank you, Leilani."

She returned my smile, still not quite the bright sunshine that was her norm, but a dim twilight that lit her face as a watercolor artwork. I felt my anger and stress subside some, relieved by her quiet acceptance of my upset. No reassurances, merely a fervent plea and a hand like an anchor.

Finally, the meal in front of me smelled like something I could consume. Using my free hand, I started in without tasting it, keeping hold of the smaller hand in mine and the claws that were oddly comforting even as they cut into my skin. I knew better, but some irrational part of me said that letting go now would leave me adrift. So I held tight, grateful for the demoness and how she intuitively knew how to calm me—like the demon I was and not the human I impersonated.

~~ * ~ * ~ * ~~

Thursday

"What are you saying?" My voice was numb, words falling flat and hollow. "Is it hopeless?"

The officer hesitated. "It's been twenty-four hours. They're with a repeat criminal offender, no one saw the vehicle, and the only witness is a non-human who doesn't speak English. The odds certainly aren't favorable."

"So that's it, then?" I choked, finding myself angry at the injustice of it all. "You stop looking? You condemn them to whatever hellish nightmare that sorry excuse of a man can think up?!"

"We haven't given up yet, but we just wanted to

make sure you understood the situation," he said calmly, hand moving toward his belt and the weapons it held.

I took a deep breath, shaking my head slowly. "Fine. Fine, then speak to my sister next time you need to 'make sure we understand'. I remember all too well how this goes."

I gave a pointed glare between his milky tone and my bright crimson before I stalked toward the old tree out back. My body was worn, charged with anxious energy sparking like lightning through my nerves. I paced between the back door and the tree guarding our family cemetery. At some point, I heard the door of a car slam shut, watched the police vehicle drive off of the property.

It took every fragment of my shattered self-control to cease my pacing. I fought for a deep breath, choking back the inhuman wails and outcries I felt building in my throat. When I turned to make my final trek back to the house, Leilani was already on her way out to meet me. She took my trembling hand in hers, uncaring of the grip I knew could all too easily crush human bone.

She was calm and steady, everything I had strived for these last months and everything I now was not. With patience far beyond what I knew I deserved for my behavior, she withstood so much more of me than I considered safe to express. It helped, having that hand to cling to as tightly as I needed to keep from drowning. More than anything else in this nightmare, she helped.

In a matter of seconds, she tempered my jaded edges to endure another bout of this forsaken waiting.

$\sim\sim * \sim * \sim * \sim\sim$

Karma Rose

There is too little time left.

Sitting in the living room was as useless as sitting anywhere else. The only difference was, there, I had company in my misery. Robert, my sister, Leilani, and the damned bottle of whiskey which would not stop whispering to me the countdown to my children's near-certain death sentence.

Just a few more hours.

I stared hatefully at the amber liquid, feeling mocked as it promised such sweet and blissful release behind the burn of these tears. It made it difficult to focus on the droning voices I had long since begun to ignore. Their speculations brought us nowhere closer to having my children home and safe in my arms. The officers were doing what they could, but with their prime suspect being from nowhere local our efforts of rallying our community were worthless. He could have been states away by now.

Still, that bottle *mocked* me!

Without thinking, I snatched it from its perch, rushing to the kitchen and the solitude I found there. My eyes fell in an instant on the stuffed animals still sitting on the table, the rabbit's crooked button eye stared at me oddly.

The bottle I clutched held a new weight, sending a pang of uncomfortable guilt shivering through me like cold oil beneath my skin. I could not catch my breath, gasping from the effort it took to stay standing. All the while, those accusing, deadened eyes were pleading with me with the same fervor I knew my children would if they saw what I warred with now.

Broken Orbit

Fighting against the weight of the drink, I lifted the bottle and undid the cap, tossing it to the counter. My hands shook violently, barely able to keep my grip firm. Heart racing with anticipation, I tipped the bottle with a groan as the familiar smell burned the air.

I choked on my breath, mouth going dry.

Tick, tock.

"You're dumping it."

The declaration was quiet despite the thunderous meaning behind those words. Robert was at my side, he and my sister at the ready to wrest the damned bottle from me. He was relieved and startled, flinching when I tossed the empty container into the sink after its contents, the glass clattering loudly. The sound of the whiskey in the drain was a new pain I could hardly stand, seconded by the unbearable silence that followed.

"You dumped it."

"I couldn't think with it staring at me," I spat, all at once relieved and desperately disappointed with my choice.

I could have had some small freedom from this, I thought wistfully.

I lumbered back to the living area, grabbing the toys from the table along the way. I found the sewing kit on the shelf where Mother always kept it, sitting down to right that poor rabbit's eye. They followed me quietly, ruffled and awkward. Leilani was still in her seat, eyes wide and uncomprehending of the weight behind the exchange.

She set a hand on my knee, timid. "Is good?"

"Yes, Leilani, I'm fine," I muttered, the room

feeling so much clearer and cleaner without that monstrous distraction present. "Thank you."

~~ * ~ * ~ * ~~

"You sleep," murmured Leilani quietly, copper eyes shimmering in the darkened living room. I saw her move, sitting beside me on the couch and setting a hand on my arm for comfort.

"I can't," I whispered, staring at where the whiskey bottle had sat, so very near defeat. First Kate, and now...I closed my eyes with a sigh. "I can't. I need to know where they are—if they're safe, or when they can come home. I need them to know they're loved. I want to do so much for them, to be their father, I I can't lose them. Not like this."

I knew she could not understand what I was saying—nor I, her—when she replied quietly in her purring language, voice tender. She gave my arm a gentle squeeze, setting her free hand hand on my shoulder. I opened my eyes to see her crying, heartbroken and worried.

"Please smile. The children and your infectious enthusiasm got me through Kate's passing, I can't lose them both," I begged, needing some boon to cling to in this. I already felt myself sinking back into grief. Seeing her upset had sent my frayed mind into a downward spiral. I realized then that, while I had cried and I had paced, I had not sat long enough to feel anything more than anxiety.

"Sad is good, is okay," she told me with a nod,

face contorting as she watched my sorrow devour me from within. She stroked my shoulder, letting me weep without saying a word. No telling me how things would get better, or heal, or stop hurting, no lying that my children would miraculously be home any second now. Only her silent acceptance.

Before I realized it, I was shaking with my sobs, unable to keep myself quiet despite my better efforts not to disturb the too-silent house. There were no children to hide my breaking from.

Leilani simply nodded, squeezing my arm again before shifting to put her arms around me, pulling my face to rest on her shoulder. I felt her tail wrap around mine, her wings enveloping me for comfort. It was odd still, alien from what I was accustomed to with humans, but there was a familiarity to it which soothed me so much more naturally.

She kept a tight hold, singing quietly. It sounded like a lullaby, the words lilting and soft, helping to calm me. Without my realizing, I had stopped weeping, chest hollow but relieved of some weight. Leilani began to rock back and forth, still singing.

My eyes finally grew heavy after nearly two days of strain, awake and alert for every second. I still felt desperately lonely and terrified. Yet, whether it was a specific action or how she so easily combined them, I finally felt it was safe to be tired.

"Thank you," I whispered, body turning to lead. Before I could think to listen for her reply I was gone, lost at last to sleep.

Karma Rose

~~ * ~ * ~ * ~~

<u>Different</u>

"They're different—*he's* different when he's with her," whispered Robert, watching Cory sleep at last. The demoness shifted to the end of the sofa, allowing the larger man to lie back, his head still tucked to her shoulder as his legs spilled off the furniture and across the floor. "Have you noticed?"

Lisa nodded slowly. "Yeah. He keeps doing things he's never done before, and he looks just as surprised as I am when it happens. The other day, they were playing with the kids and he hit Leilani with his tail—on purpose, but he didn't realize it, I guess? She just laughed."

"Ouch," he muttered, slowly realizing that, to her, it may not have felt like much more than a tap of the hand. She was just over Robert's average height, and certainly much more durable, he knew. Just how rough and tumble could demons get before play turned to violence? Where was the line drawn?

"Not really. I was scared, he was scared, and she just..." Lisa shrugged, frowning at the memory. "It's weird, Robert. I knew him so well and in a lot of ways, he's still the same. But he changes with her. He lets his guard down, and he keeps doing things that...I would expect them from an animal, not him."

"The way they communicated earlier?" cited Robert easily, and he could see that Lisa was just as unnerved as he was. It had been short-lived, Cory's stressed silence after dumping the whiskey, broken by quiet whimpers and growls so pitiful it broke Robert's heart to listen.

Leilani had replied.

As naturally as discussing the weather, the demoness had chirruped back an inquiry. Just as easily, Cory had responded with an even sadder, moaning growl. Where the humans in the room had been at a loss, the demoness simply gave a reassuring purr that had visibly eased Cory out of his mood enough to finally relax, if only to breathe easier.

Lisa nodded with a nervous sigh. "Yeah. That was something else. I'm scared of how much more might happen, Robert. What if he does turn into an animal?"

"Leilani seems pretty civilized," he offered with a shrug, but he could not shake the same concern. "I'm sure he'll be fine. Maybe a little confused for a while, but fine."

The demon's sister was not placated. "And if that confusion has one of us on the other end of his tail? Or the kids, if they ever come home? What then, Robert? He's always had to practice self-control more strictly than us; I don't think you've seen what he's capable of."

"He would never hurt his kids," protested Robert, horrified by the thought.

"He hurt me growing up, more than once," insisted Lisa fervently. "His hand slipped and I got a claw. He wasn't thinking when he got excited and clipped me with a wing. And the tail? I've seen him snap branches with it, Robert, and it looks like it's only gotten stronger since then."

Robert sighed, eyes wandering to the demons on the sofa. Leilani was now asleep, her upper body curled protectively around Cory's head and shoulders, wings wrapped over him and tail wound tight around his own. Robert could not deny that they were dangerous. That would be an idiotic lie, the same as calling a tamed lion completely harmless. It seemed unfair and unreasonable to *fear* Cory, though, after all of the work he put forth to mind his strength and his interactions. Even strained to his limit, he was so soft-spoken and mild, Robert could hardly imagine him as anything but that.

Then again, the few moments of a slip in self-control he had seen were startling, to say the least. He could recall too easily the night at Kate's house when the demon had been picked up from a police station. The sound of his tail whipping the air and the glint of his fangs when he snarled...

Robert shuddered. "I don't think he'll become dangerous to us, though. Leilani brings out parts of him, but it's all calmer things: how they're communicating or being more playful. Even holding him like that—I'm sure some part of him is much more comforted with the proper anatomy being used than if either of us tried, no matter how much of a stranger she is. She's like him. It's only natural for them."

"I still don't like it, Robert," hissed Lisa, shifting uncomfortably with a glance toward the demons. "It just feels...wrong. From my memory of him and just watching them as two people interacting."

"It's just culture shock, Lisa, he's still the same Cory we know." After the countless conversations they had shared since Cory's return to Littleton, Robert had learned just how unchanged his friend was, despite his years away. It had altered his impression of the demon from a man to a statue, weathered and worn but otherwise unyielding despite time's steady passing. Robert smiled as a new image presented itself. "He's like a dog when it meets another dog for the first time. They change, and they communicate differently with each other than us, but...they're still the same dog."

Lisa laughed quietly in spite of herself, tension easing at the comparison. "I don't think he'd appreciate being called a dog, however, I see your point. I'll try and give it some time, but just-in-case—"

"I already have just-in-case handled," interrupted Robert quietly. Since the release—and more recently, Cory's psychotic episode—he had 'just in case' at the ready. He pulled out a small device which fit in his palm. On one side, there was a small speaker, the other a switch to turn it on and off. "I used to have to keep mace and a taser, not that I told Cory, but then I got this from a doctor, Bernard. It's much more humane. It emits a tone that renders demons inert. Only works if there's not too much background noise, but out here it should do just fine."

"What the hell is wrong with you?!" hissed Lisa, glaring at the device. "I'm scared, yeah, but that's my brother! He's not some rabid—"

"Animal? Really?" Robert's words were flat and he raised one eyebrow pointedly. "I don't like it any more than you do, and I hope I never need it. I'm also never handing it over to anyone who can't keep it safe. But we also can't pretend like he couldn't hurt us if he really wanted to. Like a dog."

"You can keep it," she muttered, still angry as she looked back at the demons. Even the much more feral Leilani was a giant sweetheart, always wanting to help. "I trust them more than *that*."

"I know, I do, too, but—"

"But nothing. Possibility of accidents aside, they're the biggest teddy bears I've ever met, and *that*—something specifically to drop a demon? That's just sick," spat the older woman petulantly.

"Lisa, I know they'd never hurt us if they could help it," whispered Robert, pale face turning ashen with a new realization. "But the others he mentioned—what if *they're* not so tame?"

They both shared a look of terror, fear shivering through them as they realized with painful clarity how perfectly suited the demons were as predators. Robert felt sick coming face to face with his glaringly obvious mortality. He had spent his entire life knowing that he was the apex of predators. Humans in general, at least, despite his immediate lack of skill.

Even so, Robert could only imagine what Cory could do if he allowed himself a break in his iron-clad self-restraint. In sheer size alone, the damage was cringe-worthy, but with the claws, the fangs? Or his extra limbs—things Robert never thought of as dangerous before. Not even considering that the behemoth of a man was far from the same level of physical prowess as humans...

"Let's hope for civil," offered Lisa with a deep

breath to steady herself.

Robert nodded. "Let's."

~~ * ~ * ~ * ~~

The darkness of sleep did not last long, my eyes opening to a familiar clearing and the ruins that now stood at its center. It was empty, the world around me unnervingly calm and silent. I stepped forward, expecting company and finding none.

"Hello?" I called, not even an echo calling back to me.

An eerie stillness settled in around me, a flash of light drawing my gaze. In one of the ruin's archways, colors danced and flickered. They drew me nearer—transfixed—until I was close enough to hear tiny whispers coming through from the stone.

"Sarah, I'm scared."

My heart stopped. "Kyle?"

"Me too, Kyle, but we have to be brave. Like Dad."

"Sarah?!" I lurched forward, hands feeling the archway in search of a door that might open, some secret hinge. All I found were shimmering colors as they slowly came into focus. "Where are you?!"

"Do you think Dad will find us?"

"Yes. Yes, I will, just tell me where you are!" I begged desperately, overwhelmed by my need to move, to act. I could hear them so clearly!

"No one's coming for you little shits, least of all that animal. Stupid brats actually thought anyone wanted

you?" A new voice snapped at them scathingly, one I had not heard before.

"Our dad wants us, he said so!" screamed Sarah.

I heard a sharp smack. "Then where the fuck is he?"

"Here. I'm here, I'm right here! Sarah!" The colors sharpened, an image finally becoming clear: my daughter, holding her cheek and crying. She was angry, defiant, reminding me so much of Katelyn in her youth. "Sarah, I'm here."

"He's our dad and he wants us!" she screamed again. A hand shot out from outside the picture, striking her once more.

"NO!" My grip on the archway tightened.

"How many times do I have to tell you not to call that thing your dad?! It isn't, I am, and you'd better learn it quick or you'll just be walking bruises!"

Something twisted in my chest, angry and hurting for her. "Show me where you are, sweetheart, let me see so I can find you."

Slowly, the picture grew to fill the archway. The image of Sarah began to fade, and I lunged in after it, desperate not to let it go. I fell through the archway, the ground beneath my feet vanishing. The sharp sensation that came with those dreams of the future overtook me, every detail carving itself into my memory.

I was flying, a small motel coming into view. I dropped lower, impatient to land. I had to reach the ground, dropping farther and faster until I felt the rough pavement beneath my feet.

Four.

Broken Orbit

The number felt right, and I scanned the doors in front of me, stalking toward the one I wanted. I threw my fist against the door, hearing movement inside. The lock clicked, the handle turned, but my impatience won out and I shoved open the door with a snarl.

I recognized the pathetic excuse of a man as he was knocked to the floor, scrambling to right himself. My hand shot out to grab his shoulder, blunt claws digging in mercilessly. I dragged him close.

"Where are they?!" I hissed, resisting every urge to bury my claws and tear him apart, filed or not.

"I don't know what the fuck you're talking about," he spat back, crying out when I tightened my grip. The bone of his shoulder felt far too delicate in my hand.

I scanned the room, hoping against everything that they would be there, finding nothing but the scum I held and a pair of small travel bags. I went to inspect them, dragging my victim with me. Inside, money stared back at me, cold and careless as I wondered why he would have so much of it in such a grubby motel.

"Where are my children?" I asked again, breathless as my blood turned to ice in my veins. I fixed him with a glare, snarling again as I came dangerously close to understanding the scene around me. "WHERE ARE THEY?!"

"Fuck, I don't know!" he cried out, startled. "Probably another country by now. I don't care, I didn't ask!"

I looked back at the money with a newfound horror. "You sold them."

"Well, I—"

"YOU SOLD THEM?!" My skin felt like fire was dancing across it; I saw flames jumping and lapping hungrily at the monster in my clutches. "WHO HAS THEM?!"

"I didn't ask! They paid double!"

I bellowed, my free hand finding his throat and—

"Cory?!"

My name had me double-take, looking around a now empty and darkened room. On the mattress, I saw a small pamphlet, half-crumpled and proudly boasting the motel's name and location, as well as advertising local destinations.

"Cory!"

I pocketed the pamphlet, looking over the room quickly. I stopped in the bathroom, reaching to pick something up from beneath the sink. Just a little pink barrette, but I knew this one with its delicate heart shapes. I had put it in Sarah's hair the other morning.

"They were here." It brought little relief, finding no sign of where they could have gone or who they were with.

"CORY!"

~~ * ~ * ~ * ~~

Friday

The startled cry shattered my horrific dream, catching me off-guard. I stared up at Leilani, finding myself on the floor. The distinct smell of smoke caught my attention.

370

"What happened?" I sat up quickly, head spinning.

"You. Fire. You." She made a gesture above my hand, pointing to me. "You have fire."

"I was on fire...?" I threw the thought aside after taking a quick look for any damage, finding only singed carpeting here or there. "A problem for another day. Go wake Lisa, I know where the children are."

"No words," she moaned helplessly, watching me intently.

I gestured up toward the second story. "Lisa."

She took another moment before her eyes lit up and she nodded, running off and up the stairs noisily, calling for my sister. I shoved myself off the floor, body aching and protesting but still a secondary matter. I went to the kitchen table and the papers scattered there, finding the card for the detective and hurrying to the phone.

It seemed I could not dial fast enough, hissing in frustration at how delicately I had to handle the damned contraption to work around my claws. By the time I got it to dial through, Lisa was rushing down the stairs, still in her sleepwear.

"What, what is it?!" she demanded, breathless.

"I know where they are," I replied giddily, caught somewhere between excitement and crippling anxiety that there was little I could do in that very second.

"Hello?" The gruff, disgruntled voice that came over the phone sounded like an angel in my panic.

"My apologies about the hour, but I have news," I choked out, clinging to the image in my mind of the pamphlet.

"Mr. Lawrence?"

"Yes, yes. I know where the children are, please." Why did it seem as though my voice was crumbling in on itself? Before he could reply, I gave him the name of the motel and its address, reciting from memory.

Silence. Then, "How do you know that?"

"Intuition? Does it matter, that's where they are!" I found myself pacing, tail whipping the air behind me.

"We're about to leave that motel. It was one of our only leads, but they're not here," he replied dryly.

My blood turned cold. "What?"

"It's the offseason, they said they're closed for another month," he added, sounding frustrated.

"No, no that's not right," I muttered, glaring at the floor. "Did you check room number four?"

"I *just* said—"

"Just knock!" I begged. "Please, he intends to sell them. Knock and tell them I'll be there soon, Sarah *will* answer, I know she will."

A heavy sigh. "Fine. I'm knocking." Muffled, as if the phone were pressed into something, "Hello? I've got your dad on the phone, says he'll be here soon." Closer again, dripping with sarcasm, "I'm sure they'll be right—"

He stopped, the next sounds coming at a distance as I heard someone pounding on a door and yelling. I jumped at the crack of a gunshot, hoping painfully they were safe and wanting to know what was happening.

The line disconnected.

I stopped where I was, staring at the scorched carpet numbly. Did he find them? Were they all right? Who fired the gun?!

372

"Cory, what the hell is happening?!" demanded Lisa again, stepping into my view.

I finally looked at her, still too overwhelmed to know what I felt. The receiver fell from my nonexistent fingertips. "I had a dream. There was a motel, and the detective said they weren't there, but when he knocked there was gunfire—"

She waved her hands, trying to stop me. "A dream? There was gunfire in your dream?"

I shook my head dumbly, words falling off my tongue haplessly, "No. No, that was over the phone, after he knocked. The motel was supposed to be closed. It's an off-season."

"What the hell—Cory?!" My sister yelled out, the sound drowned by my gasping breaths as the walls closed in on me.

Who fired the gun?!

Coral dominated my vision, clawed hands gripping mine firmly. I clung to them, the smallest fraction of myself screaming that I would break bones with the force I was using, but I ignored it. If I eased my fingers at all, I would slip away, the sensation so much like being drugged as I fought to stay in control.

A thousand memories played at once, each one similar to the last as I stared into a bright light and an anesthetic flooded my system. It was the feeling of such heavy weightlessness, drowning in a dreamless sleep and barely able to breathe for the tube down my throat.

I heard something crack, and the next I knew my tail was being coiled by another. The feeling was less of an embrace and more of a hard restraint. Not comforting

373

me—pinning me.

I gasped for air, the gesture futile as my lungs could not seem to take enough in. The copper in my vision was too metallic, glinting with the same sharp light as the knives. They danced just beyond my line of sight, threatening to come closer should I close my eyes.

Damn it all, but I had clung to sanity for days now! I was so close to finding them, bringing them home, and if the detective did not succeed I would fly out and chase down whoever had my little ones. I would go to the ends of the earth, but I needed to know that I could make them safe. That was what broke me, hearing too clearly the dangers my children were in.

WHO FIRED THE GUN?!

The phone screamed in my ears and my body made to scramble away, finding the way blocked. I was being held in place by an iron grip, someone's wings pressing tightly around me like some living straight jacket. I knew I should have been grateful that Leilani was working to keep me from harming anyone. I knew this, but my instincts raged against it, mounting to a feral sound in my chest.

A sharp hiss answered, almost like a banshee's screech, reminding me of a mountain lion. It startled me enough that I was able to take a breath, vision coming into focus as Leilani's features retreated from a savage glare to her usual, gentle self. She saw my sanity returning, chirruping quickly before launching into a purr, and I nodded shakily.

"I'm fine," I gasped, nodding again. "I'm fine."

The phone rang again.

Lisa slipped past where I was still pinned to answer it. "Lawrence residence."

There was a pause that felt like an eternity as I watched her expression change. First, a deep scowl, worried, and then...

"About how long will that be?" My sister sounded faint, tears in her eyes. "Okay, thank you. We'll see you soon."

I could not breathe, waiting to hear the words that would follow tears and a gunshot.

"They'll be home in a couple hours." Lisa struggled to smile, drowning in her relief. "They'll be okay."

It took me a long moment to feel anything. My knees weakened as the words seeped into me slowly; Leilani's restraint turned to support. I laughed once, overwhelmed by my anticipation that they would be home soon, and with barely any time to spare.

~~ * ~ * ~ * ~~

The knock on the door sounded louder than I knew it was, but I could not bring myself to stand and answer. It had already happened twice now, and twice I found my children still absent. Once had been Robert returning to the house. The second had been a cousin from the orchard with their congratulations.

My sister was still phoning to inform people that the ordeal was over. All the same, I could not bear disappointment again, already having my every nerve frayed and at my wit's end. This was some cruel torment not even Beth could have created.

Robert was the one to answer this time, footsteps like some surreal countdown that preceded my hope's rise and fall. There was the subtle click of the door being opened, the quiet creak of its hinges. Where he should have been greeting our next guest I heard silence, turning to look toward the door from my place at the table.

"Kyle?!" I hurried from my seat, fumbling and tripping in my rush to the door. My daughter peered in shyly. "Sarah?!"

When they saw me they rushed inside, running to where I was still on the floor disentangling myself from my chair. I forfeited the endeavor, grabbing them both and holding them close. Their tiny little hands clung to me tightly, strong and steady despite their trembling.

"It's all right now, I've got you," I told them, finding myself crying yet again. The relief was overwhelming, drowning out every doubt and fear of the last two days. I wrapped my tail over them, closing my wings around them protectively. "Oh, I've got you, I won't let him hurt you again."

They continued to tremble in my arms, crying incoherently. They smelled foul, faces dirty and bruised. I saw where the cur had struck Sarah's cheek, hating that there was nothing I could have done to stop it.

"Oh, you were both so brave," I cried, still feeling like they were not safe enough, even hidden away in my embrace as they were. The detective watched me with a stern gaze. I ignored him, trying to help my children to calm down. "I'll keep you safe now, I promise. Would you like your stuffed toys? I'm sure they missed you, too."

Timid little nods answered, and I reached up to the table for their toys where I had set them earlier. Kyle and Sarah both snatched them up eagerly, finally releasing their grip on me to be cradled properly. I could do nothing but smile through my tears, a child in each arm.

I glanced at the window and the morning light filtering in. "What would you like for breakfast, hm? I'm sure you must be hungry."

They nodded slowly, Kyle asking quietly, "Can we have pancakes?"

"Of course, you may have pancakes, my boy," I told him gently, finally earning the smallest smile from him.

"Yum," he chirped, fiddling with his bear and still visibly nervous.

"Oh, I'm sure." I looked to my daughter, nearly catatonic now she had her rabbit in hand. "Sarah?"

She kept her gaze fixed on her toy, picking at its freshly-sewn eye. "Scrambled eggs, please."

"Of course, sweetheart. And syrup, I would guess?" They both nodded. "All right, we can make pancakes and scrambled eggs. May I get up to cook?" They both grabbed onto my hands tightly in reply, Kyle shaking his head fervently. "Very well, I can ask Aunt Lisa."

"I'll get it started." The reply startled me, coming from just over my shoulder. I had been so absorbed in my reassurances and comforting, the rest of the world had ceased to matter.

"Thank you." I smiled at my sister in gratitude,

the gesture feeling genuine for the first time in days. I looked back to my little ones and their dirty faces, feeling nothing but joy at having them home. "We should get ready, hm? I'll start a quick bath and get you both into something clean."

"Can we wear pajamas?" asked Sarah, still quiet and timid.

I nodded, hurting that the outspoken daughter I knew was so subdued. "Whatever you like today, Sarah."

She finally looked at me with a tiny smile despite the bruises I saw on her cheek, surrounding her eye. "Thank you, Dad."

I pecked her on the forehead in reply. With a tired groan, I worked to free myself from the chair to stand. The effort was well worth continuing to cradle my children, despite the aching protests of my exhausted body. Leilani materialized beside me, helping me to stand without compromising my grip on the children I held.

The demoness followed me upstairs, aiding me in the task of seeing Kyle and Sarah into clean clothing. She took my daughter for a quick bath before trading off to dress Sarah while I cleaned Kyle up. Their faces were barely the start of their bruising, arms covered and wrists raw. I recognized injuries of a struggle from my own experiences resisting in the Institute.

Still, the instant they were both bathed and dressed in their nightclothes, they were back in my arms again. Even their usual preference for Leilani was forgotten now, refusing to allow me even a moment away. I would take it. Happily, I would keep at this however long they needed for it to ease their fears. No matter the time it took, it would always be too soon for them to leave my arms again.

By the time we returned downstairs for breakfast, Kyle and Sarah had fallen asleep, clutching their stuffed toys tightly. Thirty-seven hours was too long for them to have been away. I could only imagine how exhausting it had been for them.

"Sleep well, little ones," I murmured with a smile, finding Robert finishing with the detective as I reached the last step. Leilani was just behind me, hovering close by with her eyes glued to the children I carried. I heard her stifle a quiet hiss when the detective approached me.

"I need to ask how you knew where they'd be," said Mitch quietly, eyes fixated on the sleeping children in my arms.

I hesitated, terrified of answering. If he thought me mad, would he take them from me? What if he considered me dangerous? "I...I have an exceptional sense of intuition."

"Intuition?" he echoed flatly, raising one brow. "You knew the room number based on intuition?"

"Why does it matter?" I asked nervously.

He crossed his arms, scrutinizing me. "It's just a little suspicious, is all. They get kidnapped, and two days later you call claiming they're going to be trafficked with the exact location of the meet?"

Robert came to my rescue then, overhearing the informal interrogation. He kept a cool smile as he looked to me first, "You told him about the anonymous tip we got?"

It took me a moment to grasp at the ruse, but I

nodded, dropping my gaze nervously. "Yes, of course."

"No, he told me it was intuition." It was Robert's turn to receive that stare.

Robert laughed at that. "No one's that good. No, we got a tip, and the person wanted to remain anonymous. I guess he didn't realize that we didn't have to make a cover story for the tipper. He's still getting the hang of modern social norms."

"Right. Well, if you get any more tips, let me know," he said slowly. He nodded to the sleeping bundles I held. "I had my doubts about a demon, but you do well with them. Take care."

"Thank you." I watched him leave, my sigh of relief making my entire body feel weak from the tension I released. I turned to Robert, grateful. "And thank *you*. I thought he might try to arrest me next."

"Well, he's right that it's a little fishy," explained Robert, giving me a similar stare. "How *did* you know?"

"I had a dream," I confessed quietly, wary should anyone overhear. "I saw them, I saw him hitting Sarah for calling me their dad, but she was so defiant. Then...I found the room, and they were gone. He was there with bags of money, and all that was left of them was her barrette."

Robert stared at me in amazement. "You really do have dreams like that? I mean, when you told me before I thought you were just...I don't know, superimposing false memories?"

"That would be more believable," I agreed with a shy smile. "Almost preferable, if they weren't so helpful."

"Definitely good luck in this case," he chuckled,

giddy. He shook his head, smiling at the sleeping bundles in my arms. "Why didn't you see it beforehand, though? Or sooner than tonight, since the kidnapping?"

"I...I feel that this may have been my first dream that I purposefully sought out," I admitted slowly, recalling how deliberate each action had been. "I have never commanded one to happen before, but I could not stand being so helpless. It was the only thing I could do for them."

Robert nodded slowly, watching me with a smirk as I stifled a yawn. "We can talk about it later, bud. Why don't you go get some sleep? In a bed," he amended when I made to find the couch.

I grinned. "I suppose I should. Send my apologies to Lisa?"

"You'll owe me," he teased, nodding. "I'll get it handled. Get some sleep, you look...well..."

I chuckled and nodded, sighing tiredly as I made the climb back to the second story. By the time I reached the hall upstairs, my body felt weighed down, movements heavy and sluggish. Still, I managed to settle myself into bed without waking Kyle or Sarah. Before I drifted off, I was able to recognize Leilani as she tucked herself in beside me, refusing to allow the children to leave her sight.

~~ * ~ * ~ * ~~

March 28th, 2012

My precious little monsters are home. I cannot

seem to completely accept it, terrified that they may be stolen away again should I grow too comfortable. I have done my best to ease them back into our regular routines, and in light of this, they appear to be recovering well. Robert has even volunteered to take time for informal sessions with them, as a precaution. I am eternally grateful to have such a generously kind friend and am all the more confident in my choice of guardian for my children.

Their nightmares have worsened, however, no matter how well they are acting during waking hours. My bed has turned into a grand visitation center, with the children sleeping with me most nights since they returned home. I will tuck them into their beds, and sometime in the night one or both will wander in to join me, instead. Even Leilani has taken up the habit, waking when she hears the little ones stirring and coming to check they are all right before joining our odd puzzle of sleeping space, which often ends with me half-off the bed entirely.

The seasonal break has provided immense relief in all of this. It has allowed us time for the dust to settle before the children return to their schooling. Robert has reassured me on several occasions that my confidence during the situation and strongly built rapport both have been crucial to such a swift recovery, as well. While they have relaxed considerably—and, according to Robert, should be well enough to resume our former habits—I imagine Leilani and I will only suffer in their absences for some time longer.

If only I could find the same solace as my children, to know so wholly that they are truly safe. I understand that they are doing so well because of my efforts to protect them now, however. Simply one more facet to this job I have coveted for so many years, and I am relieved to know that I have performed the task admirably enough to be beneficial.

Still, through all of this, we now have the trial tomorrow. Kyle and Sarah have been asked by Mitch to accompany me, in the event their presence may aid in a proper conviction. The detective has expressed concern that their father may walk away with little consequence, given how hurried this case has become. I will be requesting a restraining order, in the hopes it might serve as a deterrent, at the very least. Robert suspects their father will let it lie after this, something about it all being too much trouble to pursue again.

I have also learned where Lisa had gone to that day, that she was not home with Leilani at the time. Ethan had called her not thirty minutes before the incident to speak to her at the diner. The coincidence is uncanny, although neither of us have spoken of it outright. We both know that the two crooks associate together regularly, but my sister is intent to enjoy her denial of our brother's despicable nature. I fear I may not restrain myself if I see him again, and I know I will savor every second of it should it come to that.

~~ * ~ * ~ * ~~

Twenty-sixth Week After Paradise

Friday

Karma Rose

As I sat waiting, I took in the grungy visiting area nervously. The stale air was too cold, the surfaces I could see giving me the distinct feeling of being unclean. My hands shook terribly, breath hitching every other inhale as I wondered why it was I had come. I had seen more than enough of the cretin at the trial, recalling again how disappointingly lacking his sentencing was.

Just a few short months in a correctional facility, followed by double that on probation. For kidnapping and attempting to traffic my children; his assaulting Leilani was never addressed. I could only assume that the neglect of her suffering was encouraged by the new consideration for laws requiring demons to pass sentience tests.

What am I doing here? I wondered, unable to understand this compulsive need for resolution. *What is the point of this? What could I hope to gain?*

A flash of movement on the other side of the filthy viewing window made me jump, nerves frayed. There he sat, the vile monster who had caused so much trouble. He wore a haughty smirk, arrogant and proud even in his gaudy jumper.

"What, sick of the brats already? Come to beg me to take 'em back?" he scoffed at me. The comment saddened me, that he could think so poorly of the little ones I had grown to love and adore.

"No," I replied, subdued in my anxiety. "No, I love my children, I could never tire of them."

"They're not yours!" he snapped angrily, disgust twisting his already aggressive features. "You're just some dumb fucking animal! Belong in a goddamn *zoo*."

Broken Orbit

The remark should have stung, I knew, but I could not rid my mind of how keenly he detested my little monsters. I sighed shakily, doing my best to breathe deeply and evenly.

"I read to them every night," I said slowly, lost for why I thought the detail important. "Sarah asks me to help her put her hair back, and Kyle has trouble with his shoes most mornings."

"Yeah, not my problem," he snapped irritably.

"I love it," I laughed incredulously, staring at my hands as my nervousness vanished. Where I had once seen inhumanity in this crimson skin and these blackened claws, I saw the hands that my children had known as the things that could guard them, tend to them and nurture. I smiled. "It is everything I could have hoped for since I was a young man. I have always wanted to be a father. I always wanted the smiles, the toys everywhere, the playtimes and grins. Just as much as I always wanted the messes, the nightmares and sleepless nights. I love it all."

"You really aren't human."

"No, I cannot deny that. Human or not, though, I am enough of a man to act with integrity where my children are concerned," I replied bitterly. As I gained confidence, I felt cheated that his imprisonment far from suited his crimes. Not while mine had dragged on so sadistically. He had windows, he still had some shreds of freedom. All because I looked as he behaved. "As a man, I am ashamed of you. I am disgusted that you would sully the image of us who work to do better for the world. You would ruin our reputation as men, actively reject your offspring, and for what? What could be worth that?"

He smirked. "About fifty grand, cash. But I'd also do it free if it kept something like you from ruining human kids."

Ethan's selfish reasoning came to mind. "Better abused and missing than with the likes of me, then?"

He shrugged. "Gives them a better chance not going to Hell, don't it?"

After everything you have done, they know that place all too well. I glowered through the glass at him, uncaring of how severely inhuman I may appear. Perhaps my face could serve as a proper mirror for his withered soul.

"Did you never once want them?" I asked, heartbroken that my children could ever know what it was like to be treated as such a burden. "Through no selfish desires or ulterior motives, truly want them, as they are?"

"Who would ever want disgusting little shits like those?" he retorted snidely.

I nodded sadly, taking a deep breath. "I would, and I will choose them every day for as long as I live, no matter the hardships it took to get here. I have left a copy of the restraining order for you, along with a formal letter barring you from visiting my children or my property. Both are to be filed with your belongings. I would appreciate you honoring them, and allowing my children to be happy without you. I hope you get everything you deserve in life, sir."

With that, I stood and left, ignoring the angry and spiteful comments he yelled at me from the other side of the window. He could have his words, and he could have all the distasteful things he desired now. Kyle and Sarah were *mine*. Despite his bravado, I could hear it in his defiance that he knew this, and would never want to correct it beyond his judgmental bias.

~~ * ~ * ~ * ~~

Saturday

"Dad. Can I talk to you?"

Hearing the serious tone of the inquiry, I stopped my rhythmic stitching to peer at my daughter. Her face was burdened by a heavy scowl, looking much too old for her age. I set my threaded needle aside in its cushion, anticipating her needing my full attention.

"All right, Sarah." I nodded, signaling to her that she had my focus.

She hesitated, wringing her hands nervously and staring at her feet. A habit she had been nursing since their father's meddling. It was one I recognized too well as timid shame.

"Um. Can we talk somewhere else?" she asked quietly. Her voice was shaking, and I could smell her fear. I hesitated, giving the start of my seam a hesitant glance and calling the task forfeit for the moment. I had only just begun to work on this dress for Leilani; she had enough to wear that this one could wait.

"Very well," I agreed, nodding again. She took a deep breath and turned around, shuffling out of the living room to the stairs. I followed, only able to take one step to her three as she led me to her bedroom closet. She curled up into the back corner, worrying me as she

387

wordlessly confirmed just how upset she was.

I held up one hand for her to wait for me to join her. I gathered a spare blanket from the closet's top shelf, stealing the pillow from her bed and her stuffed rabbit for good measure. Settling myself halfway into the closet— and too cumbersome to fit any farther—I helped nestle my daughter more comfortably into her hiding place and tuck her into it.

"Now then, is that better?" She nodded with a quick bob of her head, still avoiding looking at me. "Good."

She picked at her poor rabbit's eye for a long moment. "Can you close the door? Please."

"Of course." I stood with a quiet groan, easing myself out of the tight space with some difficulty. I closed the door, returning to my seat and leaning against the back wall of the closet awkwardly. No matter how I tried to contort myself, I would ever be able to fit properly. "There now, are you ready?"

Sarah hesitated but nodded, little hands quaking. "Yeah, I think so."

She was silent for a long while, and I settled in patiently while she collected her thoughts. Several times, I heard her take a deep breath as if to start, only to stop herself. What could be worrying her so? What had her father done that left such a lasting mark? I struggled to keep my imagination from running away with me when she finally spoke, her timid and shaking whisper sounding like a scream after the previous silence.

"I miss my dad," she confessed in a rush, sounding like she was choking on the words. "I was happy when he came and got us. I thought maybe he wanted us."

A flurry of emotions flooded me, from aggrieved rejection to confusion, anger to denial. They were all drowned out by my sympathy for her. It was the crown act of his villainy that he left her to cry in a closet, unwanted by the man she should have been able to trust, with little more than a stranger for a surrogate. I took a deep breath to steady myself, finding it difficult with the ropes I felt wrapped tight around my lungs.

"Sweetheart." What was I supposed to say? I knew she needed some sort of consolation, even if I could only ruin the delicate balance of comfort and confidence in my ineptitude. "That's perfectly natural."

Another long silence with several starts and stops of her bracing herself. "You're not mad?"

"No, Sarah, I'm not mad," I assured her gently. Was that what she feared? That I would disapprove of what was only expected for such a young person? I remembered then that their father had beaten them for placing their loyalties elsewhere. "I would never be mad at you for that."

"Really?" She finally looked up at me, face soaked with tears, her tiny frame trembling with her fright. "Promise?"

I offered her my little finger, hating how she flinched at my movement before accepting the gesture. "I promise, Sarah. If you ever want to pursue a relationship there, I will do everything in my power to help you, so long as I could keep you safe in the process."

She lurched forward to latch onto my arm, clinging tightly with all of the tenacity of a June bug. I rubbed her back with my free hand. Again, she flinched before she relaxed into the comfort of it.

"He doesn't want us, does he?" she whimpered, voice muffled and nearly too quiet to hear.

No, sweetheart.

My heart broke, and I felt fresh anger that he would leave his daughter to suffer in this. Indignation swelled in my chest, that he would allow another man to pick up the pieces that never should have shattered, to begin with. It was my turn now to brace myself repeatedly, trying to find some way to soften the blow without fruitless lies. She deserved the truth here, certainly, but she likewise deserved to smile after this.

"I think he's too angry to know what he wants," I offered feebly. I wanted to tell her to pack her bags, that he was on his way. I wanted him to realize his errors and change for these children. For her sake, I wanted it to be true. "I think he's not well and hasn't been for a long time, sweetheart."

She keened, fingers digging in as she held on tighter. Her slight shoulders began to shake with her sobs, growing louder as she wept. There was little I could do to comfort her, not until she was ready.

"Why doesn't he want me?!" she cried. Damn it all, why could I not make this right?! "I tried to be good! I tried!"

I could not stand it any longer, scooping her up and pulling her close. Her steely grip went from my arm to my neck, latching on tightly enough that I had to shift to breathe as her shoulder buried itself into my throat. I hugged her tight, resting one hand on her hair and rocking us as best I could in the cramped space.

"Hush now, darling, you did nothing wrong," I murmured, unable to hold back my tears much longer, hearing her sobs in my ear. I breathed deeply, the sound shaky. "Sometimes..."

I faltered, unable to collect myself quite well enough to continue. I thought of Ethan, someone I knew more personally, so I could clearly compose my words now. I explained gently, "Sometimes, people get sick, Sarah. They don't feel well or think quite right. They're sick on the inside, and they do things they shouldn't because of it. They don't always know how to get better, sweetheart."

She shook her head furiously, sobbing, "I think I'm broken, Dad."

"Sarah, look at me." She obeyed, sniffling and scared that she was in trouble. I sacrificed my shirt sleeve to dry her face, looking her in the eye and telling her firmly, "You are *not* broken, Sarah. You're perfect just the way you are, and I will always take you in a heartbeat."

Her face scrunched up and she latched onto my neck again. I let her, continuing, "I always wanted a daughter like you, right down to the littlest hair on your head. You're just perfect, darling, and don't you let anyone make you feel otherwise."

"I didn't mean to want to go," she choked out with a sniffle, and it took me a moment to realize she was referring to her earlier confession. "I know you're a better dad, but I just—I wanted—"

"Sh, sh, I know," I hushed her softly as she

dissolved into hysterics. I kept up my uneven rocking, stroking her hair. "I'm not mad, sweetheart, not even a little bit."

"You still want me?" she croaked. How was it she managed to tighten her hold any further?!

"*Always*," I promised. "No matter how old you are, or the differences between us, you will always be my little girl. Nothing you want or say could change that, ever. You're my daughter, Sarah. I love you, and it's my job to always love you, to want you, and keep you safe."

My poor little girl kept at her crying a good while longer, and I knew that she had been needing this since the moment she returned home. She had needed to confess her imagined betrayal, to know that I would not forsake her so easily. I would have to be more vigilant, then, to watch her needs for reassurances. I could do that. I would, to help her feel safe, secure, and loved, in order to build her up to be the remarkable young lady I knew her to be.

My precious daughter.

~~ * ~ * ~ * ~~

Twenty-seventh Week After Paradise

Sunday (April 1st)

I sat at the table quietly, glad to see that everyone else had already settled and started in on breakfast. Not long now, then. I fought a smirk, glancing over at my sister as she took the first sip of her morning tea.

Lisa gagged and coughed, glaring at me through her disgust. "Cory, what did you do?!"

I feigned innocent confusion. "Whatever's the matter, Lisa?"

"What's wrong with my tea?!"

"I haven't the faintest."

"Don't even hide it, Charles, it tastes like you steeped it with garlic."

I chuckled at that, grinning. Oh, how right she was. "Perhaps there was something wrong with the blend?"

The children and Leilani were watching our exchange with cautious amusement. My sister glared at me petulantly while I started in on my breakfast to keep up the charade. I fought the urge to spit the bite back onto my plate, wrestling with the overly-salted flavor and nodding to myself. I never should have turned my back on her at the table.

"How's your breakfast?" asked Lisa sweetly. "As good as my tea?"

"Scrumptious," I replied with a shudder. I cleared my throat, the salt making me parched. I made to wash it down, choking when I found my glass of water laced with lime. She always was better at this. My voice was strained as I croaked, "Shall we call a truce early, then?"

"Yes, we should. I'm too old to be doing this," giggled Lisa. She stood, collecting our cups and my plate to correct the situation.

Our audience kept on watching, grinning silently as they waited for the next prank to be had.

Karma Rose

Broken Orbit

April 3rd, 2012

My dear Katelyn,

I wish I had known. I wish you had told me. I wish I could have better prepared, to say I love you so many more times than I have. Had I understood how criminally numbered the moments were, my dear, I would have said it every second.

Still, that never could have sufficed. Perhaps, to show you my affection, to hold you in my arms...I should have stolen you away to live some grand adventure as you always dreamed of doing. I should have insisted we stay home, not leave to find the others.

We should have had our wedding.

You should have told me, Kate.

My promise is as good as kept.

Happy Birthday, my dear. I intend to plant daisies for you when the season allows; I hope you enjoy them, wherever you are.

With love,
Cory

Karma Rose

Broken Orbit

Lunar Anomaly Resolved

An unexplained lunar anomaly has resolved itself after eight months of baffling experts worldwide. It was first observed early last August, presenting as a lack of new moon and giving the illusion of the lunar cycle jumping from waning to waxing.

When questioned about the perplexing new phenomenon, top scientists were unable to provide a definitive answer for the cause. It's speculated that there was an atmospheric condition creating light distortion, resulting in the unique repeat occurrences. Many experts are reluctant to discuss the matter further without the continued pursuit of solid answers.

Regardless of the cause, it's certainly good to have our full lunar cycle back! The world of astrology has never been so dissonant.

Karma Rose

Chapter Eleven:
When Worlds Collide

Twenty-eighth Week After Paradise

Thursday

"Watch for my wings."

When I woke, there was a distinct thought in my mind, nearly overwhelming to me. All I could recall of dreaming was an image of Braxen's face reflected through dark water. It was reminiscent of how I had used a mirror to speak to him, as a way to focus my intent in the hopes my words may reach him.

It seemed that my attempts had succeeded, and his to replicate the experiment had done the same.

"Braxen is visiting today," I muttered to myself, sighing tiredly as I realized that meant a need to prepare. Introducing people to Leilani had been trying enough, even with her naturally approachable demeanor. The demon I had come to adopt as a brother, however... "Lisa is going to have my head! Oh, and Robert is coming for the afternoon..."

There was a tentative knock on my bedroom door, the knob rattling as it swung open a moment later. Sarah peered around it hesitantly.

"Dad? Are you okay?" she called worriedly.

"Of course, sweetheart," I replied, sitting slowly with a habitual glance at the clock. I fell from my bed in a panic, realizing I had slept past my alarm with barely an hour left to feed and dress the children before school. "I'm awake! Bring your brush downstairs, darling, we don't have time for proper styling this morning."

"What if Leilani helps?"

"If she's awake," I agreed, stepping around my daughter and rushing downstairs. There was no time to change from my nightclothes this morning, let alone worry over Braxen.

Until I entered the kitchen to make breakfast, finding the demon already seated at the table and looking around with an intrigued smile.

Braxen grinned when he saw me. "Oh. Hello!"

By the time I was able to return inside from running the children out to the bus, the rest of our household was beginning to stir. Hearing Leilani and Lisa's shuffling upstairs, I grabbed Braxen by the shoulder and hurried out the back door with him in tow. I did not stop until we were out of sight of the house, hidden behind the old coop. I was not prepared for the commotion his presence would certainly stir up when people met him today.

"When you said you were visiting today, I hoped I might have more time to prepare than just waking up,

Braxen!" I snapped as I finally released my hold on him. Still, I could not lie to myself that I was not at least somewhat relieved to see him. The familiarity of his presence was comforting, feeling even more like a brother than the last time I had seen him.

"I meant to give you more time—I did—but then I couldn't wait any longer," he confessed, embarrassed by the predicament. He reminded me of Kyle when the boy wanted for something too excitedly to possibly be patient.

I nodded slowly, dismissing my agitation with a shrug. "It's all right, I suppose, if a mite bit frustrating. Why are you here, though? Not that I don't appreciate the visit, of course."

"Cory, I came to talk with you about the village." The way Braxen spoke, his words sounded like the admittance of an egregiously offensive criminal, guilty to voice his transgressions aloud to me. "I know you have humans to worry about now. Please, we don't have anyone else to help us anymore."

"Braxen, what happened?" I asked, knowing already that I would not enjoy the answer. I felt his worry like an echo to my own.

"Vladimir wants to evacuate the village," he told me quietly, eyes flicking up to meet mine. "I don't know who else to turn to, Cory. The Drinker has a mind for strategy, but those people look to me for leadership. I'm sorry. I need help."

"Braxen, you have nothing to apologize for," I assured him, frowning deeply as I considered the conundrum. Evacuating so many people would take weeks, at least, if not months. "You came to me for what, then, my opinion? Guidance? Companionship?"

He shrugged, lost for answers. "I don't know."

"Well, where are you evacuating to?" I prodded gently. He shook his head mutely. I sighed, his confusion all-consuming. Using the tricks Robert had taught me I breathed deeply, fingers straying to the bracelets I wore to calm myself. Gradually, I saw the same ease spreading across Braxen's face.

My attention strayed to the back fields for a brief distraction in the hopes I may better collect myself. The earth there was still far too barren to be useful for several more years, at least for planting. I would have to make do with it as a sparse pasture for some stock or other. Perhaps I could scrap it for any sort of crop. There was certainly plenty of fencing. All I would need is a proper barn for any animals I owned.

I sighed tiredly, returning to the problem at hand. "I will consider what I can do from here, Braxen. My apologies that I cannot offer more than that now."

The marigold demon nodded slowly. He appeared somewhat less strained, at least. Perhaps he had needed a confidant as desperately as myself this year. "Thank you, Cory. In the village, I have no one else I can speak to so freely, given the position we're in with the angels, and...Well, I needed my brother."

He smiled wryly, lips curling enough to show his fangs. I returned the smile, weary of the endless trials these last several months had set forth for both of our worlds. I gave him a firm pat on the shoulder.

"Come now, I suppose I should feed you," I sighed in defeat. I would have to introduce him to Lisa at some point, and Leilani was certain to enjoy having someone to speak to more naturally.

Braxen nodded, a grin breaking out on his face. "I know where everything is."

"How is it I have no privacy anymore?" I pondered dryly.

"Kyle showed me everything." He laughed at my dumbfounded expression as we meandered back toward the house. "Your kitchen isn't particularly vision-inspiring, Cory."

I chuckled at that, holding the door for him to enter first. I followed behind, ducking into the kitchen and stopping there as a mug hit the floor with a sharp *crack*. My eyes immediately found my sister's, hers bugging wide as her face drained of any color. She struggled for words for a moment while Braxen waved and grinned, brimming with enthusiasm. I heard Leilani on the stairs, her footsteps hurried as she rushed to Lisa's side.

"Lisa? Is okay?" she asked concernedly. The little demoness lifted the broken mug gingerly, puzzled as she finally followed my sister's mortified gaze. The mug fell again, breaking into even more pieces as Leilani charged at Braxen to hug him tight. Her shriek of excitement broke my sister and me from our trance. The world resumed its normal pace as she chattered in her native language at the unsuspecting Shaman.

I stepped past and took my turn collecting fragments of broken ceramics. "Lisa, I can explain, I assure you."

"You had better," she agreed faintly. I could smell her fear, and I knew that we were in for an exceptionally long day.

~~ * ~ * ~ * ~~

Saturday

"All right, *now* I'm going outside," I called, the following thunder of running children making me smile. They tore into the kitchen, all grins. "Remember that Aunt Lisa has asked for no running inside, please."

"Okay," they replied in tandem, rushing past. I saw Kyle making to shove past his sister for the door, reaching down to stop him gently.

"Not so fast, my boy." He turned to look at me, curious and guilty. I smiled to let him know that there was no reprimand. "You and I are men, we walk beside or behind women. The only time we should step in front is to help or protect."

"That's weird," he commented honestly, but he was listening intently.

My smile broadened. "Not at all. It's our job as men to do it out of respect."

"But why?" he asked, still expecting some sort of stern word. "Sarah's just a girl."

"Do you know who else are girls?" He shook his head. "Mothers, grandmothers, your aunt, even Bailey, and Leilani."

"Oh." He glanced at his sister. "But she's still just Sarah, Dad."

"And she is just as deserving of respect as your aunt," I told him, spotting the tag of his shirt and tucking

404

it without a second thought. "It is kind and thoughtful to show respect to others. It speaks volumes of who you are, as well."

He made a face and whispered loudly, "But she's still just my sister."

"You're still a kind young man," I pointed out, making him beam with pride. "And kind young men respect women, even their sisters."

"Fine." He grumbled, staring at his shoe grumpily. "Can we still go outside?"

"Yes, we can, we just let Sarah through the door first," I chuckled, patting his shoulder and turning him back toward the door in time to see Sarah sticking out her tongue. "And young ladies act with grace."

My daughter corrected herself, righting her posture quickly. She grinned sheepishly, inching for the door. I reached over them to open it, holding it ajar as they sprinted outside. The early morning light was warm and soft as I strode across the yard to see to the new hens first, the morning ritual comforting.

I sighed quietly, more than amused despite the lingering feeling that they had gleaned little. Yet I found that I would gladly repeat the lesson just to watch as, bit by bit, it stuck. Even seeing how far they had come from when I first met them made my chest swell with pride.

"Dad, look!" Sarah's excited outcry caught my attention when I left the coop, hens pecking happily at their breakfast. She beamed as I came to inspect the garden bed she was pointing at. "There's new leaves on this one!"

"So there are." I knelt, smiling at the sight as she

bombarded me with questions about everything we had planted. I had answered at least half of them twice before, I knew. Still, I could not be anything but glad for the opportunity to do so again, watching her face light up with excitement as she took it all in.

~~ * ~ * ~ * ~~

Thirty-second Week After Paradise

<u>Sunday</u>

My morning began earlier today than what had become my norm with my children's schooling schedules. There was plenty to do, given the holiday at hand. The children wanted to celebrate in many ways, giving recognition for a number of people. Namely Lisa, as the obvious option. I had a surprise ready, as well, should they desire to visit their grandmother's grave.

Awake barely an hour now, and I was already up to my elbows in damp soil, working by the light of the setting moon. Beside me were potted daisies, mature and in full bloom with their smiling yellow flowers. Sarah had been asking for some time now if we could plant anything for Kate, although the young girl seemed far too reluctant to be directly involved in the task. She still missed her grandmother terribly, I knew. These daisies were as much a gift to my daughter as they were for my late fiancée.

Before I realized I had finished with the deed, I was pressing in the loose soil around the fresh plantings. Gathering up my tools in the empty pots, I stepped back to admire my work grimly.   Katelyn's gravestone was cheery, decorated on either side and the better-looking of the four markers now tucked away in the back beside my own.   My regular grooming of the little graveyard had done the area plenty of good, bringing somber tranquility to the site that made visiting more bearable.

"Happy Mother's Day, my dear," I choked out faintly. I grimaced as my grief drew in too close, setting it aside habitually.

Not today.

Returning the items I held to the shed, I washed up at the hose before making my way inside to ready myself for the rest of this already long day.

~~ * ~ * ~ * ~~

Tuesday

Robert took a seat on the worn front porch steps, watching me work. I had fresh rose bushes to plant; Mother had always wanted climbing red roses out front. I glanced over as I buried the spade and braced it to clear the soil. In his hands, he was fidgeting with an envelope bearing an eerily familiar stamp on its front. I stifled a shudder. Something was wrong.

"Would you like anything to drink, Robert?" I asked to break the silence that stretched on. Redundantly, given how he and his family were barely considered proper guests anymore. They may as well have been Lawrences themselves, with as close as our households had become.

He shook his head with a guilty grimace. "No thanks, bud. I have something for you. I don't see why they went over your head through me, but..."

I stopped my digging, reaching out to accept the letter and dropping it in the same instant. I glared hatefully at the neat lettering that declared its sender, my fingers burning where I had touched it.

"What do they want, Robert?!" I demanded, more than done with their scheming and unwarranted abuse of me.

He was tired, pale face drawn as he grew reluctant to speak. "The Institute is requesting your cooperation for annual exams."

The spade fell from my hand with a noisy clatter. The air in my lungs choked me, skin too tight across my body. I felt the walls closing in on me, even standing in the open air with the sky above me.

I shook my head numbly. "No, Robert. I won't. They can't make me do a damned thing!"

"If they don't hear back by today, they'll schedule a liaison to make a courtesy call," he recited his words, sounding as broken as I was defiant. "I got the letter this morning. And they're closed for maintenance until tomorrow."

"They planned this," I growled, unable to stop myself from shaking. My tail lashed at the air behind me.

"I'd put money on it," agreed Robert with a nod. "I'm sorry, Cory, I know this is the last thing you need right now. We don't have much choice but to agree tomorrow, though."

I felt my heart stop in my chest. "*LIKE HELL!*"

"Cory, if they come by and find Leilani..." He sighed heavily. He had already had too long to think this over on his drive from the city. I could not tell if I was grateful for his consideration of her or hateful of his willingness to throw me to the wolves. "She doesn't have the certifications you do under the new laws, and she still doesn't speak English well enough to pass the Sentience Tests. She may as well be a stray dog to them."

"Son of a *gun!*" I swore, a string of profanities leaving me before I could stop myself. My nerves were wound tight and I had to pace to relieve some of the tension. I could not stand the thought of the mild little demoness anywhere near that hell on earth, those spattered masks with their glinting steel and stabbing needles. A vicious snarl broke free from my chest. "I won't allow them to touch her or any other demon. I would watch that prison burn first!"

A clawed hand found mine as I whirled to stalk back along the path of my pacing. The copper eyes I found were tight with worry, watching me carefully. As much as I loathed the idea to cooperate in any way peacefully, it was worse to think of her in the room I had been trapped in for too long. My voluntary acquiescence to their request was the lesser of two evils, certainly. Still only barely, though, as my veins were flooded with terror.

"Why angry?" she asked quietly. Her coral skin shimmered in the sunlight, smooth and unbroken by scars.

I grimaced, selfishly considering for the briefest second if I could spare myself returning to the pit, no matter the risk to Leilani. The wrenching guilt and sense of responsibility I felt for her told me there was no way out. I had to venture into the lion's den.

Shaking my head helplessly, I found I could not speak. Leilani nodded once, accepting my silence. If only she could join me, I knew that she would see me through with my sanity intact. Returning to her and my children would have to suffice, however. In order to spare her suffering such inhumane treatments, where I had not been considered human.

~~ * ~ * ~ * ~~

Friday

"Robert, if-if I don't—If they—" My words fell short, staring at the doors I never thought I would see again. My heart was racing, the sheer terror in my body unbearably brutal.

The lingering apathy I had been warring with no longer seemed to be a problem, at least.

His hand on my arm did little to soothe this anxiety. "I won't let you out of my sight, Cory. I've also got a failsafe so people know where we are. If either of us doesn't come back, this place will be swarmed with lawyers and news stations."

I nodded shakily. "Very well, then."

~~ * ~ * ~ * ~~

Gloved hands moved about me in an eerie, demented ballet. I clenched my teeth to keep myself from making any sounds they could perceive as threatening.

The arms of the familiar steel chair bit into my palms, I gripped it so tightly. They began to strap me in, no doubt out of habit before Robert's voice snapped out angrily.

"I don't think that's necessary." The assistants hesitated before undoing the tight bonds. "Good."

It was everything I could do to keep from devolving into madness. This place had stolen so much from me already, I despised that I had to give them even a minute more. For one criminal second, I wanted anyone else to be in that chair, so long as I could be free.

Leilani.

I could not jeopardize my friend's safety; my better virtues were deeply ashamed for the moment of weakness. Of all the things they had perverted in my life, I had clung tightly enough to my morals as a man to keep them from the worst of the damage. Bruised and battered, perhaps, but I was not an animal.

I would never give them that satisfaction.

The smell of latex was nauseating, and I stared at the painfully bright light above me for anything to focus on. I felt them preparing my arm for a blood draw, the reek of alcohol burning my nose. There was the pinch of the needle—in that second and a thousand others that had played out over the course of a lifetime. Out of a long-used habit of self-preservation, I recited my mantra, the thing that had given me the will to fight against their bonds as long as I had.

My name. My name is Cory Charles Lawrence.

"Can you grab me a couple extra vials? I want to be sure we have enough."

My parents are William and Eleanor.

411

"That's it, just one more. Almost done."

My daughter is Sarah, my son is Kyle.

They finished with their needles and led me to the room where my measurements had always been taken. Too many decades, they had treated me like little more than a wild monster. I had not dedicated my earliest years to refining self-restraint—practicing a careful balance of neglected instincts and deprived cravings—to have them be disregarded so easily. Not by me.

My name is Cory Charles Lawrence, and I am a man.

"Step here. That's a jump in weight, but it seems healthy. Good. And stretch the wings—excellent."

I am a man.

"Great. Now then, how's the range of motion in the shoulder?"

I am a man.

"Not good. It stops him from living like he used to, and any prolonged use means hours of pain."

Paul? No. No, the tone sounds right, certainly, but the voice...Robert.

"Ah. Well, then, that just leaves tissue samples. Cheek swab, horn cutting, s—"

When would it end? Please, let it end.

"Are you insane?! You know he has nerves, blood vessels—!"

I want to go home.

"We'll be careful. But especially with that drastic of a color change, we need to know what's going on there."

Let me go home.

"Just get it over with," I muttered, bracing for the pain I knew would come. I noticed someone collecting tools, all too easily recognizing the saw they always used for my horns. My fingers drifted to the woven strands on my wrist, feeling the same desperation I once had when I clung to my photos and phone calls.

My name. My parents. My children. I am a man.
I am a man.
I am a man.

~~ * ~ * ~ * ~~

Somehow, those doors opened for me again, the bright world outside so near I could smell it. My chains weighed heavily on my mind, keeping my body from moving to take those steps to freedom. There was a morbid comfort to knowing my place here, however perturbing it was. The chaos outside was nearly as mortifying as these walls now.

"There you are." My heart stopped when I heard that voice, the woman who had tormented me for decades—in the waking world and nightmares alike.

"Beth." I linked my shaking hands behind my back, finding the horror of a woman easily enough. Even withered with age she was still severe, holding power in her demeanor that I could only fear. More than I feared the angel Bravery, I dreaded her presence.

"Mr.Lawrence." The name she used was wrong, tone tamed and...respectful. What did she want from me? "It's good to see you again."

"I find it difficult to say the same," I muttered

bitterly. Where were the armed guards at her command? When would they beat me into submission, drag me back to my cell?

"I was sorry to hear about Miss Smith," she told me, ignoring my tone. To my amazement, she appeared sincere in her words. "It's a pity, losing her when she was out...exploring. Must have been quite an adventure, seen some exotic animals."

My heart turned to ice.

She knew.

"We were spending time as a family," I explained weakly. Beth was not convinced.

"Well, if you have a chance, you should come by my house for lunch. You can tell me all about that family time," she suggested, eyes flashing with hidden meaning. She handed me a small slip of paper, adding quietly, "I'm considering going into exotic animal rescue, after retiring. If you find any that need rehabilitation before being papered, let me know."

Oh, damn, she knew.

How did she know?!

I nodded shakily, tucking the paper in my pocket. "Of course. Very well, then."

After seeing Beth, I was more than ready to leave. No amount of routine could make me ignore what horrors she had contributed to in this place. So I stepped outside, breathing deeply the fresh air that smelled of spring, tears of relief burning on my cheeks.

I stretched my wings wide, savoring the feel of such open spaces and the sunlight that warmed them. I wanted to fly as I had that first time I tasted my freedom, but those chains tethered me to the earth. Instead, I tucked my wings and followed Robert to the little yellow vehicle. I passed him the keys, subdued.

"I fear I am far too distracted, Robert, if you would not mind?"

He nodded once, going instead to the driver's door. We settled into our seats, the vehicle painfully confining. I cursed that my will was too weak to fly instead. Before we pulled out, Robert busied himself with the radio and his cellular phone, connecting the two with a cord. I frowned, focusing on my curiosity for anything to distract me from what I had just endured.

"Okay, I hope this isn't too weird, but I got Leilani's help with this specifically for today," he forewarned awkwardly. There was a recorded shuffling and static, a moment of silence, and then...

"Oh," I sighed, the relief I felt instant as always when I heard the soft chirrup preceding the quiet purr which promised safety to the most primal parts of me. My eyes slipped shut as I focused on the sound, embracing that animalistic need. It was able to drown out the thoughts of the man I worked to live as, and I welcomed it.

I am a man, I told myself again. *But I am not human.*

~~ * ~ * ~ * ~~

The recordings Robert had prepared for the journey home were invaluable. They helped ease me into a tempered calm, exhausted still and far too stressed to be of any good to anyone. Still, it was a scrap of peace after enduring that hell on earth. Those primal urges I neglected so often were satisfied, at least, even as my domesticated nature dreaded the coming tasks. The simple thought of seeing my children was too much for me to bear at that moment.

Robert parked without a word, shutting off the engine and the recording with it. In an instant, the world came rushing back to me like a flood. It was suffocating, feeling like I was drowning in it all.

Without thinking of the actions, I was out of the car and trudging up the porch steps. The front door swung open, my hand falling from the doorknob weakly. The idle chatter I heard in the home was overwhelming, like the screams of a crowd to my ears. Their voices died at my entrance; the following silence was just as deafening.

My foot was on the first stair, my cowardly escape to my room interrupted by an excited shriek.

"Dad, you're back! School was so much fun today! We had a project—"

"Not now, Kyle." My tone was beaten, too tired from the day to muster anything more. I hated the stares I could feel on me, my scars burning shamefully. The missing chip in my horn may as well have been the brand that marked me a traitor to my freedom and the life I had built with it.

I could not even look my son in the eyes as I dismissed him.

"—and we got caterpillars a few weeks ago, and today—"

"Please, Kyle, I can't," I begged, desperate for any

scrap of patience that I could give him. There was nothing left to scrape for, my failed attempts catching only raw nerves.

"—they turned into butterflies! Isn't that super awesome, Dad?! They were so pretty, and when we let them go outside—"

"KYLE!"

The sound of my last shred of *anything* snapping was harsh, voice hitting the air like a slap that my son visibly flinched from. He stared at me in shock with wide, tear-filled eyes while I could only gasp for air in this aggravating exhaustion. I wanted to *want* to help him, to at least explain why he needed to curb his excitement, but I could not manage any more than that.

"Not now, my boy. Please. I can't."

Kyle was frozen in shock, his tiny frame trembling. Still, I found myself unable to give him anything more of myself. There was nothing left, barely even an excuse of a man remaining in this shambling mess of a shell.

Leilani crept over, scooping up the young boy and cradling him close. Her eyes were wary as she watched me. I shuddered, staring at the reason I had endured another day in hell. Morality. Decency. Some perverse notion that perhaps I could spare her the cruelty that had been given to me all too freely.

"Cory, are you okay?" It was Lisa who was asking, I knew it was her, a clawless hand brushing my arm.

I snarled rabidly at the sensation, like an icy burn against my skin. The humans all jumped at the sound.

"Don't. Touch. Me."

"Okay, it's all right, Cory," came the gentle tones of Robert. I nodded out of habit alone. When had he followed me inside? "You go do what you need, I'll help down here. That's it. Good, get some rest."

I climbed the stairs slowly, the racket of my children crying upsetting only due to the grating it caused in my ears. Every sound was too loud, too clear, and I heard the hushed whispers downstairs long after I was in my room, even with the door shut tight. I stared at the window in confusion.

"What was *that*, Robert?!"

"Shh, babies, is okay. Is only sad, is okay. Shh."

"Lisa, he's had a rough day."

"Rough day? Robert, I thought he might attack me."

"I don't think you understand what it was like for him to go back there, Lisa. It's going to take a few days for him to make it back home completely, so please be patient. I'll be here to help as much as I can, but if it's at all possible I recommend taking the kids somewhere else for a day or two. That way, Leilani and I can focus on helping Cory."

"Is Dad mad at us, Leilani? He never yells."

"Not mad. Sad, babies." Words in that demon language, so much softer to my ears.

"Well, I mean, I guess that makes sense..."

"Robert, why would he do this to himself? He should've said no!"

"He did it to keep Leilani hidden. They might have come looking for him here, and he didn't want them to hurt her like they did him."

That was it.

I leaned back against the door, sliding to the floor in a slumped heap. I recited my mantra, again and again, knowing I was home and safe but not feeling it. No, I felt as though I had never left that nightmare, to begin with. They never freed me, only put me on a longer leash, the chain of my collar strangling me now that I felt its presence.

My name. My parents. My children.

I am a man.

I am not human.

My brother is Braxen.

Leilani saved my family.

I went back to hell to save my friend from ever knowing its burning cruelty.

~~ * ~ * ~ * ~~

Two days.

It had taken two days of rigorous work to bring me back to myself. Robert was with us the first day in its entirety. He did not have any other appointments, in anticipation of a relapse after the NSISD. It seemed every other hour he was helping me collect the shards of myself, easing me through endless mental exercises to ground me.

By the end of that first day, the chains I felt were cut away, leaving my body weightless and exhausted. Leilani was always nearby, watchful eyes trained on me as a patient smile lit up her face; her unique way of speaking to me was a precious tool she took every advantage of.

419

Karma Rose

I could see that she wanted to help more directly, though, her fingers working even harder to keep busy with some task, but I still could not stand to be touched. If it was not from shame at my scars, it was from the razor-sharp sensation that any touch may lead to something far worse—to cuts, to cruelty and abuse.

They were patient with me, certainly far more than I was with myself. As soon as I had time to rest and recuperate even slightly, I was torn apart by how I had snapped at Kyle, that I had yelled and frightened both of my children. Without any explanation or apology, and then having them sent away? I hoped against the odds they would not despise me—fear me—that I could continue as their father when they came home.

The second day was only Leilani and me. She did everything she could for me, from cooking to comfort. I struggled through my daily work, breaking frequently to collect myself before I fell apart. By midday, I was finally finished.

Every part of me wanted to lie down and give up then. Leilani had other plans, however, determined to help me smile again. Through tenacious persistence—and perhaps more tolerance than I deserved—she finally had me at my old habits of listening to one of my favorite albums while I read. At one point, she asked me to read aloud, one clawed finger hovering just below the words on the page as I did so. She was learning quickly, considering her informal education and background.

That night, she helped me to sleep. I could finally stand physical contact, something she took advantage of as she helped me settle into bed. She would not hear any

420

of my half-hearted protests, always answering with a cheeky, "No words."

As she positioned me on my side with my back towards her, I already felt I could sleep for an eternity. Then I felt it, a delicate touch between my wings and running down my back. The pressure was light, reminiscent of having my hair stroked as she found her goal at my shoulder where my wing connected. She pressed gently, rubbing the nerves carefully.

There was a flood of emotion like I was flying. Without the rush of action to drive my heart into a gallop, however, it was only soothing. I may as well have been falling asleep amidst the clouds, drifting off with a quiet groan.

~~ * ~ * ~ * ~~

Thirty-third Week After Paradise

<u>Monday</u>

My grip on Leilani's hand was tight, eyes fixed on the living room carpet as I heard a vehicle pull up to the house. I breathed deeply, hoping to stop my nervous shaking before Kyle or Sarah came inside. I had made such an ass of myself; could they forgive me?

Car doors opened and shut, the sound of voices rang through the closed windows mutedly. Footsteps thumped across the porch, the front door opened slowly...

I released Leilani so that she could see to the children, in case they needed a moment longer to approach me. There was a calm chatter that she joined in on as she greeted them, and I felt like my heart might burst at hearing their happy voices again. Even subdued and quiet, I had missed that sound.

"Dad?"

I looked up from the faint burns on the carpet, into the cautious eyes of Kyle. He stood in the entryway, just outside of the living area, wringing his tiny hands nervously. I did not smell fear, no matter how much I knew I had earned it. I leaned forward to rest my arms on my knees, wanting to engage with him and unaware of how else to address this elephant crowding us.

"Are you still mad at me?"

"No, Kyle, I was never mad at you."

Stop shaking, please, I do not know how to fix this! I cannot stand to see you this way.

Sarah came to join him, holding her brother's hand tightly. She stared me down, black eyes scrutinizing as she searched my face. "Aunt Lisa said you were sad."

"That's the simple answer, yes," I agreed quietly. If I offered any more of an explanation, would they accept it? Was everything I had worked for with them ruined? I took a deep breath, bracing for the worst.

My daughter thought that over for a long moment, ever the skeptical little thing. "Are you better now?"

"For now, yes." She frowned, my admittance unappealing to her. I continued softly, "I've been sad, Sarah, for a long time now. It...It's a lot like being sad all of the time. Robert helps me with it, and I should be able to get better in time. But the other day...

"I went to a very sad place," I said quietly, forcing

myself to continue meeting their eyes. They were both distraught, in need of me, and yet I still felt so utterly crippled in my ability to help. "Where I was before I met you at your grandmother's. That day, I...I was just too sad to shake it. I never should have behaved that way. I'm sorry."

"I thought we made you happy." Her reply was disappointed in spite of her attempts to remain detached. Oh, sweetheart...

"You do, Sarah, the both of you, but it is not your job to look after me. Certainly not like that, not when I'm that sad," I explained gently. It began to feel like I might regain my footing, stand tall again as their father, provided they would still have me. "That's why I had to be alone for a little while. So that Robert and Leilani could help me not be so sad anymore."

Kyle looked up at his sister and whispered noisily, "Leilani's real good at that, Sarah."

She was still erring on the side of caution. "When will you be better for real?"

"It could take a while." Again, she was not satisfied, but her grimace was twisting more with her restrained tears than her anger at me. "Robert and I are working hard every day, and I should get better sooner than later. And I'm better right now."

It was everything I had to not lose control, to stay where I was and allow them to come to me. I knew they needed that from me, no matter how I despised sitting there. They needed to know that however they felt toward me, I would respect it. I had learned that lesson well enough from their father's mistakes, what few I had seen.

Through some gesture unseen to me, Sarah gave Kyle confirmation of the situation's safety. He hurried over eagerly, bouncing up into my lap before I had much time to prepare myself for him. I hugged him tightly. His arms locked around my neck as he trembled, finally caving to his upsets.

"I missed you, Dad," he sniffled. "I'm sorry you were sad."

"Oh, I'm all right now, my boy. I missed you, too," I sighed, voice thick. I saw Sarah, still just outside of the room, watching us longingly. I held out one hand as an invitation, resisting the urge to meet her any closer. She clenched her fists, and I recognized that look on her face from all of the upset her father had caused so recently. I could not hold my tongue any longer, "It's all right, sweetheart, it's still me. I'm not him, I'm still Dad."

Leilani appeared behind her, giving the girl a gentle nudge in my direction. That was all she needed, ducking her head and rushing over to join her brother in my arms. I held them both, feeling relief and joy at their forgiveness. Untainted by apathy or depression, I *felt* it.

As naturally as breathing, I was able to ease back into the role I had always longed to fill. It was not long before they were telling me about their weekend away at a cousin's house—Lisa's daughter and her family.

I grinned to hear of their adventures, frowning with them and their mutual dislike of Lisa's granddaughter and her opinions of demons. Still, I was able to bring their smiles back around, and they let me. My little ones, helping me as best as they knew how with their chatter and expressions and grand waving gestures.

424

Broken Orbit

I could see the light at the end of this darkness, at last. It had taken a detour into hell itself to break the apathy at my core, and even worse to bring me back from that raw state, but this was worth so much more than that. Leilani was safe, and I finally *felt* happy, like their father, so completely I could never doubt it.

I can do this.

~~ * ~ * ~ * ~~

<u>Saturday</u>

"This place is becoming far too familiar for comfort," I muttered, looking around at the clearing. The ruins still stood in its center, although now I had company.

A young woman that looked to be Bailey's age stood at the edge of the ruins. She reminded me of my mother, although she was far younger than I had ever seen her. Still, I recognized the oddity of how the world's color swirled around the woman, recalling the dizzying dreams she had starred in more recently than I liked. She beckoned me over with a broad, waving gesture, a mischievous smile dancing on her face.

I complied, uncertain if it would be a fruitful effort to defy this dream. "Who are you?"

"You don't recognize me?" she replied coyly. "I know, I look different without the other two, but we are a busy person, you know."

I sighed tiredly, already done with this. "And who are you, then?"

Karma Rose

"I'm Maiden," she replied proudly. "It was my idea to take a more informal approach with you from here on, especially with these recent developments of yours. Crone loves her theatrics, sorry."

"Of course, that all makes sense," I replied quietly, though sarcastically, looking at the ruins surrounding us. The Maiden led me through them without a word, stopping at a familiar place and waving me forward.

The archways were empty now, no hint of an image in their translucent surfaces. Yet I could recall too clearly the scenes I had witnessed before, of my daughter and the dream that had followed.

"What are these, then?" I asked, glancing at the young woman coming to my side. She waved a hand, the archways shimmering to life with a series of flashing colors.

"These are my mirrors," she replied, gesturing from left to right. "For the Maiden, Mother, and Crone. The threads of time I weave can be seen here."

Well, now. "When I saw Sarah...?"

"You saw through the Mother's mirror, the present moment," she explained with a youthful smile that held all of the pride of any parent. "You summoned the mirrors to use, and you used them well. However, there are still consequences..."

I followed her hesitant gaze, noticing for the first time a figure in the distance across the clearing. Judging by the hulking silhouette it cast, I could guess that it was a demon, too far away to discern much else as it strode slowly towards us. The movements were eerily graceful,

426

reminding me more of Bravery's unearthly beauty as it all but glided through its next step.

"Who is that?" I asked, expecting it to be another one of her illusions. She was fond of her theatrics, after all. One of her was, at any rate.

The Maiden's smile turned sly, eyes flashing with excitement. "You. Part of you that has been so deeply buried for so long. You woke it when you commanded our mirrors."

I swallowed back my terror of the creature. Even at such a distance, I knew it was too otherworldly to be me, too regal. "No. No, I am me. Whole and complete. That...that is something else. An imposter."

She raised one brow at me skeptically, expression nearly laughing at me. "That part of you is older than the body you wear so proudly. The reason Mother and Crone gave you someone to help shoulder the burden."

"Maiden!" Her voice whipped out behind me, an older incarnation of herself coming up on my other side wearing a hard scowl. This one I knew, my mother's wiser face the one I remembered so clearly. "Not yet, you know that."

The Maiden crossed her arms, expression petulant. "Fine, fine. I have my preferences, is all, Mother."

"And you can keep them to yourself," chided the Mother. It was disconcerting to see her arguing with herself where I was so accustomed to hearing them speak synchronously.

"I do not understand," I confessed, still shaken by the sight of that creature's approach.

The Mother smiled for me. "Soon, Prince. You're

427

where you need to be right now. Enjoy it while you can."

"Before, you tell me to 'become what I am' and other nonsense. Now, you would not tell me anything?" I scowled, frustrated by this confusion.

"I did say that," she agreed, her smile turning grim. "And you have already begun."

~~ * ~ * ~ * ~~

I groaned as I woke, my slow return to awareness shattered apart by a lurching in my stomach. I threw back the bedsheets and lurched out of bed. Stumbling out and across the hall to the bathroom, I felt my skin covered in sweat. The air was icy against me, even when I knew the night was balmy for spring.

My trembling body could not make it to my goal fast enough, lunging for the bathroom trash can instead as my stomach heaved violently. I coughed and choked, what little remained of my supper leaving me in a bout of burning acid. It was several minutes of useless spasms before my body at last accepted defeat, allowing me to slump over against the nearest wall. I shoved the trash can away from myself, unable to stand the smell.

I gasped for air, still shaking considerably. The sweat had not broken, and it took me a moment to realize that I was burning with a fever. That would have worried me, had I not been so utterly exhausted by it. My skull pounded, some cruel creature hammering away at it in time with my thundering pulse. The gentle *click* of the children's door closing had me struggling for composure and doing what I could to hide that I had already vomited.

"Dad? Are you okay?"

I smiled weakly. "Just tired, sweetheart. What are you doing out of bed?"

Sarah shrugged and hugged her stuffed rabbit. "I heard something. I think there's a monster outside, Dad."

Had I been vocalizing while I slept? I weighed my options carefully. "That was me, Sarah. I was making sure the other monsters would stay away, is all."

"Is that why you're sick?" she asked, and I knew I was foolish for thinking I could have hidden anything so obvious from her. I must have been pale, breathing heavily while the sweat was still drying on my skin.

"Never, sweetheart, those monsters can't get past me," I reassured her bravely regarding her imagined fears. Reaching out to tweak her nose, I was glad to see her smile. "I think I ate something off at supper. Just don't tell your aunt I blame her cooking," I added teasingly. There it was, that quiet giggle that meant she knew the world was safe. "Go on to bed now, Sarah. I'll be perfectly fine."

My daughter debated for a moment, bearing a deeply war-torn expression that worried me. She lifted her rabbit, kissed it and handed it off to me.

"I'll be right back, Dad, keep her safe," she said solemnly, little footsteps pattering downstairs quickly.

I listened to her frantic rushing with a tired smile, the pit in my gut churning slowly now that I had a moment to feel this illness more completely. I leaned over to the trash can, heaving dryly and without results. When I righted myself again, Sarah was standing in the doorway with a stoic expression.

There was a blanket draped across her shoulders, a glass of water in one hand and a fresh ice pack in the other. Setting the glass and pack on the counter, she pulled the blanket from her shoulder to drape it over me. Sarah fussed with the edges that failed to cover me, huffing a sigh when she finally settled for the futile results she had managed already.

"Sarah, what are you doing?" I chuckled, strength slowly returning to me.

"You're sick, so I'm being a doctor," she replied matter-of-factly. Of course, how silly of me to ask.

"Well, now, I feel better already."

She stretched up on her toes to open the cabinet above the counter, fingers straining for something. She grumbled a moment before she cried out triumphantly, holding up her small prize. She turned to me with a short-lived grin, brandishing the digital thermometer proudly.

"Open," she commanded, tucking the instrument beneath my tongue. I played along, feeling my fever breaking. Sarah grabbed the ice pack and set it atop my head, balanced between my horns. The thermometer beeped a moment later and she grabbed it with a critical frown. "Oh."

"What's the diagnosis, Doctor Lawrence?" I asked, biting back my grin.

"I don't know," she declared boldly. She showed me the tiny display. "Is that a bad number?"

"For you, yes, very. Not for me, though," I reassured her, and she let out a sigh of relief, tension visibly leaving her little shoulders. "You did a good job, Doctor."

Sarah nodded, pride making her smile as she swapped the instrument for the glass of water. She offered it to me, and I traded her rabbit for it. I sipped tentatively, awaiting my stomach's verdict before drinking more deeply.

"Thank you, darling, I feel much better." Finally, I felt like I might be able to return to bed, despite still being damp to the touch. "Go lie down and I can tuck you back in, hm?"

Sarah hesitated. "I'm scared."

I knew that look, smiling patiently. "Of the monsters?"

She nodded. "Can I sleep with you?"

"Very well." I groaned as I ambled to my feet somewhat shakily. I finished the glass of water and set it on the counter before herding my daughter back across the hall. I flicked the light on, wincing when I took in the mess of bedding. "Give me just a moment, Sarah."

I straightened the sheets, hesitating a moment when I caught sight of a burn mark. It matched the shape and size of my palm. Keeping my composure, I finished with the bedding, giving the spare pillow a quick pat.

"All right, now, into bed," I sighed tiredly, stifling a yawn. Sarah obeyed, plopping herself down where I had gestured. I tucked her in quickly. "There we are. I need to tidy the bathroom, and I will be right back, sweetheart. I can leave the light on if you'd like."

She nodded sleepily, already drifting off before I was out the door. I hurried through my tasks, namely returning the glass to the kitchen sink and setting the trash can out the back door. One more chore for the morning.

431

By the time I returned to my room, I was more than ready to lie down.

I shut off the light and shuffled to the bed tiredly, climbing in carefully and settling swiftly. Flashes of my dream replayed briefly behind my closed lids, lingering on those mirrors I had seen. The scene changed quickly, towards the morning to come and upcoming school activities I had to plan for.

~~ * ~ * ~ * ~~

Thirty-fifth Week After Paradise

<u>Tuesday</u>

What am I doing here?

The answer was simple enough, I knew, yet I could not shake this deep-seated doubt. My namesake had visited last week, with a formal invitation meet with my old rival—hand-written, signed and dated.

"Oliver mentioned something about him being reformed, but this?" I had questioned the true intentions behind the gesture, sought for ulterior motives hidden in the simply worded letter.

Corey had merely shrugged and kept on with his updates on the church's upcoming summer activities. He wanted my help with participation. I was but one of many stops for him to gather volunteers, and the distraction was welcome from the message he had delivered.

Which led me to where I was standing on the sidewalk dumbly, lost for why I should honor the request

432

at all.

Still, I stared at the diner, surprised by the nervous rush I felt. Last I had seen Richard, he had made a bet with me about a plow. He had lost with barely any semblance of grace or decency, and it was difficult to imagine him as anything but that angry young man. Regardless, I forced myself to approach the entrance, a bell ringing cheerily as I opened the door.

The interior was well furnished and clean. Several people were seated at various tables, involved in quiet conversations adding to a light chatter as a whole. I waited nervously as an older, heavy-set gentleman approached, beaming at me in welcome.

"Cory! It's good to see you," he laughed, and I barely recognized my old rival without the anger on his face.

"Richard?" I asked, having to confirm before I would believe it. I held out a hand to shake in greeting.

He nodded, ignoring my outstretched hand and giving me a quick embrace. "Welcome home, Lawrence. Gosh, it's been a minute. Last time I saw you...it was the plow!" he crowed, face lighting up.

"Is it too late to cash in on that bet?" I asked jokingly, at a loss for anything else to say.

"I insist," he chortled with a grin. "Lunch is on me. Would you mind if I joined you?"

"I suppose not, but...Richard?" He kept that grin, polite and curious despite my hesitation. "It may take me some time to adjust to...*this*."

"I expected as much," he admitted, grin fading to a look of guilt. "I, um, I was an angry young man, Cory, and

I did plenty of things I regret now. If you'll hear me out, I'd like to apologize for the way I treated you, and Kate. I've made amends with her already, but I'm sure it would help if I made an equal effort with you on her behalf," he added thoughtfully.

This was the man who had terrorized Kate and me for over a decade, sounding sincere in his desire to repent. Leading us to a quiet table near the back of the dining area, I only hoped I was not being drawn in by falsehoods. Everyone else I had conversed with about him had spoken confidently enough of his reformation, however, so I sat with the intent to keep an open mind.

Richard wasted no time to start listing his past transgressions. With each one, he apologized earnestly and explained the steps he had taken to correct himself, going so far as to repent by doing better to others where he had previously done ill. He had even aided in some of the initial petitionings for demon rights, loaning his diner as a meeting place and to host local political events before the movement gained momentum.

Discussing Kate put us both in a dour mood, his guilt weighing heavy on his aged shoulders. His eyes grew sad. "Do...Do you know about Kate's daughter?"

"I know about Ethan's involvement," I replied quietly, wanting to be angry but finding it impossible when I thought of the two little ones I would see soon.

"Yeah. That." He sighed, wringing his hands and fingering his wedding band, obviously a nervous habit. "I was there that night. I'm not sure what I expected to happen or why, honestly. I heard a couple of months later about Kate's condition through my wife, who heard it through the church—you know how word spreads around here?

"Anyway, it turns out my wife had just gotten pregnant, too. Almost the same time. And it just...hit me," he murmured, moved to tears still by the revelation he must have had. "The next day, I went to see Kate and apologize for everything. Your old man gave me a good whupping, too. But I offered to pay for her medical bills, whichever way she decided to go with it.

"And then there was Charlie." He smiled at the memory. "My wife had our son two days later. I helped where I could and when Kate'd let me, but, uh...She's always been headstrong. Eventually decided that she was done with this place and took off. I guess your funeral took more out of her than we all thought," he added somberly.

It seemed that returning to my hometown brought with it all of the little details I had not known I was longing for. One tidbit, in particular, stuck out for me, catching me off guard from the brash man I remembered.

"You helped her with Charlie?" The words were quiet, and I was worried they might lodge in my throat as I spoke them. Why? What twisted in my chest so fiercely knowing she and Kate were not as painfully alone as I had previously envisioned?

Richard nodded. "Not as much as I would've liked, but I tried."

"Thank you." I felt I had done my gratitude an injustice in those words, that there was little more that I could say. A fleeting excitement shivered through me. "What was she like? Charlie."

"Charlie? Well, I didn't see her much, but when I did, um..." He laughed, thinking back on memories I longed to see. "She was quiet, liked to sit back and observe rather than jump right into things. Once she warmed up to you, though, she was...chatty, friendly, polite. She liked her rules. And I don't know how, but she reminded everyone of you," he laughed again.

As he spoke, I could not help but recognize how he described the habits of my children—Charlie's children. Lawrences by blood and name, even if that blood was not my own. Still, I found comfort in that, feeling all the more secure in my place with them. No matter the distance, time or difference of species, they had parts of me in them, parts of the daughter I never knew.

I smiled, somber. "Thank you, Richard."

Never in my life would I have considered saying those words so sincerely to that man. But then, life these last two years had been nothing of what I could have expected.

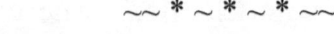

Thirty-seventh Week After Paradise

Friday

The thought I was making a mistake was impossible to ignore as it pervaded every fiber of my being. I knocked on the door in front of me, unable to shake the confusion I felt, either. The neighborhood was bright, with cheerily colored gardens and neatly trimmed

436

yards in front of every picturesquely painted home. The vehicles were all well cared for and even the sidewalks were washed.

Aside from the keen attention to its detailed perfection, I could not envision the woman who had tormented me for decades living here, in this lovely neighborhood. It was too...pleasant. This was the home of a domesticated, mild grandmother who enjoyed baking and knitting, not a certifiably mad scientist.

The door flew open. "Oh. It's you."

"Good afternoon, Beth," I greeted nervously, already feeling as welcome here as I would have been wandering into a bear's cave. I held up the worn paper scrap she had slipped me at the Institute. "You asked for me?"

She nodded, stepping aside to beckon me into her home. I ducked inside, the warm aroma of baked goods startling me. If the outside of the home had not been enough, the interior was an entirely different matter. I was reminded of a dollhouse, with how precisely the flower-patterned furniture was arranged. Bright colors were pulled together nicely, and family photos smiled at us from the pastel walls.

How had I feared this woman?

"Make yourself at home," she invited me with a wave to the seating arrangement in the living area. "I'll be back in a second with drinks."

"Is there anything I may assist with?" I offered awkwardly, unable to help myself acting properly.

"I have a couple of plates you could carry," she agreed politely, allowing me to follow her into the next room. The kitchen was overwhelming, decorated entirely with floral designs and scrawling paintings of inspirational wisdom. Beth picked up a tray with a delicate tea set, nodding to a pair of plates filled with cookies and finger sandwiches for me to carry.

As we returned to the living area and placed her adorable concoctions on the coffee table, I was all the more disturbed by her, knowing this was her home life. I could recall all too clearly how precise and steady she was with a knife. Could she possibly be the same woman who lived here, with such carefully prepared delicacies and fine, rose-painted teacups?

"You invited me for tea, then?" I asked quietly, voice still far too loud for the stiff atmosphere. I had never felt so keenly out of place. Inhuman appearance aside, I was not dainty. I was hulking, and no matter the polite manners or tamed communication I had cultivated, I was rugged and coarse compared to...*this*.

"I admit, I didn't think you'd show up," she confessed as she poured the still-steaming drink. "Cream or sugar?"

"Oh, no, thank you." I had an awkward feeling of playing at a game as I accepted my cup. It was reminiscent of tea parties with Sarah and her dolls. If only I could have enjoyed Beth's presence even a fraction as much as I did my daughter's toys.

Beth dressed up her drink, spoon clinking loudly in the uncomfortable silence. When she spoke again, it was with the familiar, businesslike tone she had always commanded in the Institute, "So, I'm retiring in six months. I'm getting the paperwork together now, it'll be ready to file next week."

I nodded stiffly. "And then you intend to...rescue animals?"

"Exotic ones. I like to keep things exciting, you know," she said with a smirk.

I stared at her, shaking my head slowly in confusion. "Beth. We are not friends. You caged me. You tortured me. The only positive thing we have ever shared is an understanding of maintaining plain honesty. What do you want from me?"

The woman nodded, setting her cup on the table and fixing me with a stern gaze. "You're right. We're not friends, but I do owe you a lot. I want to help you."

"Help me, Beth? How could you possibly help me after all you have helped *do* to me?" I retorted with more bitterness than I liked.

"How do you think your friend got that adoption pushed through so quickly?" she laughed, shaking her head. "I happen to have some sway when it comes to demons in the political world."

The shock I felt reminded me of rolling on burning pavement, raw and sharp. "You? Why would you ever do anything so considerate, least of all for me?"

"What, you don't want the munchkins anymore?" she asked with a smirk. I bit back my reactionary growl, realizing that her jest meant no harm. "Anyway, I figured you deserved a break. And it's fun to hold something over that terrible excuse of a shrink."

"Be kind to him, he does try," I said quietly, still recovering from my surprise. "He makes for a better friend, something I am certain you could benefit from."

"I know it's a long shot, but I liked you enough when we couldn't get along. If you're as forgiving as I remember and I can help enough, well..." She shrugged, gaze wandering to the photos on the wall. I recognized the same man in several of them, varying in age between the images. "As I said, I owe you a lot, regardless."

"Your son," I realized slowly. "Is he...?"

"He's fine," she assured me sharply. Her expression hardened to glare as she turned back to face me. "Ungrateful ass doesn't like that his mother was a bad guy, with all of this demon political crap going around. I don't think he realizes that you're the reason I could afford this house and his college tuition."

On this side of captivity, I could almost justify her actions against me. She had a son to care for, after all. "You stopped speaking of him as much these last couple decades. What does he do these days?"

"Complain," she sighed sarcastically. "He got a degree in finance. He's an investment consultant or some crap. My grandkids are spoiled; I guess that's all I care about."

"If he is competent, I could use advise," I offered with a smirk. "I may be well off now, but I have two children to raise these days. I need to plan accordingly."

Beth was quiet for a moment, a look of remorse seeming very out of place on her face. "Ages ago, you said I shouldn't do more than I needed. You were right. I should have found a way to get you out of there after my son graduated."

My heart stopped, blood running cold. "I beg your pardon?"

"I won't say it again," she told me quietly, still wearing that expression. "Everything I did for him, it's fine, but after that—I can't justify any of it anymore, not seeing who you are outside of that hellhole. You deserve more than that, but it's all I have."

"Thank you." The words were nearly silent, an odd weight I never knew I bore leaving my chest with them. I sipped at my cup, our conversation turning to easier topics of weather for a while. I kept my eye on the time, eventually having to hide my smile of relief when I had reason enough to excuse myself. "My apologies, Beth, but I need to get home and start supper. My children will be home soon."

She stood with me, seeming uncharacteristically reluctant to see me leave. "Can I send you with anything? I think I might've made too much for lunch."

"Oh, no, Beth, that is not—"

"Stop being polite for a second and just take some damn cookies," she snapped. Why was it that I was more at ease with her irritability? "It's not like I'll eat them all, and I only see my grandkids for Christmas. At least let me spoil yours."

"Very well," I agreed, although as quick as she was to pack up the extras I felt I had little choice in the matter, to begin with. "Thank you."

She shrugged and handed me the bundle of goods. "What can I say? I like kids."

I smiled at that, seeing a disgruntled grandmother instead of a sadistic madwoman. Without thinking, I pulled out my wallet and offered it to her, opened to the photos I carried with me. Beth's face lit up, first with curiosity and then adoration as she looked over Kyle and Sarah's smiling faces.

"Those are my children. Kyle is seven and Sarah is nine," I told her quietly, unable to hide my pride. Nearly as powerful was a feeling of contentment, knowing that I had helped brighten this lonely woman's day.

"They're so lucky they don't look like you," she commented, dry humor still what I remembered.

I laughed and nodded, pocketing the wallet again. "They certainly are."

Beth saw me to the door, mulling something over idly. As we reached the exit, she finally spoke, voice detached as if she were reciting a lesson, "You know, horses used to be considered exotic."

I raised one brow, confused. "Beth?"

"Now, they're kept in barns by the dozens," she added, tone a bit sharper as she shrugged. "No one bats an eye about animals, Mr.Lawrence. You could house hundreds. As long as they're fed and watered, with so much space per head. The permits are usually cheap, and I think the hardest part is making sure you've got proof of ownership."

My blood ran cold as I realized she was speaking of demons. "How do you know about Leilani?"

"Oh, did you get a dog?" she asked too innocently. She sighed sharply, frustrated quickly by my lack of understanding whatever she meant to say. "I don't know a damn thing about anything that isn't papered or tagged. Not until *after* I retire. But if you decide to get more dogs, make sure you follow the recommended guidelines for housing and care. And make damn sure your current bitch wears her collar," she added sharply, angry guilt twisting her features.

I nodded shakily. "Very well, Beth, I will take it all into consideration."

She nodded, relaxing some. "Good. Go take care of your brats. Don't be a stranger."

I hesitated a moment, thinking over the indirect invitation to visit again. "Weekends are preferable, provided you would not mind my bringing my children?"

"If you have to," she grumbled, but her smile was unable to hide how she was partial to the idea. I smiled and excused myself, ducking out of the house and onto that street filled with its too-neat houses. As I made my way home, I felt a pang of pity for my old adversary. I could not entirely grasp why, but I knew of the two of us I had been the luckier one, in the end.

Recovery

Robert and Lisa sat on the front porch swing, rocking slowly. The afternoon was pleasant, warm for the season despite the lazy breeze playing through the air. They watched the most unorthodox little family dancing in the empty front fields. The sounds of both joyful laughter and bestial glee mingled together naturally.

"You know, I keep giving him a hard time, but he's better at this than I ever was," sighed Lisa with a smile. She shook her head slowly, her brother tumbling to the ground dramatically as the human children pulled him down. "I don't know if it's because of what they are. He just seems so much more involved. I love my kids, but I think I would go crazy if I spent as much time with them as he does with his."

"I think it's a difference of experience, as much as anything else," replied Robert with a smile. The children ran to hide behind Leilani now that their father had gotten back to his feet. "We take a lot for granted that he's never really had access to, like having kids. It stands to reason he'd be more inclined to spend as much time with them as he can."

Lisa watched their rambunctious playing for a

moment, laughing as the kids started trying to pit the two demons against each other, crying for the demoness to save them. "Whatever the reasons, I don't think those kids could be loved any more than they are now."

Robert chuckled and nodded in agreement. "It's not a conventional situation by any means, but you're right. They know it, too. It's certainly helped them bounce back after—"

"Run, Sarah!" screeched Kyle. The two children scrambled to the porch in a fit of giggles. Their plan had worked, with Leilani acting as their champion in the task of taking down the hulking demon they fled from.

Leilani waved back to the children, dodging the unenthusiastic swipe from Cory. She grinned, letting out a playful chirp before pouncing, looking more like a feline than anything in her movements. The two demons collided, tumbling head over tails before landing with Leilani perched on top. She raised her hands in triumph, the children cheering her on.

The pin was short-lived, Cory sitting easily and tossing the demoness over one shoulder effortlessly. He made his way to his feet, oblivious to the little woman's efforts to free herself. Leilani dropped her wings to hang limp, the abrupt change of weight knocking her adversary off-balance. Cory was thrown back to the ground, Leilani pinning him again. The children ran out to pile atop the demon with her.

Robert laughed at the sight. "That's not something you see every day, is it?"

"Around here, you do." Lisa smiled. "I think he lets her win. Just don't tell the kids, they'd be put out if

445

they knew no one could beat him fairly."

"I'm sure." Robert nodded to himself, glad to see his friend doing so well. "He's acting more like himself. Since Kate passed, I've been worried, but this is good."

"You're not here to see it all the time, Robert, but Leilani helps him," said Lisa, keeping her voice quiet to avoid being heard over the raucous laughter. "A lot more than he helps her, I think. It made me nervous at first, but...you're right. It's like watching a pair of dogs."

Robert smirked. "I won't tell him you said that."

"You'd better not, young man," she warned playfully. Lisa sighed. "I wish Mom could've seen him like this. He's always had a lighthearted side, he's just never had someone to really explore it with. After Cory was about twelve, both of our brothers were just too breakable to him."

"Leilani seems pretty sturdy," agreed Robert with a smile. "It really is good to see him like this, though. He was always so serious when I first met him, as though he couldn't relax. Even once he'd reconnected with Kate. I feel like this is a side of him he's never gotten to express much."

"It isn't." The demon's sister smiled. "I'm glad Leilani's here for him. He's needed someone like him for a long time."

At the declaration, the pair on the porch could only laugh as the demoness in question used her tail to smack her companion on the shoulder. She darted away, easily more agile than the behemoth that chased after her.

Chapter Twelve: Fatherhood

Thirty-eighth Week After Paradise

Sunday (June 17th)

"Dad. Dad!"

I groaned, stirring slowly to whispers and little hands on my face. With a disoriented glance at the dark window, I frowned when I saw dawn was still some time away. My frown deepened when I realized that both of the children were on the bed with me. I propped myself up on my good arm to see them better.

"What's wrong?" I whispered groggily. "Are you two all right?"

Kyle jumped excitedly, landing on my middle and knocking some of the wind from me. He kept his grin, too elated to calm down. "Oops, sorry."

"Careful now," I groaned, shifting him so that I could recover my breath. Was he made of lead now?! "Come now, was it a nightmare? What woke you both?"

"We haven't slept," confessed Sarah, sharing her brother's grin. I glanced at the clock, certain I must have

447

only been asleep a short while, then.

I groaned again, seeing the clock's bright little numbers declaring that it was barely an hour until I usually woke to start breakfast. Oh, they had not slept *at all*, then?! I mentally braced myself for the day, knowing well what tempers they had when they did not get the rest they needed.

"Why are you two awake?!" I laughed in a maddened whisper. "It's hours before you should be up!"

"We couldn't sleep," my daughter continued her confession. I closed my eyes, trying to collect myself. Their tiny hands began prodding my face again.

"Yes, yes, I'm still awake." I peeked my eyes open, unable to resist smiling at those grins. "Now, would you please tell me why we're all three awake at such inhuman hours?"

"Well, you're not human," listed Sarah as if it were the most natural thing in her world. I nodded at her infallible reasoning. How was it that grin could get any wider? "And it's Father's Day! We've never celebrated before so we were too excited to sleep."

"Yeah, and we made you stuff!" chirped Kyle, beginning his excited bouncing again. Before he could make a solid effort at rupturing my organs, the young boy mercifully stopped himself. "Aunt Lisa and Leilani and Robert and Bailey all helped, too."

"But it was our ideas!" chimed Sarah proudly, refusing to let her credit slide by.

"Father's Day?" I echoed, stunned. I had utterly forgotten Lisa's reminder of the upcoming holiday, let alone been prepared for an onslaught this early in the morning. I made a dramatically skeptical expression to toy with the little monsters. "Are you sure it's not Christmas? The only day you both are up before dawn is Christmas."

"We're sure!" insisted Sarah eagerly.

"Yeah, super sure! Aunt Lisa said!" agreed Kyle with a bobbing nod.

"Oh, well if Aunt Lisa said..." My sarcasm trailed off, wasted on their tired, over-stimulated little faces. I could not help a quiet laugh as I finally caved, "Very well, what did you two have planned?"

"Well, first, we fed the chickens," declared Sarah proudly.

Oh, no. "You fed the chickens?"

"Yeah, we did!" Kyle beamed. "And we made breakfast."

Oh, heavens, no. "*And* you made breakfast?"

"We even made the tea, but we didn't know which kind you'd want so we just put it all in," admitted Sarah in a hushed babble. "But you and Aunt Lisa like it so much, we figured you'd like it a lot more that way. I hope you like it!"

Did no gods have any mercy? "That's not quite how it works, but thank you."

My daughter's expression fell, tired eyes welling up with her disappointment. Oh, we were in for a day. "Oh. Well. I mean..."

"I'm sure I will enjoy it all the same, darling," I amended gently, glad to see that grin come back to life so quickly. I bit back a tired sigh. "Now then, what shall we do first?"

Karma Rose

~~ * ~ * ~ * ~~

"Oh, a march in my honor?" I asked as I sat to watch the news with Lisa. Angry faces with banners both clever and dull declaring there should be laws restricting demons, treating them as little more than the animals they were. As if the most recent enactment of mandatory Sentience Tests were not enough. "They're too kind, truly, they shouldn't have. I have already received plenty of these! More than I know what to do with, in all honesty."

Lisa looked over at hearing my dry witticism, raising one brow skeptically. "Really? This doesn't bother you at all?"

"Oh, it does, certainly," I agreed, smiling over my fresh cup of tea. "But it's Father's Day, I finally have an herbal cup that is not some unfortunate chimera made with love, and both of my children are down for a nap at once. They can have at their marching, I already won this day."

"Cheery," she commented, mood as pleasant as bathing with wet sandpaper. She looked back at the television. "I can't believe this is still going on, though."

"What now? Some 'evidence' of my evil ways linking back to Dante and his works?" I smirked bitterly. "*That* was entertaining."

"No, it's actually a pretty solid argument this time," she sighed tiredly. "Aggravated assault against a group of men?"

I frowned thoughtfully. "Oh, which set? The one I stopped from beating a woman, or the one which so generously gave me need of nineteen stitches and three months' flight restriction? Either way, I suppose I should send a card to apologize."

"Wow, you're *chipper* today," she noted with heavy-handed sarcasm. "I thought Ethan was supposed to be the snarky one?"

"Oh, I am exhausted, and no matter how much patience I wake with it all goes to those precious little monsters," I sighed affectionately, settling into my seat and sipping at my cup. On the screen, a slim reporter was speaking at us sternly. "Besides which, both of those incidents were resolved already. These people will get bored and move on to some new angle soon enough."

My sister shifted to stare at me incredulously. "Seriously? They're demanding you be locked up again, and you really don't care?"

"Of course, I care," I protested, wishing she could have let it lie as I felt the stirrings of panic accompanied by blinding flashes of too-clean steel. "I despise that place. I hate the color white, the shine of polished steel, and the smell of bleach and starched cloth. Almost as much as I detest the feel of stitches in my skin, and the medications in my system."

I saw the horror in my sister's eyes as I continued, "But I can't dwell on that when those children wake up in two hours. And they will because I will be cooking a proper breakfast and the smell always gets them out of bed. Why should I care what these people think or how I feel about white sheets with that on the horizon?"

"They could take you away again, Cory," she whispered, eyes pleading with me desperately. "Away from those little monsters that you love so much."

I had known since my release that it was always a possibility to be taken into custody again. After all, was that not the reason behind Robert's being offered my case? Of course, I had known, although it had always remained some secondary concern. The way she put forth her argument now, however, made my heart race with a spike of panic.

I had lost so much the first time. Previously, the thought of returning was terrible, yes, but nothing that felt so completely shattering. How was it that now when I thought of being torn away it was so much more crushing, as though the life should be drained from me? Like I should not survive the injustice again, and yet I *had* to endure it all until I could return?

"Daddy?"

The tiny voice I heard answered my questions with her own, my daughter drawing my attention to where she stood at the edge of the living area. She clung to her stuffed rabbit, startled and terrified despite the obvious sleep still in her eyes.

"Sarah?" My heart stopped. How much had she heard? I motioned her over, glad when she shuffled to where I sat. Setting my cup on the coffee table, I hoisted her up into my lap, hugging her close. "Why aren't you in bed, sweetheart?"

"I had a bad dream," she whispered nervously, settling quickly in my arms. She looked up at me, eyes as depthless as Kate's when she had been upset. In an instant, I was wrapped around that little finger of hers. "Who's taking you away?"

I glanced at Lisa quickly, giving her a stern look to

keep her silent. "Robert. He and I are going to be having lunch someday soon."

"Oh." She relaxed some, resting her head on my arm with a yawn. "But you said they. Is someone else going with you?"

"Yes," I continued the charade readily. As much as I loathed lying to my daughter, I could not bear the idea of her knowing the truth. I had to protect that perfect smile of hers for as long as I could.

"Who?" she wondered sleepily, already drifting off.

"It's a surprise," I whispered, pecking her on the forehead. She shifted slightly, adjusting herself for a long nap with me.

"Okay," she mumbled eyes slipping shut. She smiled, giving her rabbit a squeeze. "I love you, Dad. Happy Father's Day."

I stared at her sleeping face, utterly captured. How could I ever leave that face? The thought was brutal, anguishing, and I was horrified that I may need to consider the possibility. What would I do for them, if I was torn away again? This was my life now, these two children and everything being their father entailed. What would I do if I lost the time to watch them grow? I could barely stand that I had missed so much already.

Lisa tapped my shoulder, and I was drawn back to the news abruptly.

"In other news, a breakthrough for demons today, when local Iowan lawmakers made the first declaration of its kind this morning. If a demon has passed their Self-Awareness and Sentience tests, the state intends to honor the certification with all of the rights granted to human citizens. This is being considered a preemptive safety net against the possibility of other changes to demon rights in the future. Isn't that great, Tom?" asked the female anchor, expression heartfelt.

Her colleague forced a smile, genuinely perturbed beneath his cool exterior. "Wow. How did that happen, Kim? That's...well, that's something else!"

The delight in her eyes was oddly comforting. "Well, Tom, it seems that it started with rural communities near Littleton wanting to protect one of their neighbors. They banded together and kept at it like any good community, and the rest makes history."

"That's quite a story," the man said tightly, his smile growing bitter.

"Wholesome, isn't it?" she asked pointedly, beaming at her audience. "We'll have more for you after a quick break."

Lisa silenced the screen with her remote, stunned. She turned to me, a grin slowly spreading across her face, punctuating the wrinkles at her eyes. I felt a weight being lifted, having borne it so long I had forgotten its existence. But my shoulders were lighter, making it easier to breathe.

"Well." My sister chuckled despite her shock. "Happy Father's Day."

I looked at my little girl, overjoyed to know I was never going to leave her. "Yes, it is."

~~ * ~ * ~ * ~~

Thirty-ninth Week After Paradise

Broken Orbit

Monday

Lisa crossed her arms, narrowing her eyes at me. "You're building a barn?"

"What of it, Lisa?" I returned her gesture firmly, wondering how it was she could come off as so much more intimidating when I had two feet on her in height, never mind sheer size.

"You're hiring contractors to build it," she stated flatly, tone accusing me of some criminal act.

I shrugged. "I lack the time to build one myself, with summer break so near."

"Okay, but why do you need a barn with over twenty stalls, a break room, and a vet office?" She raised one brow at me. "Are you breeding horses or something?"

"Nonsense! I only want to make the most of that back plot as a pasture. If I'm installing a barn, I may as well have the job done right."

"Charles!" Lisa was unconvinced, refusing to be deterred by anything I said. Obnoxious, meddlesome little gnat. "Stop insulting me. You're a farmer, not a rancher. Does this have anything to do with your...*brother*?"

The word was awkward when she said it, her distaste obvious. I debated my answer for a moment, considering the information at hand. I sighed heavily, nodding. "Yes. He leads a village, and needs someplace safe for his people to stay for a time."

Oh, dear.

"Are you serious?! You're already stretched thin, Charles! And what about your kids? Who's taking care of

455

them while you're off playing hero? I don't care if he's blood, he's been who knows where while we've been family! He can't just drop in out of nowhere asking stuff like this of you, it's not right!"

I waited for her to calm down, her indignant mood settling slowly. Holding up my hands in a plea for patience, I explained, "He never asked it of me, Lisa. He came to me concerned for his village, and I offered assistance. I am not doing anything more than that, providing assistance. I can't turn a blind eye to people in need, the same as you, and I am in a unique position to be able to help. So I will.

"As for my children, they greatly enjoyed the company of other demons. More than I did, at times. Besides which, I fully intend to keep them as my priority, and Braxen understands such," I added, seeing her bracing to protest again. "Once the demons have no more need of the structure, the barn will provide an invaluable asset to restoring this farm, as well. The market is always good for cattle."

"Fine. It's your property," she relented in a tone that told me the matter was far from settled. She shrugged and left me to review the paperwork at the table. The remainder of the morning, I felt her glaring daggers at me from her living room chair until I left to busy myself with the work outside.

~~ * ~ * ~ * ~~

Fortieth Week After Paradise

456

Broken Orbit

<u>Wednesday</u>

"Leilani, let me see your wrist." I gestured for her to present her hand to me, holding out the bracelet I had acquired for her. She obeyed, watching as I did up the clasp of the simple chain. My fingers brushed the identification tag that hung daintily from her coral wrist. I sighed, an odd pit settling in my gut to read what was effectively my claiming ownership of her. "I need you to wear this at all times, Leilani. Please, understand that."

Her copper eyes watched me, worried by my quiet severity. "No words...?"

I groaned in frustration, tapping her wrist and the bracelet there. "I need you to wear this. Never remove it, ever, for any reason. It should keep you safe, Leilani, from-from this!"

I gestured to the scarring on my arm, startled by the intensity of my worry for her. She appeared equally disturbed, my mood causing her to watch me with deeply rooted concern. She took my hand in hers, chirping once in question. I took a deep breath, nodding slowly. I tapped the bracelets she had given me, and understanding lit up in her eyes immediately.

"Good lick!" she realized with a grin. She rolled her eyes, the gesture making me chuckle in spite of my prior upset as she corrected herself, "*Luck.*"

"Yes, Leilani, for good luck," I agreed with a guilty smile. With the best of luck, that little piece of metal might keep her safe in the face of the tumultuous social atmosphere rising just outside our door. Looking at that brilliant smile, I knew that if the tag were not up to the task I would find another answer. Whatever it took, Leilani would be safe.

~~ * ~ * ~ * ~~

Forty-second Week After Paradise

<u>Thursday (July 19th)</u>

"Are the kids settled?" asked Lisa, her purse settling heavily as she slung it over one shoulder.

I nodded, heart racing nervously. "Leilani has them busy, but I could check again. Just to be safe."

"They'll be fine."

"Well, now, but it would be ill-advised to leave the three of them alone—"

My sister's hand latched onto my wrist, fingers barely wrapping around it. "Come on, Charles, no more delays or we'll be late!"

"A bit of comedic irony for the occasion, perhaps?" I offered, but I followed her stiff march. I would hate for her to injure herself in a doomed effort to tow me along. She shot me a glare. "I take it there are also no exceptions, then."

"Come on, people have been waiting decades for this, you can't back out now! Get your tail in the air and hurry up to the diner, I'll be right behind you."

Of course. Decades. The diner. This was the day of the annual memorial. *My* memorial. While I could appreciate the conceited implications of me arriving at such a somber dedication in my honor, my sister disagreed. This was my welcome home, a true welcome home, the grand gesture I would be loathe to deprive the town of after they had held such a long vigil on my behalf.

Perhaps I could feign a migratory pattern for the season and return once it was over.

"And no side stops!" yelled Lisa after me as I started my way to take flight. I should have known that she would guess my less than honest inclinations.

The flight to the diner could not have been shorter, be it from my trepidation or my stronger wings. I circled twice, frustrated to find—despite all of the vehicles below—their drivers had been considerate enough to leave me a landing strip, complete with traffic cones and ribbons.

So I lowered myself gradually, dragging out the seconds before I recognized Lisa's car approaching from down the road. I dropped down, landing more swiftly and tucking my wings. I shuffled them habitually, hands linking behind my back as I strode out to meet Lisa where she parked toward the front.

"You made it!" she cheered sarcastically, adjusting her purse strap and gesturing to the diner. "Your party awaits."

My mouth went dry as I opened the door for her to enter. Before I even stepped foot inside, there was a round of genial greetings and rambunctious cheers. I grimaced, Lisa grabbing my wrist again to drag me inside.

It was festive, that much was certain. Decorations were strung from the ceiling, strewn across tables, taped to walls. Across the far wall above the kitchen bar hung a giant banner. Its bright lettering of 'Welcome Home' stood out boldly despite all of the other streamers and ribbons draped around it.

I turned on my heel, hand outstretched for the door's handle, but the mischievous little imp I called sister was two steps ahead and blocking my exit. She crossed her arms with a huff. I smiled sheepishly, shrugging in defeat and turning back to the congregation.

There were a handful of old faces I knew well: Richard, Jeff, Jeanine. Even Dustin was there, locked in conversation with Corey, neither seeming to notice the commotion that came with our entrance.

The majority, however, were new faces I did not recognize. They were children and grandchildren of the people I had known, and I saw in their excitement the impact I must have made without ever realizing.

It was then I noticed the photos covering the walls, treasured moments of my existence which never should have been documented. Newspaper clippings were intermingled of my disappearance, of Littleton's uproar at their abducted citizen. Then the steady gain of attention Katelyn's efforts received, leading to her triumphant success and the rights I had so long been denied.

"Hey, welcome to the party, stranger," greeted Richard, shaking my hand firmly in greeting. He followed my gaze to the walls, grinning broadly. "What do you think? It's normally a more depressing atmosphere."

"It is all so much," I mused breathlessly, unable to look away from those countless photos. There was proof I was existent, that I had a home here. "I was never supposed to have lived so...substantially."

Richard shrugged. "You didn't. Not for a while,

anyway. People had a picture or two scattered here and there, but when we started coming together...Well, it added up. We even dug up some old videos, courtesy of Kate, mostly."

Still, I could not look away, moved by the gesture. Had I truly left such a mark? "I was never supposed to exist like this."

Richard laughed and gave my shoulder a solid pat. "It's all right, you'll adjust. Come on, say hi to everyone! Lunch is about ready and then we'll start up the movie."

"Movie?" I echoed, but I had little time to ponder as I was thrust into the fray of the excited social gathering. Time blurred by in a whirlwind of exuberant introductions and heartfelt hellos from old faces. Jeanine still insisted on her ridiculous nickname, some of the younger crowd finding genuine humor in it. Oh, and I had been hoping it might mercifully stay restricted to only her dry witticisms.

Before I knew it, we were settling in for the film that Richard had mentioned. It played like the home videos I had been sorting through from the study. The grainy images were windows to moments so frivolous I never thought to remember them this distinctly previously. I felt as if I was watching someone else's life entirely. The young man being featured was so far from who I was now it was eerie and disorienting.

Had we always been so unrelentingly happy?

The face changed to a ghost of perfection, framed by tight ringlets of hair and black eyes smiling out at us mercilessly. Slowly, I felt my grief closing in on me. Fresh and raw, it raked against my heart and lungs brutally. The video of Katelyn—*my* Katelyn, the woman I had loved so deeply and so long—now drove home the final wedge that shattered the fragile self-control I had clung to for the children's sake.

They were not here to glue it together again.

"Excuse me," I choked, needing some way to escape. The exits were blocked by spectators, so I made my way for the bathrooms, hoping for a lock. The door swung open and slammed shut behind me in the same numbing second, its lock clicking quietly beneath my trembling fingers. I leaned back against the door, knees weak and knowing my weight would barricade it shut if anyone sought to disturb me.

I cried.

Like I had never had the time to, never had the complete and horrible realization to grieve, I cried. My chest should have split open as the vivisections had once done. I could feel the scars burning, white-hot flames running along the fault lines so clearly etched across my skin. I should have shattered. I should have crumbled to ashes, unable to bear the weight of this.

I cried.

It seemed unending, this wrenching pain and the searing wet across my cheeks. Could her death demand any less of me? She had always had such a solid grip on my heart, on the soul I had long doubted myself having. They were hers. Always, I had belonged to her, since the very first moment when she had reached out to touch me in my dreary prison of a room. She was the moonlight across my dark existence, the doorway into a world with light and laughter, a possibility beyond what I could simply settle with.

Broken Orbit

For her, I cried.

All of those years, *stolen*. The act was so much more criminal now, knowing it was her life with me which had been stripped away. In its entirety, short of the year which we had scavenged in the end. They had destroyed so much more for her than they had for me.

These scars were nothing to that precious time.

These weighted memories meant little compared to what it had cost her.

Katelyn.

My Kate.

I felt the door tremble as voices worried from the other side. Their words were meaningless to my ears as their fists fought to catch my attention, to bargain with me to come out. Why should I? What worth was out there anymore? It felt as if I had died with her, now just some shambling and hollow husk of the man she had once given life to.

A new voice made its way to me, quieter than the others had been. Robert's familiar and gentle tones made sense, even in this endless turmoil.

"Hey, Cory. Sorry I'm late, but the girls couldn't figure out what to wear," he joked. I managed a weak smile in spite of myself, knowing the sort of ordeal that was with his daughters. "The way they were fussing, you'd think they were going to have tea with the Queen of England."

The short pause in his careful words brought my attention to how painfully loud my sobs had become, the unrelenting anguish twisting in them. I did what I could to quiet myself, although it felt like a futile effort. My chest was hollow, my veins empty of a pulse.

"You wouldn't believe how excited they've been to see you again," he told me. He sounded amused. "Even Vanessa couldn't stop gushing. As it is, they're both glued to the walls looking at some of the pictures that are posted up. They really look up to you."

Even broken down in a diner bathroom?

Oh, the cruel humor of Fate, that their ill-chosen idol should be devastated so easily. At my very own memorial, no less, but I could not stand to see the silent smiles of my parents and my Kate. Even Charlie had a place of her own, the gorgeous daughter I had never known—*would* never know. Sarah had her smile, while Kyle had her eyes. My brother's eyes.

"Hey, Cory? I brought something for you. Can I come in and show you?" He was quiet for a moment, continuing his case, "I won't lie, I'm also really wanting to take a break from all of these people. I'd rather sit with a familiar face, you know?"

I hesitated, loathing the idea of disturbing my solitude, yet unable to leave him to the mercy of those endless masses of people. I unlocked the door and stepped back, opening it for Robert to enter before locking it and barricading it again. He looked around and gave me a calm smile.

"It's homey," he commented, leaning against the wall opposite from me. I stared at him wordlessly, still gasping for air as it felt I should not be able to breathe. There should have been nothing left of me, this pain was so absolute.

I was not ready to face losing Kate.

Broken Orbit

Robert appraised me for a moment and nodded, settling in against his wall to wait. It could have been hours before I slid down the door to sit on the floor, drained of anything and everything. Time ceased to have meaning, yet still, he remained patient, watchful. I leaned my head back, horns knocking against the door with a painfully loud *clunk* after such a long silence. Robert mimicked me, taking a seat and settling in.

"Why now?" My whisper was uneven and hoarse, barely escaping me before I felt a fresh stab of grief.

Robert frowned, somber. "I don't know, Cory."

"She should be here." The words burned my tongue. I gasped for air, my heart wrenching again.

"She worked hard for this party to happen," he agreed quietly, nodding. He sighed, shifting against the tile floor. "Kate was something else."

I closed my eyes, feeling my face contorting unnaturally with this pain. "I miss her, worse now than I ever had in the Institute. I need her, Robert, and she's gone."

"I know," he murmured, sounding distraught. He cleared his throat. "You've every right to be angry and sad right now, Cory. No one's going to blame you for it."

"I am!" I choked faintly. My eyes opened to take in the world, but I felt it was a wasted effort, pointless. "I am livid and utterly broken. I don't know how I have held on this long without her."

Robert's smile was perverted by sorrow. "You have your kids. You do what you have to for them."

"They deserve better than this," I hissed, unsure if I spoke of myself or the situation as a whole. "They deserve to have their mother. They more than deserve to have their grandmother."

"You deserve to have her, too," he pointed out gently, igniting a fresh wave of tears from me. I shook my head slowly, horns scraping against the door. The sound made me hate this all the more. "You do, Cory, and it's okay to be upset that she isn't here now. Yes, it is, because you love her and she left you behind, all three of you. It isn't anyone's fault, but it's definitely not fair, either."

I grit my teeth against fresh anguish. I wanted him to be right. I wanted to be able to have someone to blame, anyone to be angry with. I needed her to know the injustice of this, how she had tormented us with this absence. Although, if there was anyone to stake the blame with...

"I yelled at her," I confessed brokenly. Surely, my blood must have turned to acid again, to create this burn in my veins? "So much was happening. She was so worried, and I yelled. I was angry, and she was there, and....she collapsed. Even her stubborn grit couldn't help her heal from it. And I was the one—*I* yelled at her. Why? It's so trite now."

Robert was nodding slowly, eyes fixed on my face. "It's not your fault."

"I never should have yelled," I protested numbly.

"It's *not* your fault."

"I never should have sought out the demons."

"It's not *your fault*."

"I never should have left home."

"Charles." His attempt at being stern was feeble,

the name sounding awkward and wrong compared to the commanding tenacity I was so accustomed to when hearing it said. "Cory. Just humor me and say it, please. It's not your fault. All of those years of sadness, when these people got together, Kate's death, your mom getting sick—none of it is your fault."

"It's not my..." His words sank in more quickly than I could speak them. I was just a man, doing the best I could with this terrible hand I had been dealt. How could it have been my fault? Would I have issued the same blame had it been anyone else? "...my fault."

Why was this so much more difficult to feel than guilt? How was it that lacking responsibility could be worse? Knowing that everything had unfolded in such an unjustified, callous fashion—it robbed me of the demented safety being this monster had always provided. How could I explain the kidnapping and inhumane torture of an innocent man? How could the resulting destruction of my family be written off so easily if I was not the key to it, not the vile creature to shoulder the blame?

Robert shifted, coming to my side and setting a hand on my shoulder. "It's all right. It's a lot for one day."

"Morning feels like a lifetime ago," I whispered, struggling to come to terms with this. I lifted my head from where it rested on the door. "This can't be one day."

"Well..." He glanced at his watch, letting out a whistle. "It's seven at night, so close enough to a lifetime, I'd say."

"It's almost time for bed," I murmured, thinking of the little ones waiting for me at home. A sudden longing filled the emptiness, a need to see their faces. The world never mattered, so long as they could smile. The woven strands on my wrist were a firm reminder of such.

"Are you ready to get out of here?" asked Robert, holding up a hand to calm my immediate panic. "You don't have to be. And you certainly don't have to stay for any social obligations, either. It's all up to you."

"Thank you, Robert," I sighed. I knew I should have felt relief, but it was lost in the numb ache of sorrow. "I want to see my children. I saw them so recently, I know, but I miss them. Isn't that just the darnedest thing? Even on the worst of days, I can never get enough of them."

My friend smiled knowingly, the expression changing abruptly with a realization. He held up one finger for me to wait, pulling his cellular device from his pocket. He pressed a series of buttons before holding the screen out for me to see a recording playing. Kyle and Sarah's exuberant little voices echoed out against the tile walls. It must have been from one of their visits to Robert's home, Bailey's voice sounding out despite her not being in sight.

"Okay, guys, one quick message and then it's beddy-bye! Whatcha wanna say?"

Sarah's face popped into view first, black eyes so lit up with her excitement they were nearly brown. "Um, hi, Dad! I'm having fun, but I love you!"

Kyle bounced into view beside her, wearing that smile of his that looked so much like a grin. "Me, too! Oh, and Aunt Lisa, I guess, but I miss you more, just don't tell her, 'kay?"

I laughed in spite of myself, feeling my chest swell

at the sight of them, recording or not. Those were the faces I was so helplessly compelled to keep smiling. Even now, if I found them needing me, I knew I could scrape myself from the floor.

"Okay, now say bye!"

"Bye! Bye, Dad!"

"Bye, Daddy!"

The recording ended abruptly, leaving me with an overwhelming need to see my children. I sighed shakily, taking in my surroundings for the first time since locking myself away. Robert's initial assessment was accurate: overall, the room was homey. Still, it was too small and far from where I desired to be any longer.

"All right, Robert. I feel I may be ready," I relented, ignoring the thoughts of anything that stood between me and my little ones. None of that mattered, not when I had a story to read and monsters to check for in the dark.

Robert's smile was relieved and he stood, offering me a hand to help stand. "I'm glad. Come on, bud, I'll help wrap things up here."

I spared him the effort of pulling me to my feet, easing myself from the floor on my own. "Thank you. Mind Lisa, she may be put out with me over this ordeal."

"Bah, how bad could she be?" he joked as I opened the door. My sister was waiting on the other side, arms crossed and looking like an irate punchline to his dismissal.

"Ah. I will be going home, then," I announced, the comment as much for Lisa as it was for Robert. I slipped by, ignoring my sister's frustrated cries for me to stop.

She had more than earned my ire, as well, all but dragging me by the tail to this event.

The crowds had thinned considerably in my absence, for which I was thankful. It seemed only the more familiar faces remained, making my exit far less awkward than I had anticipated. Richard was waiting for me by the door, wearing an incredibly kind expression that still seemed out of place for the antagonistic young man I remembered.

"It was a lovely event, Richard, and you have my apologies for my rude behavior, but I—"

He waved it away with an amicable shrug. "It's fine, Lawrence, really. It wouldn't have been the same if someone hadn't fallen apart in the bathroom. Just take care of yourself and be sure to stop by before next year. Deal?"

I nodded, relieved to find that he took everything in such even stride. *This* man I could consider keeping company with. "Very well, then. I suppose I could see my way to taking an evening off from cooking supper sometime soon."

"I look forward to it." He smiled broadly as I excused myself, ducking outside before my sister could break away from her conversation with Robert.

I was more than ready to be home, even with this pit of grief still cutting in my chest. That old house certainly was home again, the ghosts silenced by the countless new memories my children had built in its halls. Even Leilani had helped in its revival, the fairy of a demoness bringing new light to the rooms. It was a place I missed now, separate of any attachments I had formed before my captivity. Without Kate or my parents, our little family had made it our home.

~~ * ~ * ~ * ~~

Saturday

I watched Jeff's vehicle pull away, what little patience I had woken with leaving with my children. They had a day of adventures ahead of them, so much more than I could provide after what happened at the diner. I waited until the car was out of view, taking a deep breath of air I scarcely tasted and ambling back toward the house.

My morning work blurred by, barely demanding enough of me to be considered as a distraction. While I certainly felt better than I had Thursday evening, I had not fully recovered from the event.

Keeping my hands busy with the garden only helped in that I did not sink further into this freshly awakened grief. It did me little good for finding a way to freedom from the pain I sought to ignore. Faster than I realized, the work was done with and I found myself taking a moment to rest out back under the old tree. I stared at the cluster of headstones listlessly.

It was odd, seeing my name etched in stone beside my loved ones' graves. Had anyone sat here like this for me, hoping to find any scrap of familiarity to alleviate this agonizing feeling? Kate had left within a year of my funeral, I knew. Had she visited me? Across the distance of time, could we be sitting together? My eyes strayed to the tree's worn bark and the initials I had dug into it decades ago.

"Foolish," I muttered, glaring again at the small graveyard, hoping I could banish the memories from my mind's eye. They played regardless, unrelenting, forcing me to remember all of those happy moments, the life I had taken for granted. The farm I never thought I would leave behind, all but utterly ravaged with time and neglect now. It would take years to revive the land alone if I was lucky enough to rebuild it to its former glory at all.

"What would you do, Father?" I asked of the stone nearest me, my isolation made all the more painful by the silence that replied. I sighed, shaking my head and focusing on my freshly filed claws. "Perhaps I could take the children and travel, explore everything like I never could..."

I pursed my lips, raising one brow at the graves. My grief inched ever-closer to the surface. I stood, pacing slowly and finding little relief in it. All the action served to do was agitate me, the sensation reminiscent of using a sleeping limb.

"Terrible company," I muttered, shaking my head in disappointment. What had I expected? Some answer? How would I receive it, when the persons I spoke to were six feet deep and decaying? I winced at that thought, gritting my teeth to imagine Kate—my Kate—as anything but vibrant, her skin glowing, black eyes alight with her unyielding spirit.

I gasped for air, finding its presence was lacking as my chest burned with an overwhelming cocktail of anger and sorrow. It built to a strangled sound in my throat, a mangled chimera of a snarl and hiss.

The need to move lit my nerves on fire, fueled by the unending grief I had found myself drowning in of late. I needed to act, and I remembered too clearly what destruction had followed last time I had been consumed by instinct this way. I barely had time to imagine what that could mean for my children, my sister, my home—

I was running, wind in my membranes as I shot through the air as quickly as I could manage. In two quick strokes, I was soaring away. Still, I was choking on these feelings, adding to my urgency to flee. I would not allow this dangerous mood to threaten them.

Out of a buried, terrible habit, I soon found myself in that clearing I had mauled once, the new growth still so young compared to the older trees nearby. Even that archway was too new, comparatively infantile to its aged brethren. My landing was clumsy, body confused by the mad surge of relief that I was away from civilization, adding to the already-overpowering needs that thundered in my veins.

Katelyn's disparaged sigh caught my attention as she rolled over, practically flailing with how impassioned the movement was. I peered over the top of my book at her, watching the sun playing across her face as it filtered through the leaves above us.

"Did I miss something?" I asked concernedly, setting my book aside slowly. She huffed again pointedly. "Kate?"

She groaned and stared at me, tossing a wrinkled magazine toward me. It looked like it had been thrown away twice before she had had her turn with it. I lifted it

473

carefully, taking in the article and then looking back to Kate confusedly. I shrugged and handed her back her media.

"You're upset because of Marilyn Monroe?" I asked skeptically. "I thought you were a fan."

"I am! She's so pretty and all of the girls at school are dressing up like her and—What's that stupid grin for, mister?! Are you laughing at me!" she gasped in mock horror.

My chuckle broke into laughter, booming in the calm of our lazy afternoon. "I'm sorry, Kate, but I never thought someone like you..."

I caught myself, blushing deeply and ducking my face to hide behind my book again. I swallowed loudly, nervous that I had nearly let slip my admiration. Kate snatched the book away, careful that my claws did not catch the paper, and tossed it to lie with her battered magazine.

"Like what?" she demanded, eyes black and depthless as she challenged me. I was captured, at her mercy. She had ended any more attempts to flee then and there.

"Well...you're beautiful, Kate. I never thought you would ever be envious of Miss Monroe, let alone her poor imitations," I explained quietly, gaze dropping to my hands shyly.

There was a rustle of papers, and I was staring at a photo of Marilyn. "You're telling me you don't think that she's just gorgeous? I mean absolutely unfair levels of stunning?"

"She's attractive," I agreed with a nervous glance

at Kate's breathtaking face. I cleared my throat anxiously. "I have a preference for chocolate to vanilla, so to speak, and I find it would only be unfair to the results to attempt comparing the two."

Her answering blush was enough to set my heart galloping wildly with passion.

My yearning to sink my claws into something was sorely disappointed, the option removed by my recent filing. I snarled, my good shoulder slamming into a tree instead. My body moved of its own volition, driven completely by raw instincts best unleashed in solitude.

My gaze was drawn to the end of the aisle, past its rows of pews, falling on Katelyn as she entered the church. My eyes widened and it was everything I had to keep from gawking outright as I took her in, stunned.

She was wearing a breathtaking shade of my favorite blue, her gown falling to her calf just past her knees. It clung to her waist and shoulders, cut low to show the graceful curve of her neck and collar. The sleeves sat daintily on her shoulders, hanging to her elbows. Her face was done up, lips painted my shade of crimson and pulling into a broad smile when she saw me. I barely noticed how her hair was styled up in a bun, floral pins decorating her even further.

Dustin's bride could have been right beside her, and I never would have noticed; Katelyn was as outwardly stunning as she was inwardly perfect.

I wanted to forget my place at the altar, waiting for Dustin to be ready for his wedding to begin. I wanted to walk away from the hateful droll of my grandfather's pompous blathering. I wanted to forsake a proper *proposal and borrow Paul's services after my brother's ceremony.*

Damn it all, but I wanted that woman to be my wife.

"Oh, look, and someone invited those? Probably your mother," came the snide mutter of my grandfather with a pointed sneer at Katelyn and her friend, Jeanine. I bit back a reactionary growl at the comment, not wanting to upset Father by inciting an altercation with my despicable elder. Charles huffed a sigh. "At least they're better than you. I can't believe the best man is as good as a rabid cur in a cheap suit."

The words cut deep, the cruel sounds that gave all of my inner doubts and demons an outer voice. As wrong as he was about his comments towards Kate and Jeanine, he was right about me. I had to take a deep breath to force my composure to remain calm, feeling those inhuman urges to act an animal stirring as my heart shattered.

This was the best I could hope for at a wedding, the closest I would ever be to the altar. Best man, watching life pass me by with everything I wanted and could never hope to have both so tantalizingly within my reach.

Still, I memorized that glimpse of Kate looking so cruelly gorgeous. I could steal that one image, and I could pretend I was the man she deserved.

Feral.

No other word did this sensation justice, feeling backed into a corner with my life in jeopardy. I was the danger, I knew, with the absolute magnitude of my grief.

Broken Orbit

My body was less intuitive, needing anything to maim and fight for life against. Even my crippled shoulder was forgotten, right arm lashing out. I regretted the action in the same instant, nerves dipped in gasoline and set aflame.

"AGH!"

I draped my wing over us to hide from the sunlight in the room. Still, it made its way through my membranes, staining the light red. Kate was cast into a stunning shade so very near my own. I was surprised by how much I enjoyed the color on her.

"Can you promise me something?" she asked in a whisper, grinning mischievously.

"What's that, my dear?" I asked, following her cue to whisper so nothing but our pillows might hear.

Her eyes glittered, changing from brown to black as I watched. "Promise me that you'll love me when I'm all wrinkly and pruny and gray."

"You are getting old," I teased, laughing in a whisper when she smacked at my shoulder. "Is this because my mother is noticing her gray hair? Father means well to point it out with his humor, you know."

"I mean, yeah, but I still want you to promise, mister," she giggled before stopping herself, shocked that she had so rudely broken our unspoken treaty for hushed conversation. She resumed her whisper, adding, "Oh, and no teasing when I get there."

"I refuse," I retaliated, chuckling at her frustrated scowl. I kissed her deeply, lingering to enjoy the taste of her before I amended, "I will love you beyond then, and I will cherish every second of it, my dear. I will also poke what fun I can since you're sure to age better than I am."

Karma Rose

She wrinkled her nose but accepted my terms with a kiss of her own. "Deal, mister."

I felt a brutal shudder run through my bones as my horns made contact with a tree. A sharp crack sounded before I felt the bark caving to my brute strength and savagery. I bellowed, pushing into it, the force against my shoulders giving some satisfaction. My tail felt like a whip behind me as it caught against something firm. A hand gripped it tight, claws pressing into my skin.

Whirling with a rabid snarl, I barely caught myself from attacking before I recognized Leilani. Confusion flooded me quickly, disorienting me.

No one had ever seen me like this. I had made certain that no matter how I slipped or what parts of my more primal nature were glimpsed, *this* was never part of it. This was dangerous, primordial, some of the darkest shards of myself that I was too deeply ashamed of to completely acknowledge it as my own. Yet here that little demoness stood with my tail in hand, copper eyes worried and head tilted in question.

As easily as humans might inquire about a sour mood, she chittered quietly. The sound startled me, reminding me to breathe through my shock. She chittered again, more urgently, but I could barely think through the shame.

"What are you doing here?!" I demanded sharply, worried that I may lose control again should this feeling fade enough. Solitude was essential right now, for her safety as much as my personal preference.

"You is not happy." Her reply was casual as she released her grip on my tail, watching it carefully until it was safely behind me.

Her words were lost on me. What did *that* have to do with her following me into the lion's den?! "*How* are you here?!"

Then I saw them, the wings on her back, and realized that she must have followed me. No one had been able to do that before, not if I truly wished to be alone. I could go where no others could. For so long, that was how my world had worked. Now there was Leilani, living with the humans as I had done my entire life.

Nerves taught and wound to the point of snapping, I found that this unique companionship left a bitter taste in this aspect.

I hissed, baring my fangs instinctively. She took a subtle step back, chirruping quietly. A question, to which I answered with a warning growl. Shame and terror spiked in my chest, heart racing faster than I had ever felt before. Leilani's lips parted and she inhaled deeply, tasting the air. Could she smell the rancid reek of these emotions in my veins? Did she taste them the way I could, like chewing the waxy rinds of citrus fruits?

Slowly, she tilted her head back to bare her throat to me, a low purr emanating from her. I felt my nerves easing, away from that too-tight sensation that made me wonder if this was how it would feel to be fiddle strings made of glass. Still, I growled, the sound considerably less threatening to my ears and more relaxed.

She stepped towards me again, throat still exposed, purr soothing to my frayed senses, coaxing me to calm down until she was close enough to touch. She started slow, her fingers brushing mine until she was able to take my hand in hers.

The rush of panic faded quickly, her firm grasp draining everything else with it to leave me hollow and shaking. I fell to one knee, panting to catch my breath. Had I not been breathing? The way my lungs burned at the intake of air, I thought I must have neglected that most basic function.

Leilani was on her knees beside me, hands on my face and inspecting me with a worried scowl. Her fingers prodded at the base of my horns gently while she muttered to herself words I did not know. The area was tender, reminding me bitterly how I had acted rashly. Her copper gaze flicked to the hunch of my right shoulder, hands testing me there. The slightest touch made me groan in pain, shoulder flaring indignantly now I was calming down.

"Why not happy?" she asked gently, finished with her quick appraisal and taking my hands in hers.

I felt my shame return, understanding completely in my sobriety that she had seen me, the creature I fought to suppress, the inhuman monster. *Me*—for everything I was and everything I loathed about this body even more than my own naturally mutilated face. She had seen it and not once had she flinched, not a second had I smelled fear. Humans, even my own family, had feared me for far less.

It drove home the fact that she and I were of the same breed. For all of our lingual difficulties, Leilani understood me more completely than anyone else had come close to before. Because she could withstand the force if I was not in complete control, and she could speak to me when no words made sense.

Broken Orbit

Suddenly, everything I had missed of Katelyn was sated, knowing I was not alone in this world of humans who judged so harshly. By no means did the little demoness replace Kate's companionship. Yet Leilani lifted from me this crushing isolation I had not known was bearing down on my shoulders.

I breathed in deeply. It was that inhale I had been waiting for since Katelyn's final words were spoken. At last, I tasted nothing but air for the first time in nearly a year.

I met Leilani's gaze, unashamed as I could finally feel Kate's absence without the pain of fear. Leilani could understand just how deeply I felt my inner monster that stirred with it. "I miss Kate."

Leilani sighed patiently and nodded, sympathetic. She gave my hands a firm squeeze, the feel of her claws nothing but comforting. "Yes. Is sad, no Kate. You is not alonely."

"No. I'm certainly not alone anymore," I agreed, this crippling emptiness filling in my chest some. It was not healed, but it felt eased. Perhaps it could mend, though, now that the thorn had been pulled from my wound. I bit back my customary apology at losing my strict control over myself, knowing she would neither need nor want for it. I tried something else, the words awkward and wrong in the face of all of my years of restraint and self-blame. "Thank you."

Leilani's answering smile was bright and kind, lighting up the world better than the summer sun above us. "You are happy?"

"No," I sighed, finishing before she could end her

infectious smile, "But I feel like perhaps I can be. Truly, completely happy, not dulled by heartache."

She knew enough of what I said to relax. "Good."

I nodded, grief rearing again. It was so much more painful with this numbness leaving me, every nerve in my body feeling it. I cried, an inhuman whimper of a growl leaving me. Leilani chirruped back sadly, leaning forward to allow my horns to rest in her hair as she gave me one more way to brace against her.

I had never felt this before, this knowing that I did not need to hide what I was and allowing it to fill me instead of fighting against it. To have it welcomed so wholly was a consolation all its own. At last, I could feel myself letting my dearest Katelyn go, unafraid of whatever consequences I would face should someone see this side of me.

Without the burning need to fight, I felt my body collapsing slowly. Still, there was no worry that the little demoness might reject what I was, the inner animal we shared as a common ground. I felt safe, falling into my friend's welcoming embrace as she sheltered me in my sorrow.

Broken Orbit

Katelyn,

These last several months have been trying, to say the least. While I have done everything in my power to keep you near—to not let you go again—I have found myself time and again doing just that, setting aside our past in favor of my present and the future you will never see.

I miss you. I fear that I may never stop missing you, my dear, but I will not sacrifice this world for the obsessive preservation of your memory. We both want better than that, I know.

I am uncertain I may ever feel again for another what we shared, and in spite of that, I am not alone. I have my family, I have good friends, and I even have faces like mine to share this world with. All of it is thanks to you, Miss Katelyn, and your unrivaled passion to see the world bettered for us all. You never once left me behind but pulled me forward to stand alongside you all—as much an equal as you alone could manage to make us. Rest well knowing that I will see those efforts honored.

As for my promise, I must apologize. I will not keep it. I no longer care for the children on your behalf, Katelyn. They are mine, now and always, and whatever I give them or however I love them will forevermore be my own. I can only hope you understand why I am breaking my word to you, and that you forgive me. They need so much more of me than an aging promise. They deserve a proper father to love them of his own accord, and that is what I will give them.

I understand that this is not the end of my grieving you. That will take quite some time. I have the most magnificent friend to help me, however, who does not mind who and what I am. Leilani stays steady at my side, regardless of how untamed I become. I am not alone any longer.

No matter how deeply this wound still cuts me, now is the time for goodbye. I love you, as I have always loved you, my dear, and as I always will. Katelyn, my Kate.

Farewell,
Cory

Chapter Thirteen:
The Devil You Know

My cluster of letters felt like lead in my hand, too heavy for such light little pieces of paper. I had not realized how my grief and neglected desires weighed so greatly. Now that I had someone to brace against, however, I had to wonder how I had managed to stand on my own for so long.

There was a quiet chirp behind me. The matchbox I clutched tightly rattled as I turned to see Leilani dancing after me at a sprint. Without saying a word, she matched my gait to follow me out to the little cemetery beneath that faithful old tree. I stopped at Katelyn's headstone, her daisies still blooming through the summer by some magic, I knew.

Katelyn Smith—Beloved mother, grandmother— changed the world.

I stared at the neatly carved writing, allowing my sorrow to reach me no matter how desperately I wanted to bury it beside her. "My dear, you will always be so much more than any words would only fail to describe. I promised you once, that we would remain friends. I hope I was able to deliver as well as you deserved, Kate."

485

Karma Rose

I knelt, my every action feeling disconcertingly vivid. I had held on for too long now, that I had begun to believe my half-spun lies that this nightmare might end. This was not the Institute. This was my freedom, in all of its bitingly wondrous glory.

My hands were shaking as I struck a match and held it to the corner of my stack of letters. The paper took only a moment before it caught the flames, burning black and curling in as it was devoured. I set the stack atop her headstone to watch my intentions turn to ashes.

The feeling of grief that came over me was deep enough that I swore I could feel those letters burning in my veins, my every nerve on fire with it. Wings embraced me tightly as I began to shake with sobs. Beside my ear, there was a gentle purr that was different from the ones I had heard before. It was less earnest, as though Leilani was reminding me that she was beside me rather than adamantly convincing me of the role she played.

I clutched at my friend, feeling desperation to sink my claws into something and steady myself. There was no change in her tone or posture to indicate any discomfort from my strong grasp. Without realizing, I braced my horns against her shoulder, eased in an instant by the sensation of giving in to these cravings.

"Thank you, Leilani," I gasped through my tears, the dying embers of my letters blurred in my eyes.

"I has you," she replied gently, stroking her claws through my hair and humming what sounded like a lullaby. I knew the sound of it, from a dream and well before this mess of life had played itself out. The

486

recognition was short-lived, drowned out instead by the satisfaction of a well-met need.

~ * ~ * ~ * ~

Forty-third Week After Paradise

Monday

The phone dialed through, the other end of the line ringing loudly in my ear. Perhaps I was simply nervous, but it sounded much too noisy at the moment. The ruckus that trio of mischief was making upstairs certainly did little to help, either.

"Hello?" A polite voice finally answered after what felt like an eternity.

"Good afternoon, my name is Cory Charles Lawrence, I am calling for Doct—Bernard," I corrected myself quickly.

"I'm sorry, what?"

"My name is Cory Charles Lawrence, I am calling for—"

"I'm sorry, I can't hear you, can you speak up a bit?"

My children must have been much louder than I realized. "My name is Cory Charles Lawrence, and I am calling to speak to Bernard. Is he available?"

A loud laugh replied. "Okay, sorry, but you've missed me. This is Bernard's phone, leave a message after the beep. BEEP!"

An obnoxiously shrill tone rang out, making me

flinch. "I beg your pardon? Bernard? Hello? I have already said, but this is Cory Charles Lawrence. I have important business to discuss—"

"The voicemail-box of the number you are trying to reach is now full," interrupted a woman's voice, sounding detached.

"What on earth is a voicemail-box?" I asked the operator nervously, straining to remain polite. The woman did not answer, a series of high-pitched chimes sounding off before the line went dead. "Hello? Blast it!"

I scowled as I replaced the receiver on its cradle, baffled by the entire call. Had he not been able to hear me? Perhaps there was something wrong with the phone itself? It did seem to be aging rather poorly.

The phone rang, startling me from my musings.

"Lawrence residence, this is Cory speaking."

"Hey there, fiend-o!" The cordial greeting was familiar, voice sounding all too clear now. "I got your message. What's the big important business, huh?"

"My message?" I echoed confusedly. "Bernard, I must apologize in advance for any inconvenience, it seems my phone may be malfunctioning. I called you only a moment ago, but you did not seem able to hear me properly."

"Yeah, that was my voicemail," he dismissed with a snicker.

"I beg your pardon?"

"My v—Wait, has no one seriously explained this to you yet?" he asked hurriedly. "What's next, the Internet?"

"I know what an Internet is," I replied a bit too

enthusiastically. "Is the voicemail related?"

"Look, I think I'll let someone else explain all this to you, I don't want to go and risk teaching you something inappropriate," he grumbled, sounding torn between frustration and amusement. "Now, big important business, what is it?"

"Ah, yes." I smiled, listening to the sounds of laughter on the floor above. With any luck, I could help to provide a safe place for more demons to laugh like Leilani was able to these days. "I require your medical expertise for demons, Bernard. I will be providing and furnishing the facilities for your work, as well as an apartment for living and a small allowance for personal use. All I ask is your restraint regarding your...recreational habits."

"And what's in it for me? Doesn't sound entirely worth it, to up and move, quit my job, not even starting on the fact that my recreational habits are my business," he added belligerently.

"On my property, they are my business. I have an opportunity I am willing to offer you, studying demons who volunteer to be your patient for regular medical care," I replied patiently, keeping the explanation deliberately unrefined with its details. "Barring a preference for personal equipment, everything will be provided, as I said, and if you require an assistant—"

A shrill squeal had me pulling the receiver away from my ear with a wince of pain. Even so, I could easily hear his exuberant reply, "When can I move in?!"

~~ * ~ * ~ * ~~

Karma Rose

Tuesday

"Let me see, then. What was your favorite thing about the village?" I asked. The brick wall we walked beside understood more of my words, guessing the way Leilani stared at me. "Very well, not quite there, then. Oh, let me think. Ah! Your favorite animal?"

Still, I received that confused stare, paired with an awkwardly apologetic smile. "No words?"

I shrugged and waved it away. "No need to worry. I seem to be rambling anyway. You must forgive me, I never had friends much. Not so casually, I mean. Oh, thank goodness you do not understand a word of my idiotic blathering."

She snickered. What word was it that had done the trick? Had she been playing at her befuddlement? I blushed, embarrassed at the thought, and focused my eyes on the sidewalk as we strolled down the little town proper.

"Perhaps you should have a turn at speaking," I suggested in a shy mumble.

The demoness grinned at me with glinting fangs, startling a poor woman as she passed us by. Leilani's eyes were thoughtful for a moment, and I wondered if she understood my futile attempts to converse with her were to know her better. She must have, her happy face lighting up with an idea.

"You have make babies?"

I choked on my air, eyes wide as I stared at her in shocked horror. "I beg your pardon?!"

"No Kyle-Sarah babies," she continued, no clearer than a thick fog. She tapped her face and gestured to my own. "Like you-I, babies?"

It took me a moment longer to grasp that she was not making advances. I laughed, giddy with relief.

"Have I fathered any children? No, heavens no." I shook my head with a smile. "What about you, Leilani? You do so well with Kyle and Sarah. Certainly, you have your own? Oh, of course, no words, then...Ah, do you have babies?" I simplified my question.

Her face fell, eyes dropping to her feet as she hunched in on herself some. She crossed her arms over her chest and shook her head mutely. She looked aggrieved, heartbroken at some loss. I thought of the angels and the war-torn world she had come from, my heart turning to stone in my chest.

"Leilani, you have my condolences and apologies, for what little they are worth," I said quietly, hating to think that she had suffered any loss of the sort.

Seeing her so timid and ashamed, I wanted to bring back that sunny smile somehow. What could I possibly do to help her when we could only just bridge the gap in our language? Taking a deep breath, I offered her my hand. She stared at it in surprise for a long moment, reaching out and taking it tentatively.

Why was it so startling to her, when she had done the same for me on countless occasions? Her fingers held tight, claws pressing against my skin. The sensation was still oddly natural to me.

"Thank you," she mumbled shyly, still clutching my hand tightly.

"Of course, Leilani." I sighed quietly, finding us in front of a quaint little shop. I read the name on the sign, smiling as an idea came to me while peering into the craft store's window. "Come now, let's see what we can do about getting that smile of yours back, hm?"

I led us into the shop, a bell jingling brightly at our entrance. It only took an instant for Leilani's mood to change, recognizing the various crafts supplies. An entire wall was laden with yarns and strings, another shelf with beads and still more hobbies' worth of items filled the rest of the shop. After a moment of our browsing, an older gentleman shambled to the front counter. He must have been at least Jeff's age, and certainly bored of retirement if he was working at all while hobbling with his cane.

It took another moment before I recognized the resemblance to Richard with a pang of panic. My hand tightened around Leilani's, unwilling to risk her wandering away in the slightest.

"Good morning, good morning, how can I—Oh. *You.*" Richard's father sneered at me spitefully, and I knew we were in for some sort of unpleasantness. "Unless you've got IDs for proof of sentience, get the hell out. We don't serve *animals.*"

"Very well. Ah, will this do, then?" I offered both my license and the card I was given upon release. He inspected them both with a cynical glower, nodding sharply after a moment. "Thank you."

"What about that one?" He jabbed his cane in Leilani's direction. She sniffed at him, curious as always but knowing enough now to wait for and follow my cues.

"She is with me," I replied firmly, presenting the bracelet on her wrist with its little tag.

"Is that a joke?" he spat hatefully. His hand

whipped out, grabbing the bracelet and breaking the delicate chain with a solid yank. Leilani whimpered and flinched, the sound twisting in my gut. "You've got an unleashed animal running around? And now it's lost its collar! That's a hefty fine. Get it out of my shop, I'm calling the cops."

"Return that bracelet! She is perfectly safe—"

"Out! Or I'll find something to press charges with, you worthless demon! And make sure you take that *thing* with you," he added with another jab at Leilani. I allowed myself a moment's lapse with my features, glaring at him. He stumbled back, startled. "Monster! Get out!"

"Yes, sir," I muttered bitterly, guiding the little demoness out ahead of me. I did what I could to keep her hidden from his view, infuriated by the entire exchange.

I had become complacent of late, in this little world where my family had carved out a place for me to live. I had neglected to think much of prejudice these last few months. The brief span it took us to flee to the farmhouse gave me more than enough time to consider it all before we landed and the little demoness began her silent inquiry into what had transpired.

Looking at Leilani's startled face pleading with me to explain, I found myself torn between disappointment and self-disgust. I had grown too comfortable with my new privileges, forgetting entirely that I needed to prepare Leilani for the new Tests. No matter how wretchedly abhorrent the whole practice was, for reasons like this afternoon we had little choice but to play along.

"I'm sorry, Leilani," I apologized, desperately wishing that she could understand that I never intended for her to see this side of my world. She had followed me here to help, and now she was being exposed to the same cruelty I had known my entire life. I felt that I had failed her somehow, this innocent pixie of a woman that always danced and smiled so readily. Her world was lovely, made of nothing but forests and beauteous scenes from the most fantastical of dreams.

"I'm not...I'm not like you, Leilani, this is more home to me than any other place, in this world or yours. Bigotry and all, this is where I belong, but you...I suppose I should oversee you returning to the village. I can't possibly ask you to endure what's to come here, nor forgive the wrongs done to you when you've acted in no way deserving of them. I'm sorry, Leilani, but you deserve to be safe from this treatment."

"No words." Her smile said otherwise, saddened too deeply to be right. She took my hand easily, giving it a firm squeeze. With her free hand, she gestured to the porch in front of us. "Home now, is safe. No you have sorry."

"What will I do with you?" I wondered quietly, sighing heavily. Her adamance was obvious in her tone and the confidence her slight shoulders held. It was different from the stubbornness I was familiar with, Katelyn's being set to convince me of my need to reconsider the way of things. Leilani's conviction was nearly silent, patiently viewing the world and waiting for me to see the apparent truth of it that I was blind to.

It was her silence that spoke so loudly to me. The same as how her gentle words and broken English had become unquestionably clear of late. All of it was accepting, an unyielding anchor against the currents of this world.

Leilani shrugged, her smile breaking free from this somber mood, coral face brimming with her infectious enthusiasm. There was a dance to her step again as she tugged me along toward the porch. I made a show of stumbling and dragging my feet, grinning at her frustrated chirps of laughter. By the time she had gotten me up the steps and to the door, our moods had turned around to leave the bitterness of the day forgotten.

Wednesday

I inspected the new construction, satisfied with the work and hopeful of what it could mean for the refugees Braxen had mentioned. The closed stall system was ingenious, twenty-two easily fitting into the single large barn. The building was also outfitted with a full range of amenities from water spigots in the stalls to a fully functional kitchen and clinic—for our employees, of course.

Never mind that the animals we house will be trained to use them, I thought, embittered by the need to consider my brethren so callously. I knew that Braxen would not approve, no matter how desperate the village became. Still, it was a solid shelter with electricity and running water.

On the other end of the barn, I heard a vehicle approach slowly. Car doors opened and slammed shut as I made my way down the lane of stalls. Even at a distance, I recognized the eccentric and mad laughter of my guest.

"Good afternoon, gentlemen," I greeted, seeing Robert wearing his most patient expression as he smiled tightly at Bernard. From behind the vehicle, a young woman near Bernard's age shut the trunk and hefted two large suitcases along with her. "Madam. May I help you?"

"No one touches my babies," she replied, quick and stern despite her apparent disinterest in her surroundings. She set one case down with the utmost care, offering me her hand. "Terry Evans, I'm Bernard's wife. I'm very excited by this opportunity, Mr.Lawrence."

I glanced at Bernard as I released her hand, uncertain of my choice suddenly. "Bernard...?"

"Personal equipment," he clarified with a nod to the case his wife lifted again. He grinned nervously. "So, where's our broom closet?"

I chuckled and shared a quick look with Robert. He had visited plenty during this building's construction. Even the smaller tool rooms were too large to be considered a closet. "This way, then."

At the end of the lane on the lefthand side, I entered the "veterinary" clinic easily, its doors built to allow for large horses. A generous assumption on my part, should demons grow larger than Braxen or me. Inside, the lights flickered to life automatically and I held the door for the small troupe that followed me.

"This will be your office." I gestured to the interior. It was large and open with several workspaces lined with tables. The steel counters were bare, the room

496

primarily vacant save for a set of livestock scales at the front by the door and a set of measuring lines on the door for ease. Along the back wall, several doors led to smaller rooms for living and medical practice. "I was uncertain regarding equipment or medical supplies, and thought it better to wait for your professional recommendations."

"This'll work." Terry smiled broadly, the first bit of any expression I had seen break free from her stoic mask. She carried her luggage to the tables, already unpacking.

"We get to work *here*?" gasped Bernard excitedly, laughing like Kyle when I mentioned an early desert.

"With an additional person," I clarified. "He is a licensed veterinarian, which rounds out our needs nicely, I suspect. Corey Ericson, my namesake and son of the most brilliant man I have ever known to study me."

Bernard gaped at me. "This is perfect. Beyond perfect! This is amazing! Like Christmas, except even better! Thank you, sub-terrestrial Santa!"

A familiar screech interrupted our discussion, bringing a swell of comfort to my chest at the gleeful sound. I peered out into the aisle outside, finding Kyle sprinting the length of the barn and darting between my legs into the office. Only seconds behind him, Leilani barreled into view, Sarah on her shoulders and both wearing grins.

"Leilani!" I called, catching her attention. She hurried down the aisle, copper eyes searching around for my mischievous son. "I take it you lost Kyle?"

"Kyle ran," she huffed, hands on her hips. She looked like a disgruntled fairy, tiny and adorable as she shifted her wings in her irritation. "You see?"

"Yes," I chuckled, nodding my head. "He ran inside. Come in, you should meet the new doctors, in any case."

Leilani entered as I held the door ajar, closing it behind her and careful not to catch her tail. Kyle giggled, hiding behind Robert's legs. The demoness caught sight of him, crying out triumphantly and scooping him up with a chirping laugh.

There was an animated outcry, startling us all.

"Is that a female?" squeaked Bernard excitedly. He laughed giddily at my confused nod. "Terry, they're sexually dimorphic. Do you see, she doesn't have horns!"

"I have eyes, and my ears function just fine, too," she replied pointedly, but that deadpan face held a new curiosity as she approached. "Spur-like bony growths on the face and extremities. Neat."

"Dad, what are all the big words," whispered Sarah, leaning over from Leilani's shoulders to reach my ear.

I smiled. "They mean that Leilani looks differently than I do, because I'm a man and she's a woman, but I can explain better later, sweetheart."

"Also notably docile with offspring not her own," commented Bernard, joining Terry's quiet speculation. He frowned. "She's really small."

"Yes. I am small," she said the words slowly, focusing on her pronunciation. I nodded when she looked to me for approval. "My name is Leilani."

"Leilani. That sounds human in origin," mused Terry in a murmur. "Where did you say you found her?

Were there any others? What kind of social dynamic do you two have, given the obvious assumption of predatory ancestry? Does she speak English as her primary language, or secondary?"

"Babe," intoned Bernard with an apologetic smile. Poor Leilani was utterly baffled, unable to keep up with the rapid interrogation.

"We have plenty of time for questions," I reassured them both. "Leilani lives in the main house with me. She commonly helps with the children, but if she should have free time she would like to volunteer, I will accompany her for any conversations or exams."

"Perfectly acceptable," agreed Terry with a nod. She smiled at Leilani in admiration.

"Now then, I will get supper on the stove. You both are welcome to join when it is ready," I invited them. I opened the door to usher Robert and Leilani outside, both children still held all too easily by that little woman. I gave a final smile and nod to the odd pair. Whirlwind though they were, their curiosity was honest and patient. Perhaps this could work better than I had dared hope.

~~ * ~ * ~ * ~~

Thursday

"You said you'd be bringing kids, and now I've got two dozen cookies and not a brat in sight," accused Beth venomously. I could tell that she was disappointed, making it difficult to determine where her vitriol ended and her playful tone began.

499

"My apologies, Beth, but their grandfather asked to teach them the starts of their orchard's apple season," I apologized with a shrug. Jeff had been all too happy when I agreed, only days before planning to visit my old tormentor.

"Apple farmers?" she scoffed, shaking her head as she took her seat across from me and began to prepare her tea. This felt easier than my first visit, at least, and with how naturally we had both set our area I wondered if we might make a habit of it. "I'm not sure I ever told you, but it's incredibly embarrassing to see something like you doing anything so mundane."

"Something like me?" I echoed, wary but hoping for the best.

She took a sip of her cup, nodding. "Look at you! So many better career choices, and you pick playing with dirt. You know the kind of crap I had to put up with from the military?"

"I would make an atrocious soldier," I chuckled wryly.

"But a good bodyguard, and intimidating as all hell," she cackled gleefully. Beth sighed nostalgically. "Oh, Paul beat me to the punch on telling those insufferable leeches off, though. The good old pastor only ever had to whip up some speech about resisting the Devil's temptation and people just went along with it! Absolutely ridiculous."

"Is that jealousy I hear?" I teased. "From the great Beth? I may faint of shock."

"Aren't you cute?" she snapped with a sneer. Still, there was humor in her eyes that could not hide that she was enjoying the afternoon visit. From the kitchen, there was the beep of a timer. "Oh, that's more cookies it looks like kids aren't eating."

"Your overabundance of confections is only convincing me of the wisdom to leave them with family," I warned her playfully. She struggled from her chair a moment before I stood quickly to assist her. She waved me off at first, taking a dangerously unbalanced step.

I steadied Beth carefully, startled by the strength of her grip despite how faint she appeared. It reminded me of Katelyn, the way her fingers dug into me. She seemed to lose her balance again, the feel of it wrong, as though she was pulling on me deliberately. Somehow, she managed to get a grip on my hair, yanking my face down to hers.

"They're still watching you," hissed Beth into my ear. Her grip on me was becoming painful, like a vice—much more like the woman I knew. "It isn't safe for the woman you're keeping. They think you know where more of them are, Cory; they're waiting until there are enough demons to act. You have to keep the others safe."

I felt my breath leave me for a moment, panic settling in and constricting my chest. I followed her cue, whispering in reply, "What can I do? Who is watching us?"

"Powerful people who are interested in using what you are for their gain," she replied sharply, still keeping her voice hushed. Her grip on my hair tightened painfully, no doubt to ensure she had my attention. "You're an exception, you're documented as sentient, but the rest of them are as good as chattel now unless they pass tests we both know they're not ready for. You have to keep them safe."

"What do I do, Beth? The new laws tie my hands," I murmured, wincing as she kept up the charade of her faulty balance, pulling at me again. "I need to keep Leilani safe."

"You need to keep them all safe! They're cattle, but it gives you an advantage, too. If they treat them like animals, you have to do the same. You can't own people, Cory, but they're not people. Act like they're the animals the law says they are." She finally steadied herself, releasing her grip on me and patting my shoulder. "Thank you. You're such a gentleman."

"Of course, Beth." I watched her carefully, stepping back. She was smiling as pleasantly as she had been previously, looking as though little more than a fit of poor footing had happened. An odd sense of gloom settled in my veins, weighing down my heart. I had to keep Leilani safe. I owed her that much and more. "Whatever is needed of me."

~~ * ~ * ~ * ~~

Friday

I stared in the mirror intently, feeling completely this was a moment of change. No matter how ridiculous it must have looked, my talking to myself in the bathroom. The barn was ready, and the Evans had settled into their clinic much more quickly than I had anticipated. There was nothing left to delay this, then.

"Braxen." I stopped to take a deep breath, overwhelmed by this undertaking abruptly. I had to remind myself that it was simply lodging, nothing more. I was not their leader, that was Braxen's role. I was not some savior to be owed for my actions. I was a man, doing what he could to better the lives of others—nothing more than that. There was no reason to be anxious about refusing to turn a blind eye to these people's needs.

"Braxen, I took the liberty of building a place for your village, at least a small part of it," I began, my nervousness fading easily. "I will be arranging for more accommodations to be built shortly. I do not know how much more I can do, but you have a safe place here should you need it."

I felt a rush of gratitude not my own, and I knew he had heard me.

~~ * ~ * ~ * ~~

Saturday

Leilani and I landed after our regular evening flight, the both of us gasping through our giddy laughter. The winds higher up had taken an abrupt turn, in direction and strength alike. A storm was likely coming in soon, and we had very nearly suffered the sky's punishment.

"Oh, that was thrilling!" I crowed. My heart was thundering in my chest, and I found the danger was not quite so mortifying when faced with good company. It felt excitingly addictive, a boastful pride blooming in me to have fought against the force of nature with her. "Dare I say, fun?"

Leilani grinned, nodding enthusiastically. "Fun!"

I guffawed, the sound rolling from my chest to echo deeply across the fields. "You were fantastic, as well! I may have practice with tricks, but you are simply deft and graceful, my dear."

My words caught in my throat, sticking to my tongue painfully as I realized what I had said. I took a deep breath in the hopes to ease this sudden stab of grief in my chest. It was a mistake, simply enough. A slip of the tongue, and yet it still burned in my veins.

The poor little woman did not understand my abrupt upset. Taking my hand in hers firmly, she chirped at me inquisitively before asking, "Is okay?"

I nodded slowly. "A bit of sadness is all, Leilani."

"Is Kate?" she asked, ever the observant little thing. I nodded again, and her replying smile was warmly inviting. It reminded me of spending a brisk autumn evening in front of a fire. "Is okay, not alonely."

"I know," I replied quietly, feeling this sorrow easing already. "Thank you."

Leilani nodded, although she seemed far from satisfied just yet. She dropped my hand, moving in a blinding flash of coral to throw her arms around my front. Her wings wrapped around me tightly, and I was unable to resist the overpowering relief that came with the embrace.

It no longer felt alien to be welcomed so wholly, just as I was. Her wings were comforting and warm against me, easing any remaining spikes of grief instantly. After a long moment, she sighed and nodded, releasing me.

"Thank you, little pixie," I murmured with a smile. The nickname was easy, feeling right when I spoke it. Leilani smiled that infectious smile of hers, coral cheeks flushing to my crimson. "Oh, dear. Have I embarrassed you?"

"No words," she mumbled shyly, copper eyes flicking away toward the road.

I chuckled nervously, taking a deep breath to steady myself. Before we could continue with our newfound awkwardness, however, I heard something in the distance. It almost sounded like...thunder? The pattern was all wrong for it, though, and despite the earlier winds, the sky was clear this evening. I frowned, looking in the direction of the sound.

Leilani heard it, as well. Her reaction was much different, and I realized she must have recognized what was happening. Her smile turned to a grin, eyes lighting up like I had not seen in some time now. She grabbed my arm and tugged on it with an overjoyed squeal.

"Fly!" she squeaked through her grin, pointing to the horizon excitedly. I saw them then, looking like warped birds at first. The figures grew in size every second I watched—dozens of demons, flying this way. I felt a shiver run down my spine and through my tail, cowed at the sight.

"Oh, dear," I muttered under my breath, unable to stop myself shaking as they drew closer. The sound grew louder, to the point I thought I might feel it in my bones if I joined them in the air. Leilani scarcely noticed my unease, cheering happily to see so many of our brethren.

The sky should have fallen, shaken from its perch

and replaced by that motley of reds.

"Cory, do you hear that?!" I glanced behind myself to see that Lisa had run out to the front porch, worried. She saw the nearing mob of demons and froze, paling to a ghost. "Oh. *Shit*."

I jumped, startled as they began to drop from the sky and land in the fields around us. Leilani's dainty movements were nothing to compare to this visual onslaught of predatory prowess as, one after another, demons hit the earth with all of the regal command of wild panthers. They collected themselves just as easily, moving towards us without missing a beat. I could not help but feel myself as their helpless prey, watching such magnificent monsters stalk forward, gliding through their movements.

Braxen landed in front of me and I fell back with a scream. He and Leilani both stared at me in confusion as I scrambled back to my feet. My heart was thundering in my chest, my pulse pounding so heavily that I felt it in my horns. The entire scene was mortifying, out of place for my world of humans. Could they smell it?

"Braxen, I-I wasn't expecting you so—" I stopped myself to swallow back another surge of fear, voice shaking uncontrollably. "That is, I...I thought you would be walking, not...Heavens, but this is a surprise."

Braxen laughed at my startled expression, patting my shoulder. "You look so human! No need to be afraid, it's only a few women, the children, and a couple bulls. I got your message."

"I gathered that, Braxen," I replied, still faint. Leilani grabbed my hand firmly, helping to steady me as I took in all of these inhuman faces. Here, in this world of humans, on my family's old farm. Where once I had found such suffocating solitude, I now saw it all ground into the dirt by clawed feet. "I'm afraid I don't have a proper supper ready."

"You have already given us more than enough, Cory," he reassured me with a smile. I could not shake the sensation he was keeping something from me, no matter how sincere he sounded. I could feel him hiding it from me, the ominous sensation reminding me of shivering against a floor of cold, wet tile.

"Of course, Braxen." I linked my hands behind my back out of habit. I braced myself to lead these people to their new home, glad I had Braxen's help with it. "Whatever is needed of me."

<u>Epilogue</u>

"Beth, you've got someone here to see you."

The older woman sighed tiredly, glancing at the clock on her desk. Ten minutes until the day was over. Of course, someone would wait until *now* to bother her. They had better not be bringing her any paperwork.

"Send them in, Stewart," she replied, frustration adding a bitter edge to her tone. Not that she cared; she was in charge because she was good, and everyone else knew it. Polite social manners only went so far in her line of work, anyway. A strong stomach and flexible morals were much more valuable.

A moment later, her door opened. A youthful man entered her office wearing a pleasant smile. His skin reminded her of clay, earthy with the slightest hint of a burnt-red undertone. His silky black hair was pulled back into a long braid. He was on the shorter side of things, just below average, and his already wiry frame seemed even more minuscule in his rumpled, baggy clothes. His eyes stood out, a vibrant blue that almost seemed to glow despite the harsh lighting of Beth's office.

"Who are you and what the hell do you want?" She wasted no time getting to the point. In eight minutes, she was going home, damn it.

The man continued to smile, expression serene. "It's me, Doctor Lysse? Balthazar? People used to call me Bliss as a bad joke, remember? We've worked together for years, Beth."

"No, we..." Her protest fell short, an odd calm overtaking her. She frowned, confused as she struggled to remember. He was trustworthy, she knew that. Slowly, she began to recall working with him, despite how foggy the details were. "Right. Right, of course, sorry. Did you have something you needed, Balthazar?"

"The Lawrence files, actually," he replied coolly. "The damn thing thinks he can go behind my back moving demons around, playing *hero*. I'll remind him what he is in this world."

Beth faltered a moment, offended on behalf of the man she had recently befriended. "Excuse you?"

"Forget that little rant," sighed Bliss, bored. The woman blinked, disoriented briefly.

"Balthazar? Did you need something?" asked Beth. Why was he just standing in her office?

"The Lawrence files?" he prompted gently, biting his tongue firmly against his bitter sense of betrayal. That was unimportant right now.

"Oh, right, I forgot you needed those," she sighed with a glance at the clock. Two minutes until quitting time. "I'll do it first thing in the morning, Balthazar, I'm about to head home for the day. Did you need the recent results from his last visit, too?"

"Everything," he persisted eagerly. He was used to having sway over others, but humans were just too

509

easy! At least demons knew they were being played. "I'm compiling something of a book, for educational reasons. Make it easier to train new people, you know?"

"Good idea," praised Beth, standing from her desk and sparing him a smile. "I'll see you in the morning, Balthazar. You're bringing coffee, right?"

Bliss grinned. "Don't I always?"

About the Author

Karma Rose was an unschooled student and has always been a writer at heart. Although she began with poems and short stories, she has now since completed two installments in her *Gravity* series, *Demon Rising* and its sequel, *Broken Orbit*. She spends her days tending her own small farm.

For updates on current and future projects, look for Karma Rose on various social media platforms!

www.ingramcontent.com/pod-product-compliance
Lightning Source LLC
Chambersburg PA
CBHW03074503726
47497CB00001B/132